P9-ARV-592

# FOLKTALES OF *Norway*

*Folktales*
OF THE WORLD

GENERAL EDITOR : RICHARD M. DORSON

# FOLKTALES OF
# *Norway*

EDITED BY
*Reidar Th. Christiansen*

TRANSLATED BY
PAT SHAW IVERSEN

FOREWORD BY
*Richard M. Dorson*

THE UNIVERSITY OF CHICAGO PRESS

Library of Congress Catalog Card Number: 64–15830
The University of Chicago Press, Chicago 60637
Routledge & Kegan Paul, Ltd., London E.C.4
© 1964 by The University of Chicago. All rights reserved
Published 1964. Second Impression 1968
Printed in the United States of America

# Foreword

Everyone in the English-speaking world knows the pioneer collection of folktales made by the brothers Grimm in Germany, but relatively few are familiar with the second major collection, assembled in Norway by Peter Christen Asbjörnsen and Jörgen Moe. In its day their *Norske Folkeeventyr* achieved a full measure of celebrity. On intellectual grounds it won fame for bolstering the thesis of Jacob Grimm, that an oral literature of the Aryan peoples had filtered throughout all the countries of Europe. The same tales discovered in Germany were now collected in Norway, and clearly their counterparts must exist in neighboring lands. Popular appeal may explain why Norwegian folktales have flourished ever since, translated and published under such enticing titles as *East of the Sun and West of the Moon*.

From its beginnings, Norwegian interest in folk materials coincided with the stirrings of nationalism and the vogue of romanticism. Norway gained her independence from Denmark in 1814 and throughout the nineteenth century sought to promote her national identity. In the wake of the Grimms, Norwegian collectors began to gather tales and songs of the villagers, supplying evidence for a living speech and an ancient mythology distinctively Norse. These newfound traditions were believed to mirror the craggy fjords and forest-covered slopes of the northern land. The question of *landsmaal*, or peasant speech, around which the debate over a national language raged, became deeply involved with the new science of folklore, for the oral literature of the people was expressed, and recorded, in the tongue of the people.

When the first book of Norwegian folktales was issued, by the

minister Andreas Faye in 1833, under the title *Norske Sagn*
(*Norwegian Legends*), it deplored the superstitions of the peasantry. By the time the second edition was issued in 1844, the
rationalistic disdain of the uneducated, inherited from the
eighteenth century, was yielding to the mellow romanticism of
the nineteenth, which saw the humble cotter not as an ignorant
peasant but as nature's nobleman. Faye's revised title, *Norske
Folke-Sagn*, introduced in the word *folke* this new spiritual
notion. Immediately, Faye was challenged by Peter Christen
Asbjörnsen (1812–85), who considered Faye's work unwar-
rantedly didactic. In the 1830's Asbjörnsen had begun collecting
traditions in the countryside, and when destiny threw him into
contact with Jörgen Moe (1813–82), first at school in Norderhov,
and later at the Royal Frederik University in Christiania, he
found a kindred spirit. The two friends and collaborators were
to follow quite different careers, for Moe became an ordained
clergyman and finally a bishop, and Asbjörnsen earned his
living as a zoölogist and forest-master. The quiet, reflective Moe
wrote lyrical poems of some merit, and the outgoing, hearty
Asbjörnsen translated Darwin's *Origin of Species* into Norwegian, but their most zealous endeavors in the 1830's and '40's
were devoted to folklore.

In 1840 Moe published a collection of popular songs in local
dialects, of which one-third came from oral, folk sources. In his
native inland district of Ringerike, Moe had grown up in the
midst of traditional lore. Asbjörnsen, a city youth from Christiania, also engaged in a preliminary effort, issuing in Christmas,
1837 a picture book for Norwegian children titled *Nor*, with
Bernt Moe, a cousin of Jörgen. The first half, contributed by
Bernt, dealt with celebrated Norwegian heroes of history and
saga; the second half, by Asbjörnsen, presented folktales, and
this section attracted the most favorable comment. Now the
two friends, informed through the Grimms of oral peasant
tales and sensitive to the rising spirit of Norwegian patriotism,
prepared to launch their *Norske Folkeeventyr*. A prospectus
written by Moe in 1840 stated, "No cultivated person now
doubts the scientific importance of the folk tales ... they help

to determine a people's unique character and outlook."[1] And he promised to reproduce the stories as faithfully as had the Grimms in their admirable *Kinder- und Hausmärchen*.

In 1841 the first pamphlet of folktales appeared, in complete anonymity, lacking title, collectors' names, foreword. Three more pamphlets followed in the next three years. Collectively they constitute the first edition of the *Norske Folkeeventyr*.

The ensuing years saw considerable and intensive fieldwork by the collaborators, who were assisted by university grants. Directly inspired and motivated by the *Kinder- und Hausmärchen*, Asbjörnsen and Moe corresponded with and sought the assistance of Jacob Grimm. Seeking a renewal of his scholarship to study folklore, Jörgen Moe wrote Grimm for a letter of support to the members of the University Council. His request to Grimm has an eerily contemporary ring.

Last year I applied for and received such a stipend in order to study our folk poetry in relationship to that of related races. It was only with great difficulties that the scholarship came through, not because those in charge were in doubt of my competence but because this subject could not be brought under any academic discipline. Consequently many of our highly learned people were very much in doubt about the scientific value of such studies. (*October 12, 1849*)[2]

In the same letter Moe speaks of the common principles which he shares with his illustrious German colleague. He writes that "comparative studies of folk poetry" will yield as valuable results to the historian as to the student of comparative linguistics. "Especially now may such studies be an actuality; with the awakening nationalistic strivings of peoples the particular poetic creations by the folk everywhere are more and more the subject

---

[1] As quoted in Oscar J. Falnes, *National Romanticism in Norway* (New York: Columbia University Press, 1933), p. 215. I am much indebted to Falnes' excellent treatment of the folklore movement in Norway.

[2] *Briefwechsel der Gebrüder Grimm mit nordischen Gelehrten*, edited by Ernst Schmidt (Berlin: Ferd. Dümmlers, 1885), p. 270. This and other translations from the Norwegian letters written to J. Grimm have been made for me by Barbro Sklute. Her assistance in the preparation of the whole manuscript has been invaluable.

for attention and careful collecting." Such a statement well reveals the synthesis of comparative and nationalist emphases, and
the stress on fieldwork, that distinguish the work of both the
German and Norwegian folklorists.

Turning aside from the wonder tales of magic to legends of
spirit beings, Asbjörnsen on his own published *Norske Huldre-
Eventyr og Folksagn* in 1845. He followed this with a second
collection two years later, and in the ensuing years he re-edited
and reprinted them (1859, 1866, 1870). In this work Asbjörnsen
introduced the fictional device of a frame setting with an imaginary village narrator relating the olden stories. This manner of
presentation, which did at least suggest the verisimilitude of the
recited narratives, had been adopted by an early field collector,
T. Crofton Croker, who in 1825 published *Fairy Traditions of
the South of Ireland*. Jacob Grimm translated the book into
German the following year as *Irische Elfenmärchen*, and Asbjörnsen spied it in that form. The fairies of Ireland corresponded
to the *huldre* folk of Norway, belonging to the same order of
bothersome goblins of house and field. In calling attention to
traditional belief in demons, Asbjörnsen performed a valuable
service, since this form of folk narrative is usually slighted in
favour of fictions.

Four terms had now been introduced into the vocabulary of
Norwegian folk-narrative: *eventyr, sagn, folke, huldre*. They
were employed in various combinations, and tended to blend
together—Asbjörnsen used all four in the title of his 1845 collection—but they contributed distinct concepts to the young field.
*Eventyr* designated fictional tales or *Märchen*, usually called
fairy tales in English, but the word was also used in a wider
sense, like folktale, to cover all oral narrative. Thus it was possible to speak of *huldre-eventyr*. *Sagn* derived from the German
*Sagen* and similarly meant legends connected with particular
places, such as haunted castles. *Huldre* stood for a class of un-
natural creatures, ranging from elves to monsters, which were
sighted and encountered and talked about by village people.
(*Hulder* in the singular signifies a wood nymph.) *Folke* indicated the oral and traditional as opposed to the polished and
literary character of twice-told tales offered to the public.

Asbjörnsen and Moe claimed to offer scientifically accurate specimens of Norwegian folk literature in their *Norske Folkeeventyr*. They proposed to improve upon the Grimms' methods, feeling that the brothers had taken too many liberties in rewriting oral texts. Nevertheless, the Norwegians shared with the Germans a belief in the artistic value of the tale set before educated readers. The sponsor of the tale acts not only as a faithful collector-reproducer, but also should serve as a writerartist, who seeks to convey the personal style and mannerisms of the teller and the full sense of the story. Since the narrator can use gestures and intonations denied to the writer, a written tale needs additional words to compensate for these lacks. In the case of outstanding folk tellers, little interpolation is required, but an inept narrator yields a sketchy text on which the writer-reporter must elaborate. Asbjörnsen and Moe thought of the reciters of Icelandic sagas as the ideal and prototypical Norwegian storytellers, and sought to achieve this ideal standard when their informants fell short. They thereby deviated from the present-day view that all texts, garbled or ample, should be recorded literally. But their end product so appealed to Jacob Grimm that he described them as the best *Märchen* in print.

Directly related to the question of accuracy in printing oral texts was the matter of language. Could and should the local dialect forms be rendered? Here the issue of *landsmaal*, the native speech as opposed to the cultivated tongue, flared forth. In general the Norwegian collaborators strove for a middle ground, giving the flavour of the local phrasing without jeopardy to the sense. Asbjörnsen drew a clear distinction between *eventyr* and *sagn*, employing many more proverbs, sayings, and dialect expressions in the legends than in the *Märchen*, on the premise that legends were more firmly rooted in specific localities, where the fairy tales drifted about the general population.[3]

Language in turn involved nationalism; the speech of the *landsman* reflected his character, his character was molded by the fjords and forests, and so, according to the theory of nature

[3] The theories of Asbjörnsen are carefully discussed by Knut Liestöl in his biographical study, *P. Chr. Asbjörnsen, Mannen og Livsverket* (Oslo, J. G. Tanum, 1947). See especially pp. 85–86, 161–74.

symbolism, the *eventyr* and *sagn* embodied the deepest and purest strains of the Norwegian soul. They were "nature poems," living specimens of the ancient Norse mythology, said Asbjörnsen. How then could the same peasant tales be found throughout Europe, as the Grimms' hypothesis of a common Aryan origin specified and the evidence supported? Moe puzzled over this question in his introduction to the 1851 edition, and at length saw an answer: the plot outlines of the European tales did indeed mirror their common ancestry, but a given national stock, like the Norwegian, still expressed the special characteristics of the people transmitting, and transmuting, the traditions. The details of place and personality, and the metaphorical expressions, breathed the spirit of Norway.

The notion of separate racial heritages of folklore—Celtic, Teutonic, Anglo-Saxon, Scandinavian—was first voiced by the poet Johann Gottfried von Herder in the late eighteenth century, and was avidly seized on by cultural nationalists. Norwegian intellectuals, smarting under the Danish domination which since the Reformation had foisted upon them a foreign clergy, bureaucracy, and burgher class, sought further to refine the Scandinavian inheritance by isolating unmistakably Norwegian elements. Moe endeavored to define these qualities. He spoke of the balance between humor and terror, arising from a self-assured people living on a harsh terrain. The youthful hero Askeladden, counterpart of the boy dragon-killer in fairy tales throughout Europe, in Norwegian folk-narrative exemplified the confidence of the *landsman* in a mysterious power on high guiding his destiny. As late as 1957 a newspaper article in Oslo described Askeladden as "a crafty, clever, glib Norwegian farmer with the necessary sense and power to win half a kingdom."[4]

Asbjörnsen theorized chiefly about folk beliefs and legends. Following the nature-symbolical school of interpretation, he construed such figures as the *hulder*, the *nisse*, and the *jutul* as reflections of physical nature recast into eerie forms by the folk.

---

[4] Jan Brunvand, "Norway's Askeladden, the Unpromising Hero, and Junior-Right," *Journal of American Folklore*, LXXII (1959), 14. Brunvand distinguishes between the actual dusty Askeladden of the folktales and the glamorized hero.

Harsh, forbidding crags and fjords shaped the malevolent *jutul,* verdant hills and gentle slopes fashioned the wood-nymph called *hulder.* In the wake of Jacob Grimm he accepted the historical-evolutionary thesis that these supernatural creatures were further molded by the ancient Germanic pantheon, from which they had degenerated to their present forms. Yet a third reading, the historical-psychological, regarded non-rational folk beliefs as primitive conceptions of the race revived in the soul of the peasant during special moods and stages. The philological mythology of Jacob Grimm, the pastoral romanticism of Herder, and the evolutionary biology of Darwin were thus synthesized in Asbjörnsen's thinking about folk beliefs in spirit beings and the tales they engendered. While these ideas were derivative, Asbjörnsen did introduce a new concept, the distinction between personal and general traditions. Individual accounts of dealings with spirit creatures he called *huldre-eventyr.* Oft retold narratives of personal and historic episodes took on an epic pattern over the centuries, and became *egentlige sagn,* or genuine legends. Unfortunately, the term *eventyr* was inappropriate, since it suggested invented tales rather than accepted beliefs.

During the 1850's the reputation of the *Norske-Eventyr* rapidly grew, both at home and abroad. Asbjörnsen and Moe brought out a second, enlarged edition in 1851, with a one-hundred-and-fifteen-page appendix of comparative notes and an extended scholarly introduction by Moe. From this edition the English scholar George Webbe Dasent rendered a translation in 1858, *Popular Tales from the Norse,* destined for fame. In a letter to Jacob Grimm, Asbjörnsen commented on the difference in reception accorded the tales in England and in Germany.

Our Norwegian folktales seem to be much more appealing to the English than to the Germans. At Christmas a new translation was published in Edinburgh and London with, according to the reviews, a new and enlarged introduction which received fine reviews in the *Times,* the *Athenaeum,* the *Saturday Review,* and many other English papers and magazines. Already in March another and much larger edition was issued, from which it is indicated that the book will become very popular in England. In Germany, on the other hand, there still exists only the Brese-

mann translation from 1847 in the first edition and that at a
price that is hardly more than 1/5 of the price of the English
translation. (*May 6, 1859*)[5]

In the lengthy, impassioned, and eloquently Victorian "Intro-
ductory Essay on the Origin and Diffusion of Popular Tales,"
by Sir George W. Dasent,[6] we can perceive the intensity and
even violence of the controversies aroused by the newly discovered oral literature of European peasants. The whole course
of civilization is bound up with the theories of the origin and
migration of folktales. Vehemently Dasent attacks the tyrannical
classicists who assert Greco-Roman origins for Aryan institutions
and traditions; the Jewish race, "the most obstinate and stiff-
necked the world has ever seen," who blocked Christianity and
progress and tampered with the Old Testament; the Christian
fundamentalists, who blindly deny the evolutionary truths of
Natural Science; the Roman Catholic Church, which embraced
idolatry in the eleventh century when Pope Gregory VII commanded the priests to celibacy. Even the highly cultured people
of India, whose Sanskrit language and sacred writings are the
fountainhead of the Aryan tongues and learning, suffered, according to Dasent, from a racial lethargy which permanently
arrested their development. Only in the Aryan race and Protes-
tant faith in Europe—where the miserable remnants of the Mon-
golian invaders, the Lapps, Finns, and Basques, had been swept
aside—does modern civilization bloom and flourish.

And how did the popular tales of the Norse enter into this
sweeping racial theory of the march of mankind? The key to
the theory lay in the premise that the Indo-Aryan tongues were
derived from Sanskrit. Nineteenth-century philologists believed
that the history of a nation was found in its language. The
corollary followed that India had sired the civilizations of
Europe. Along the westward routes of the ancient tongues had
traveled the popular tales now scattered from the Scots to the
Chinese. Jacob Grimm had effectively documented for the folktales what Max Müller had proved for language, that India was

[5] Schmidt, *Briefwechsel*, p. 267.
[6] *Popular Tales from the Norse* (2nd ed.; London: George Routledge &
Sons, n.d.), pp. 1–87.

the parent and the source. No longer should the traditions of the peasantry be regarded as fragments of the myths inherited from Greece and Rome. They came from the majestic East.

Upholders of the theory of Greco-Roman origins had still another powerful argument against the Sanskritists. For if they yielded to the overwhelming evidence of Indian and European parallels, still they contended that the fables and tales of the East had penetrated western Europe through two thirteenth-century translations, the *Directorium Humanae Vitae* and the *History of the Seven Sages*. Dasent vigorously criticized this "copying" theory, with examples of widely distributed tales that must have preceded such late translations. As instances of "primeval" stories, he cited the familiar traditions of William Tell, and his counterparts, who shot the apple from his son's head, and of the faithful dog Gellert who saved his master's babe from a wolf, and was charged with the child's death by the false wife pointing to his bloody jaws. Both these "events" transpired in many places in different centuries. In the very collection of Norse tales he was translating Dasent found close connections with Sanskrit originals; the magic bowl, staff, and pair of shoes, which endowed their possessor with powers to fly and vanish, appeared in the eleventh-century *Katha Sarit Sagara* and in the nineteenth-century Norwegian tale of "The Three Princesses of Whiteland" (in this collection "The Three Princesses in Whittenland").

If these Norse traditions, then, shared a common character with other Aryan tales all transmitted from a common source in India, what was particularly Norse about them? The national character of Norway was shaped by the ancient mythology and the towering landscape. Thus the isolated Icelandic settlement, and the late conversion of the people to Christianity, had nourished the old Norse mythology, which left its imprints on the modern popular tales. Here Dasent relied heavily on the doctrine of survivals in folklore inherited from early stages of cultural development, a doctrine developed by his countrymen with great persuasiveness. So Dasent saw magic wishing objects and animals as reflections of the Norse god Odin or "Wish"; God and St. Peter as Christian counterparts of early pagan wanderers; the Virgin Mary as a mythic guardian of the heavens in "The Lassie and her Grandmother." The ancient Norse conception of Hel as a not overly unpleasant place was apparent in "The Mastermaid." Survivals of heathenism from pagan times could be read in the incidents of witchcraft and transformation and the appearance of giants and trolls throughout the tales.

Dasent concludes his essay with a ringing pronouncement on the cultural traits discernible in the popular tales of all peoples.

> The tales of all races have a character and manner of their own. Among the Hindoos the straight stem of the story is overhung with a network of imagery which reminds one of the parasitic growth of a tropical forest. Among the Arabs the tale is more elegant, pointed with a moral and adorned with tropes and episodes. Among the Italians it is bright, light, dazzling, and swift. Among the French we have passed from the woods, and fields, and hills, to my lady's *boudoir*—rose-pink is the prevailing colour, and the air is loaded with patchouli and *mille fleurs*. . . . The Swedes are more stiff, and their style is more like that of a chronicle than a tale. The Germans are simple, hearty, and rather comic than humorous; and M. Moe has well said, that as we read them it is as if we sat and listened to some elderly woman of the middle class, who recites them with a clear, full, deep voice.[7]

But in contrast with these national varieties, Dasent, following Jörgen Moe, perceives a clear Norwegian stamp.

> These Norse Tales we may characterize as bold, out-spoken, and humorous, in the true sense of humour. In the midst of every difficulty and danger arises that old Norse feeling of making the best of everything, and keeping a good face to the foe. The language and tone are perhaps rather lower than in some other collections, but it must be remembered that these are the tales of "hempen homespuns," of Norse yeomen, of *Norske Bönder*, who call a spade a spade, and who burn tallow, not wax; and yet in no collection of tales is the general tone so chaste, are the great principles of morality better worked out, and right and wrong kept so steadily in sight.[8]

[7] Dasent, p. 78.
[8] Dasent, p. 81.

The pride of Norwegians in their folklore, so clearly voiced by Dasent, has continued unabated to the present day.[9] Jörgen Moe's son, Moltke Moe (1859–1913), achieved a fame as a folklorist equal to that of his father, and he perpetuated the work of the two pioneer collectors in a spirit of both filial and national piety. Beginning in 1878, as a youth of nineteen, he traveled each year through the villages in quest of oral traditions. On his first trip, to Telemark in the southwest, Moltke garnered a rich harvest of tales and ballads, including accounts of the *oskorei*, the army of specters and demons hurtling across the mountain ranges during the storms of winter. That same year he provided detailed notes to the collection of *eventyr* made by Kristoffer Janson from the eastern province of Sandeherad. In 1886 members of the Storting invited him to serve as professor of the vernacular languages at the University of Christiania, and he accepted on condition that the post also include the responsibility to lecture on popular traditions. In 1899 his title was altered to professor of Norwegian popular tradition and medieval literature. The university chair gave an official sanction to his life work, the preservation and presentation of Norwegian folk materials; he prepared a standard edition of the Norwegian ballads, issued new printings of the fairy tales, and corresponded with collectors all over the country and accumulated their manuscripts in addition to his father's and his own. His dedication to these enterprises has been set forth in a touching memoir by the eminent Danish folklorist, Axel Olrik:

> I noticed from his books, his speech and everything, how closely allied Moltke Moe was not only to his own life-task, but also to that of his ancestors, to the work of his father, whom he had loved and followed with deep respect, and of Peter Christen Asbjörnsen, whose friendship during his youth had had such great influence on him, and had made intelligible to him the nature of the people and the popular poetry. Every step on their road was to him identical to a piece of Norway's history; every notebook or leaflet a document for which he not only was

[9] A succinct history of Norwegian folktale collections is given by Reidar Th. Christiansen in "The Norwegian Fairytales," Folklore Fellows Communications, No. 46 (Helsinki, 1922), pp. 3–14.

accountable to them and to science, but of which he had charge
on behalf of the Norwegian people, and of which he should
draw forth an extensive biography, containing a thorough scientific, artistic and linguistic appreciation of the work of the two
great narrators.[10]

As early as 1876 Moltke Moe began collaborating with Asbjörnsen on the successive editions of the *eventyr*, and after the
latter's death in 1885 Moltke continued the process of revision,
according to testamentary provision, adding more and more
flavour of the Norwegian dialects and striving still for perfected
forms of the fictions. All the manuscripts and folklore books in
his possession he bequeathed to the government for safekeeping,
and these formed the basis of the Norsk Folkeminnesamling,
established on his death in 1913 as a folklore archives in the
university library. One can find today on its shelves the crabbed
handwriting of a tale written by Jörgen Moe on horseback, or a
volume inscribed to Asbjörnsen by Hans Christian Andersen.[11]

Moltke Moe was succeeded by Knut Liestöl, who held the pro-
fessorship of Norse popular tradition from 1917 to 1951. Liestöl
edited the collected writings of Moltke Moe in three volumes
(1925–27), and wrote a perceptive biography of Asbjörnsen (1947),
analyzing closely his theories of legends and folk beliefs. He
also prepared as co-author with Moltke Moe a selection of Norwegian ballads from the middle ages (1912). A major work of
his own, available in English translation, is *The Origin of the
Icelandic Family Sagas* (1930), a skilful treatment of oral narrative style and techniques as practiced by the reciters of Icelandic
sagas. In his comment on the nature of oral historical tradition,
Liestöl was able to draw from the accumulated knowledge of
peasant storytelling in modern Norway. A memorial volume of
ballads, folktales, and legends he had collected was edited in

[10] Axel Olrik, "Personal Impressions of Moltke Moe," Folklore Fellows
Communications, No. 17 (Helsinki, 1915), p. 16.

[11] Sigurd B. Hustvedt, *Ballad Books and Ballad Men* (Cambridge, Mass.:
Harvard University Press, 1916), pp. 167–68; and Warren E. Roberts,
"Folklore in Norway: Addendum," in *Folklore Research Around the
World,* ed. R. M. Dorson (Bloomington, Ind.: Indiana University Press,
1961), pp. 35–36.

1955 by his assistant and successor, Reidar Th. Christiansen.

Reidar Christiansen has devoted a lengthy and productive career to the study of Norwegian traditional narrative. In 1921 he constructed a type index of *eventyr,* based on the system first proposed by the Finnish scholar Antti Aarne in 1910 for identifying traditional European folktales. When revised editions of Aarne's type index were prepared for all Europe by Stith Thompson in 1928 and 1961, they duly incorporated the Christiansen references for Norway. Moving from the *eventyr* to the *sagn,* Christiansen in 1958 devised a completely new original type index, *The Migratory Legends.* The subtitle, "A Proposed List of Types with a Systematic Catalogue of the Norwegian Variants," indicated both the general and the restricted character of the work. Where Aarne had made an inventory of the whole European stock of fictional tales available to him, and identified popular tale-units which national collectors could recognize in their own countries, Christiansen constructed the legend index entirely from texts known in Norway, but intended that it too could guide legend cataloguers elsewhere in Europe.

This undertaking presented difficulties which had deterred earlier folklorists from attempting to classify the slippery materials of legend. Unlike the more firmly patterned animal and magical and romantic fictions, these retellings of personal experiences with ghosts and demons, or of exploits of local heroes and heroines facing invaders or robbers, lacked sharp and clear episodic structure. As the archives filled with all manner of local traditions, the evidence showed that many alleged happenings were in truth wandering fictions. To draw a line between the individual and the generic text, Christiansen employed a distinction already foreshadowed by Asbjörnsen and made explicit by the Swedish folklorist Carl von Sydow with the terms *memorates* and *fabulates.* Many a villager or townsman might describe his or his neighbor's encounter with a revenant, a witch, the Devil, a troll, and this formless account was a *memorate;* but frequent repetitions of such incidents gave them a definite sequence of motifs, and these were *fabulates,* or traveling legends. They fastened onto a churchyard, a boulder, a mound, a grove, a river, a fiddler, an old woman, a soldier on leave, as they

moved from one community to another, and from one country
to another. From this latter group Christiansen abstracted some
seventy-seven legend types, many of which are represented in
the present volume.

A wide-ranging scholar, Christiansen has not confined himself to the Norwegian repertoire, but has considered the relation
of Scandinavian tales in general to Irish and Scottish lore, and
of European narratives to their variants in the United States. A
year as visiting professor of folklore at Indiana University in
1956–57, followed by a year with the Irish Folklore Commission
in Dublin, contributed to the perspective of these comparative
studies. In English alone he has published extensive monographs
on *The Vikings and the Viking Wars in Irish and Gaelic Tradition* (1931), and a sequel, *Studies in Irish and Scandinavian Folktales* (1959), while a different line of comparison produced
*European Folklore in America* (1962). These investigations de-
parted from the customary style of tracing the life history of a
tale by the so-called Finnish historic-geographic method, a
method which Christiansen himself criticized as reducing the
study of folklore to a dry list of statistical tables and charts. Instead, Christiansen has attempted, and succeeded, in viewing
the similarities and differences in bodies of folktales as results of
cultural and environmental circumstances affecting the narrator
and his tradition.

It is only fitting that the present edition of Norwegian folktales be prepared by the leading folktale scholar of Norway, who
continues the memorable enterprise commenced by Peter Asbjörnsen and Jörgen Moe.

RICHARD M. DORSON

# Introduction

Both legends and folktales may be included under the term *oral narrative tradition,* in itself a province of the more extensive category of *folklore.* There is no universally accepted definition for folklore, but the suggestions listed in Funk and Wagnall's *Dictionary of Folklore, Mythology and Legend* (1959–60) emphasize the traditional, unliterary origin of the elements involved. A precise definition may be useful, but folklore may also be considered as a special cultural complex, rooted in the distant past, yet persisting in the present because some of its main concepts are so deeply ingrained in the human consciousness that they still color the attitudes of a certain percentage of the population—especially in regions where the influence of modern industrial civilization has not been dominant. To us such traces seem irrational or "superstitious," because they do not conform to what is taught in schools or to what is accessible in print. A better understanding of the relationship between the different branches of folklore may be obtained if they are considered as coherent parts of a special type of culture.

Every type of human society—savage or civilized, ancient or modern—has had some kind of emotional outlet as a relief from the problems of existence. One may call it *art,* in its broadest sense, without entering upon the vexatious question of origins. Music, with or without the accompaniment of dancing, and the drawing of rough pictures have this function, combined perhaps with some practical purpose. By analogy the folklore complex had its literature: poetry and prose. In our day both confront us in print (in folklore) as ballads and songs and folktales. The analogy may be extended to history—the record of what has happened or is believed to have happened. To us, history is a vast conglomeration of facts, speculations, and interpretations, too vast for any individual to master.

The urge to connect, somehow, the past to the present seems to be inherent in human beings at every stage of development. In the oral tradition, history has, as its counterpart, the legends. A better term is the one in use in some European countries—*Sage, sagn*, etc.—while *legend* is reserved for a religious, pious tale. The etymology of these terms indicates the difference between them. *Sage* is something told or spoken; legends are read, as in religious teaching and services.

Such generalized considerations serve to illustrate the essential difference between legend and folktale. The latter is akin to fiction, the former to history. Both, to a certain extent, may overlap, and a folktale may ultimately be founded upon a legend. In the main, however, both storytellers and listeners are fully aware of the difference, and where the telling of folktales still has a social function, it is addressed to adults, not exclusively to children.

The term *fairy tale,* used for folktale, is misleading and was coined in a milieu where the fairies no longer interfered effectively in the life of man, but, by literary influence, figured as diminutive ballet dancers, removed at a safe distance into an imaginary world. Actually, the fairies, or by whatever name they might be known, were legitimate denizens of this world, even if they might have a "secret commonwealth" of their own.

In classifying legends with history, one has to remember the essential change in the conception of Man, Nature, and the Universe during the last few centuries, especially on one important point: The implicit belief in the constant interference in everyday life by non-human powers has ceased to play a decisive part, even if traces of such belief may still color and influence the belief and behavior of individuals everywhere.

According to traditional, i.e., legendary, history, such powers interfere actively, and even if some legends do not refer to them, it is curious to note that legends primarily associated with some real event also have a tendency to introduce, at one point or another, a non-human factor. This tendency is probably connected with the function of the legend, which is to explain anything that seems to call for an explanation, corresponding, according to Malinowski, to the function of the myth in primitive society.

At the same time, however, a legend is told in a strictly realistic manner, as something which really did happen, but with the reference to the out-of-the-ordinary being the very reason for its being remembered at all. Legends may sometimes combine into a whole cycle, a *saga,* and when compared with documentary evidence, may turn out to be a fairly accurate reflection of a period, and even some insignificant and striking feature may turn out to have a foundation in fact.

Only rarely, however, do legends offer important additions to our knowledge of history, and the reason is obvious. Accounts in a fixed text remain unchanged, while in oral tradition the contents are subject to a further development. The surprising tenacity of folk-memory is well established, but in oral transmission a more or less unconscious rearrangement sets in, until a definite pattern is evolved in passing from generation to generation. The process is highly complicated, and, by its very nature, extremely difficult to analyze in detail.

Because legends are told as actual truth, the contents are determined by folk-belief, while, in a folktale, the choice of motifs is determined by the exigencies of the pattern, and strange happenings are accepted without comment. To a modern mind, legends may include episodes equally as fanciful even if they are presented as facts, because they are rooted in conceptions that we now label "superstitious." Yet, in some form or other, they retain their hold on the mind and affect our behavior, if only in small matters like avoiding walking under a ladder or touching wood. After all, to quote Graham Greene, "Man has to resort to some kind of superstition. They are the nails in his boots that keep him on the rock."

In the present selection of Norwegian legends, the traditional classification of *historical* legends and *mythical* legends is used. The distinction is useful, with the reservation that the former are not history and the latter are not myths. Both classes are represented, and in the Introduction, a short survey of the various themes is given, as well as a brief sketch of their general background.

The legends called *historical* record some event in the past, are associated with some definite locality or object, or center around an individual striking enough to be remembered. As a rule, their horizon is limited to a single region, and only rarely is their subject something that concerns the history of the country as a whole. In Norwegian tradition such subjects are the National Saint, St. Olav (Hellig Olav); the Black Death, the Great Plague that devastated the country around the year A.D. 1350; and, to a lesser degree, past wars and searches for buried treasure.

The National Saint, St. Olav, the perpetual king of Norway (*rex perpetuus Norwegiæ*), has left a strong imprint upon oral tradition, and there are traces of his activities in all parts of the country. To quote the first printed collection of Norwegian legends by Andreas Faye (1833):

> Throughout the country traces of the activities of the Saint and king exist. Springs welled forth where he suffered from thirst, and were vested with healing powers when he drank from them. Mountains split at his bidding, passages opened where he needed them. Churches were built, and in St. Olav the trolls found an antagonist equally as formidable as Tor, the god, whose flaming beard the Saint inherited.

As the king who converted his countrymen to the Christian faith, he is, by legends, accredited with building any number of churches. He is even said to have enlisted the assistance of a troll in the building of the most famous church in Norway, Trondheim Cathedral—a story also told of churches elsewhere (as of the cathedral in Lund, Sweden). Common also are tales about his conflicts with trolls and other beings.

The second period of Norwegian history remembered in the oral tradition is the Great Plague. In the tradition of one western Norwegian district, the year is remembered in this way: It was the year of a grill (M), three sausages (CCC), a cramp (L) and a spear (I), i.e., MCCCLI, or 1351. It is estimated that about two-thirds of the population died, among them a comparatively large number of members of the clergy. Whole districts were laid waste, farmsteads decayed. It was a national disaster and explains the country's subsequent decline. In these stories the Plague is personified as an old hag, wandering through the parishes with a broom and a rake. Legends tell of encounters with her, of men ferrying her across a lake, as well as of the few survivors and their fates, about the troubled years, or of the farms and even churches found many years afterward in the wilderness.

Years of wars and famine are also subjects for legendary tradition, especially such dramatic episodes as of a guide leading an enemy troop to destruction. In eastern Norway, incidents from the wars with the Swedes are remembered, and along the south and west coasts a favorite theme is the blockade-running during the last phase of the Napoleonic Wars. Even the German occupation is reflected in legends gradually adapted to the traditional pattern: rivers flowing red with blood, and so forth.

Stories of outlaws and robbers are also known. Extremely popular is the tale of the girl taken captive and her escape. The theme of the legends is often associated with some landmark, with a building such as a church. The churches were the only conspicuous buildings, the only ornamental structures to be found. Stories are told of the intervention of non-human beings in changing building sites. It has been contested that such stories may be based on the fact that the churches were often built upon the site of a pagan cult center, but such conclusions are rather hazardous. Everything connected with the churches or church ritual was thought to possess some mystic power, and might play an important part in traditional remedies against afflictions of many kinds. Church bells resisted removal to a new location, as did an altarpiece, like the famous one in Ringsaker church.

A theme even more popular in the legends is the search for buried treasure, as current in all parts of Norway as it is everywhere else. Buried treasure has played an important part in the collective imagination. People try to recover these hoards, and sometimes even find them. But usually, by breaking some rule or by the intervention of the guardians of the treasure, they lose them again immediately.

The other group, the *mythical* legends, is more varied and, as has been mentioned, more widely current. Such legends are not distorted pagan myths, but may well be rooted in the same ground as the ancient Norse mythology. The term is here employed in the sense of legends in which non-human elements play a decisive part. At the same time, however, these legends are told as actual facts, with an obvious tendency to work in some realistic touch in order to stress the truth of what is being told. This is done by somehow identifying the person to whom it happened as, e.g., "... an old woman my grandmother knew well"; or the locality where it occurred as, e.g., "... at a farm up toward the North"; or the date, "... about a hundred years ago"; or by pointing out an object or landmark associated with the event, as in the case of the tale about the drinking cup stolen from the *huldre*-folk.

With the mythical legends the question arises as to the relationship between two different types, for which the terms *memorat* and *fabulat* have been suggested. The former is defined as the firsthand account of an individual experience with non-humans, while a *fabulat* means a story that has been developed, by oral transmission, to conform to the traditional pattern. The distinction is difficult to maintain, because such a direct, firsthand account is not objective but is explained at once by the observer according to the traditional complex of ideas. He or she may have experienced something out of the ordinary, but it is unconsciously interpreted in accordance with what traditionally happens when a person encounters these neighbors.

Such accounts—and any number exist—would scarcely be called legends in the strictest sense, but, rather, illustrations of current folk-belief, and they serve as conclusive evidence of the reality of such belief in a "secret commonwealth" coexistent with man. In a way, they are the rough materials out of which legends have developed. Accounts of individual experiences are, further, usually presented to us in the records of a collector, and most collectors will be familiar with the phrase: "Pity you did not come when so-and-so was alive. He would have had something to tell."

In a category between historical and mythical legends falls a cycle of legends about the art of magic and its practitioners.

Some of these legends are international and migratory, especially tales about the experts. Others may be taken rather as illustrations of folk-belief. The belief in magic is probably universal, and in ancient Norse literature—in the sagas as in the poetry—references to magic and witchcraft are numerous. Witches, shapeshifting, spells, and magic words are often mentioned, and Odin the god is past master of magic, possessing the right spell for every occasion. In later oral tradition, vestiges of these conceptions are easy to trace, but the actual legends are, on the whole, derived from the belief in witchcraft, systematized and acknowledged as a vital part of the teaching of the Church, and, consequently, regarded by the secular authorities as a sinister crime. They could point to the words of the Bible itself, commanding "Let not a wizard dwell among you" (Fifth Book of Moses 18.10). The belief held sway almost to the end of the eighteenth century, and its shadows lingered much longer, with the whole complex furnishing rich materials for legendary tradition.

These materials were not exclusively Norwegian, but migratory. Stories were current about the School of Magic, assumed to be situated at some famous university, as, e.g., the one at Salamanca. In Norway the full impact of the belief in witchcraft coincided with the introduction of Lutheranism by royal decree in 1536. It therefore seemed a natural conclusion that this Black School was situated in the chief Lutheran city, Wittenberg, in Germany. Only pupils from this school, later ministers, were qualified to handle their textbook, the dreaded *Black Book,* copies of which have sometimes been claimed to have been found "in a marble chest at the castle of Wittenberg."

The book is often called *Cyprianus,* after a legendary master of magic, and has a very complicated pedigree. A large number of manuscript copies exist, popularized and with copious additions from current tradition. Concerning the school, a well-known legend is told. One pupil, in this case a Norwegian who later became a renowned minister, escapes by tricking the headmaster, who is entitled to keep for himself the last pupil to leave the school at the end of the term. In this case he is tricked into grasping at the shadow, so that afterward the pupil has no

shadow at all—a fact often mentioned by witnesses to vouch for
the truth of the story.

The activities of these wise and venerable clergymen supply
the themes for a large number of legends, and tradition seems
to have preferred those who, in some way or other, were different
and more striking than their colleagues in looks or behavior—
or those who had written a book. One of them, the Rev. H. Ruge,
had published a book called *Curious Speculations upon Various
Matters* (1754), in which he devoted a chapter to the "invisibles",
the *huldre*-folk. Widely known throughout the country, especially in the south and west, is the story about the minister who has
the Devil carry his cart when one of the wheels drops off. The
same story is told about St. Boniface, and in German churches
pictures are extant showing the Saint enjoying a ride of this
sort.

Another story, equally popular, relates how one of these
venerables once exorcised the Devil. A stranger has joined a
party of card players and is a constant winner. A card is dropped
on the floor, and someone picking it up from under the table
notices the stranger's feet and knows who he is. The minister
is fetched, and after a heated dialogue he succeeds in making
the stranger leave through a tiny hole in the window.

In addition, there is the well-known story of what happens
to some inexperienced lad or girl who gets hold of the *Black
Book* and happens to summon the Evil One. To keep him busy
they give him the task of making ropes from sand, an old motif,
thus keeping him busy until the minister's return.

In many countries these magic experts used the assistance of
demons for quick transportation. The famous Scottish wizard,
Michael Scott, did so in order to go to Rome, and in Norway it
was done by the Rev. Petter Dass. He was in charge of a parish
far to the north, and the author of a description of his district
which he called "The Trumpet of Nordland." (There is an
excellent English translation by Prof. Th. Jörgensen, published
by St. Olaf College Press, Northfield, 1954.) Petter Dass also
wrote poems and popular hymns, and his famous journey to
Copenhagen is well known in various districts. Similar quick

passages over large distances in other legends are due to the assistance of trolls or one of the *huldre*-folk.

Inasmuch as the belief in witchcraft persisted until two centuries ago, stories about individual witches are numerous, and their names may be checked by reference to documents from the witchcraft trials. Legends tell of their annual convocations, held in certain churches or on mountains, and of the fate that befalls whoever tries to follow a witch. Stories of witches are recorded from many countries in Europe and from the United States as well. How such dangerous powers might be inherited is illustrated in a story about the daughter of a witch who has been sentenced to die on the pyre. The girl has been adopted by a benevolent clergyman who wants to save her. It turns out, however, that she is already conversant with evil practices, and she suffers the same kind of death as her mother.

While most of these tales had their origin in the medieval witchcraft complex, there is one legend which has a more direct connection with ancient Norse ideas: the tale of the Finn messenger. Some person, far away from home, is deeply worried about not having news of his family, and his companion is a Finn who promises to get news quickly. The Finn falls into a trance after ordering that no one is to touch him until he comes to himself. When he returns, he has good news and also brings back some special object, a silver spoon perhaps, in confirmation of his visit. Later it is learned that the spoon unaccountably disappeared from the home on the very day of the messenger's visit. The story corresponds remarkably well to what is told in the Vatnsdöla-saga. One of the prospective emigrants to Iceland employs two Laplanders, i.e., Finns, to find a suitable place for a settlement. He gives them a silver goblet, which they are to bury at the chosen spot. When the Norseman reaches that place, he finds the goblet. The fame of the Finns as experts in the magic arts is deeply ingrained in the Norwegian tradition from ancient times and, to a certain extent, still persists. In the tale "Driving out the Snakes," the stranger called in for this task is usually said to be a Finn. He drives out the snakes but perishes himself.

Although Norwegian legends about witchcraft were mainly

derived from a comparatively late, officially accepted complex of ideas, other cycles of legends are founded upon conceptions far more ancient, not to say universal, such as legends concerning the human spirit or the soul, by whatever name it be known. It can manifest itself both before and after the final separation in death.

Stories about ghosts, or revenants, are equally familiar elsewhere, even in states like New York, as is evidenced by a very interesting paper, "Some Characteristics of New York Ghosts," *Journal of American Folklore,* LVII (1944), p. 320. Ghosts usually have some message to deliver or some wrong to redress. But it may also happen that a mortal becomes involved in their activities by mistake, thereby running a fearful risk—as the person who attends "The Midnight Mass of the Dead," a legend recorded in several districts in Norway, and in other countries. The version reprinted here was recorded around 1850 and has a wealth of local touches. The Mass was held in the main church of the capital, and even the name of the old woman to whom it happened is all but remembered.

The human soul may also move freely about, even before its final separation from the body, and its appearance, in popular belief, is considered an omen of impending death, or a forerunner (Norw. *vardögr*, Scottish *fetch*) of an arrival immediately afterward. In a widely-told legend, the soul was seen on an expedition of its own, as in the case of the soul of Guntram, the king of the Burgundians, as recorded by Paulus Diaconus, a contemporary of Charlemagne. Variants of the story are still current in Norway as well as in other countries.

Associated with the same theme—the human soul and its vagaries—are legends concerning shapeshifting, stories about persons under a spell and able to assume for certain periods the shape of some dangerous animal, in Norway usually a bear (more rarely a wolf), corresponding to the werewolf of international fame. The Laplanders of the far north tell numerous stories about persons assuming animal shape at their own will, and even describe how it was done. A popular legend concerns a married couple, with the husband under such a spell. On one occasion, as he is leaving her, he warns her of a probable attack by a bear. She is attacked but saves herself, and when she later finds out what kind of bear this is, the spell loses its power and he is freed.

It might be said that legends about magic and the human soul have this in common: in both, a human being, even if involuntarily, is the main factor in what happens. In another group of legends, far more extensively known, the central point is the relationship between man and the "unseen powers," the beings, not human, of whose existence he is firmly convinced and about which he could offer innumerable stories in evidence. His attitude toward these beings is a strange mixture of fear and respect, coupled with a certain superiority toward them as belonging to a race inferior to mankind. In both extent and popularity, this cycle comprises the largest number of legends recorded, a fact which illustrates how deeply such belief is rooted in the human mind. It also illustrates how tales of this kind, by constant transmission in oral tradition, develop more or less consciously into well-balanced, if not indeed artistic, compositions. Consider vivid snapshots like these:

"They were standing behind the corner of the house, listening to some of the *huldre*-folk passing by, and overheard one of them saying, 'If one could only live in the world of the sun.' " (*Setesdal*)

"At a farm, husband and wife were always quarreling. One day, during a meal, they kept on in their usual way, when the door was thrown open and one of those dwellers under the ground looked at them and said, 'The same thing here as with us!' And then he slammed the door and vanished." (*Numedal*)

Some kind of systematic arrangement is necessary for a survey of this mass of legends, and usually these beings—the term *spirits* may be misleading, as there is very little that is spiritual about them—are grouped according to the sphere of their activities, as spirits of the sea, of the air, of the hills and wilderness, and household spirits. An arrangement of this kind is similar to a zoölogist's classification of animals, but does not take into sufficient account the fluidity, the interchange, of stories and motifs among these groups. The attitude towards them varies in accordance with the sense of risk and danger involved in any contact with them, but does not justify ascribing to each group a separate origin, even if their appearance or behavior is colored by their sphere of action.

The remaining impression is that such belief is ultimately rooted in a complex of conceptions inherited from a distant past —even if gradually altered through transmission from one generation to another—but still accessible as expressed in tales told even today. This belief has been called the most persistent survival from the past, but has never been worked into a system, into some kind of theology.

Naturally the sea has given a characteristic color to the beings assumed to be living in it. The long coast line and the multitude of islands made a large percentage of the population familiar with the sea, dominating their way of living and their imagination as well. There is an old saying: "The sea is a big storehouse." According to Pliny, there are ten times as many creatures in the sea as ashore, or, to quote a Norwegian proverb: "If there are so many kinds of creatures on land, how many would there not be in the sea!"

At the same time the sea represents constant hardship and danger. "The sea is taking so many," is the refrain of a Norwegian ballad. The *draug* is almost a personification of this attitude. He is a sinister, malevolent being, and his appearance is an omen of impending disaster. In the tradition his name is explained in a way that corresponds to the name itself. It is identical with Old Norse *draugr*, i.e., ghost, or more precisely, "a living dead person," and in some dialects the word *draug* is still used in this sense. In northern Norway, the *draug* is equally familiar with the Laplanders' *rawga,* which shows that they took their conception from the Norwegian. He is said to be someone who had drowned at sea, and had never been given a Christian burial within the sacred precincts of the Church—the necessary condition for being accepted into Heaven. The force of this idea is illustrated by the general sense of duty in securing a decent burial for those who were drowned at sea.

An illustration of the antagonism between those who had been buried and those who had not is the story about the battle between the sea *draugs* and the land *draugs*. The *draug* has a malignant, sinister character. He has been seen testing the seats in a fishing boat to find out which member of the crew would lose his life. He is a constant danger. If a stone covered with moss happens to be taken aboard, it may be the *draug*; in one shape or another he may be taken aboard and then grow so heavy the boat is overturned. His shrieking, heard from the sea, is a sure sign of disaster, as is his appearance in stormy weather, sailing in half a boat. Seen at close quarters, his face is a bundle of sea wrack.

Other sea spirits are less frightening, and the attitude toward them less colored by fear. The merman may actually show his gratitude for a gift. His pedigree goes a long way back, as he is mentioned in "Half's Saga," and called the *Marmennil* (the Sea-mannikin), a tiny creature sitting in a fish hook, giving good advice. Mermaids are also reported, half-fish, half-woman, occupied in the traditional pastime of combing their long tresses. They are sometimes said to have enticed young men to follow them to the bottom of the sea, but on the whole they seem to be later immigrants.

More closely related to the *huldre*-folk on land are the inhabitants of the mysterious islands—in Norway referred to as *Utröst*, Röst being the outermost island in Lofoten, and Utröst, accordingly, beyond Röst. Visits to it are recorded, with the visitors well received. There is an account of a shipwrecked sailor who happens to be present at the Christmas festivities of these islanders, on a tiny isle (Sandflesa) where no one had ever lived. Tales of such islands, visible only at certain intervals, are current in most countries around the North Sea, and some of them (the Irish *Hy Brazil*) have figured on maps even down to fairly recent times. An authentic report of the discovery and a visit to this enchanted island is even in print (Londonderry, 1674). Similar islands later become visible and accessible like ordinary islands. At a farm close to the sea, the farmer is worried by a strange bull coming to land and leading his cows away. He decides to follow them and comes to an island unknown to him. He lights a fire, or happens to be carrying a piece of iron with him, and the island then becomes an ordinary island.

The legend of the sea serpent and the sea horse is known

only in the southwest. It is maintained that sea serpents are reported from various parts of the coastal districts. They breed in inland lakes, and, at a certain age, try to get away to the open sea. Most famous, perhaps, is the serpent in Lake Mjösen. A picturesque ancient account of how it was killed, at some point between 1520 and 1530, reads just like a traditional legend. The *fossegrim* and the *nökk* live in waterfalls and rivers. From the former, many eminent fiddlers have learned to play. The *nökk* is less friendly and often appears in the shape of a white horse grazing by the side of the lake. He tempts young boys into mounting upon his back and then jumps into the lake. An ancient story, recorded as early as the Middle Ages, tells of the *nökk* claiming his due from some river or lake. His due is a human victim, and he claims his due, despite every effort to prevent the catastrophe.

The *oskorei,* "the terrible host," sweeps through Norwegian valleys on winter nights, especially before Christmas time. This is a distinct cycle of legends, recorded in the inlands, Telemark and Valdres, and to some extent farther south and west. Much has been written about the *oskorei,* and various theories have been advanced as to its origin. The name has also been interpreted in different ways. It has been associated with a word *osku* (Old Norse, "terror") and also with the name of the ancient pagan gods (plural *Æsir*), making out that the degraded ancient pagan gods, in the course of time, have become such a host sweeping through the air. Whatever the name may originally have meant (and other names as, e.g., the *jolerei,* are also known), the conception of such a host of evil spirits is by no means exclusively Norwegian. In other countries in northwestern Europe, stories about such hosts are recorded, hosts of ghosts that, for some reason or other, can find no rest. Evidence exists from northern France, around the year 900, of stories of apparitions from Normandy that evidently belong in the same class.

In Telemark, it was said that the host consisted of those who were neither bad enough to go to Hell nor good enough to be admitted into Heaven. In northern Norway the term is *gangferd* and refers to restless, unhappy ghosts that sometimes compel living persons to follow them about. In the tradition, naturally enough, notorious criminals have been seen in the host, and, equally naturally, it happens that observers have recognized persons in the host. Names from fiction and from ancient romance are mentioned, such as *Guro* (Gudrun Gjukesdatter), and *Sigurd*, who by now is said to be old and decrepit, "... his eyes being held open with threads of brass."

In Scotland and Ireland the *sluagh*, i.e., host, is well known. They are restless spirits constantly on the move, "like leaves driven before the wind." In these countries, as elsewhere, they are hostile to mankind. Persons are often carried away by them and may find themselves transported to a distant place. The *oskorei* may settle down for a while at a farm with considerable noise, and such visits are considered a sure sign of fighting and killing. It may be noticed in some of the tales about being carried away by the *oskorei,* how difficult it often is to make a distinction between the host and the *huldre*-folk; thus compare the story about the Valdres girl who was taken on Christmas Eve (tale No. 32) with the story of the host taking possession of a house, as in the tales of the Christmas visitors (tales No. 53a, 53b). These latter are, as a rule, the *huldre*-folk coming from the hill close to the farm.

The classification of such "spirits" according to the sphere in which they operate is open to the qualification that the classes often overlap, so that one is left with the impression that all these beings belong to the same family. In the Norwegian tradition this family group is covered by the name *huldre*-folk, meaning the "hidden people." Equally common is the term *under-jordiske,* meaning "those under the ground." They are also called *hauge*-folk, "people of the mounds," *berg*-folk (especially in eastern Norway toward the Swedish frontier), meaning "people of the hills," and by other names as well.

Before going into a characterization of this race, some mention must be made of the trolls. In international use, the name covers all such "mythical" beings, while in the Norwegian tradition a line of distinction is drawn between the trolls and the *huldre*-folk, despite the fact that the same legend is associated with both, as in the story of the strange journey made by Johannes Blessom in the company of a *jutul* or troll (tale No. 35). In many versions the strange fellow-traveler is one of the *huldre*-folk. Some aspects of the traditional view may clarify the difference. One is that the trolls evidently belong to a distant past. Furthermore, there is a marked difference as to their appearance. Trolls are huge and grotesque, may have only a single eye in the middle of the forehead, and very often three heads. They are terribly strong but are also stupid and are easily tricked by a quick-witted person.

Such aspects point to the conclusions that the trolls have long since passed out of actual folk belief, or, in other words, from the sphere of belief into that of the imagination, of free fantasy. Such a conclusion is confirmed by the fact that trolls figure frequently in ballads and folktales, while in legends they are mentioned only in explaining some conspicuous landmark, such as a huge boulder in the middle of a field or a huge rock-fall. Throughout the countryside, such boulders are said to have been thrown by a troll at a newly built church because the sound of churchbells is abhorrent to the troll race. So they threw stones at, but missed, the church, and the stone is still there as evidence. Occasionally someone may also have met a troll moving all his belongings to a distant mountain where he wishes to be left in peace. It may also be noted that trolls have a predilection for eating human flesh, another point in which they differ from the *huldre*-folk.

Nonetheless, trolls have an established position in Norwegian tradition. They are closely related to the *jotuns* (also *jutul*) who, in ancient Norse mythology, were the constant enemies of the gods, more especially of Thor, the god of strength who is identified by his hammer. In the sagas of adventure, and later in a special group of Norwegian ballads called the *trollviser*, they remain true to their nature, carrying away princesses to their homeland—the dark, ice-covered land of Trollebotn, the huge bay which, according to the ancient geographers, stretched deep into the frozen continent assumed to bridge the distance from Greenland to the north of Scandinavia or Russia.

Whether the trolls and *huldre*-folk came from the same stock or had different origins altogether is a difficult question to which no definite answer has been given. The belief in the existence of a race of giants is of long standing, and the trolls, the *jotuns*, and the giants, e.g., Polyphemus, the Cyclops of the Greeks and Romans, seem to be of the same kin, and tend, as creatures and offspring of human fantasy, to be independent of any historical or geographical background.

In any event, no doubt could exist as to the fact that the *huldre-folk* are much more closely related to man. The belief in their existence is deeply rooted, and where references to them in earlier documents and sources are rare, the reason may well be that contacts with them were such everyday occurrences that they were not thought worthy of notice. About 150 years ago, when country people and their world became a subject of general interest, writers considered such beliefs to be superstition. Their serious objections to it are evidence of the tenacity of such conceptions.

Even today firm believers exist, although they are growing rarer every year. They are not inclined to talk about such things, partly from their fear of ridicule, but also from the semi-religious aura which surrounds references to the other race. As the beliefs were never arranged into any definite system, contradictions—apparent and real—are frequent within this vast mass of legends. They were told not as entertainment but as constantly renewed proof of the necessity not to deviate from the traditional code of behavior. This code had to be observed in order to avoid running any risks from contacts with these invisible neighbors.

Some of the names by which "they"—perhaps the safest way of referring to them—were known have been noted above. Most of these names refer to the places where they were supposed to be living. The term *underjordiske*, in a general way, expressed the opinion as to the whereabouts of their domain, which also included the ground under the houses. Compare the term *kjellerman*, "cellar man," which is sometimes used. More realistic was the belief that they might use one of the houses on the farm, one not in daily use and rarely visited by man. But they often lived literally under a building, e.g., in a stable or a cowshed. One may notice the numerous stories about the farmer being asked to remove his stable or cowshed, as it was a nuisance to those below.

As of old, grave mounds were a part of the farmstead, and the *huldre*-folk were thought to occupy the grave mounds. Thus, they are often referred to as the *haug*-folk ("dwellers in mounds"), or *haugetusser*. They were further removed to a safer distance when they were housed in a hill near the farmstead or in the cabins at the mountain pastures occupied in the summer, the *seter*. Here they moved in when the farmer's people left in the autumn, and these, on their return in the spring, had to ask the winter dwellers for permission to enter. According to Snorre the historian, King Olav, the royal saint, once had to spend a night in a *seter*. He did so despite warnings, and weeping and lamenting were heard when the *vetter* (i.e., the *huldre*-folk) had to move away, "burnt by the king's prayers." Thus they lived on the fringe of the sphere of the farm people. But one might equally well happen to see their cattle unexpectedly in the woods, or hear them singing and playing, or even find oneself suddenly inside their house, situated in a place where nobody had ever seen a house before. In intercourse with them, there is a certain latitude between an actual coexistence and chance meetings in places far afield.

As to the appearance of the *huldre*-folk, most observers seem to agree that they look very much like human beings. They were often mistaken for people, and the many tales about inter-marriage with their race point to a similar conclusion. At the same time, however, there is also a tendency to conceive of them as being small. Some names in use point in the same direction, and authorities on such matters have emphatically stated that it is so. In a complex colored more by emotion than by reasoning, contradictions of this kind need not be surprising. There is also the plausible conjecture that dwellers in the mounds were small of stature.

In the same way, in Scotland and Ireland, the dwellers in the *raths* (subterranean dwellings) were believed to be tiny creatures. Somewhere in the Hebrides, a set of chessmen was found during the excavation of such a *rath*, and the immediate reaction of one of the diggers was, "Were they really as small as this?" The idea of size may also be an expression of the attitudes of supe-riority held toward them. They might be beautiful, as are the young *huldre* girls when they try to capture some young lad, or they might be grotesque, with abnormally long noses. And even a *huldre* girl (sometimes called a *hulder*) gives her true nature away by revealing a cow's tail—appreciates a gentle hint to hide it. Such attributes may also express the consciousness on the part of human beings of stepping outside their natural and legitimate boundaries, by having intimate intercourse with a member of another order of beings.

Another conception, not consistently held, is that in the *huldre* world nothing is what it seems to be. What looks to us like splendor is actually squalor and misery. A mortal may acquire the faculty of seeing their world as they see it themselves by applying some kind of ointment to his eyes—as in the stories of the woman who acts as midwife to the *huldre*-folk (tales Nos. 49a, 49b)—or by having a slight slit made in his eye (as in Ibsen's *Peer Gynt*). On the other hand, most visitors to their houses have given testimony of opulence, in descriptions modeled upon the interior of some well-to-do farm. And girls who ended up marrying into their race, at some chance meeting with people long afterward, have told that they were living as if "every day was like Christmas day."

Mortals and *huldre*-folk may be closely related, but they are essentially different. Every contact with them involves a risk, and even talking about some such chance encounter before sleeping on it, or answering when they call you by name, may have serious consequences. This attitude is apparent in a vast number of legends where the theme is their insatiable desire to capture a human being. They steal infants in the cradle and leave one of their ugly brats instead. The changeling is a heavy burden to a family, even if means of getting rid of him exist. Young boys and girls are often their victims. If a young girl about to be married is left alone at a *seter*, she is in serious danger of finding herself married to one of the *huldre*-folk. In most stories she is saved in the nick of time. It may be noted how this type of legend also explains the birth of abnormal or deformed infants, or the disappearance or premature deaths of some young person. Visitors to the houses of the *huldre*-folk have, in many cases, recognized captured persons there, and such visitors had better know that they should not touch either food or drink offered to them. In general, the *huldre*-folk are known to be tricky neighbors, especially as they can appear and disappear at will.

It has been repeatedly stressed that there was never any system in this congeries of beliefs, even if the tradition does explain the origin of the *huldre*-folk. They were the children of Adam and his first wife (tale No. 38) or they were the children of Eve (tale No. 39). Once, when our Lord came to see her, after they had been driven out of Eden, she had only washed some of her children. She hid the rest away. Our Lord knew this and decreed: "Those not revealed shall remain concealed" (*huldre*, from the verb *hylja*, meaning "to cover or conceal"). A third explanation is that they belonged to the party of angels that rebelled against our Lord and were driven out of Heaven. Some of them were not as bad as the rest and remained in the air between Heaven and Hell. Their ultimate salvation is an open question, but they are also said to have churches and clergymen of their own, and some of them are said to be so strict that they cannot stand to hear cursing or swearing.

Traditional explanations of this kind do not in any way give an answer to the problem of the ultimate origin of the belief. The problem is very difficult; no attempt can be made here to enter upon this discussion. However, some general lines must be indicated. A belief in the existence of a class of beings, not human but belonging to the world of man, seems to be universal. But the conception of them varies and is altered for every new country. New aspects, new characteristics, have developed in new surroundings. In Norway, as well as in the other northern countries, we note the persistence of the ancient pagan conception of the nature of man. He is not conceived of as consisting of two elements, the one surviving on the destruction of the other, but remains himself, continuing in some way to live on and on, to remain alive and active.

This strange being, "the living corpse," presents a serious problem to the survivors. In the sagas, many instances are mentioned of the difficulties caused by these shadowy but intensely human ancestors, more malignant and active than any ghost. They had to be placated. Quarters had to be provided for them

in the burial mounds, and huge, empty grave mounds testify
to such efforts. They might also have to move into a hill close to
a farm. A Norse immigrant to Iceland is said to have chosen a
site close to the mountain in order "to die into the mountain."
Removing the ancestors to a safer distance would mean a certain
relief from the constant pressure involved by their presence. However, it might turn out that they were very close neighbors after
all, living under the farmhouse itself, making their presence
known and insisting upon being treated with respect and consideration.

As the centuries passed there was a further development, to
a considerable extent due to the teachings of the Church. And
gradually these non-human beings were conceived of as a race
apart, were referred to by a new set of terms, some of them pre-
serving the ancient associations (*hauge*-folk, "the people of the
grave mounds"). Also inherited from the past were some of their
characteristics: the desire to capture mortals for their own world,
the evidence of visitors to their houses of having met people
there they once knew who had died before their visit. The
persistence of the belief in the *huldre*-folk and the preservation of
the ancient characteristics justify the verdict of an archeologist
that this belief "is the strongest link extant with a distant past."

Finally, another group of such beings calls for attention: the
household spirits. Somewhere in eastern Norway a boy happened
to see a tiny man sitting on a stone. "Don't be afraid of me,"
he said to the boy, "I will do you no harm." The one who told
the story reflected, "But whether this was one of the *huldre*-folk
or a *nisse*, I could not tell." Both belong to the same race, but
the *nisse* has been evolved out of a mixture of elements, some
introduced fairly recently and some quite ancient conceptions,
as a being that has specialized as a guardian of the farmstead
and its fortunes.

The *huldre*-folk may certainly inhabit the house, but they are
not thought of as its guardians, a position ascribed to the *nisse*,
who is actively interested in the prosperity of the people living
there. He may have certain claims but, if treated with due consideration, is a staunch defender of the welfare of his hosts. The
*nisse* is of diminutive size, even though inordinately strong. He

wears a red cap with a tassel and seems to be a fairly recent arrival in Norway.

His pedigree extends through Denmark to Germany, to St. Nicholas, and through him he is related to Santa Claus, by now an international and, to a large extent, commercialized figure. However, the conception of a guardian of the farm is far more ancient in Norwegian tradition, and, while the *nisse* is best known in the eastern and southern districts, in the west and north the *gardvord*, i.e., "the guardian of the house," or the *tunkall* or *godbonde*, still figure in belief and stories. He is a more sinister type. He is very big; in fact, he has been seen leaning his elbows on the roof of the house. A room had to be reserved for him, or at any rate a bed, and a photograph of one actually exists. He resents intruders, and handles them roughly, but he is also a good guardian against dangers of any kind.

The national characteristics of Norwegian folktales are far less in evidence and are accordingly more difficult to define than is the special Norwegian flavor of the legends. The reason seems apparent. As has been emphasized, folktales are to be classed with fiction, while legends are akin to history and determined by folk-belief which is a steady growth of centuries, with lines running back to prehistoric times. Legend motifs are often migratory and international, but when introduced, they are transposed into a Norwegian key.

The first collection of Norwegian folktales by Asbjörnsen and Moe has, in the course of time, become a national classic, and the pertinent remarks of J. Moe in his Introduction to the second edition (1852) are still instructive today. One notes his appreciation of the right approach to the storytellers, by many, he wrote, "supposed to be an easy matter," but it has, as a necessary qualification ". . . a tact developed through practice and knowledge . . . ." To a would-be editor, another problem even more difficult was the rendering of the tales recorded into a readable text, as the current literary language of Norway at that date was far removed from the daily speech of the countryside. For centuries the language spoken, and even more, the one written and in official use, was closely modeled upon Danish, with the Old Norse tongue surviving only in the vocabulary and grammar of the country dialects. The gap between the two was apparent enough to everyone.

Both Asbjörnsen and Moe possessed the necessary qualifications: both were intimately acquainted with the people of the countryside. Both had a sure touch, which explains why their collection became a classic, sharing with the Bible and the Book of Hymns the privilege of constant revision in order always to correspond to spoken and written Norwegian. This was left as a special legacy by Asbjörnsen to later editors, and his instructions have been followed with every new edition.

J. Moe also raised another question: to what extent could one talk about *Norwegian* folktales, except in the sense of tales being recorded in Norway? He was well aware of the fact that all the tales in his edition had their counterparts, even to minute details, in collections from other countries. He was familiar with the writings of Jacob Grimm, accepted his views, and was familiar with most collections published at that date. This amazing unity of folktales has since become increasingly evident, and the problem he posed—does any Norwegian folktale, unique in pattern or in manner, really exist?—has become even more puzzling. Accordingly, national characteristics, as has already been pointed out by J. Moe, have to be looked for in the manner of retelling the story and in the presentation of the standard types of persons introduced in the tales.

A precise interpretation of such possible characteristics is often equally applicable to the folktales of other nationalities as well. Nor is the way of telling a tale the same in all Norwegian districts. Most of the tales in the collections of Asbjörnsen and Moe were recorded in the eastern Norwegian districts, and they differ in manner from the Telemark versions, where the folktale tradition was best preserved. And both in turn are different from the shorter, more pointed way of telling stories in western Norway and in Tröndelag—where pauses and gestures bridge gaps effectively—and the more prosy rendering of the stories in the north.

Another factor to be taken into consideration is the contribution of the various editors in giving definite shape to the tales they recorded. Such considerations make a precise definition of the characteristic Norwegian folktale hazardous. When J. Moe asserted that the style of Norwegian folktales is "a distinct continuation of the saga manner," he qualified the statement: that the continuity was not in the diction but in the presentation of the chief actors and their reactions.

To illustrate his point, J. Moe adds some instances, but the problem seems as imponderable as any attempt to determine the special characteristics of the Norwegians. And yet, the folktales have undergone a process of being attuned, making their types Norwegian, easily recognizable as their own by the Norwegians themselves. The best expression of this feeling is perhaps to be found in the illustrations to the stories made by Norwegian artists. An artist like Kittelsen has shown us once and for all with a troll looks like. Another artist, Werenskiold, has retained the regality of kings and princesses within the frame of Norwegian peasant surroundings and accessories.

In summing up, one might quote the words of Moltke Moe, son of the collector and, for many years, at the center of collecting and studying Norwegian folklore, as well as professor of this subject at the University of Oslo, in his Introduction to the centenary edition of *Folke og Huldre-eventyr* (1911): "In Norwegian folk tradition we recognize some salient features: the sound common sense, the cool objectivity, the manly pose; but also the wealth of contradictions, the gigantic exertions with long, quiet intervals—but sometimes with an undertone of the charm of a summer evening, a strong imagination that lends to the marvels of imagination and illusion of reality . . . a presentation episodic, impressionistic, with an epic-dramatic turn—the decisive episodes side-by-side, like a ridge of blue mountains, the rest in mist and dust, for the fantasy to fill in."

More than a hundred years have passed since the first collection was published, and our knowledge of Norwegian folktales has widened, perhaps not so much as regards their history, but as a result of the number of versions recorded and their diversity. They once heralded what Norwegians call the National Revival, because at that time an ancient traditional strain, the continuation of the language and culture of the centuries before the decline of Norway and the years of union with Denmark, had gone underground and persisted in the tradition of the countryside. This "hidden Norway" again emerged and was absorbed in the main stream of Norwegian life and culture as a vivid and powerful element. Since that time, folklore, in the forms of poetry and prose, music and dancing, arts and crafts, has enjoyed a more prominent position in Norway than in most other countries.

A student of Norwegian Folktales has, by now, some 4,000 to 4,500 recorded versions at his disposal, in print and in manuscripts, mainly in the Archives of the Norwegian Folklore Institute at the University of Oslo. A systematic catalogue of the folktales was printed in 1921, with several later editions. In Norway, as elsewhere, the telling of folktales has lost its hold upon the public. Modern ways of living, intercommunication, the general, rapid spreading of news leave scant room for traditional stories. They are, of course, still favorite reading for children, and adults enjoy a good actor's reading of the old favorites, preferably the humorous tales. They have been a source of inspiration to artists, and students have found puzzling problems in them. Some general lines have become apparent. As to the chronology, few dates exist, and references to folktales in earlier writings are extremely rare. One is to be found in the saga of Sverre the King, where the writer refers, with an almost academical disdain, to the tales told by youthful herdsmen about evil stepmothers and king's sons, saying no one knows whether they are true or not. From later writings, evidence is equally scarce, so the only sources available are the folktales themselves.

One may ask: Are some special types of folktales more popular than others in Norway? Statistics show that the tales most often recorded are equally popular in other countries. One fact may be noted, however, and that is that tales about fights with trolls and giants are special favorites, as are, to a slightly lesser extent, stories of marriages between a mortal and a being of the other world. Thus, of the cycle Types 300 to 303, some 350 versions have been recorded, and from Types 400 to 425, some 150. The theme of fighting trolls, referred to above, was always a favorite in Norwegian tradition, and from the later romantic sagas, into the ballads and the folktales, the same popularity seems to have persisted.

The geographical distribution of the types may offer additional indications. If they were entered upon a map, some facts would become apparent. One is that from the Telemark district there is a far greater number of versions than from other parts of the country, but the explanation is that collecting activities for several decades were directed to Telemark at a time when the folktales were still common property. Another suggestive fact is the remarkably close parallels between the tales from the southwest and the Danish folktales, especially those from Jutland, following in the wake of constant communication across the narrow stretch of sea. In eastern Norwegian districts, along the Swedish frontier, the close connection with Swedish folktales is very much in evidence. In the north, the folktale tradition reflects a far more mobile life at sea. During the large seasonal fishing expeditions people from far off places, even from northern Russia, came to Norway. When they were forced to stay ashore during stormy weather, storytelling was the favorite pastime. Farther north, the folktale tradition of the Laplanders reflects the intercourse and exchange with both Norwegians and Finns, and even Russians.

Such indications, however vague, are still suggestive. They show that folktales have gradually developed and that not all the types have been accepted by Norwegian tradition at the same time, but as they were introduced, one by one, perhaps on many separate occasions, through an intercourse to which no definite dates can be assigned. In a way, the bearers of such tradition, the storytellers, were artists, careful to retell a tale in the right way, and, if keeping to the familiar pattern, still intent upon retelling it in an effective manner. There was room for their creative powers, even if the well-known story followed the age-old lines.

Much has been written about the characteristics of the folktale as a special kind of fiction, and such characteristics probably exist. At the same time, however, every good storyteller is aware of the fact that each different type of tale—dramatic, epic, novelistic, humorous—requires a special manner of rendering, and a storyteller might have a predilection for one kind of story. Too little is known about the great Norwegian storytellers of earlier years, but some bits of information are available. The stock of tales of one storyteller was recorded by two collectors at an interval of some ten to fifteen years, and both records were almost identical, with the same choice of words, the same phrases. The first collectors, in the 1830's, were perhaps more intent on recording than on observing their informants, but we have some of their notes showing old men and women with a stock of some hundred stories and definite ideas as to how they should be told.

REIDAR TH. CHRISTIANSEN

# *Contents*

## VII. LEGENDS ABOUT HOUSEHOLD SPIRITS

## VIII. FICTIONAL FOLKTALES

# Part I
# Historical Legends

# ·1a· King Olav, The National Saint

*Norway is full of folk traditions about King Olav, who ruled from 995 to 1030. See Introduction, p. xxii, and Bø,* Heilag-Olav i norsk folketradisjon. *This text was recorded by A. Röstad before 1930 in Verdal (Tröndelag), the scene of the battle in which the king was killed. Printed in* Norsk Folkemin-nelag, *XXV (1931), 156, and reprinted in* Norsk Folkedikting, *III, 118, 226. The Motifs A941.5, "Spring breaks forth through power of saint" and D1567.6, "Stroke of staff brings water from rock," are present.*

· ONCE, WHEN St. Olav, the king, came to Leksdalen, he saw how hard it was for people to travel back and forth. To get to Verdalen they had to cross a big lake and go over Klingen Mountain. The king made the farmers this offer: he would build a bridge over the lake and make a road through Klingen, while the farmers, for their part, were to give him one calfskin from each farm. This they agreed to, and he started building the bridge. But after he had been working there for a while, a man came and said that the king would not be getting any calfskin from him, and with that there was an end to the construction work. But the remains of the bridge, which the king started to build, can still be seen. The shallow bottom goes out in the water for a hundred yards, and this bottom is made like a road.

One day, when St. Olav was busy with the work up on Klingen, he became exceedingly tired and thirsty. He spoke to the mountain, and at once a spring bubbled forth right out of the hard rock. This is called "Olav's Spring" to this very day.

On Bjartnes farm there lies a big stone which resembles a huge bowl. It is said that St. Olav had thought of making a drinking vessel out of this stone, but he did not get it finished. Another time, when the king was going to ford the Trongdöla River, he led his horse across, and deep tracks of both horse and man can still be seen in the hard stone. Down in the lowlands there is a field which is called "Olav's Field," and from time to time something can be seen shining down there. These are small tongues of flame which flicker up in the tracks where St. Olav has walked.

Not a snake is to be found between Verdal River and Stjördal River, and this is because St. Olav once drove out all the snakes into a big cave, and no one has seen snakes there since. One day a man with a load of hay came up from Björge, and was going to cross the bridge over the Verdal River. When he came to the middle of the bridge, a snake popped out of the load of hay and hurried back.

A story is told of a fiddler from Verdal who had been on a journey all the way to Russia with the famous fiddler Ole Bull. It seems they'd had a falling out, and the fiddler from Verdal went home by way of Sweden. But on the way home he became sick, and he grew worse and worse as he came closer to home. It was all he could do to come up to Stikklestad, where St. Olav fell in battle and where the monument to him stands. The man was barely able to crawl over to the monument and touch it, and suddenly he was well again. It was as if the sickness had been stricken from him.

## • *1b* • King Olav and the Gyger

*This legend was collected by A. Faye in Ringerike (in eastern Norway) in the 1840's and printed in A. Faye,* Norske Folkesagn *(1844), 110.*

• ONCE, WHEN St. Olav came to Sten Farm in Ringerike, he had plans for building a church at Sten, because it is said that his mother once lived there. Now a *gyger*—who lived in a mountain, which is called Gyrihaugen to this very day—did not like this one bit, and she proposed that the king go along with a wager:

"By the time you finish your church, I'll have built a stone bridge over the fjord here," she said.

The king said he'd like to try, but before she was halfway finished with the bridge, she heard the bells ringing from St.

Olav's church. Then she became furious, took all the stones she had gathered for the bridge and threw them, from Gyrihaugen, at the church on the other side of the fjord. But none of them hit it. Then she grew even angrier and wrenched off one of her thighs and threw this at the church. What happened next is a matter of dispute. Some say she managed to knock down the tower, others think she aimed too high. But everyone knows that the thighbone fell down in a mud hole behind the church, and this is called Gjöger Puddle to this very day, and a bad odor always comes up out of this mud hole.

Up in the mountains, on the same side of the fjord as Gyrihaugen, a steep road goes down into a narrow valley called Krokkeleiva. Once, when St. Olav came along this road, a *gjöger* ran out of the mountain and shrieked at the king:

> "St. Olav, with red beard and all,
> You ride too near my cellar wall!"

But St. Olav only looked at her and said:

> "Stand here in stock and stone,
> Until I come this way alone!"

And there she stands to this very day!

# • 2a • King Olav, Master Builder of Seljord Church

*Motif H521, "Test: guessing unknown propounder's name"; R. Th. Christiansen, The Migratory Legends, 7065, "Building a Church. The Name of the Masterbuilder"; Type 500, The Name of the Helper. This legend has been collected throughout Norway and in many parts of Sweden. The variant connected with the cathedral in Lund, Sweden, is famous. "The lullaby is often found independently as a well-known nursery rhyme" (The Migratory Legends, p. 210). In its fairy tale form, the story is extraordinarily popular in Denmark, Finland, Germany, and*

*Ireland. Rumpelstiltskin and Tom-Tit-Tot are two of the secret names of the supernatural helper.*

*The legend of the Seljord church in Telemark was recorded by Reverend M. B. Landstad in the 1840's. It was first printed in Norsk Folkeminnelag, XIII (1926), 38–39.*

• IN BRINGSAAS MOUNTAIN, in Seljord, there lived a *tusse* (troll) who was called Skaane—others say he was called Vinfjell. St. Olav had many churches to build, and had to get people to help him wherever he went. He came to an agreement with the troll in Bringsaas, that the troll was to build the church at Seljord and have it ready by a certain time. If, by that time, the king was not able to guess the troll's name, the payment for the building would be the sun and the moon—and St. Olav's head!

As might be expected, the work went fast, but the king could in no way find out what the troll's name was. Time went by, the church was finished except for the spire and the vane, and they were to be put up the next day. And still the king did not know anything about the name.

St. Olav was in great distress, and prayed to God for help. Then, in the evening, the troll went up towards Bringsaas to find a fine, straight billet out of which to make the spire. Then St. Olav heard someone singing inside the mountain. It was the troll's wife singing a lullaby for her baby:

> "Bye, bye baby,
> Skaane's coming soon,
> Bringing St. Olav's head,
> And the sun and moon,
> As playthings for the baby!"

Now St. Olav was saved. On the next day, when the troll had raised both spire and vane, he stood there proud of his work and certain of his payment. Then he shouted to the king, "Well, King Olav, which way is the church facing now?"

"East and west, Skaane!" answered the king. But then the troll became so angry that he fell down from the church tower and was killed. Since then the church has always been called "St. Olav's Church," and it stands there to this very day.

## • 2b • King Olav, Master Builder of Trondheim Cathedral

*This legend was recorded by A. Faye in the 1830's and printed in* Norske Folkesagn *(1844), 5.*

• THE CATHEDRAL in Trondheim is one of the most magnificent churches in the lands here to the north. It has been like that from time immemorial, especially the way it was, when it had its tall, beautiful spire, St. Olav could build the church, all right, but he was not able to put up the spire. He did not rightly know what to do, but in his dilemma he promised the sun as payment to the one who could carry out the work. But there was no one who dared take upon himself the job of putting up the spire, until a troll came who lived in Ladehammeren, a mountain just outside the city. He promised to set up the spire for the payment that was promised, and on the condition that St. Olav was not to call him by name, if he should find out what it was. The king did not know how he was going to get the sun for payment or how he could find out what the name of the troll was.

It happened one night around midnight that St. Olav sailed past Ladehammeren and came below a place called Kjerringa. Then he heard a child crying, while the mother sang to it to make it go to sleep, and comforted it saying that Tvester was coming soon with the "heavenly gold." The king was happy and hurried back to the church. When he got there, the troll was already busy putting the golden knob on the vane of the spire. Then the king shouted, "Tvester, you're putting the vane too far to the west!"

And when the troll heard his name mentioned, he plunged down from the tower and was killed.

# ·3· The Plague as an Old Hag Is Ferried across a River

*R. Th. Christiansen*, The Migratory Legends, *7085* (a subdivision of the legend cycle about the Great Plague). Recorded by S. Nergaard in Aamot, Österdal (in eastern Norway) about 1900 and printed in Norsk Folkeminnelag, III (1921), 109. This legend and Nos. 4, 5, and 6 are part of a cycle about the Black Death. The Great Plague cycle is widely known throughout the country and seems to be primarily Norwegian (The Migratory Legends, p. 214).

· WHEN THE Black Death ravaged Aamot, an old hag went ahead with a rake and a broom. Wherever she used the rake, some people survived. But if she used the broom and swept a farm clean, everyone died there. First she kept to one side of the river, but one day she went down to Sundet and shouted to the ferryman to take her across.

The ferryman did not know who it was, and rowed over to fetch her. When the Black Death entered the boat with the rake and the broom, he understood what kind of person she was, and said, "Well, if I'd known it was you, I certainly would not have come over to fetch you. But surely you'll spare me, who took you over the river."

"I can't promise to spare you," said the Black Death, "but I can promise you one thing; if I must take you, you shall have an easy death." She kept her word, for at the very moment they stepped out of the boat, the ferryman fell down dead.

## · 4 · The Horse That Carried the Corpses across the Mountains

*This legend was first printed in a newspaper in Fedraheimen and reprinted in* Norsk Folkedikting, *III, 159-60. The relationship between the folk tune "Förnesbrunen" and this legend is discussed in Rikard Berge, "Förnesbrunen, Segni og Slaatten,"* Norsk Folkekultur, *XXI (1935), 3-18.*

· THERE IS a folk tune called "Förnesbrunen" (Förnes Brown), about the Black Death. At the time the plague ravaged Mjösstrand, they had a brown horse on Förnes farm, which has since become renowned. It was so clever that people only had to lay the corpses of the plague victims on a sledge and send the horse on its way. Then the horse trudged through the forests and over marshes to Rauland church. At that time there was no church at Mjösstrand, so the dead had to be carried all the way to the church in Rauland, a distance of fourteen miles. When Förnesbrunen came to the hill outside Rauland church, it neighed so loudly that people on the nearby farms could hear it, and they came and took the corpses off the sledge. But the horse left right away, and on the next day it came back with a new load.

It kept this up for a long time, for there were many who died in those days. But in the end the horse was so worn out—because it did not rest, and probably did not get the right food either—that one day it fell down dead when it came to the hill outside the church. People believed—and they were right—that there was something unusual about this horse, and so they dug a big grave on the spot where it had died, and buried Förnesbrunen there. The grave can still be seen, and is called "Hestedokken" (Horse Hollow).

In the folk tune named after this horse one can hear in the music how the horse struggles on the way until finally it cannot manage any longer.

# · 5 · The Jostedal Grouse

*R. Th. Christiansen, The Migratory Legends, 7090. Collected by Olav Sande, Sogn (in western Norway) before 1893 and printed in Olav Sande, Segner fraa Sogn, II, 102. Reprinted in Norsk Folkedikting, III, 158–59. In the latter source (pp. 226–27) is also reprinted Ramus' first recording of the legend in 1735. This is probably the best known of all the legends concerning the Great Plague. Variants from other parts of Norway are connected with various other prominent families.*

· WHEN THE Black Death ravaged the land here, many of the best families in Sogn moved up to Jostedal in order to avoid the plague. They settled down here, cleared fields, and built houses. They had made an agreement with people down by the fjord that they were not to visit them until the plague was over. If anyone wanted to write to them, he was to put the letters under a certain stone, and this stone is called the Letter Stone to this very day. The ones remaining down by the fjord could then fetch an answer from under the same stone. It lies beside the road from Jostedal to Luster.

But no matter how careful and foresighted these people were, the plague came to Jostedal too, and it came so hard that everyone died except a little girl on Björkhaug farm. Some say that seven cows without a herdsman, with the bell-cow in front, came straying over the mountains to the neighboring parish in Gudbrandsdal. When no one came to look for the animals, it occurred to someone that they must have come from Jostedal, and people went over there to see what had happened. If this was the case, then things must really have been in a bad way. Houses stood empty everywhere, and many of the dead had not been buried. They went all through the valley but saw no smoke from a single house, and no sign of life was to be found anywhere.

When they came to Mjelvesdalen, they saw footprints in the

new snow. They followed the tracks, and at Björkhaug they saw
a little girl. As soon as she caught sight of them, she ran into
the birch forest, but at last they caught her. They questioned her
about various things, but she did not understand them nor they
her, except for these words: "Mother, little grouse."

It is told that when her mother was dying, she left food on
the table, put the girl in a feather bed, and put food near the
bed so the girl would not starve to death. When she was found,
some of the feathers had grown fast to her.

The men took her home with them, and she grew into a fine
and clever young woman. Some say she married and settled
down at Björkhaug, but most people think she settled down at
Runnöy, all the way out in Gaupnefjord, where people from
Jostedal drive down to the sea. They called her the "Jostedal
Grouse," after the words her mother had spoken to her. Her
descendants are called "the Grouse Family," and they are known
as generous and influential people. Characteristic of this family
was "bird skin"; that is to say, they had big holes in their skin
as if from the feathers that had grown fast to the girl.

# · 6 ·   The Church Found in the Woods

*This story concerns Hedal Church, Valdres (in eastern Norway).
It was collected by A. Faye about 1835 and printed in his* Norske
Folkesagn *(1844), p. 152. A somewhat earlier reference is to be
found in J. E. Kraft,* Historisk topografisk Haandbog over
Norge, *p. 208. Similar stories are told about other churches, e.g.,
the church in Tuft parish, Sandsvaer; see* Norsk Folkeminnelag,
*XXXI (1934), 42.*

· IN THE REMOTE mountain valleys in Valdres, the Black Death
struck with overwhelming force. On many a farm, in many a
valley, everyone died. The farms lay deserted and forgotten,
until, at long last, people started moving in from the outside.

Once there was a hunter who was out shooting grouse. It
must have been a long time ago, for he was using a bow and

arrow. He caught sight of a bird sitting in a tree and shot at it, but a strange clang was heard as though the arrow had struck a metal object. The hunter went over to see what it was, and underneath some huge trees stood an ancient church. He thought at first that this church must belong to the *huldre*-folk, and to keep it from disappearing right away, he took his fire-steel (*ildjern*), and threw it over the church. On the spot where it landed lies a farm today called Eldjarnstad.

When he had done this, he went over to the church to have a closer look at it. The key was in the door, which, as a matter of fact, was halfway open. In the middle of the floor stood a huge bell, and up by the altar an enormous bear had made its winter lair. The man managed to shoot the bear; afterwards, as a reminder, the huge bearskin was hung on the wall of the church, and old folks relate that they remember when some bits of it were still left. In addition, they found some pictures, a little church made of brass, which had most likely been part of a chest of relics, and more bells, four large ones and a small one. The strange clang had been caused by the arrow striking one of these bells.

The smallest bell was hung in the church, and it is said that if anyone loses his way in the forest and hears the sound of this bell, he finds the right way back at once. People decided to take the biggest bell to the main church, but as they were carrying it across a lake, it slid out of the boat and sank. People said it probably did not want to be separated from its sister. It can still be seen on the bottom when the water is clear, but it is not so easy to get it up. For this, seven brothers are needed, and they must not say a single word while they are trying to get it up. Once there were seven brothers who tried, and they got it all the way up to the edge of the boat when one of them said, "God be praised! Now we have it here!" But at the same moment, the bell slid back into the water again and sank.

# ·7· *Over the Cliff*

*R. Th. Christiansen,* The Migratory Legends, 8000. *Under this number is treated a cycle of legends about the wars of former times, especially against the Swedes. This story was collected in Namdal (in western Norway) by Knut Strompdal about 1920 and printed in* Norsk Folkedikting, III, 167–69. *A ballad about the event localized in Midjaa was printed as a chapbook in Tromsö. This legend is current in northern Norway, especially near the Swedish border. It is adapted to different localities; the enemies may be Russians or Finns as well as Swedes.*

• DURING THE WARS with Sweden, there was once a whole troop of Swedish soldiers who lost their lives while crossing the mountains near Midjaa Farm in Namdal. The troop came from Sweden and had intended harrying the Norwegian border parishes. They heard that a big wedding was going to take place at Midjaa Farm, and they decided to go there. They came by way of the mountains, and up there they met a Finn who stayed in a sheepcote at a spot called Midjaa Seter. The way down to the parish was steep and rugged, and the Swedes wanted the Finn along as a guide. He was not any too willing, but there were a lot of Swedes and they bullied him into doing it. There was no other way out, for otherwise they would have beaten him to death. But this being so, he decided to do it in his own way. He delayed the Swedes with talk and preparations, and when they tried to hurry things up, he said it was best they rested up and waited. Down at the farm all the wedding presents were handed out in the evening, and that was the right time to arrive there. The Swedes thought this sounded likely. They settled down at the Finn's cote during the day, and it was already growing dark when they set out in the evening. It was winter and the snow was deep, so they were all wearing skis. The Finn went first with a pine torch in his hand so the others could follow him.

He knew the mountains well, and dark as it was, he found his way. He was no fonder of the Swedes than the ones who lived there, and he figured out a plan to trick them. In many places in the mountains near Midjaa there are steep cliffs with huge rock-falls below them, and toward one of these the Finn set his course. The Swedes suspected nothing but followed in the ski tracks of the Finn wherever he went. The snow was dry, and they were going fast. The Finn headed right for the cliff, but at the very last moment he managed to fling himself to one side and avoided plunging over the edge. But he threw the torch over the edge, and the Swedes followed it. Maybe they thought the speed was great, but they relied on the Finn and kept on going. The last one in the troop became suspicious, when he saw the Finn clinging fast to a bush. He could not stop, but he wanted to drag the Finn with him at any rate. But he could not grab hold of him and plunged over the edge after the others. They were all killed on the stones down below.

The Finn managed to crawl up again, took another way around, and came down to the farm where the wedding was taking place. When he told what had happened, they would not believe him at first and wanted to take him prisoner as a liar and a cheat. The Finn replied that they could go over and have a look at the rock-fall under the cliff, and there they found all the dead Swedes. Then they set the Finn free, thanked and praised him, and gave him a reward into the bargain.

There was an old black wooden table at the farm, and as a reminder they hammered nails in it for every dead Swede—an iron nail for every enlisted man, a copper one for every officer. This table is still supposed to be at the farm to this very day.

## • 8 •   *The Girl and the Robbers*

*R. Th. Christiansen,* The Migratory Legends, *8025, "The Robbers and the Captive Girl." Collected by A. Faye,* Norske Folkesagn *(1844), pp. 224–25. Earlier references are to be found in a poem from 1828 and in* Topografisk Journal, *XXX (1805), 184.*

*The legend has been collected in some hundred variants from most parts of Norway, except from the north, and it is also known in Sweden. "The tale is generally told in explanation of the verse which is still more widely known"* (The Migratory Legends, p. 215). *Faye cites three different variants of the verse; see* Norske Folkesagn, *pp. 224–27.*

• TYVENBORG (Thieves Fortress) is the name of a high mountain between Soknedal and Aadal, in Ringerike. It is told that in the old days it was a hideout for thieves and robbers. Only one steep path led up to it, and around their lair the robbers had built a wall, so they were safe from being taken by surprise. They stayed there, and used to steal cows from the herds that grazed in the forest below. Once they also took along with them a shepherd girl. She was from a farm called Oppen. She was a prisoner up there, and went about wondering how she could send word down to the parish. At last she had made up a little song:

> Tove, Tove, little friend,
> In the forest are twelve men!
> Tiny babies they do beat!
> Little sheep dogs they do eat!
> Bell cows to the stake they tie!
> Bulls they stick until they die!
> Me they'll rape below the hill,
> In the forest deep and still!

She tried to blow this song on a *lure* (a horn), in case anyone could hear her, but she was a long way from any people, and it was not easy for them to understand what she blew.

One of the robbers wanted to marry her, and at last she pretended she was willing, and suggested that they let her go down to the farm and steal the bridal silver. This she was allowed to do on the condition that she promise not to speak to a living soul. She came down there one night, and did not see anyone, but when she heard that the farmer was awake, she told the chimney everything that had happened. She also said that she would clip into tiny bits some red and white cloth she had with her, and to show the way would drop the pieces after her when she went back. She also said she would hang out an apron when they had celebrated the wedding and all the robbers were drunk. This is exactly what happened, and the people from the parish came to Tyvenborg. To escape, the robbers plunged off the cliff. One of them wanted to drag the girl along with him, and grabbed hold of her apron, but the farmer from Oppen was so close that he caught hold of her, and she was saved.

## • 9a • *The Disputed Site for a Church at Voss*

*Motif F531.6.6.1., "Giants by night move buildings built by men in day"; R. Th. Christiansen, The Migratory Legends, 7060, "Disputed Site for a Church." This legend is told about many Norwegian churches; some 125 variants are reported from all parts of the country.*

*The first variant given here was collected by Ivar Aasen in Vossevangen (in western Norway) in 1844 and printed in* Norsk Folkeminnelag, *I (1923), 81–82.*

• AT THE TIME when they were going to build a church at Voss, in Vang parish, people first thought of building it on Böjarmo, a wooded plain about two furlongs above Vossevangen. They started to build it there too, but the work did not go very well, for everything they built during the day was torn down at night, and no one knew how it happened.

Now there was an old man who was so clever and wise that he was known far and wide. They sent for him, and asked what they were to do. He replied that the church should be built where four valleys meet, and that could not be at any other place but Vossevangen.

It is also related that there was an ax which had been left behind on Böjarmo, and this ax moved a bit every night until it had come all the way down to Vossevangen, and there it stayed. Then they started building where the ax was lying, and everything went so fast that it was as if the work went by itself. There was a mountain just above the spot where they were building, and here they found the kind of stone they wanted to use in the church. They also found some lead there too, and they melted the lead into slabs, and used them to cover the choir. But since then, no lead has ever been found there, nor the kind of stone from which the church was built.

## • 9b • The Disputed Site for a Church at Slagen

*The second variant given here was collected in Slagen (in western Norway) by Kristoffer Bugge about 1900. A reference from 1593 to a similar variant of the tale is to be found in Bishop Jens Nielssön,* Visitatsbog, *p. 37.*

• WHEN THEY WERE going to build a church at Slagen, in Vestfold, it was decided to build it on some land belonging to Ilebrekke Farm, and here they hauled the stone and the materials they were going to use. But the night after this was done, the stone and other materials were moved right across the valley, and this is why the church stands where it does to this very day. People understood that the only thing to be done was to build the church there. But when they moved the stones, they did not take all of them. Some were left behind at Ilebrekke. These are called the "Free Stones," and they can still be seen there. A stretch of woods is also there which is called the "Free Stone Woods."

## · 9c · The Disputed Site for a Church at Hosanger

*The third variant given here was collected in Hosanger (in western Norway) by A. Leiro about 1920. See manuscript by A. Leiro, No. 7, p. 35, in Norsk Folkeminnesamling (Norwegian Folklore Institute).*

· WHEN THE CHURCH in Hosanger burned down, the parishioners were charged with getting materials for a new church. They got hold of timber, which they floated and towed in to the shore at Hosanger. But there was a dispute as to whether or not the church should be built where it had stood before. One night all the timber came loose and drifted down to a place called Eknes. Everyone thought it was probably *tusse*-folk who had been at work. But somehow the church came to stand at Hosanger.

## · 10 · The Altarpiece in Ringsaker Church

*R. Th. Christiansen, The Migratory Legends, 7070ff., "Legends about church-bells." A cycle of Norwegian legends deals with sacred objects such as church bells that refuse to be removed from their location. This variant was collected by P. Chr. As-björnsen in Ringsaker (in eastern Norway) in 1835 and printed in Hedmarks Historie, I, 427.*

· IN THE OLD DAYS, hundreds and hundreds of years ago, there was once a princess in England who was so badly tormented by the Devil that at last she was completely possessed by him. Her father, the king, sent for clergymen from every land and kingdom. Yes, he sent his messengers almost the world over to get hold of the most God-fearing minister, and one who was best trained in the use of the Black Book. But they could not find anyone who was able to drive out Old Erik. One day they managed to draw it out of the Evil One himself that at Ringsaker, in Norway, there was a minister who was so God-fearing and so experienced in black magic that he was the only one who could drive him out. They sent for the Ringsaker minister at once, and when he came he cast out the Devil on the spot.

"Now you can wish for whatever you'd like," said the princess. She was so happy that she did not know how to repay him.

"I desire nothing for myself," said the minister, "but, with your permission, I would like an altarpiece for my congregation."

"Oh to hell with it!" said the Devil. "If that minister had asked for something for himself, I'd have rushed in and tugged and clawed at both body and soul!" he said, and then away he flew.

The princess sent word to Holland and ordered the finest altarpiece that was to be had, and it is hanging in Ringsaker church to this very day. The minister is buried in the cellar, and looks as fresh as if he'd been buried yesterday.

During the wars with the Swedes, in 1567, the cathedral at Hamar was destroyed. A company of Swedes also went up to Ringsaker, ravaging and burning on the way, and they used the church as a stall. They thought of taking the altarpiece along with them, but when they had loaded it onto a wagon and were going to leave, the horse could not pull it. They harnessed horse after horse to the wagon, but it was no use; and not until they had harnessed twelve horses did the wagon begin to move. But when they came to Sveinhaug, it stood quite still again. Then they gave up. A yearling foal was all that was needed to pull the load back to the church again.

## • 11a • Hidden Treasures: The Silver King

R. Th. Christiansen, The Migratory Legends, 8010f., "Hidden Treasures." Stories about hidden treasures are common all over Norway, as they are in many parts of the world. Still, they reveal an individual, local character, even if certain international motifs recur, such as breaking the taboo not to speak, seeing strange apparitions, and so on. See The Migratory Legends, p. 215.

The legend of the silver king at Meheia was collected by the Reverend M. B. Landstad in the 1840's, first printed in Norsk Folkeminnelag, XIII (1926), 58–60, and reprinted in Norsk Folkedikting, III, 89–91.

• THERE WAS A MAN in western Telemark who was so heavily in debt that he was in danger of losing his farm. He was not able to borrow any money in his own parish, so he went to town. But he did not get any money there either, and he had to set out for home again. His knapsack was empty and his spirits were low. He walked along wondering what would become of his wife and children.

He had come as far as Meheia, and there he sat down on a stump by the side of the road to rest. As he sat there moping, an old man came and sat down beside him. They started talking together, and the old fellow was so pleasant and sympathetic that the farmer grew very fond of him and wanted to treat him to something. He took out his snuffbox, took a pinch of snuff himself, and offered the rest to the old fellow. The old man emptied the whole box. They started talking, and the farmer told about his affairs and how badly off he was.

After they had been talking like this for some time, the stranger said, "It's getting late. It's a long way to the parish. You'd better come with me, and then you'll have a place to stay tonight."

The farmer thanked him. He had walked all the way from Drammen that day, so he was quite worn out. They cut across the road and headed into the deep spruce forest. Neither of them said a word. It had grown quite dark, and the farmer noticed that the ground felt strange beneath his feet—as if he were walking over a bridge. When they were well on the other side, they came to a big, magnificent farm. Other farms were lying around it. It was just like a city.

"This is where I live," said the old fellow.

The farmer said with a sigh, "Well, you've really got a fine farm!"

"In this parish I am king!" said the old man, and now the farmer noticed that he was wearing a silver belt around his waist and carrying a silver staff in his hand, and the heelplates on his shoes glittered as if they were of silver too.

When they got inside the house, the old fellow said to his wife, "I brought this man home with me. I got such good snuff from him."

"Well, well," she said, "we'll have to try to give him something in return."

The man from Telemark could hardly keep his eyes open with all the gold and silver that glittered and shone on the walls. He was given good things to eat and drink, and the old fellow showed him around. It was just as magnificent everywhere. But in the middle of the floor stood a terribly big stump. It was so huge that it almost filled the room.

The guest wondered about this, and at last he said, "If I were a man like you, I wouldn't have that ugly old stump here inside the house."

A black cloth was lying over the stump, and the old fellow went over and took it off. The entire stump was of purest silver, and it sparkled and shone like the sun.

"This is the trunk!" said the old fellow. "They've got hold of the roots down in Kongsberg!"

When the farmer set out the next morning, the old fellow filled his knapsack with silver and said he was to pay off the debt on his farm with it.

"If you come this way again, you must look in on me," he

said, and the farmer promised to do so if he could find the way. The old fellow thought he could, for people had started coming to his farm now, he said.

## • *11b* •    Hidden Treasures: Rakbjörg Treasure

*The story of the treasure in Rakbjörg woods was collected by Karen Svensen in Melhus (in western Norway) in 1935 and printed in R. Th. Christiansen, Norske Sagn, p. 147.*

• THERE'S SUPPOSED to be silver up in the woods in a mound called Rakbjörg Mound, on the west side of the Gula River in Melhus. But where this mound lies, no one knows. A couple of hundred years ago—or maybe it was many more—there was a mill by one of the streams up there, as there often were in the old days.

One evening, as the miller was busy grinding flour, a Finn woman came in and asked for a little food. He gave her some flour in her bag, to make some porridge with. The old woman was poor, and she had nothing to pay for it with, she said. He would get what she had to give him, and when she left, she took her staff, pounded it on the floor, shook the dust from it, and said the man was to have this for the food she had received.

When the man went to see what it was, he found she had shaken pure silver dust off her staff. She had put the staff in a brook when she went past it, she said, and that brook was supposed to have so much silver in it that it clung to the staff if she but dipped it down in the water. That was only the "calf" he'd got there, she said, but if he was clever at searching, he'd probably get the "cow" too. Norway was a poor land, she said, and it was going to be so impoverished that people would own nothing. But then they would find so much silver and ore in the mountain that Norway would be the richest land in the world.

But where that stream was, the miller did not know. Many have searched for it, but no one has found it yet.

A blacksmith lived somewhere nearby, and everyone thought he must be rich, for he went about selling objects of silver to people. There were many who wondered where he got the silver from, but they could not get it out of him. Most of them thought he got it from a place out in the forest.

Now one day he was at an inn getting something to drink. Then he started talking about the silver, and bragged that he could shoe his horse with silver if he wanted to. Someone took him up on that, and the blacksmith promised to show them the next time he came to town. Then his horse would be wearing silver horseshoes.

But that same day, on the way home, he became sick, and died shortly afterward; and although many have searched for his mine, no one has ever found it.

## · IIc · Hidden Treasures: The Copper Cauldron

*The legend about the copper cauldron was collected by R. A. Quitzen in Stördal (on the Swedish border) in 1835 and printed in R. Th. Christiansen,* Norske Sagn, *p. 156.*

· DURING THE Seven Years War, the Swedes invaded Trondheim county in 1564, and the farmers in the parishes buried in the ground what valuables they had. When the war was over, the story goes that they started digging up these goods again, but they say there were not many who found their possessions. But then there was a wise old woman who said they had to dig on Midsummer night when the moon was full.

There were not many who believed this, but one farmer, one moonlit Midsummer night, took along a hoe and a spade and went out to dig. He dug and he dug, and all at once the hoe struck something hard. He became more and more eager, and at last he dug out a big copper cauldron filled with money and valuables. The man sat down to rest and wipe away the sweat. All at once he heard someone come driving by, and when he turned to look, he saw a cock pulling a load of straw. He stood watching this until both the cock and load were out of sight. Then he turned to the cauldron, but that was gone too.

On the same night there was another man who was digging for treasure right by his farm, and he also got hold of a big copper cauldron. He managed to pull it out of the ground, put it down to catch his breath, and happened to look over at his farm. There it stood all ablaze! He dropped everything, left the kettle there, and started running toward the farm to wake up the people sleeping inside. He happened to look back at the cauldron, but it was gone, and the farm lay as before. The fire was out, and everything was as usual.

# Part II
# Legends about Magic and Witchcraft

# · 12 · The Black School

*Motif S241.2, "Devil is to have last one who leaves black school,"
R. Th. Christiansen,* The Migratory Legends, *3000, "Escape
from the Black School at Wittenberg." This variant was collected
by R. Th. Christiansen about 1920 in Vang, Hedmark (eastern
Norway). It is printed in* Hedmarks Historie, *I, 520. The
Reverend Peder Dohn, referred to in this story, died in 1776.
Similar legends about priests or ministers are found in other
parts of the Christian world. See, for instance, A. Aarne,*
Finnische Märchenvarianten, *"Sagen," No. 30; R. S. Boggs,*
Index of Spanish Folktales, *No. 325. A tale about an escape
from the Black School is told about the famous Scottish magician
Michael Scott.*

· IT'S A WELL-KNOWN fact that it was mostly the clergy who were
skilled in the black arts, and in the Hedmark parishes it was
the minister in Vang, Peder Dohn, who had attended the Black
School in Wittenberg. There it was the custom that, when the
training period for a class of pupils was over, the master could
take one of the pupils, and that would be the last one to go out
of the door.

It so happened that Peder Dohn was the last one this time.
But as he went out of the door, he said: "There's one behind
me! Take him! And you can keep him until I put on two
stockings of the same pair!" But the one behind him was his
shadow. After that Peder Dohn had no shadow, and he always
saw to it that he wore stockings that did not match.

People say there is a picture of this minister still hanging in
the church, and that he was not like other people. And besides,
he had been a minister up north in Finnmark, and up there he
had probably learned more of the same sort of thing!

# · 13 ·  Making the Devil Carry the Cart

*Motif G303.22.4, "Devil helps man place cart wheel when it becomes unfastened"; R. Th. Christiansen, The Migratory Legends, 3010, "Making the Devil Carry the Cart." Collected by P. Chr. Asbjörnsen in Romerike (eastern Norway) and printed in P. Chr. Asbjörnsen, Norske Huldreeventyr og Folkesagn (1870), pp. 211ff.; new edition (1949), pp. 40ff. The story is one of several told by Asbjörnsen under the title "Planke-kjörerne."*

*Some thirty Norwegian variants of this legend have been collected, mostly from the eastern and southern parts of the country. Christiansen cites references in Danish, Swedish, and German traditions. The clergyman referred to in this and the following story is Christian Holst, the minister of Röyken parish, who lived from 1743 to 1823.*

· IT TOOK A righteous man to exorcise the Devil, not one who was sly and conniving or full of mean and scurvy tricks. He had to understand the Black Book just as well as the catechism, and then some.

I have heard tell of a minister who was the man to do it. This was the minister in Röyken. My mother's brother told about it, for he was at Branes and in Röyken parish at that time. This minister had the Black Book, and could read it backward just as well as he could read it forward. And he could loose and bind at the same time. Lord save us! What a man he was, both at holding forth and exorcising the Devil!

It happened one time, when my mother's brother was still a young lad, that he was with the minister one Sunday afternoon down at Tangen, with a man the Devil was playing terrible pranks on. (I do believe he was a merchant.) There had been a whole crowd of ministers and other folks there, who had tried to drive him out as best they could, but it was no use. The Devil only grew worse and worse for every day that passed. At last they sent for the Röyken minister. It was still early in the autumn, during the worst rainy period. Well, he drove down to Gullaug in Lier and went across Dramsfjord to Tangen on Sunday evening, and my mother's brother was with him. But scarcely had he come inside the house before there was a shrieking and a whimpering in every last chink in the wall.

But then the Röyken minister said, "There's no use your whining, you'll just have to move!" And scarcely were the words out of his mouth before the Devil flew up through the chimney like a cloud of black smoke, and there were lots of people who saw it. Then everything was quiet, as you can imagine, and the minister went back across the fjord again, and drove home. But when he had come part of the way up on Gullaugkleiva, it grew dark, and all at once as they were driving—mother's brother was even walking alongside—the cariole axle broke off in two places, so the wheels rolled down the hill.

"Aha! So that's what you're up to!" said the Röyken minister. "Well, by God, you're going to have something to carry! Get on, Per, and hold on tight!" he said to my mother's brother.

And then I dare say they moved. No living soul has ever come from Gakken to Grini so fast before. My mother's brother said he would be willing to go to court and swear to it, and hope to die, that they flew more through the air than they rode on the ground. But when they did stay on the ground for a little while, mud and sparks showered about their ears, so they looked worse than the Devil himself when they came to the parsonage.

"Well, now you're to have thanks for the ride, my boy!" said the Röyken minister, and I dare say you can guess who he said that to. "But now go back and fetch my cariole wheels in Gullhaugkleiva and weld together the axle you broke to pieces, so we can be quits this time," he said. And my mother's brother had not even got out one of the harness pins before the axle was as whole as when they had started out with it. But both horse and axle smelled of sulphur for at least three weeks.

# · 14 ·  The Cardplayers and the Devil

*Motif G303.4.5.3.1, "Devil detected by his hoofs"; R. Th. Christiansen, The Migratory Legends 3015, "The Cardplayers and the Devil." Collected by P. Chr. Asbjörnsen in Romerike (eastern Norway) and printed in P. Chr. Asbjörnsen, Norske Huldreeventyr og Folkesagn (1870), pp. 211ff.; new edition (1949), pp. 40ff. Asbjörnsen combined this legend as well as the preceding one, No. 13, in the story "Plankekjörerne."*

*This legend type has been reported throughout Norway and is well known in Danish, Swedish, German, English, and French traditions. For Finnish variants see A. Aarne, Finnische Märchenvarianten, "Sagen," No. 34.*

· ONE TIME, at Stor-Valle, they were playing cards at Aage Sandaker's place, and swearing and carrying on. The other players were doing badly, but Sandaker won one round after the other, and he was ruining them all. Suddenly, one of the players dropped a card on the floor. When he bent down to pick it up, he saw the Devil sitting under the table, clutching the foot of the table with his claw. The Devil was helping Sandaker. Then they sent for the Röyken minister, and he was there inside the hour, for it did not take him long to be on his way when he was to exorcise the Devil. He lit two altar candles and put them on the table. Scarcely had he started reading, before the Devil let go the foot of the table and threw the cards at the minister, he was so riled!

"So you're thinking you'll get me out, Christian black-smock!" said the Devil. "Well, you're a thief! You stole a spool of thread and a crust of bread!"

"I took the spool of thread to mend my robe, and the crust of bread to stay my hunger," answered the minister, and went on exorcising. But the Devil would not go out. Then the minister began chanting and chanting, until there was a cracking and a creaking in the Devil, for it was wearing him down too hard.

"May I go through the chimney?" asked the Devil.

"No!" answered the minister, for if he had been allowed to do that, he might have carried the roof off with him.

"May I go through the chimney?" said the Devil again.

"No, here's where you're going out, my man," said the minister, and bored a tiny hole through the glazier's lead with a needle. And the Devil had to go out this way, no matter how he whined and carried on. Out he had to go!

Then everything was quiet for a while, but around the time Aage was going to die, the Devil again ran rampant in Lier, both at Stor-Valle and elsewhere. About this time there was a girl on a farm near Linnes who had given birth to a baby out of wedlock. One Sunday afternoon, as she was standing on Viker Bridge and staring down at the water, the Devil came to her in the shape of a big, black dog and licked her hand. At the same moment she threw the child into the river.

At Stor-Valle they were at the end of their wits. And this was not surprising, for the Devil hung about there, one year after the other, waiting for Aage to die. But Aage kept right on living, he did, and in the end people started thinking that he had cheated the Devil too. Yes, he was quite a fellow, that Aage, but an uglier man has never been seen!

Well, they knew of no other way out than to send for the Röyken minister. When he was well inside the house and had said "Good evening," he was going to sit down on a chair. But at the same moment, someone came and yanked the chair out from under him, so the minister landed on the floor.

"Bring an empty whiskey keg, Mother," said the minister, for now he was angry. And when he had the keg, he started chanting and chanting, so that a shudder went through everyone in the room. And all at once the Devil came in through the keyhole, and, whining and wagging his tail like a dog, crawled across the floor to the Röyken minister. And down in the keg he had to go.

When he was well down inside, the minister popped in a cork and said, "Well Devil, damn you, you're mine!"

Since then, they've never seen the Devil at Stor-Valle!

# · 15 · *Inexperienced Use of the Black Book*

*Motif H1021.1, "Task: making a rope of sand"; Type 1174,
Making a Rope of Sand; R. Th. Christiansen, The Migratory
Legends, 3020, "Inexperienced Use of the Black Book. Ropes of
Sand." Collected in 1921 by R. Th. Christiansen in Land
(eastern Norway) and printed in Boka om Land, II, 205.*

*The Reverend Nils Dorph, subject of this variant, was
minister in Land from 1734 to 1786. Over a hundred variants
of this legend have been collected in Norway, with the chief
concentration in the west. It is also common in Sweden, and
scattered examples are reported from Ireland to Russia.*

· Most of the legends in this tradition are about the minister
Nils Dorph. He had the Black Book and knew how to use it,
but one day things almost went wrong, because he had not kept
it hidden.

Over on the west side of Randsfjord lay the curate's farm,
Haga, and one day the minister was over there on a visit. Then
it seems that Mr. Nils had left the Black Book lying about, and
one of the farm hands saw it and started reading, and as ill-luck
would have it, he happened to conjure up Old Erik himself.

He came and asked what he was to do, for it is a well-known
fact that the Devil must be given a task to perform. The boy
had enough presence of mind to send Old Erik down to the
fjord and set him to making a rope of sand. He went down and
started to make a rope. But over at the curate's Mr. Nils happened to look out of the window and saw the sand spouting high
in the air. Then he came home as fast as he could, and bound
Old Erik before he could do any harm.

## · 16 ·  *Carried by the Evil One*

*Motif G303.9.5.4, "Devil carries man through air as swift as wind (thought)"; R. Th. Christiansen, The Migratory Legends, 3025, "Carried by the Devil or by Evil Spirits." Collected by S. Nergaard in Rendal (eastern Norway) and printed in* Norsk Folkeminnelag, *XI (1925), 202–04. Reprinted in* Norske Bygder, *II, 218.*

*The Reverend Petter Dass lived from 1647 to 1707 and became minister at Alstahaug in northwestern Norway in 1689. He is famous as the author of* Nordlands Trompet (The Trumpet of Nordland), *a poetical description of Tromsö district. Tradition has made him into a master magician (see Introduction of this book, p. xxvi). This legend has been collected in some thirty-five Norwegian variants and is well known in Sweden and Denmark as well. In those countries Martin Luther is sometimes the minister, and he is brought to Rome. For references in Finnish and Estonian tradition see A. Aarne,* Finnische Märchenvarianten, *"Sagen," No. 37, and A. Aarne,* Estnische Märchen- und Sagenvarianten, *"Sagen," No. 37.*

· HAVE YOU HEARD about what happened the time Petter Dass went to Copenhagen? He was a merchant at the same time he was a minister. Now it once happened that the king was in Bergen, and there he caught sight of Petter Dass selling fish, while his ship lay at anchor there. When he found out that he was a minister, he wanted to know what kind of minister this could be. People maintained that Petter Dass was just as learned as other clergymen, for he could do more than the others. Then the king wrote a letter to Petter Dass, saying he was to preach in the church in Copenhagen on Christmas Day. And he sent the letter to the bailiff with the order that the minister was to receive it on Christmas Eve. Only then and not before. Then he would see if Petter Dass was so much better than other clergymen.

Well, early Christmas morning Petter Dass said to his wife, "Today I'm going to preach for the king in Copenhagen!"

"Yes, of course," she said, "so am I!" She thought he was joking. But he told her to get his clothes ready, and this she did, for she had seen enough to do what he said when she saw he was serious. Then he sat down at a table and rapped three times, and someone came in.

"How fast can you carry me?" asked the minister.

"As the bird flies!"

"Too slow! Out again!" Then he rapped a second time, and someone else came in. "How fast can you carry me?"

"As weather and wind!"

"Too slow! Out again!" He rapped a third time. "How fast can you carry me?"

"As fast as human thought!"

"Then carry me at once to Copenhagen!"

"What'll I get for it?"

"The souls of those who sleep in church today!"

So off they went up through the air. But out over the sea his carrier grew tired and tried to trick Petter Dass into saying "In Jesus' name!" For then he would have the power to throw him off his shoulders.

"What did Saint Peter say when he was in distress at sea?" he asked.

"Onward and upward, faster and faster! Straight to the city gates of Copenhagen!" answered the minister.

He got there in plenty of time, and the sermon was supposed to be lying on the pulpit. Petter Dass went up in the pulpit, and there lay a piece of white paper without a letter on it.

"There's nothing here," he said and turned the paper over, "and there's nothing here. And out of nothing God created the earth!" Then he preached a sermon the like of which no one had ever heard before.

When they were going home, the Devil was cross.

"Well, how many souls did you get today?" asked the minister.

"How was I to get any souls the way you were raving and carrying on?" said the Evil One.

## · 17a · Following the Witch

*This story and the story that follows were collected by P. Chr. Asbjörnsen in Eidsvoll (eastern Norway) in 1845. They are printed together as parts of "Gravereens Fortaellinger" in P. Chr. Åsbjörnsen,* Norske Huldreeventyr og Folkesagn *(1870), p. 118; new ed. (1949), p. 72.*

*Motif G242.7, "Person flying with witches makes mistake and falls"; R. Th. Christiansen,* The Migratory Legends, *3045, "Following the Witch." About twenty Norwegian variants of this tale have been collected. The well-known Danish folklore collector, Evald Tang Kristensen, cites a similar legend; see his* Danske Sagn, *VI, 222. For references in German and Spanish traditions see* Handwörterbuch des deutschen Aberglaubens, *III, 1889, and R. S. Boggs,* Index of Spanish Folktales, *No. 746.*

· ON A FARM in Ringebu there was a witch who was terribly mean. But there was a boy who knew she was a witch. He went there one Sunday evening and asked for a night's lodging, and he got it too.

"You mustn't be afraid if you see me sleeping with my eyes open," he said. "I'm in the habit of doing so, but I can't do anything about it!"

Oh no, she would not be afraid of that, she said.

All at once he was snoring and sound asleep with his eyes open, and as he lay there like that, the woman took out a big horn of salve from under a stone in the hearth and anointed the broomstick.

"Up here and down here to Jönsås!" she said, and away she flew, up through the chimney, to Jönsås, which is a big mountain with *seters* and summer pastures.

The boy thought it would be fun to follow her and see what she was going to do up there. But he thought she had said, "Up here and down here to *mönsås* (crossbeam)!" So he took out the horn from under the stone in the hearth and rubbed the salve on a piece of wood.

"Up here and down here to mönsås!" he said. Suddenly he began to fly up and down between the hearth and the crossbeam of the house. This kept up the whole night, and he was almost battered to death because he had said the wrong word. After that he was given work there. A year later, on the evening of that very day, he was fixing a sled. When he got tired, he went over and lay down to sleep on the bench, staring straight ahead of him with his eyes open. All at once the witch took out the horn from under the hearth and anointed the mop, and then she flew up through the chimney again. The boy watched where she had hidden the horn, and when she was well on her way, he took it and rubbed a little of the salve on the sled. But he did not say anything. The sled set out, and they never saw any more of the sled or the boy. The farm where this happened is called Kjæstad, and the Kjæstad Horn is renowned to this very day.

## • 17b • *The Witches' Sabbath*

*This story contains Motif G234, "Witch's Sabbath," and is a variant of legend 3050, involving experiences with witches, in R. Th. Christiansen,* The Migratory Legends. *Stories about the witches' sabbath are generally told as personal experiences and follow no epic pattern* (The Migratory Legends, *p. 48*).

• BUT THEN THERE WAS a woman on a farm at Dovre who was also a witch. It was a Christmas Eve. Her hired girl was busy washing a brewing vat. In the meantime the woman took out a horn and anointed the broom, and all at once she flew up through the chimney. The girl thought this was quite a trick, and took a little salve and rubbed it on the vat. Then she also set out, and did not stop until she came to Bluekolls (Blue Knoll). There she met a whole flock of witches, and Old Erik himself. The Devil preached to them, and after he had finished, he looked over to see if they had all come. Then he caught sight of the girl, who was sitting in the brewing vat. He did not know her, for she had not written in his book. And so he asked the woman who was with her if the girl would sign. The woman thought she would. Old Erik then gave the girl the book and told her to write in it. He wanted her to write her name, but she wrote what schoolchildren usually write when they try out their pens: "I am born of God, in Jesus' name!" And then she was able to keep the book, for Old Erik was not the one to touch it again.

Now there was an uproar and a commotion on the mountain, as you might know! The witches took whips and beat on whatever they had to ride on, and they set out helter-skelter. The girl did not wait; she also took a whip, beat on the vat, and set out after them. At one place they went down and rested on a high mountain. Far below them was a wide valley with a big lake, and on the other side was another high mountain. When the witches had rested, they laid on the whips and swooped over the mountain. The girl wondered if she could also fly over it. At last she beat on the vat and came over on the other side too, both safe and sound.

"That was the devil of a hop for a brewing vat!" she said, but at the same moment she lost the book. And then she fell down and came no farther, because she had spoken and called him, even though she had not written her name in the book. She had to go the rest of the way on foot, wading through the snow, for she did not get a free ride any more, and there was many a mile to go.

## · 18 ·   The Witch's Daughter

*Motif D2083.1, "Milk transferred from another's cow by squeezing an ax-handle (or the like)"; R. Th. Christiansen, The Migratory Legends, 3035, "The Daughter of the Witch." Collected by P. Chr. Asbjörnsen in Gausdal (eastern Norway) in 1845 and printed in P. Chr. Asbjörnsen, Norske Huldreeventyr og Folke-sagn (1870), p. 116; new ed. (1949), I, 115.*

*Some thirty Norwegian variants of this tale have been collected; few of these are from the northern parts of the country. The motif of the producing of milk by sympathetic magic is common in English and Scottish tradition. See T. Davidson, "Cattle-Milking Charms and Amulets," Gwerin, II (1958–59), 22–52. In a current American example from southern Indiana, a girl milks from a towel and causes a neighbor's cow to die" (Alice J. Harmeyer, "More Folklore from Smithville," Hoosier Folklore Bulletin IV, 1945, 16.*

• SOME HUNTERS were out watching the mating dance of the black grouse one Easter night. Suddenly, as they were sitting in their shelter in the grey light of dawn, they heard such a rushing and whirring in the air that they thought a whole flock of big birds was coming to light on the marsh. But damned if *those* were birds! When they came out over the tree-tops, it was a flock of witches that had been out to the Easter Sabbath. They came riding on brooms and shovels and dungforks, on rams and goats and the most preposterous things imaginable. When they were close by, the hunters recognized one of the witches, for she was the neighbor of one of them.

"Maren Myra!" he shouted. Then she fell down in a fir tree and broke her thigh, for whenever anyone recognizes them and calls them by name they have to come down no matter how high they are. They picked her up and took her to the bailiff, and in the end she was to be burned alive. But before they got her up on the pile of wood, she asked if they would take the cloth from her eyes for a moment. Yes, this they would do, but first they turned her so she was not facing meadows and fields, but a far off ridge. And wherever her eyes looked, the forest was singed quite black.

But that witch left behind a daughter, and she was sent to a minister up in Gudbrandsdal. She could not have been more than nine years old, but she was bad and full of a witch's caprices. One day the minister told her to pick up some chips, which were lying out in the yard, and carry them into the kitchen.

"Pooh! I can get them in, even if I don't carry them!" she said.

"Is that so?" said the minister. "Let me see."

Well, right away she broke wind so the chips flew right into the kitchen. The minister asked if she could do anything else. Yes, she could. She could milk, she said, but she did not like to do it because it would hurt the cows. The minister asked her to go ahead and do it, but she did not want to. At last she agreed to do it. She stuck a sheath knife in the wall, put a pail under it, and as soon as she touched the knife, milk spurted down in the pail. After she had been milking for a while, she wanted to stop.

"Oh no, keep on milking, my child!" said the minister.

No, she did not want to, but the minister talked her into doing it some more, and she started again.

"Now I must stop," she said after a little while, "or else only blood will come."

"Oh, keep on milking, my child," said the minister, "and don't worry about that." She did not want to, but at last she gave in and went on milking.

After a while she said, "Well, if I don't stop now, your best cow'll be lying dead in the stall!"

"Keep on milking, my child, and don't worry about that," said the minister, for he wanted to see what she could do.

She did not want to, but the minister kept asking until she gave in and went on milking.

"Now the cow fell down!" she said, and when they went out to the stall to look, the minister's best cow was lying dead on the floor. Then they burned her too, just the way they had her mother.

# • 19 • *The Finn Messenger*

*Motif E721.2, "Body in trance while soul is absent"; R. Th. Christiansen, The Migratory Legends, 3080, "The Finn Messenger." Collected in Seljord (Telemark) from Anne Godlid, a story-*

*teller of note who lived from 1773 to 1836, and printed in Rikard Berge,* Norsk Sogukunst, *pp. 3-4, a book containing essays about Norwegian folk narrators and their oral styles.*

*Some fifteen variants of this tale have been collected in Norway, mostly in the north. In Norwegian folk belief, the Finn (Laplander) possesses extraordinary magical abilities (see Introduction p. xxvii). Similar tales have been collected in Swedish Lapland. As far south as Denmark, a tale about a Norwegian sailor and a Finn messenger has been reported; see Ernst Arbman, "Shamanen, extatisk andebesvärjare och visionär," in* Primitiv Religion och Magi, *ed. Å. Hultkrantz (Stockholm, 1955), pp. 52-55.*

• NERI OLAVSSON lived at Sönstveit for a while. His wife ran the farm while he was at sea. A strange thing happened to him one Christmas Eve, while he was off the China coast, and, according to Anne Godlid, it was this.

It had been necessary for him to leave his wife while she was with child, and he was quite worried about her and very homesick.

"If only there was some way of finding out how things were at home!" he said to one of his shipmates, a sailor who happened to be a Finn and was said to know more than the others. "I had to leave my wife when she was with child," he said, "and Heaven knows how it's turned out!"

"What'll you give me if I bring word from home for you tonight?" said the other.

"You certainly couldn't do that!" said Neri.

"If you'll give me a pot of spirits, it's in order!" said the sailor.

"I'd gladly give you five, if anything like that is humanly possible," said Neri.

"Well, if you have something at home you'd recognize again, I'll fetch it," said the sailor.

Why yes, they have a queer silver spoon that had come from the *huldre*-folk and which they never used. It stood in a crack in the wall over the window. "Fetch that!" said Neri.

The sailor said they had to stay as quiet as mice as long as it lasted, and this they promised to do. Then he chalked a circle on the deck and lay down inside it just as if he were dead. They all saw how he became paler and paler and lay there without moving a limb until the onlookers were downright terrified. He lay this way for some time, but suddenly he gave a start, got to his feet, and he was holding the spoon in his hands.

"Here's your silver spoon again," he said to Neri. "Now I've been to Sönstveit."

"So I see," said Neri; he recognized the spoon. "How was everything there?"

"Oh, just fine," said the sailor. "Your wife's had a lovely big boy. Your mother was sitting inside a black house, spinning on a distaff. She was a little poorly, she said. But your father was down on his knees, out by the chopping block, cutting wood."

Neri wrote down the date and the hour right away.

When he came home, he found out that everything was just as the sailor had said.

"But the old silver spoon has disappeared!" they said. "One day there was a rumbling so the whole house shook. We never were able to figure out what it was, but since then we haven't seen anything of the spoon!"

"Well, here it is," said Neri. "It's been all the way to China!" And then he told them how it had happened.

## • 20 • *Driving Out the Snakes*

*Motif D2176.1, "Snakes banned by magic"; R. Th. Christiansen, The Migratory Legends, 3060, "Banning the Snakes." Collected by K. Braset in Sparbu (Tröndelag). Printed in K. Braset, Hollra-Öventyra, p. 134.*

*Some thirty Norwegian variants of this theme have been collected, mostly from the western districts. Accounts of banning snakes in Finnish and Estonian tradition are cited in A. Aarne, Finnische Märchenvarianten, "Sagen," No. 79, and in A. Aarne, Estnische Märchen- und Sagenvarianten, "Sagen," No. 79.*

*The Finn is well known in Norwegian folk tradition for
various magical skills (cf. Tale No. 19 and Introduction,
p. xxvii). In northern European folklore there are many tales
about* Linnormen. *Fire is a common means of exorcising snakes;
in ritual sacrifices in India, for instance, snakes are forced to
throw themselves into fire* (Handwörterbuch des deutschen
Aberglaubens, *VII, 1182*).

• IN THE OLD DAYS, the parishes in Trondheim were so badly
infested by big, ugly snakes that people agreed at last to go to a
Finn who was known for his remarkable skills and ask if he
could put an end to the snakes and all the damage they did.

This he agreed to do, and when he came he made everyone
help him make a big clearing in the forest, which they did. In
the middle of this clearing they left a big fir tree standing. And
then they gathered all the branches and tops of the trees they
had chopped down and piled them in a ring all around the
clearing and the fir tree.

When this was done, the Finn set fire to the ring, and when
it was all ablaze, he climbed up in the top of the fir tree and
started chanting his spells. The snakes came rushing up from
all sides and wanted to put an end to the Finn, but they perished
in the fire—every single one.

Then the *Linnorm* (dragon) came. It is thirty ells long and
has a mane on its neck. The *Linnorm* rushed right over to the
fir tree, took the Finn in its jaws, and headed out toward the
ring of fire. But there they both burned up.

Now, whether there really were so many snakes here before,
I do not know, but I do know that there has not been a snake
here since.

# Part III
## Legends about Ghosts, the Human Soul, and Shapeshifting

# · 21 · *The Midnight Mass of the Dead*

*Motif E492, "Mass (church service) of the dead"; R. Th.
Christiansen, The Migratory Legends, 4015, "The Midnight
Mass of the Dead." Collected by P. Chr. Asbjörnsen in Kristiania
about 1843. Printed as "En gammeldags Juleaften" in P. Chr.
Asbjörnsen, Norske Huldreeventyr og Folkesagn (1870), p. 79;
new edition (1949), I, 104.*

*Some twenty-five variants of this legend have been collected
in Norway, and it is known throughout north-central Europe.
Jewish and Catholic stories about midnight religious services
have been reported from New York (Louis C. Jones, "The
Ghosts of New York: An Analytical Study," Journal of Ameri-
can Folklore, LVII, 1944, 242). The theme occurs in the Middle
Ages, for instance, in the Old French Perlesvans from the twelfth
century. Anatole France has given the tale artistic expression in
L'Etui de Nacre; see Alexander Krappe, "The Spectres' Mass,"
Journal of American Folklore, LX (1947), 159–62.*

· WHEN MY MOTHER was still a girl, she used to come now and
then to a widow she knew who was called —— Yes, what was
her name now? Madame —— No, I can't think of it, but it
doesn't matter. She lived up in Möllergaten, and was a woman a
little past her best years. Now it was a Christmas Eve, just as
now, so she thought to herself that she would go to the early
service on Christmas morning, for she was a regular churchgoer,
and she put out the coffee so she could have something warm
to drink and not have to go on an empty stomach.

When she awoke, the moon was shining in on the floor, but
when she got up and looked at the clock, it had stopped and
the hands stood at eleven-thirty. She did not know what time
of night it was, so she went to the window and looked over at
the church. Light was shining out through all the church windows. So she woke the girl and had her boil the coffee while she
was getting dressed, and then she took her prayer book and

went to church. It was very quiet on the street, and she did not see a soul on the way.

When she came in the church, she sat in her usual pew, but when she looked around, it seemed to her that people looked pale and strange, just as if they could all be dead. There wasn't anyone she knew, but there were many she thought she had met before. But she could not remember where she had seen them. When the pastor came up in the pulpit, he was not any of the city ministers. He was a tall, pale man, and she thought she recognized him too. He preached quite well, but there was not the noise and coughing and clearing of throats usually heard during the early service on Christmas morning. It was so still that one could hear a pin drop on the floor. Yes, it was so quiet that she grew quite uneasy.

When they started to sing again, a woman who was sitting beside her leaned over and whispered in her ear, "Throw your coat loosely about your shoulders and go, for if you stay here until it's over, they'll put an end to you. It's the Dead who're holding service."

Now the widow became frightened, for when she heard the voice and looked at the woman, she recognized her again. It was her neighbor who had died many years ago. And when she now looked about the church, she remembered well that she had seen both the pastor and many members of the congregation, and that they had died long ago. A chill went through her, she was so afraid. She threw the coat loosely about her shoulders, as the woman had said, and got up to leave. But then it seemed to her that they all turned and grabbed after her, and her legs shook beneath her so that she almost fainted on the floor of the church. When she came out on the steps, she felt them take hold of her coat. She let go of it and let them have it and hurried home as fast as she could. When she reached her door the clock struck one, and she went in almost dead with fright.

In the morning, when the congregation came to church, the coat was lying on the steps, but it was torn to a thousand shreds. My mother had seen the coat many times before, and I believe she saw one of the shreds too. Enough of that, it was a short, pink cloth coat, with a rabbit lining and trim, the kind that was still in use in my childhood. Nowadays it's strange to see one like it, but there are still a few women here in town, and at the Old Folks' Home in the Old Town, that I've seen at church at Christmas time wearing that kind of coat.

## • 22a • *The Human Soul Out Wandering as a Mouse*

*Motif E721.1, "Soul wanders from body in sleep"; R. Th. Christiansen, The Migratory Legends, 4000, "The Soul of a Sleeping Person Wanders on its Own ("The Guntram Legend")." This short legend is to be found in an eighth-century history of Italy written by Paulus Diaconus. The Guntram legend has been reported throughout western Europe, across central Asia, and is common in Japan. Keigo Seki, in Folktales of Japan, a companion volume in this series, gives an excellent Japanese variant, pp. 157–60.*

*The first variant given here was collected by Moltke Moe in Böherad (Telemark) in 1880. Manuscript by Moltke Moe, No. VII, 4, in Norsk Folkeminnesamling (Norwegian Folklore Institute). Another variant from Böherad collected by Moltke Moe is printed in Norsk Folkeminnelag, IX (1925), 73.*

• ONCE THERE WERE two noncommissioned officers who lay down to rest beside a little brook. One of them fell asleep. The other one saw a little mouse come out of his mouth. It wanted to go over the brook. The one who was awake took his burnished sword and laid it over the brook. When he did this, the mouse ran across it and over to a little mound. Then the mouse came back and crept into the sleeper's mouth again, and he woke up.

"My! You ought to know what I've been dreaming!"

"What did you dream, then?" asked the one who had stayed awake.

"Oh, I dreamt I went over a bridge that was so fine that I can't describe it. It was all of steel!" he said.

# · 22b · The Human Soul Out Wandering as a Fly

*This brief tale was collected by A. Leiro in Bruvik (western Norway) in 1927. From a manuscript of A. Leiro, No. I, 23, in* Norsk Folkeminnesamling (*Norwegian Folklore Institute*).

· When one dreams, a little fly crawls out of one's mouth.

Two women once lay down beside a pond. One of them fell asleep. Then the other one saw a little fly come out of her mouth, rush in and out among the leaves, and sink into the pond. The one who slept moaned and carried on in her sleep. When she awoke, she told the other woman that she had dreamt she had been in danger of losing her life at sea.

# · 23a · Shapeshifting in Fäarland

*D113.2, "Transformation: man to bear"; R. Th. Christiansen,* The Migratory Legends, *4005, "The Werewolf Husband." Collected by S. Böyum in Balestrand, Sogn (western Norway) in 1928. Manuscript of S. Böyum, No. K, 3, in* Norsk Folkeminnesamling (*Norwegian Folklore Institute*). *Printed in J. Laberg,* Balestrand En Bygdebok, *I, 136.*

*Some fifteen Norwegian variants of this legend have been reported, although none from the northern parts of the country. Werewolf traditions are widespread over the world; of this particular legend Christiansen cites Danish, Swedish, German, and Italian references. The story has also been found in French Canada (Marius Barbeau, "Anecdotes populaires du Canada,"* Journal of American Folklore, *XXXIII [1920], 205ff.).*

· There was a strange belief in the old days that some people, at times, had to take on a bear-hide. There was something about them that was under a spell. In Fäarland, in Sogn, there was once such a man-bear. One time, when his wife was with child, he said to her, "Now I have to go away for a while. If a bear should come to you while I'm gone, throw your apron at it, and run away."

A while later, sure enough, a bear did come and attack her, and she did as the man had said and got away. When the man came home, and sat down to eat, he started picking shreds of cloth out of his teeth, and the wife saw that they were shreds of her apron. Since it had now been discovered, he was freed from the spell, and was not a man-bear any longer. Some time after that he was talking with a man who had lost his bell-cow, and many other bell-cows too. "Go up on Vallerhollen. There you'll find fourteen bells under a flagstone. You can have them," he said.

Man-bears usually prefer to kill bell-cows.

## • 23b • *Shapeshifting at Harvest Time*

*Same source as 23a.*
*See R. M. Dorson, Bloodstoppers and Bearwalkers (Cambridge, Mass., Harvard University Press, 1952), pp. 76–77, for a bear that turns into a man after being shot, in the French-Canadian tradition of northern Michigan.*

• THEY TELL ABOUT A MAN who had a bear-hide. One summer he and his wife were out in the fields threshing. They were sleeping in an outhouse. One evening the man wanted to go home, but the wife stayed behind. Before he left, he said, "If the bear gives you any trouble, take the long scythe and hit at him." "You'd better not go," said the wife. "Oh, yes, I have to go," he said. Late that night the bear came, and the wife took the long scythe and hit at him. In the morning the man came back again. He had slivers of meat and hair between his teeth. He had lost one of his thumbs and his hands were bloody. He had been a bear during the night.

# Part IV
# Legends about Spirits
# of the Sea, Lakes,
# and Rivers

*The Battle Between the Sea* Draugs
*and the Land* Draugs

*Motif E271, "Sea-ghosts"; R. Th. Christiansen, The Migratory*
*Legends, 4065, "Ghosts from the Land Fight Ghosts from the*
*Sea." Collected by O. T. Olsen in Nordland (northern Norway)*
*about 1870 and printed in O. T. Olsen, Norske Folkeeventyr*
*og Sagn, samlede i Nordland, p. 14.*

*Ten variants of this legend have been collected in northern*
*Norway; further south only passing references and incomplete*
*texts are available. The draug is a malevolent spirit, sometimes*
*identical with "a living dead person" (see Introduction, pp. xxx–*
*xxxi). It has entered Lappish tradition; cf. variants in J. K.*
*Qvigstad, Lappiske Eventyr og Sagn, I (1927), 360–63, recorded*
*in Varanger; and IV (1929), 56–59, recorded in Lyngen. Stallo*
*in the form of a giant, a shaman, or the weak youngest brother,*
*is the hero of many Lappish narratives. He figures in some Lap-*
*pish variant of this story.*

· IN THE YEAR 1837, it happened on the Island of Luröy that the
servants at a farm were carousing on Christmas Eve after they
had eaten supper. They ran out of spirits, but no one wanted to
go down to the boathouse to fetch more. Then the farm boy got up
enough nerve and set out with a pottle and the lid in one hand
and a lantern and the boathouse key in the other. He got down
to the boathouse safely, unlocked the door, and filled the pottle.
But when he had locked the door behind him and was going to
go back across the bridge from the boathouse, a man without a
head was sitting there blocking the way. The boy knew at once
that it was a *draug*. When he saw that he could not get by, he
swung at him with the lid, so the *draug* tumbled down off the
bridge with a shriek. The boy headed up the path by the sea,
but all at once he heard a strange commotion behind him, and
when he looked around, he caught sight of a tremendous number

of *draugs* coming up from the shore. The graveyard lay right in his way, and the flock of *draugs* would catch up with him again if he ran around it. So he hopped over the graveyard fence, sprang across the graves, and cried:

"Up, up, every Christian soul, and save me!"

At the same moment the clock struck twelve midnight, and the earth shook under the boy's feet. When he was well over the fence on the other side, he looked back. He saw the flock of *draugs* coming after him in hot pursuit like a flock of sheep, in over the graveyard. But there they were met by a great host of dead souls who wanted to help the boy and stop the unholy *draugs* from coming onto consecrated soil. It was a bitter struggle. The land *draugs* used boards from coffins, while the sea *draugs* had sea-tangle for weapons. But the boy dared not look on. Pale and half out of his wits, he ran into the servants' quarters, put down the pottle of spirits, dashed up to the attic, and went to bed with the covers over his head. On Christmas morning he came to his senses and told what he had experienced during the night. The other servants doubted it a little, but when they came down to the church with the rest of the congregation, they saw for themselves. Over the whole churchyard were strewn boards from coffins, sea-tangle and sea spittle (jellyfish), and everyone could tell that the land *draugs* had battled the sea *draugs*.

## • 25 • *The Grateful Merman*

*Motif F423, "Sea Spirits"; R. Th. Christiansen, The Migratory Legends, 4055, "Grateful Sea-sprite Gives Warning of Approaching Storm." Collected by Knut Strompdal in Nesna, Helgeland (northern Norway), about 1930 and printed in Norsk Folkeminnelag, XLIV (1939), 47–48.*

*The fifteen recorded Norwegian variants come mostly from northern Norway. This legend is well known also in Swedish, Danish, and Irish traditions.*

• A CREW FROM NESNA was fishing in Lofoten. One day, while they were out hauling in their nets at a leisurely pace, they suddenly caught sight of the figure of a man which thrust itself up out of the water close to the boat.

"*Huttetu!* I'm freezing!" he said. One of the men in the Nesna boat pulled off one of his mittens and threw it to the stranger. Scarcely had the stranger taken the mitten before he sank down into the sea from whence he had come.

Not much was said on the Nesna boat about what had happened. They finished hauling in their nets and rowed toward land. Nothing happened after they had come ashore—not until they had finished their evening chores and were in their bunks. The man who had thrown the mitten to the merman had scarcely shut his eyes when someone came into the shelter and went over to him and said:

"Hey there, Mitten-Man, who gave the glove to me,
There's lightning to the north and thunder in the sea!"

The man who lay there was wide awake at once. It occurred to him that he and the other fishermen had not drawn their boats up on shore after they landed in the evening. The weather had been so fine that they had not thought it necessary to go to the trouble. He woke his companions in a hurry. They dragged the boats way up on land and tied them fast, and when that was done the storm broke over them. And many another fisherman had his boat destroyed by the storm and the great waves that broke over it.

## • 26 • The Cormorants from Utröst

*Motif F212, "Fairyland under water"; R. Th. Christiansen, The Migratory Legends, 4075, "Visits to 'Utröst.'" Collected by P. Chr. Asbjörnsen in 1844 in Nordland (northern Norway) and printed in Asbjörnsen, Norske Huldreeventyr og Folkesagn (1870), p. 337; new ed. (1949), II, 216.*

*Utröst is "the Blessed Land," the dwelling of the supernatural*

*beings under water (see Introduction, p. xxxi). The stories about*
*visits to Utröst are generally told as actual experiences, like other*
*visits to fairyland. A reference to Utröst from 1676 is available in*
*D. Brinch,* Prodromus Norvegiaesive Descriptio Loufoudiae.
*Belief in a fairyland under water has been reported from many*
*parts of the world—e.g., in both Irish and Japanese tradition.*
*The story of Urashima Taro is one of the best known Japanese*
*tales of this type. A good variant appears in* Folktales of Japan,
*a companion volume in this series, pp. 111–14.*

• ON THEIR HOMECOMING, it often happens that fishermen in
Nordland find straws of wheat fastened to the helm, or grains
of barley in the stomachs of the fish. Then they say they have
sailed over Utröst, or one of the other *huldre* lands about which
there are legends in Nordland. They appear only to pious or
second-sighted people who are in danger at sea, and they rise
to the surface where no land is otherwise to be found. The
hidden beings who live there engage in farming and raising
cattle, fishing and sailing their boats, the way ordinary people
do. But here the sun shines over greener pastures and richer
acres than anywhere else in Nordland, and happy is the one
who comes to, or catches a glimpse of, one of these sun-drenched
islands. "He is saved!" the Nordlanders say.

An old song, in the style of Petter Dass, contains a complete
description of one such island off Træna, in Helgeland, called
Sandflesa, with waters filled with fish, and abounding with game
of every kind. In the middle of Vestfjord, now and then a large,
flat field appears, which only comes up high enough for the
spikes of grain to stand above the water. And off Röst, on the
southern tip of Lofoten, they tell of a similar *huldre* island, with
green slopes and acres of golden barley. It is called Utröst. The
farmer on Utröst has his *jagt* (boat), like other Nordland
farmers. At times it comes toward the fishermen and other *jagt*
skippers at full sail, but at the very moment they think they will
collide with it, it disappears.

On Væröy Island, close to Röst, there once lived a poor fisherman called Isak. He owned nothing more than a boat, and a

couple of goats, which the wife kept alive on fish offals and the few blades of grass they managed to gather on the mountain, but his hut was full of hungry children. Nonetheless he was always satisfied with the way Our Lord had arranged things for him. The only thing he complained of was that his neighbor would never leave him alone. This was a rich man who thought he should be better off in every way than a wretch like Isak, and he wanted to have him out of the way so he could have the harbor that was outside Isak's hut.

One day Isak was fishing several miles out to sea when a dense fog came over his boat. All at once such a violent storm blew up that he had to throw all the fish overboard in order to lighten the boat and save his life. Still, it was not easy to keep afloat, but he turned the vessel quite neatly in and out among the heavy seas that were ready to suck him down at every moment. After he had been sailing at great speed for five or six hours, he thought he ought to be coming to land somewhere. But he sailed on and on, and the fog and the storm grew worse and worse. Then he began to realize that he was heading out to sea, or else the wind had turned. At last he knew it had to be true, for he sailed and sailed and did not reach land. All at once he heard a terrifying shriek ahead of the bow, and he thought it was none other than the *draug* singing his burial hymn! He prayed to Our Lord for his wife and children, for now he understood that his last hour had come.

All at once, as he sat there praying, he caught a glimpse of something black, but when he came closer there were only three cormorants sitting on a floating log, and whoops! he was past them. On and on he sailed, both far and long, and he became so thirsty and hungry and tired that he did not know what to do and sat half asleep, with the helm in his hand. But all at once the bottom of the boat scraped against land, and it stopped with a jolt. Then Isak opened his eyes. The sun broke through the fog and shone over a beautiful landscape. Hills and mountains were green all the way up to the top, fields and meadows sloped up to them, and flowers and grass seemed to have a sweeter fragrance than he had ever noticed before.

"God be praised! Now I'm saved! This is Utröst!" said Isak

to himself. Right in front of him lay a field of barley, with spikes so big and full of grain that he had never seen anything like it. And through the field went a small path leading up to a green, peat-roofed earthen hut that lay above the field. On the roof grazed a white goat with gilded horns, and its udders were as big as the udders on the biggest cow. Outside, on a stool, sat a little, blue-clad fellow, sucking on a briar pipe. He had a beard so bushy and long that it hung way down on his chest.

"Welcome to Utröst, Isak," said the old fellow.

"Blessings on the meeting, father," replied Isak. "Do you know me then?"

"That very well might be," said the old fellow. "I dare say you'd like me to put you up for the night."

"If that were possible, then the best is good enough, father," said Isak.

"The trouble is with my sons, they can't stand the smell of a Christian man," said the old fellow. "Haven't you met them?"

"No, all I met was three cormorants, sitting and shrieking on a floating log."

"Well, those were my sons," said the old fellow. Then he knocked the ashes out of his pipe and said to Isak, "You'd better come in for the time being. I imagine you must be both hungry and thirsty."

"Much obliged, father," said Isak.

But when the man opened the door, it was so richly furnished inside the hut that Isak was out-and-out dazzled. He had never seen such wealth before. The table was decked with the tastiest dishes: clabber and haddock, reindeer steak, great piles of Bergen twists, loaves of bread and fish liver covered with molasses and cheese, spirits and ale and mead, and everything good! Isak ate and drank as much as he was able, and still the plate was never empty and the glass was just as full. The old fellow did not eat much, nor did he say much either. But suddenly, as they were sitting there, they heard a shrieking and a rattling outside the door and then he went out. After a while he came back in again with his three sons. Isak started a little when they came in the door, but the old fellow had probably managed to calm them down, for they were quite gentle and good-natured. And then they said he would have to mind his manners and remain seated and drink with them, for Isak had wanted to leave the table. He had had enough, he said. But he humored them, and they drank dram after dram, and in between they took a drop of the ale and the mead. They became friends and were on good terms, and at last they said that he was to sail a few voyages with them, so he could have a little to take home with him when he left.

The first voyage they made was in a violent storm. One of the sons sat by the helm, the second by the tack, and the third was halyard man. Isak had to use the big bailer until the sweat poured off him. They sailed as if they were raving mad. Not once did they reef the sail, and when the boat was full of water, they sheered up on the waves and ran before the wind, so the water poured out the stern like a waterfall. After a while the storm abated, and then they started fishing. There were so many fish that they could not get the sinker to the bottom for the shoals under them. The sons from Utröst hauled in fish without stopping. Isak also had good bites, but he had taken his own fishing equipment along, and every time he got a fish to the gunnel, it got away again, and his creel stayed empty. When the boat was full, they rushed home to Utröst, and the sons cleaned the fish and hung it up on flakes to dry. But Isak complained to the old fellow because it had gone so badly with his fish. The fellow promised that it would go better the next time, and gave him a couple of fishhooks. And on the next voyage he pulled in fish just as fast as the others, and when they came home, he was given three flakes filled with fish as his share.

Then he grew homesick, and when he was ready to go the old fellow presented him with a new, eight-oared fishing boat filled with flour and fine sailcloth and other useful things. Isak thanked him, and as he was leaving the old fellow said he was to come back in time for the launching of the *jagt*. He wanted to take a cargo of fish to Bergen along with the next group of *jagts* from Nordland, and then Isak could come with him and sell his fish himself. Well, Isak was only too willing, and asked which course to follow when he wanted to come back to Utröst again.

"Straight behind the cormorants, when they head out to sea.

Then you're on the right course!" said the old fellow. "Good luck on your journey."

But when Isak had shoved off and wanted to look around, he saw no more of Utröst. He saw nothing but the sea as far as his eye could reach.

When it was time, Isak showed up for the launching. But such a *jagt* he had never seen before. It was so long that when the mate, who stood watch in the prow, wanted to shout to the man at the helm, the fellow could not hear him; and so they had to put a man in the middle of the vessel, beside the mast, who shouted the mate's call to the helmsman. And even then he had to shout as loud as he could. They put Isak's share of the fish in the prow of the *jagt*. He took the fish off the flakes himself. But he could not understand how it happened: new fish constantly appeared on the flakes in place of the ones he took away, and when he left, they were just as full as when he had come.

When he got to Bergen, he sold his fish and got so much money for them that he bought himself a new *jagt* that was fully equipped, and with a cargo and everything that belonged to it, for the old fellow had advised him to do so. And late in the evening, before he was going to sail for home, the old fellow came on board and told him not to forget the ones who lived the way his neighbor did, for now he'd become a rich man himself, he said. And then he prophesied both good fortune and prosperity for Isak with the *jagt*.

"All is well, and everything will withstand the storms," he said. By this he meant that there was someone on board that no one could see who supported the mast with his back when things looked bad.

From that time, Isak always had good fortune. He knew well where it came from, and he never forgot to leave something good for the one who stood watch during the winter, after he put the *jagt* up in the autumn. And every Christmas Eve, lights blazed from the *jagt,* and they could hear the sound of fiddles and music and laughter and noise, and there was dancing in the cabin.

# · 27 ·  The Tufte-*Folk* on *Sandflesa*

*Motif F213, "Fairyland on island"; R. Th. Christiansen, The Migratory Legends, 6015, "The Christmas Party of the Fairies." Collected by P. Chr. Asbjörnsen in Luröy (northern Norway) about 1845 and printed in Asbjörnsen, Norske Huldreeventyr og Folkesagn (1870), p. 343; new ed. (1949), II, 254. This legend, a redaction of the legend about the interrupted Christmas party, has been reported in twenty Norwegian variants, primarily from the coastal districts. The story has entered Lappic tradition (J. K. Qvigstad, Lappiske Eventyr og Sagn, IV [1929], 227), and is also known on the Shetland islands (G. Douglas, Scottish Fairy and Folktales, pp. 134–37).*

· FAR AT SEA, right out from Trena in Helgeland, lies a little bank called Sandflesa. It is an excellent fishing ground, but hard to find, for it moves from one place to the other. But the one who is lucky enough to come across it is sure to have a good catch. If he leans over the gunnels in clear and calm weather, he will see a small hollow on the bottom, like the keel of a large Nordland *jagt,* and a huge crag shaped like a boathouse.

This bank has not always lain at the bottom of the sea. In the old days it was an island belonging to a rich farmer from Helgeland. As a shelter from storms, during the summer fishing, he had put up a fishermen's shanty there, and it was bigger and better than such shanties usually are. There are those who still believe that, from time to time, Sandflesa thrusts itself up above the surface of the water as a pretty island. This I shall leave unsaid, but in days gone by things were not quite as they should be on that deserted isle. Fishermen and travelers said, and they were sure of it, that they had heard laughter and noise, music and dancing and hammering and other sounds, and chanteys being sung as though for the launching of a *jagt,* when they sailed past there. For this reason they usually set their course a little around it; but there was no one who could say that he had seen a living soul on Sandflesa.

The rich farmer I spoke of had two sons. The elder was called Hans Nikolai and the younger, Lucky Anders. The elder son was not easy to figure out. He was not a good fellow to get on the wrong side of, and he had an even better head for business than most people from Nordland usually have—and they seldom have too little of this gift of God. The other son, Lucky Anders, was wild and reckless, but always in a good humor, and no matter how badly things turned out, he always said that luck was with him. If he was out robbing eagle's nests, and the eagle slashed his face until the blood flowed, he would say the same thing as long as he came home with a baby eagle. If his boat overturned, which happened not seldom, and he was found hanging to the keel, half drowned and numb with cold, then he'd reply, whenever anyone asked how he was, "Oh, tolerably well. After all I'm saved, luck is with me!"

At the time their father died they were grown men, and some time after this they were both going out to Sandflesa to get some equipment that had been left behind after the summer fishing. Lucky Anders had along his gun, which was always with him wherever he went. It was late autumn, past the time when fishermen usually go out to the fishing grounds. Hans Nikolai did not say much on this trip, but he probably had a lot to think about.

They were not ready to start for home until it was getting on toward evening.

"Listen, do you know what, Lucky Anders? There's going to be a terrible storm tonight," said Hans Nikolai, looking out over the sea. "I think we'd better stay over until morning."

"There won't be any storm," replied Anders. "The Seven Sisters [seven mountain peaks in Helgeland] aren't wearing their cloud bonnets. Let's get started."

But then the other one complained that he was tired, and at last they agreed to spend the night there. When Anders woke up in the morning, he was alone. He saw neither his brother nor the boat until he was up on top of the crag. Then he caught sight of it in the distance, like a sea gull flying toward land.

Lucky Anders could not understand the meaning of this, for the box of provisions had been left behind, and an anchor, and the rifle and various other things too. But Anders was not the kind to ponder over something for long.

"He'll probably come back this evening," he said, and started to eat. "Only a poor wretch has a faint heart before he has an empty stomach!"

Lucky Anders waited day after day, week after week. Then he understood that his brother had left him behind on that deserted island so that he could keep the inheritance, undivided, for himself. And this was his older brother's idea, too, for when Hans Nikolai was close to shore he overturned the boat and said that Lucky Anders had been drowned.

But Lucky Anders did not lose heart. He collected driftwood at low tide, shot seafowl, and gathered mussels and angelica [a type of wild carrot]. He made a raft from the logs of the drying racks and fished with a coalfish pole which had been left behind. One day, as he was busy with this, he caught sight of a hollow in the sand, shaped like the keel of a big Nordland *jagt,* and he could clearly make out marks from the twists of the ropes, all the way from the shore to the crag. Then he thought to himself that he was not in any danger, for now he could see that what he had often heard was true, that the *tufte*-folk came here and carried on considerable trade with their *jagts.*

"God be praised for good company! They are good people. Yes, it's just as I say: luck is with me!" thought Lucky Anders. Perhaps he said it out loud too, for he certainly needed to talk a little now and then. Thus he lived throughout the autumn. Once he saw a boat. He tied a cloth to a pole and waved it, but at the same moment the sail was lowered, and the men took to the oars and rowed away at breakneck speed. They thought the *tufte*-folk were waving flags.

On Christmas Eve he heard the sound of fiddles and music far out to sea. When he went outside he saw a light. It came from a big Nordland *jagt* that glided in to the shore. But such a *jagt* no one had ever seen before. It had an enormous square sail, which he thought was made of silk, and the thinnest rigging, no thicker than steel wire. And all that went with it was as fine and magnificent as any Nordlander could wish for. The *jagt* was filled with tiny, blue-clad people. But the girl who stood by the helm was dressed as a bride and looked as splendid as a queen, for she was wearing a crown and costly clothing. But he could see that she was a mortal, for she was bigger and prettier than the *tufte*-folk. Yes, Lucky Anders thought he had never seen such a pretty girl before, she was so beautiful.

The *jagt* headed toward the spot where Lucky Anders was standing, but quick-witted as he was, he rushed into the shanty, grabbed the gun from the wall, and crept up on the big shelf over the hearth. There he lay completely out of sight, but still he could see what was going on in the room. Soon it was teeming with people. It was jammed full, but still more and more came in. The walls started to creak, and suddenly the room began to stretch out on all sides. It was fixed up so fine that it could not have been finer at the richest merchant's. It was almost like the king's castle. The table was decked with the costliest dishes and plates and saucers, and all the utensils were of silver and gold.

When they had eaten, they started to dance. During the commotion Lucky Anders crawled out through the louver, which was on one side of the roof, and climbed down. He ran down to the *jagt*, threw his fire-steel over it, and for safety's sake, carved a cross in it with his sheath knife too. When he came up again, the dancing was in full swing. The only one who did not dance was the bride, and every time the bridegroom wanted her to join in, she shoved him away from her. But otherwise there was no end; the fiddler did not stop for breath or to tune the fiddle but played without stopping, with his left hand, and beat time with his foot until the sweat poured off him and he could not see the fiddle for the dust and smoke.

When Anders felt that he was also standing there keeping time with his feet, he said to himself, "Now it's time to give them a shot, or else he'll play the ground out from under my feet!"

Then he turned the gun around, stuck it in through the opening, and fired it over the bride's head, but straight up— otherwise the bullet would have come back and struck him. At the same moment as the shot was fired, all the *tufte*-folk rushed

out through the door, one after the other, but when they saw
the *jagt* was bound, they wailed and carried on. Finally they
crept into a hole in the crag. But all the gold and silver finery
was left behind, and the bride sat there too. It was as if she had
been restored to her senses. She told Lucky Anders that she had
been taken into the mountain when she was a little girl. Once,
when her mother went down by the wickets to milk the cows,
she had taken her along. But her mother had gone home on an
errand and left her there in the heather under a juniper bush.
She could eat the berries, she said, as long as she said three times:

> "I'm eating a juniper berry, blue,
> With Jesus' cross upon it true.
> I'm eating a whortleberry red,
> With Jesus pining, and Jesus dead!"

But when her mother was gone, she found so many berries
that she forgot to say the verse, and she had been taken into
the mountain. The only sign that she had been in there was
that she had lost the last joint on her little finger. She had been
well off with the *tufte*-folk, she said, but it did not seem to be
the right company, she thought; it was as if something were
nagging her, and she'd been badly pestered by that *tufte* fellow
they had wanted her to marry. He was after her from morn till
night.

When Anders heard who her mother was and where she was
from, it turned out that she was one of his distant relations, and
they were soon friends and on good terms. Now Lucky Anders
said, and he had reason to, that luck was with him. Then they
journeyed home, taking with them the *jagt* and all the gold and
silver and costly things that had been left in the shanty, and now
Anders was much richer than his brother.

But Hans Nikolai had his ideas about where all these riches
had come from, and he did not want to be any poorer. He knew
that *tufte*-folk and trolls were usually abroad on Christmas Eve,
and so he went to Sandflesa at that time. On Christmas Eve, he
saw fire lights too, but it was phosphorus that was spark-
ling. When it came closer, he heard splashing, and blood-curd-
ling howls and cold, piercing shrieks, and there was a terrible

odor of feathers. In his fright, he ran up to the shanty, and there he saw the *draugs* coming ashore. They were short and fat as haycocks, and had on complete leather outfits—long leather jackets and sea boots—and great mittens that hung almost down to the ground. Instead of head and hair, they had tangles of seaweed. When they crawled up on the shore, it shone after them like flaming birch bark, and when they shook themselves, the sparks showered about them. When they came up to the shanty, Hans Nikolai crawled up on the shelf as his brother had done. The *draugs* carried a huge stone up with them and started beating their mittens dry, and now and then they shrieked so a chill went through Hans Nikolai up on the shelf. Afterward, one of them sneezed in the embers to start a fire on the hearth, while the others carried in moss and heather and driftwood, as soggy and heavy as lead. The smoke and the heat were enough to choke Hans lying up on the shelf, and in order to get fresh air he tried to crawl out through the louver. But he was stockier than his brother and stuck fast and could neither come out nor in. Now he was really frightened and started shrieking, but the *draugs* shrieked even louder, and they howled and carried on and made a terrible racket and pounded both inside and out. But when the cock crowed they were gone, and Hans Nikolai got loose too. When he came home he was half-witted, and afterward, in outhouses and lofts, or wherever he was, they could hear the same chilling, piercing shriek which, in Nordland, they attribute to the *draug*. Before he died, however, he was restored to his senses again, and he was put in consecrated earth, as they say.

After that time, no mortal has set foot on Sandflesa. It sank, and it is believed that the *tufte*-folk moved to Lekangholmen. With Lucky Anders all went well. No *jagt* made such prosperous voyages as his. But every time he came to Lekangholmen, there was a calm. The *tufte*-folk would come on board or go ashore with their wares. After a while he would get a favourable wind, no matter whether he was going to Bergen or back home again. He had many children, and they were all healthy and fine, but on each one the last joint of the little finger was missing.

# · 28 · "The Hour Has Come But Not the Man!"

*Motif D1311.11.1, "River says, 'The time has come but not the man.'" R. Th. Christiansen, The Migratory Legends, 4050, "River Claiming its Due. The hour has come but not the man." Collected from the famous Norwegian author Björnstjerne Björnson in Söndre Land (eastern Norway) by F. Bätzman and printed in Boka om Land, II, 299.*

*Thirty-five Norwegian variants have been collected, chiefly from eastern Norway. Almost every Norwegian river has a similar legend, states Joh. T. Storaker in Norsk Folkeminnelag, X (1924), 128. The legend is well known elsewhere in Europe, and has been studied by Robert Wildhaber, " 'Die Stunde ist da, aber der Mann nicht.' Ein europäisches Sagenmotiv," Rheinisches Jahrbuch für Volkskunde, IX (1958), 65–88.*

· ONE EVENING, as it was getting on toward spring, a family was sitting together in a little house which lies close by the spot where the road turns down onto the fjord.

Then they heard loud shouting and shrieking several times from the fjord: "The hour has come but not the man! The hour has come but not the man!"

They listened, and it was not long before the shouting came again from the fjord: "The hour has come but not the man!"

Then the farmer told two of the hands to go out on the road and keep a lookout there. They were to stop the first one who came driving along, and no matter if he begged or threatened, they were to bring him into the house. This they did, and it was not long before they heard someone come driving along the road. They did as the farmer had said, and stopped him. It was a young man. He jumped out of the sleigh and wanted to know what they meant by stopping a man on his journey. He was determined to go on, and threatened them, demanding that they

let him pass. But they said he had to go into the house first and
talk with the farmer.

It was no use. At last he had to go in with them. He was
furious, and when he came in the house he stamped his foot on
the floor and said he had just received word that his father was
dying and that he was going across.

"You're not going over tonight," said the farmer. "Randsfjord
isn't safe. I've heard this sort of thing before. You'll have to stay
here until tomorrow!"

"But this is outrageous!" cried the traveler. "Do you intend
to keep me by force, now that you know the errand I'm on?
I know that people have driven over Randsfjord earlier today,
and if the ice has held for others, it'll hold for me too!"

"That makes no difference," said the farmer, "you'll have
to stay here!"

But the traveler became more and more upset, and all at once
he started to laugh and cry at the same time. His features became contorted; he was seized with a fit and fell to the floor.

"Oh, what a terrible thing this is to watch!" said the farmer.
"Go down and fetch up some water from the fjord!" This they
did and poured it into his mouth, and at the same moment he
breathed his last.

## • 29 • *The Sea Horse and the Sea Serpent*

*Motif B91.5, "Sea serpent"; Motif B71, "Sea horse"; R. Th.
Christiansen, The Migratory Legends, 4085, "The sea horse
and the sea serpent." Collected by T. Mauland in Suldal
(western Norway) about 1880 and printed in Norsk Folkeminnelag, XXVI (1931), 7-9.*

*This legend has been collected in some fifteen variants from
the coastal regions of southern and western Norway. A. Erbe, in
his Skipperlögne og andre historier fra Skjärgaarden (Christiania, 1892), p. 18, refers to a seamen's yarn about sailors who
have seen the sea horse defeat the sea serpent in a fight far out
at sea.*

· Once people were badly off in Hjelmeland. It has long been rumored that a sea serpent was out in the fjord, and people hardly dared go out on the water. One day a man was going to row across the fjord, and all at once he caught sight of something coming after the boat. He could tell it was the sea serpent and knew it was a matter of life or death. Then he hit upon something. He cut his finger and let the blood drip down on a seat. Then he put the seat in the water, and the sea serpent took time to lick the blood. Then the man got so much of a headstart that he came to land; but the sea serpent stayed there in the fjord, and made it unsafe for people to go out on the water.

Later, the sea serpent blocked the fjord lower down so that many people were not able to get to church, or anywhere else for that matter, even on a necessary errand. Farther up the fjord, food started getting scarce, and people were in trouble in many ways. Then they went to the minister and asked for advice, and the minister said they would have to hold a day of prayer in the church.

They gathered in the Hjelmeland church, and the minister went up in the pulpit and started to pray. When it was over, they heard something neighing. People streamed out of the church and down to the shore, where they caught sight of a sea horse, which came rushing in from the sea. He came from Boknfjord and Finnöyfjord and neighed three times before he was there. He neighed the first time when he was off Finnöy Island, and that neigh was so loud that it could be heard over seven parishes. He headed in across a sound, so the sea serpent could not come out, and then the sea horse set out after it. That was a chase well worth watching! The island, of course, was large—as many as two parishes lie on it—and the sea horse chased around this island at least three times before he caught up with the sea serpent.

They met way up in Hjelmelandfjord, and there was a battle the like of which has never been seen here in this world. It was so violent that the sea horse lost one of his hooves, but he did get hold of the sea serpent and bit it right in two.

The whole fjord was colored red with the blood. The comb and the front half of the sea serpent drifted into an inlet, which is called Fårekammsvika (Front Comb Inlet) to this very day. They got the comb ashore, but the back half lay out there in the bay and rotted, and there was such a stink that the animals died and the trees rotted on the closest farms, and, in general, leaves withered as far as the eye could see. The hoof drifted in to Hjelmeland, and they used it for a corn bin at the parsonage. It held forty-eight bushels of corn. When the battle was over, the sea horse headed out to sea, and no one has seen him since.

## • *30* • *The Sea Serpent in Lake Mjösen*

*Motif B91.5.2, "Lake serpent (monster)"; Motif B87.1.1.1, "Giant ox." A German writer, Ziegler, heard this story from some Norwegians in Rome. It is related in* The Hamar Chronicle *(1540) as told by Ziegler. The tale is also printed in* Hedmarks Historie, *II, 123.*

*Concerning Lake Mjösen there is an early report from approximately* A.D. *1600.:*

*"It is a treacherous and deceptive body of water, and takes many people away. It is muddy and frightening to behold, and is more dangerous to sail upon than the sea because of the great whirlwinds and squalls that can come and because fresh water is more easily agitated than salt water. For this reason, people are so superstitious of this same lake that, whenever they journey across it, they will not call it by its name Mjösen, but speak of it, instead, as 'The Fjord.'"*

• "IT HAPPENED ONCE, at midnight, that all the bells started ringing in Hamar cathedral, and the organ started playing by itself. When the bishop heard this, he got up and looked outside. There, in the cathedral and the choir, it was as brightly lighted as if it were broad daylight. The bells also rang in the Church of the Cross and in the cloister. During the night there were so many ghosts in the episcopal residence, looking as if two armies had come into battle, that the watchmen and everyone else were terrified. At the same time, in Lake Mjösen, a terribly large sea serpent appeared. It seemed to stretch all the way from Helgöy Island to the shore by Hamar. At the same time a monstrously big, horned ox was seen going from Gillund, in Stange, over to the island. It looked as if it walked on the water but nonetheless went straight ahead like an arrow from a steel bow. Day after day many sea serpents were seen as well. They writhed and arched their backs up to the sky, and afterward came the most enormous sea serpent. It ran and played along the shore, and at last it rushed up onto a rock outside the cloister at great speed. It came so far up out of the water that it had difficulty getting loose from the rock. Its eyes were as big as the bottom of a barrel, and it had a long black mane that hung down over its neck.

"Then one of the boys at the bishop's residence—he was a bold fellow—started shooting at the sea serpent's eyes with a bow and arrow. So much green fluid came out of them that the water was colored quite green. The sea serpent was multicolored, and a terrifying sight. At last it was killed by the arrows, and lay there on the rock. The following night there was a violent rainstorm, so that the serpent came loose from the rock and floated over to Helgöy Island, and there was such a stink there that people sent for the bishop and asked how they were to get rid of the serpent and the stink. The bishop ordered that, from the surrounding parishes, each farm which usually paid two or more hides in tithes was to send one strong man. This they did. The men who came together on the island were strong, full-grown fellows. They worked together to burn up the hideous serpent so people could be rid of the poisonous stink that came from it. Some chopped wood, others dragged it out into unbelievably large piles, and they burned up as much of the serpent as they could. Many hundred loads of wood were needed before the stink finally went away.

"But the bones remained and lay there on the shore for many years. Then some able artisans came. They were allowed to take whatever they could use. A grown man could hardly carry a piece of the backbone. They carried off many a load with them. The boy who had shot the sea serpent received praise and payment from people for miles around."

# Part V
# Legends about Spirits of the Air

## · 31 · *The* Oskorei *Fear the Cross*

*Motif E501, "The Wild Hunt," and F382.1, "Fairies fear the cross." There is in the inlands of Norway a distinct cycle of legends about "the terrible host," Oskoreien or Jolereien. The latter name indicates that the host is particularly dangerous around Christmas time. In the coastal districts of Norway the host appears like a group of restless souls of the dead (see Introduction, pp. xxxii). Legends about such spirits of the air exist in various parts of the world. Theories have been proposed connecting "the terrible host" with the followers of Indo-European gods, such as Rudra in India and Odin in Scandinavia. See for instance Jacob Grimm, Deutsche Mythologie, II, 765–93. The traditions about "the terrible host" have furnished inspiration for several musical compositions, such as "Le chausseur illaudit," by C. Franck (1883).*

*The legend given here was collected by the Reverend M. B. Landstad in Telemark in the 1840's and printed in Norsk Folkeminnelag, XIII (1926), 10–11.*

· A MAN FROM NATADAL had been over in Hjartdal, the neighboring parish, and it so happened that it was late in the afternoon when he started for home. By the time he had come to a valley farther up the sun had set, and when he had come up on the mountain at Valler, on his way toward a valley farther in, it was the quietest sort of summer night and not a single bird was chirping any longer. As he walked there, he heard a terrible commotion. He turned around to see what it was and knew it was the *oskorei* (evil spirits) who were rushing along. Bridles jingled and weapons clinked, and he heard them quarreling among themselves. The *oskorei* wanted food, and the leader—Guro Rysserova—said they would have to wait until they came to Natadal. There they would eat their fill, for there they would find "Friday-baked bread and Sunday-raked hay!"

When the Natadal man heard this, he did not feel any too

comfortable for they were talking about his own *stabbur* (store-house) and barn. But the *oskorei* were so close behind him that there was no chance of running away. He ran off the road a little way and, flinging himself down in the grass on his back, he stretched his arms straight out on each side so that he was lying there in the form of a cross.

When the host of *oskorei* came up, they stopped, and Guro shrieked, "Uff! Look at that cross!"

Then they dared not ride past him, but went a long way around. When the man understood this, he jumped up and took to his heels as fast as he could. He had a slight headstart and hurried home. He managed to make the sign of a cross above the wicket in the road down to the farm and on all the doors. In this way he fooled the *oskorei,* which dared not ride in to the farm.

In the old days people believed that on Friday, which was a day of fast, no work must be done in which a swinging or rolling movement was involved. Thus they could not bake oatcakes. And it was a sin to work on Sunday. Then the evil powers had the right to take the fruits of this labor. But they were always powerless against the sign of the cross.

On Dalen farm in Kvitseid, the *oskorei* came several times. Once they unsaddled their spirit horses there and threw the saddles on the roof. Then misfortune followed: there were seven murders on the farm, and there was never peace to be had at night. There was always a disturbance and a commotion, and the front door would never stay shut no matter how they locked it. Once, at Christmas time, the people from Dalen were invited to a feast at Hvestad. There was no one home and the doors were locked, but the food stood on the table as was the custom at Christmas. When the people came home a few days later, they could see that the *oskorei* had been there. They had drunk up the Christmas ale and eaten heartily of the Christmas fare. But worst of all, a dead man was hanging from the pothook over the hearth. By his clothes they could tell he was from Numedal, a valley to the east, and he had silver buttons on his vest. The *oskorei* had probably taken him along over in Numedal and had ridden so hard that it had killed him.

# ·32· *The Girl Who Was Taken*

*Motif F382.1, "Fairies fear the cross." This tale was collected by O. K. Ödegaard in Valdres (eastern Norway) before 1913. It is printed in O. K. Ödegaard,* Gamal Tru og Gamal Skjikk ifraa Valdres, *p. 103.*

*Tradition has given the girl in this story the name of Guro, which is generally associated with the leader of "the terrible host." The members of the host are in this tale called* haug-*folk (the people of the mounds) since legend tellers tend to call different supernatural beings by the same generalized names.*

· GURO LJÖSENG went out to the *stabbur* for bread one *Imber* evening [one of the three evenings before Christmas]. She did not come in again, and for all they searched, no trace of her did they find. Then it occurred to them that she could have been taken into a mountain, and so they were given permission to ring the church bells to get her out again. They rang for three days. But the ringing did not help, and so they stopped, because they knew that the ones who had taken her would not let her out again.

At Hansebu, at that time, there lived some spry fellows. They were called The "Hansebu Boys." One of them, ol' Jacob—Hanse-Jacob he was called—got drunk one *Imber* evening. Then he started bragging loudly and showing off. Among other things, he swore that there was no such thing as *haug*-folk!

Ol' Fosse sat listening to this, and became angry at such nonsense and said, "You'd better be careful about saying things like that, Jacob. If you dare to lie down by Ljöseng wicket tonight, it just might happen that you'll get to see what you least expect!" There's a fork there, a crossroads, and it's just at such crossroads that one can see *haug*-folk on an *Imber* evening.

"Well," said Jacob, "I'm not afraid to do that!" And later on that evening, just at midnight, he wandered up to Ljöseng wicket and lay down full length in the snow by the fork, and then he stretched out his arms so he looked like a cross. He had not been lying there long when a great company came riding up. First rode a huge, blue-clad man on a splendid black horse. He had a nose so long that it reached all the way down to the pommel of the saddle, and his legs were so long that they all but dangled down on the road. All the others had splendid horses too, and fine saddles and bridles, and halters with rings in them, so it almost sounded like they were full of sleigh bells.

When the first rider saw Jacob, he said, "Ow! There lies a cross!" And all the others said the same thing too when they saw Jacob. But last in the company rode a woman, and when she laid eyes on Jacob she said, "That's no cross! That's just ol' Hanse-Jacob!" Then he recognized her; it was Guro Ljöseng. He asked her why she had stayed away so long, and how she had come to be in such a company. "Things have gone well with me," she said. "My husband is Tostein Langbein, who's riding first. He took me up on his horse one *Imber* evening, when I went out to the *stabbur* for bread, and rode with me to a hill by Okshoved in Slidre. It was good they stopped ringing. When they did, I'd come all the way down by the fence at Ljöseng. If they'd kept it up just a little longer, I would have come home, but then I would not have had a day's good health since. Now I'm Tostein's woman and live as well off as if it was Christmas all the time!"

Hanse-Jacob looked at her, and she had on fine clothes all the way down to her feet, but around her feet she had bound some rags. Then he asked why that was. That, she said, was because her people had given all her clothes away to beggars, but not the shoes. She asked Jacob to tell her folks that they had to give away the shoes too; then she'd get good shoes on her feet, she said. Now she was on her way to Ryseberg to a feast; and away they rode.

But since that time, ol' Hanse-Jacob was not so sceptical when there was talk of *haug*-folk!

*Part VI*
*Legends about Spirits*
*of Forest and Mountain*

## ·33· *Trolls Resent a Disturbance*

*Motif G312, "Cannibal ogre"; R. Th. Christiansen, The Migra-tory Legends, 5000, "Trolls Resent a Disturbance." Collected by Edvard Langset in Hustad (western Norway) in 1918. From the manuscript by Langset, No. VI, 186 in Norsk Folkemin-nesamling (The Norwegian Folklore Institute).*

*Over fifty Norwegian variants of this legend have been col-lected, but none from the northern part of the country. This legend type is well known in Sweden, where it can be traced back to the Middle Ages; see Svensk Fornminneförenings Tids-skrift, V (Stockholm, 1912), 113.*

· OL' LANKY TOR never would stay home in his parish. He wanted to go into the mountains and shoot game and live just by hunting. Most of all, he wanted to live by himself. When he was in the mountains he did not know the difference between a Sunday and a weekday.

Now it happened once that he had been wandering about, far and farther than far, when he caught sight of lights in a hill a little way off. He went over toward the lights, and then he saw that *huldre*-folk were living in the hill. Then he heard one old wife in there say to another:

"Can I borrow that big cheese cauldron of yours?"

"What are you going to do with it?" said the other. She probably thought it strange that she wanted to borrow the big cauldron at that time of day.

Then the other old wife replied, "I want to cook Lanky Tor, who never will go home!"

By now Tor became frightened and took to his heels. Then he heard a great booming behind him, and when he looked back he caught sight of a big troll coming after him—a really big, ugly troll! He ran headlong down the hill as fast as he could, to get away from the troll, but soon he came to a big lake. The ice was so slippery that he could not get across.

Then someone shouted to him from another hill—it was probably a troll who wished him well: "Take off your shoes! Then
he can't catch up with you again!"

Well, Ol' Tor did just that, and he got across the ice in his
stocking feet. The troll did not come over. As Tor came down
to the parish, he saw lights burning in many places. He asked
someone he met, and found out it was Christmas Eve. Then he
went home to his parents and never went back to the mountains
again.

## ·34· *The Old Troll and the Handshake*

*Motif F571.2, "Sending to the older"; Motif F625, "Strong
man: breaker of iron"; Type 726, The Oldest on the Farm;
R. Th. Christiansen, The Migratory Legends, 5010, "The Visit
to the Old Troll. The Handshake." Collected by the Reverend
M. B. Landstad in Telemark in the 1840's and printed in Norsk
Folkeminnelag, VIII (1926), 36–38.*

*Eighteen Norwegian variants of this legend have been col-
lected, all from Telemark and other parts of western Norway.
R. Th. Christiansen has suggested that the close similarities between Norwegian and Gaelic variants point to a direct transmission of the story from one group to the other; see his "Gaelic
and Norse Folklore," Folkliv, II (1938), 328. Modern North
American versions of Type 726 are in R. M. Dorson, Negro
Folktales in Michigan, p. 181, and note 145, p. 229, and Buying
the Wind (Chicago, University of Chicago Press, 1964), pp.
86–87.*

· THERE WAS ONCE a man who went up on Skorve—a big mountain—to look for his horse, but he could not find it. Then, all
at once, a thick fog surrounded him, so he could not see his
hand in front of his face. But suddenly, as he was walking, he
came out onto a green field. He thought this was strange because
he knew his way around the mountain well, and he had never
seen anything but rockpiles and boggy hollows there before. A
little farther on, he came to a farm with many buildings, just

like any other farm. Outside he saw an old man, who was down on his knees, cutting and chopping wood. Our man went over to him and asked if he had seen anything of his horse.

"Ask my father," said the old fellow. "He's sitting inside by the hearth."

The man went in, and there he saw a very old fellow who sat in front of the hearth, cooking bacon on a stick. His head jerked to and fro, and his hands shook, and he looked like a dry fir tree full of lichens. The man asked about his horse which was gone. But he replied, "Ask my father, he's hanging in the horn on the wall." The man looked over at the wall, and there hung a mighty big horn, and in the horn was a man who was so old that he could neither see nor walk.

"Oh, poor you," said the man in the horn, "you're looking for your horse. We had to take it and shut it in, for it got into our field; but it hasn't suffered any harm. But where are you from?"

"From Seljord," said the man.

"Are folk in Seljord just as strong now as they were in the old days? Give me your hand so I can see if there's still marrow in your fingers," said the old one in the horn. But the one who was sitting by the hearth said that if the Seljord man wanted his hand back in one piece afterward he should hand the old fellow in the horn an iron bar that was standing there. He did so, and the old fellow squeezed the iron bar so hard that water oozed out of it.

"Ha!" he said. "There's nothing but ewe's milk in the fingers of folk from Seljord nowadays. It was different in the old days. Haven't you ever heard of me? I'm called Skaane, and I'm the one who built Seljord Church for St. Olav. I was living in Bringsaas then, but when the big bell came in the church, I had to move. I was strong, but St. Olav was stronger than me."

When the Seljord man was leaving, they warned him not to look behind him but hurry back the same way he had come. His horse had become so fat and fine that it fairly shone. "Thanks for the loan," said the old fellow. "Thanks yourself," said the man, and seating himself on the horse he said, "Now, in God's name then." But, when he turned to look around, he saw nothing but the big mountain, and it was as black and grey as it always had been.

## • *35* • The Jutul *and Johannes Blessom*

Motif D2121.5, "Magic journey: man carried by spirit or devil"; R. Th. Christiansen, The Migratory Legends, 5005, "A Journey with a Troll." Collected by P. Chr. Asbjörnsen in Vaage (eastern Norway) in 1842 and printed in Asbjörnsen, Norske Huldreeventyr og Folkesagn (1870), p. 124; new ed. (1949), p. 178.

Most of the thirty Norwegian variants of this legend are from eastern Norway. The Danish historian Saxo Grammaticus refers in his major work Gesta Danorum to a similar tale (around A.D. 1200) about a man named Hadding and his journey with the god Odin. A medieval reference in Swedish to this tale appears in Fornsvenskt Legendarium, II, 1208.

• ABOVE VAAGE PARSONAGE soars a fir-crowned ridge, or small mountain, with fissures and steep walls. This is the *jutul*'s mountain. By a freak of nature a doorway appears in one of the smooth walls. If one stands on the bridge over the boisterous Finna River, or in the meadows on the other side, and looks at this doorway, it takes on the shape of a double portal, joined at the top by a Gothic arch. This is no ordinary doorway or portal. It is the entrance to the *jutul*'s palace and is called Jutul's Gate. It is a tremendous gateway through which the biggest troll with fifteen heads could easily pass without bending his neck.

In the old days, when there were more dealings between mortals and trolls and someone wanted to borrow something from the *jutul*, or talk with him on other matters, it was the custom to throw a stone at the gate and say: "Open up, *jutul*!"

One of the last people to see the *jutul* was Johannes Sörigarden from Blessom, the neighboring farm to the parsonage. But he probably wished he had not.

This Johannes Blessom* was down in Copenhagen to find out about a lawsuit, for in those days there were no courts in Norway, and if anyone wanted to go to court, there was nothing else to do but go down there. This Blessom had done, and this his son did too, for he also had a lawsuit. Now it was Christmas Eve. Johannes had talked with the big shots and finished his business, and now he walked down the street in low spirits, for he wanted to go home. As he was walking, a man from Vaage suddenly strode past him in a white jacket, with a leather pouch and buttons like silver *dalers*. He was a great big man. It seemed to Johannes that he knew him, but he was not sure, he went so fast.

"You walk fast, you do," said Johannes.

"Yes, I have to hurry," answered the man, "for I'm going to Vaage tonight."

"Oh, if only I could go there too!" said Johannes.

"You can stand on behind me," said the man, "for I have a horse that takes twelve steps to a mile!"

They set out, and it was all Blessom could do to stay on the runners, for they were off through the air so fast that he could see neither heaven nor earth.

At one place they went down and rested. Before he could figure out where it was, they were suddenly off again. But he thought he saw a skull on a stake there. When they had come a bit on the way, Johannes Blessom's hands started to freeze.

"Ach! I left one of my mittens back there where we rested. Now my hand is freezing!"

"You'll just have to stand it, Blessom," said the man, "for it's not far to Vaage. There where we rested was halfway!"

Before they came to the bridge over Finna, the man stopped at Sandbuvollen and let Johannes off.

"Now you're not far from home," he said, "and now you're to promise me that you won't look back if you hear any rumbling or see any gleam of light!"

Johannes promised he would not look back and thanked him for the ride. The man drove on over the Finna bridge, and

* Customarily Norwegian farmers were called by the name of their farm.

Johannes headed up the hill toward Blessom farm. But all at once he heard a rumbling in the *jutul*'s mountain, and it was suddenly so light on the road before him that he could have picked up a pin. He forgot what he had promised and turned his head to see what had happened. There stood Jutul's Gate wide open, and the light streamed out through it as if from thousands and thousands of candles. But from that moment Johannes Blessom's head was half-turned, and he remained that way as long as he lived.

# • *36* • *The Urdebö Rockfall*

*This legend was told to Andreas Faye in 1840 by the Reverend S. O. Wolff in Telemark. It was printed in* Norske Folke-Sagn *(1844), pp. 3–5; it is reprinted in* Norsk Folkedikting, III, *"Segner,"* 116–17. *The earliest recording of this tale is a 1777 text found in E. Michaelsen,* Historisk Beskrivelse af Telemarken.

*This is the only legend collected in comparatively modern times about the old Norse pagan god Thor. It is not common, and Christiansen gives no references for it in* The Migratory Legends.

*In* The Poetic Edda, *as well as in this tale, Thor is conceived of as the strong but stupid glutton whom the other gods ridicule. Faye's informant said that he heard the story from a farmer who told it with a definitely comical touch (*Norske Folke-Sagn, *p. 5). "Thrymskvida" ("The Song about Thrym") in* The Poetic Edda *also tells of an incident in which Thor loses his famous hammer, Mjölnir, in the land of the giants, the jotuns.*

• BETWEEN URDEBÖ AND ÖYGARD farms, above Lake Totak in Rauland parish in Telemark, lies an alarmingly big rockfall right across the valley. It looks as if the mountain on the northern side of the valley has toppled over and filled the whole valley. A very old legend tells how this rockfall got there.

In the old days there was supposed to have been a whole parish in the valley. Once there was a wedding at one of the farms, and the wedding guests drank and reveled with all their might. Then came a mighty mountain troll called Tor Trolle-bane, who wanted some ale. He was huge, and he had a huge stomach, but nothing seemed to satisfy him no matter what they gave him to eat and drink. At last they had to refuse him more, for they were afraid he would drink up all the ale they had and spoil the whole feast for them. But now Tor was really angry. One of the men from a nearby farm saw this. He was a little more kindhearted, and he took Tor along to his farm and let him have a whole barrel of ale he had. And it was not long before the troll emptied the whole keg. By now Tor was so kindly dis-posed toward this man that he took him and his family along to a safe place so they could see what would happen. Then Tor took his hammer and smashed the mountain above the valley to bits, and the stones rained down over the whole valley. Only the people Tor had taken with him were saved, and to repay the man for the damage he had suffered Tor cleared up Urdebö farm for him.

But Tor struck so hard that his hammer swung off the handle and was lost among all the stones. Tor was now in such trouble that he promised to make a road through the rockfall so people could come across, if he could find the hammer again. He found it, and the road is still there. This was fortunate for people who later had to go through the rockfall.

## · 37 · *The Prospects of the* Huldre-Folk *for Salvation*

*Motif V520, "Salvation"; R. Th. Christiansen,* The Migratory Legends, *5050, "The Fairies' Prospect of Salvation." Collected in Heddal, Telemark, before 1880 by H. Tvedten, who printed it in his* Sagn fra Telemarken, *p. 78.*

*Eighteen Norwegian variants of this tale are on record, eight from western Norway. Close affinities are evident between Nor-wegian and Gaelic beliefs about the redemption of fairies; see*

R. Th. Christiansen, "Gaelic and Norse Folklore," Folkliv, II (1938), 330.

• ON HEFRE FARM, in Heddal, there lived a man named Ole, and he owned a couple of other farms, too. He married a girl from Leine farm in Sauland. One Saturday evening, before he was married, he was on his way over to Sauland to go courting. Late in the evening he came to a mound right alongside the road, way up in the parish. There he heard singing and music inside the mound, and sounds of dancing and gaiety and merriment. Ole was not afraid, and stood there listening for a while. When he was about to go on, he said aloud, "There's little use for you to be so happy. You won't share in the glory of God all the same!"

Then they replied from inside the mound, "We hope to share in the glory of God too." But Ole replied, "It's just as impossible for you to share in the glory of God as it is for flowers and leaves to grow on this dry staff I'm holding in my hand!"

Then at once it became silent in there, the dancing and music stopped, and instead he heard them begin to cry and wail. But Ole did not think any more about it. He was completely taken up by the thought that he would soon meet his sweetheart. It was late at night before he came to Leine, and when he went in he left his staff on the porch. He did not tell his sweetheart anything about his experience, for you should never talk about such things before you have slept on it, or else you will be sick.

When he was to go home in the morning, he was greatly astonished. There stood his staff, and it was completely covered with flowers and leaves which had grown on it. Then he remembered what had happened the evening before, and he walked as fast as he could to get to the mound. And when he came to it, he heard them still crying and wailing inside there. Then he shouted to them as loud as he could: "You mustn't cry and carry on any more. You can be happy now, for in truth you too will share in the glory of God. Last night leaves and flowers grew out on my staff!"

When he had said that, he heard great rejoicing inside the mound, and they started playing again and shouting to one another. Ole went home and pondered over what he had experienced, and with quite different thoughts from those he had had the evening before.

# ·38· *The Origin of the* Huldre-*Folk: the* Huldre *Minister*

*R. Th. Christiansen,* The Migratory Legends, *5055ff., "The attitude and position of the fairies toward the Christian faith." Collected in Setesdal by J. Skar and printed in his* Gamalt fra Setesdal, *I, 445.*

*Christiansen points out that various legends about the reactions of the fairies to Christianity are found in Norway, but that no distinct story pattern has developed* (The Migratory Legends, *pp. 90–91).*

· THERE WAS ONCE a farm up in the highlands, far to the east, and there folks had quite a lot of dealings with the *huldre*-folk, for a *tusse* was in the habit of coming there and borrowing one thing or another from the man on the farm. The minister had heard tell of this, and so one day he took it upon himself to journey up to this man and ask if there was anything to what people were saying.

"Yes," said the man. "If you'll sit down for about an hour, you'll see him. He's borrowed a pot of ale, and the next time the clock strikes, he's coming back with it." The minister sat down, and when the clock struck, the *tusse* came. When he saw a stranger there, he put the pot of ale on the table, bowed to the man, and wanted to go out again right away. But the minister got there first and blocked the door. He started talking to the *tusse*. He preached a sermon from the New Testament, he told of "the little babe"; he took everything from the beginning and explained and held forth as though he wanted to convert the *tusse,* for he probably thought it was a devil. The *tusse* struggled and wanted to go out, but the minister held

onto the latch and quoted and talked from the scriptures, from
the one to the other.

The *tusse* never answered a word, but at last he said, "I'm
not so learned that I can talk with you," he said, "but if you'll
sit down and wait a bit, I'll fetch my brother. He's a minister
just like you." He promised that the brother really would come,
but the minister dared not let him out; he was afraid he would
get away from them.

"You can safely let him go," said the man. "If he's promised
his brother will come, then he'll come all right. He never lies."
So the parson sat down and waited, and after he had been
sitting there a while, the *tusse* minister came, in frock and ruff
collar, and with the Bible in his hand.

"Do you know the book of Genesis?" asked the *tusse*. Yes,
that he did.

"It says there that, in the beginning, God created a man and
a woman. Do you know that?" Yes, he knew that too, and
then the *tusse* showed him what it said in the scriptures. "But
when the world had been created according to the second chapter,
God then made a woman out of Adam's rib. Do you know
that?" said the *tusse*. Yes, that he knew.

"Then Adam said: '*This time*'—why did he say '*this time*'?
Do you know that?" said the *tusse*. No, the parson did not know
that.

Then the *tusse* said, "That woman, who was created in the
very beginning, was Adam's equal in every way, and would
never be under him in anything. She considered herself as just
as good a creation as he. But God said that it wasn't good for
man and woman to be equal, and so he sent her and her offspring away, and put them into the hills to live. They are
without sin, and they stay there inside the hills, except when
they themselves want to be seen," he said. "But in the second
chapter, God took a rib out of Adam's side and made a woman
out of it, and then Adam said '*This time*,' because she was
taken out of the man. Her offspring have sin, and that's why
God had to give them the New Testament. The *tusse*-folk only
need the Old."

The minister had to give in to the *tusse* in everything, and he never went back in the pulpit again. The name of Adam's first wife is never mentioned in the Bible. She's called Lilli—or was it Lillo? But there's not much difference.

Sveinung Harstad was the one who told me this story. Sveinung had come from the east. I was old enough to go with him to the mill, and then he told this story on the way.

## · 39 · *The Origin of the* Huldre-Folk: *the Hidden Children of Eve*

*Motif F251.4, "Underworld people from children which Eve hid from God"; R. Th. Christiansen,* Norske Eventyr, *"Aitiologiske Legender," No. 10b, p. 105, "Evas ulike börn." Collected by O. K. Ödegaard in Valdres (eastern Norway) before 1917 and printed in O. K. Ödegaard,* Gamal Tru og Gamal Skjik ifraa Valdres, *p. 103.*

*Throughout Europe, stories about Eve's offspring are told as explanations of the existence of different social classes and peoples. See Type 758, The Various Children of Eve; Motif A1650.1, with the same title; and Bolte-Polívka, III, No. 180, "Die ungleichen Kinder Evas."*

· THE HAUG-FOLK? Yes—I dare say it was Our Lord who created them, too. Eve, Adam's wife, lived a long time and had an incredible number of children, even long after she was past the time when one has children, and at last she became downright ashamed at having so many. So it was, once, that Our Lord came by and looked in on Eve, and then he asked to see her children. She brought out a whole flock, but left some behind, because she thought it embarrassing to have so many now that she was getting to be so old. Our Lord understood this all right, and was a little hurt, and said to Eve: "If you're hiding children from me, then they'll be hidden from you!"

Then Eve could not see these children any longer. They were turned into *haug*-folk and mountain trolls, each and every one, and it is not often that anyone catches sight of them, although it does happen once in a while. Those who have "second sight" have the power; they can find out how they look, and how they're getting on. There is probably not such a big difference between them and us, because the same one has created them. But they are not Christians like we are.

## · 40 ·    *The Changeling Betrays His Age*

*Motif F321.11, "Changeling deceived into betraying his age"; F321.1.1.5, "Changeling calculates his age by the age of the forest"; F321.1.2.2, "Changeling is always hungry, demands food all the time." R. Th. Christiansen,* The Migratory Legends, *5085, "The Changeling"; Bolte-Polívka, I, 368–70. Collected in Telemark by H. Tvedten and printed in his* Sagn fra Telemarken, *p. 46.*

*This is a widely told Norwegian legend, especially in eastern Norway. An extensive treatment of folk traditions about changelings is in E. S. Hartland,* The Science of Fairy Tales, *pp. 93–134.*

· On LINDHEIM FARM, in Nesherad, there was supposed to have been a changeling. No one could remember when he was born or when he had come to the farm. No one had ever heard him speak, but all the same they were afraid to do anything to him or make him angry. He ate so much that the people at Lindheim had been living from hand to mouth, generation after generation, on his account.

One day a wise woman came there and gave them advice and told them what to do. They were to take a big pot, and in it they were to cook only as much porridge as was needed for a tiny baby. Then they were to put the pot in the middle of the parlor floor, with a little clump of porridge in the bottom, and as many spoons as there was room for. When this was done, they all went out so the changeling was left alone inside. He pottered

over to the pot and peered down in it. Then they heard him
speak for the first and last time.

He said: "Well, I'm not rightly old and I'm not rightly
young, but I've seen Lindheim forest chopped down and grow
up three times. But never before have I seen such a big pot
with so little food and so many spoons in it. But when they
burn down the shack on Guldhaugen, then I'll die!"

As you might expect, it was not long before the shack on Guldhaugen was all ablaze, and as for the changeling, it happened
as he had said.

## · 41 ·  *Disposing of a Changeling*

*Motif F321.1.4, "Disposing of a changeling." Collected by Ivar
Aasen in Midthordland (western Norway) in 1884 and printed
in Norsk Folkeminnelag, I (1923), 51.*

· THERE WAS ONCE a wife who had a tiny baby, and like so many
others, she took it along with her in a little cradle when she was
out working in the fields. It so happened once that she had to go
away from the cradle while the baby was asleep, and when she
came back the child had been taken away. Another baby was
lying in its place, but it was both tiny and ugly, and as black
as dirt.

Then she shouted to her husband to come right away. He
came and took the child and carried it out in the field and put
it down. Then he shouted over toward the forest that whoever
owned the child had to come and take it back and leave his own
child instead. If they did not, they would never be left in peace
again. He would shout and crash about in the forest so the
ground would shake. Then he left the child lying there and
went back to his work again. But as he turned and looked back,
he saw a *hulder* come and swap the children, and slip back into
the forest as fast as she could. But both the man and his wife
were overjoyed, as could be expected, when they got their own
child back again.

## • 42 • *The Sickly Changeling*

*Motif F321.1.3, "Changeling is sickly." Collected by Knut Strompdal in Nordland (western Norway) in the 1920's and printed in* Norsk Folkeminnelag, XIX (1929), 149.

• IN SKOTSVAR there lived a newly married couple who had a baby only a few weeks old. One day, while the husband was out fishing, the wife went up on a hill to see if he would be back soon. When she came home again, her own child was gone and a strange baby was lying in its place. It looked quite ragged and tattered. Three whole years passed without their hearing anything about their own child, but the strange child was still with them. They took good care of it, but the child did not seem to thrive. It did not get better and wouldn't grow. They felt, as the saying goes, "neither blessed nor at rest with this child." Then they went to the pastor in Tjötta and asked him for help and advice. He told them to bring the child to be christened, and then something would be sure to happen with it. Well, they rented a boat with three sets of oars and started out for Tjötta with three men to row, and the wife sat in the bulkhead in the stern with the baby.

Halfway between Tjötta and Skotsvar, another boat with three sets of oars came rowing up, and a woman was also sitting in the stern. This boat came right over to them, and was so close that they were not able to row. The head man on the other boat wanted to know where they were going.

Up to now they had never heard this child speak, but now it suddenly answered before any of the others could say anything: "We're on our way to Hellepung to drop fiddle dung!" which in their language meant "We're on our way to Tjötta to be christened!" And when he had said that he dived right into the sea, and at the same moment the strange boat was gone.

Now, of course, they had no reason for going to the pastor in Tjötta, and so they rowed home again. But when they got home, their own child was sitting on the steps crying. The mother recognized it again right away, and she was happy, as you might know!

## · 43a · Food from the Huldre-Folk on the Mountain

*Motif F361.15, "Fairies punish mortals who refuse to eat fairy food given them"; R. Th. Christiansen, The Migratory Legends, 5080, "Food from the fairies." The two variants printed here were collected by R. Th. Christiansen in Land (eastern Norway) in 1921 and printed in Boka om Land, II, 276.*

*Some twenty Norwegian variants of this tale have been collected, half from the northern parts of the country. Celtic folklore is full of traditions about churning fairies. Thus see the detailed version of this legend given by Malcolm Mac Phail in "Folklore from the Hebrides, II," Folk-Lore, VIII (1897), 380-81.*

· IT COULD BE dangerous to have anything to do with the *huldre*-folk. Two boys found this out once. They were out herding and sat down on a hill and started whittling on their staves. Then they clearly heard someone churning inside the mountain.

"Shall we call them and ask for oatcakes with new butter, and buttermilk to drink?" said one of the boys. The other one thought they had better not, it could be dangerous. But the first boy did so all the same, and they came out with what he had asked for. But now he would not have any, so the other boy took it, and it tasted very good.

But soon the first boy who had offended them became sick. He was so poorly by the time he got home that it really looked bad; at last his father knew of no other solution than to take him back up to the mountain where this had happened. And there he had to apologize to the *huldre*-folk for offending them by not eating their food.

# · 43b ·  Food from the Huldre-Folk at Ellefstad

*This variant was collected in Valdres and is printed in Svale Solheim,* Norsk Setertradisjon, *p. 462.*

· Two GIRLS from Ellefstad were out looking for their calves one day, and at last they had wandered all the way up in the mountains. As they were walking about searching, they suddenly heard the sound of churning inside a little mound they were going past.

Then, just for the fun of it, one of the girls said, to no one in particular, "Come out so we can taste your cream!"

The words were scarcely out of her mouth before a beautiful maiden was standing outside the mound holding an oatcake covered with cream. The girl who had asked the *huldre* maiden to come out started to laugh at her standing there with the cream. And the *huldre* did not like this one bit, it turned out.

Then the other girl asked, "You haven't seen anything of some calves we've lost, have you?"

"Why yes, I've seen them. You'll find your calves again soon, but the calves of the other one who laughed at me have been torn to pieces by our big hog!" answered the *huldre* maiden, and with that she was gone.

And what she had said came true. After they had searched for a while, one of the girls found her calves. But the calves of the girl who had laughed had been taken by the bear. For it's quite true that the bear is the *huldre*-folk's big hog.


# · 44 ·  The Haug-Folk Help a Man

*Motif F451.3.4.3, "Dwarfs do farming"; R. Th. Christiansen, The Migratory Legends, 6035, "Fairies Assist a Farmer in his*

*Work." Collected by Ivar Aasen in Hosanger (western Norway)
about 1860 and printed that year in a newspaper in Dölen; reprinted in* Norsk Folkeminnelag, I (*1923*), *55–58.*

*Legends concerning assistance in farm work by fairies have no
definite epic pattern; they generally refer to supposedly actual
happenings* (The Migratory Legends, *p. 167*).

• IF YOU WILL LISTEN, it might be fun to tell about what happened
once at Seim, and how that beautiful table, which they have
always had there, really came to the farm. It is such an unusually
fine table that everyone who has seen it has been quite astonished
at it.

Nowadays there are many farms at Seim, but at one time this
was all one big farm. Today there are lots of fields there, but in
those days there was one big field, and it was so big that one
could hardly see where it ended. This was a really big farm,
and the man who owned it had every possible reason for being
pleased. But it had its difficulties too. It was not easy to get
enough help, for there were not as many people in the parishes
in those days as there are now. The worst pinch was in the
autumn, when the grain was to be harvested. It could happen
that it remained standing outside until it was spoiled, and if
there was frost, things were in a bad way.

Now it happened once that it really looked bad. There had
been nothing but storms and rain the whole autumn, and when
good weather finally did set in, frost could be expected any
night. There was no help to be had, and the farmer at Seim did
not know where to turn.

But there is an old saying, "When need is greatest, help is
closest at hand." And one evening, as the farmer was walking
around the farm, he was so afraid that the grain would be
spoiled that he wrung his hands and was almost on the verge
of tears, and he said aloud, "What is one to do? There's no
help to be had here!"

Then he heard someone reply from the hills above the house,
"There's help to be had here!"

"What kind of help could that be?" said the farmer.

"If you'll just do as we ask you to, you will have such good help that you will never regret it!"

Then the farmer understood that the *haug*-folk were offering to reap the field for him, and he found out what they wanted him to do.

Well, he was to go home and brew the biggest cauldron he had full of ale, put the cauldron in the middle of the floor in the best room in the house, and place another cauldron beside it upside down. If that was all, thought the farmer, he would certainly do it. He went inside and started brewing.

But the field came to life during the night. It was teeming with tiny *haug*-folk, and they all had shiny scythes in their hands. They started cutting the grain, and they sang the whole time:

> "We can cut the grain for you,
> But bind it up we cannot do!"

When a sheaf of grain is bound together, a knot is needed, and that is so like a cross that the *haug*-folk cannot make it. They cut the grain, and the work went fast, and in the morning the people on the farm came and bound the grain into sheaves and got it inside.

Now that they had finished, the workers were to have a feast, and in the evening things were lively in the big parlor. There were so many people that there was hardly any room; there had never been so many there before. No one was allowed to watch, but they could hear the commotion for miles around, and it kept up until daybreak.

In the morning the farmer went into the big parlor. Both cauldrons were gone, but in their place stood a table, so fine that no one had ever seen anything like it. It was highly carved and painted with many colors. It was in payment to the farmer because he had been such a good host the night before.

Many years have passed, and the table has become old and worm-eaten, but it has been allowed to remain at the farm, for the people believe that as long as it stays there, good fortune will never leave Seim.

# ·45· A Woman Helps a Hulder

*Motif F330, "Grateful fairies"; Motif F343.9, "Fairy gives man horses, cattle, etc." Collected by R. Th. Christiansen in Land (eastern Norway) in 1921 and printed in* Boka om Land, *II, 288.*

• It could happen, now and then, that these other, unseen beings lived close up to people and did their chores along with them. Once there was a woman who was at a *seter* up on the mountain at Nysetra, on the west side of the ridge. Now one evening, as the sun was setting, and a huge fir tree out in the field cast a long shadow on the wall right where the door was, the woman was standing there busy fixing some pine branches that lay in front of the door. Suddenly a woman stood beside her, and she saw at once that she did not know her.

"Good evening," said the stranger. "You wouldn't by any chance do me the favor of milking my cows and straining the milk, so I can get down to the parish and stand godmother to my daughter's son?"

"Why, yes, I can do that all right," said the woman. "But how will I find your cows? I don't know where you're staying." She understood this was a *hulder* and wanted to do as she asked in order not to make an enemy of her.

"It's not hard to find the way," said the other. "Just follow me. You need only lift this pine branch. I live right under your doorstep!"

Then they lifted the branch, and they were at the *hulder*'s *seter*. They went around to the stall, and the stranger showed her how she was to milk and attend to everything. "You mustn't make any kind of sign over anything here," said the strange woman, "for then my milk will go down."

The woman did everything she had been told and took good care not to make the sign of the cross over anything. All went well. The strange woman came back and thanked her for helping her, and then she did not see any more of her the whole summer.

But as she was on her way down to the parish in the autumn, and they were out on Okshoved marsh, a big brindled cow with a milk pail on its horns came running after her, mooing and lowing.

"You can take the cow home with you," said a voice over in a hill. "You're to have it as thanks for helping me this summer. If you feed it, and butcher it instead of selling it, then good fortune will follow for nine generations to come."

It was a good cow. It was not any bigger than the others, but it gave milk constantly and steadily.

## • 46 • Removing a Building to Suit Those Under the Ground

*Motif F451.4.4.3, "Dwarfs request that cow stable be moved because it is above their home"; R. Th. Christiansen, The Migratory Legends, 5075, "Removing a Building situated over the House of the Fairies." Collected by Edvard Grimstad in Fron, Gudbrandsdal (eastern Norway), about 1900 and printed in Norsk Folkeminnelag, LXII (1948), 44–45.*

*This is one of the most widely reported Norwegian legends, collected in some three hundred variants. It is well known also in Sweden and Denmark.*

• AT STANDAR SETER there was supposed to have been a whole cluster of houses belonging to the *huldre*-folk. They were quiet and peaceful folk and were not afraid of having dealings with Christians. The farmers could see them and now and then they talked with them too. It was almost as if everyone up there belonged together.

One day a *huldre* woman came to one of the dairymaids and asked if she could borrow a little bread. The farmer happened to be at the *seter* on that particular day, and the dairymaid asked him if she could lend some of the bread.

"Just let them have anything they ask for," said the farmer. "I don't like to be on bad terms with them."

It often happened to one of the dairymaids that her goats got out during the night, so she had to go out and put them back in again. This happened not just once but time and time again. The dairymaid could not understand it, for she took extra pains to lock the door in the evening.

But one day a *huldre* woman came to her and said, "You'd better stop keeping the goats inside, for the pen is standing in such a spot that our food is being spoiled!" Then they had to move the goatpen to another place, just to be able to keep their goats in peace.

One of the farmers, who had a *seter* there, went up to it shortly before the *seter* time had begun. When he came up there, he saw a newly built, re-painted house which had not been there before. Out in the enclosure was a horse he thought he recognized. He did not give it much thought but went in the house to pay his respects to the new people who had come. He said it was nice that they had settled down at the *seter* so they would be neighbors.

Two women dressed in red were inside, and one of them said, "Oh, we've been neighbors for twenty years!"

Then the man understood what kind of people he had come to. They offered him a little milk to drink, but he dared not accept it and only went out again. Then he went over to the horse, which started neighing when he came up to it, and he saw that it was his own horse which had disappeared the year before.

Then the man no longer felt quite at ease up at the *seter* but hurried home as fast as he could, now that he had seen that the ones living up there were not completely honest. Not that it made much difference. Folks like that are certainly to be found down in the parish too—the kind that help themselves to things without even saying thanks.

# · 47 · *Escape from the* Huldre-*Folk*

*Motif F375, "Mortals as captives in fairyland." This motif forms the dominant theme in E. S. Hartland,* The Science of Fairy Tales, *a classic study dealing not with Märchen but with legends.*

*The legend given here contains Motif R112.3, "Rescue of prisoners from fairy stronghold." It was collected by Ivar Aasen in Valle, Setesdal (southern Norway), in 1844 and printed in* Norsk Folkeminnelag, I *(1923), 38–40.*

· THERE WAS ONCE a hunter who had gone up in the hills to shoot wild fowl. He came into a forest and walked along staring up at the treetops looking for birds. Before he knew it, he found himself inside a place he had never seen before. It was a big farm, and there were so many houses with long verandas on all sides that there was no end to them. He wandered aimlessly about until at last he grew tired of it. He did not see any people, and he could not find the way out. Finally, he thought he heard someone inside one of the houses. He opened the door and looked in, and there sat a girl quite alone. He spoke to her and asked what kind of people were living on the farm. She said that *tusse*-folk lived there, and it was the kind of farm that no one could see before he was inside, and from it no one could ever come out again. This is what had happened to her. She had been there for a long time, and she did not know how to get home again.

The hunter grew frightened and asked again if she was certain she knew no way out. She said she could indeed give him advice, but then he would have to promise to come back and take her away from this farm. This he promised to do.

"Now follow me," she said, "and open the door I point out to you. In there, they're sitting around the table eating. The one sitting at the head of the table is their king. He's bigger and handsomer than the rest, and you'll know him as soon as you look inside the room. Then you're to take your gun and aim it at the king, but you mustn't shoot. They'll be afraid and chase you out, but they won't dare to harm you for you have the gun. Then you're saved, and then you must think of me. You're to come back here on the first Thursday evening and the second and third Thursday evenings too, and then it's certain that I'll go home with you."

Then she went out and showed him the door he was to open. He went inside, and there they sat around the table, eating and drinking. He took the gun and aimed it at the one who was sitting at the head of the table. Then they grew frightened and jumped up at him and he got away. They chased him all the way out, and in this way he got away from them and came safely home.

He went up there to the hill on the first Thursday evening after that, and on the second Thursday too, and talked with the girl both times. But on the third Thursday evening, which was the most important, he did not come. Whatever it was that hindered him, I have never found out.

Then it happened once that the hunter was up on the hill again. It was at least three or four years later. Then he heard someone crying and carrying on badly and complaining about how sad and unpleasant it was to have to stay there by herself all the time and not be able to come home. He stayed there for a long time, looking and searching in every direction, but he was not able to find anything except marsh and forest, which is all that there is up there.

## • 48a • Living with the Huldre-Folk in a Knoll

*Motif F322, "Fairies steal man's wife and carry her to fairy-land," and Motif D1983.2, "Invisibility conferred by fairy." This legend was collected by P. Lunde before 1920 in Sögne (southern Norway) and printed in* Norsk Folkeminnelag, *VI (1923), 125.*

• THE HULDRE-FOLK had carried off a wife from a certain place, and the husband had been left behind alone. Some time after this, the husband was in the forest chopping wood when he heard a mighty pounding in a knoll, and then he heard his wife's voice close beside him.

"Are you here?" she said, but he could not see her. He thought it was only his imagination, but then the wife said, "Hold out your hand and I'll give you the brooch you gave to me. Then you can tell you've been talking with me."

The man held out his hand, and she put the brooch in it. He asked if she was coming back to him.

"No," she said, "you can't have me back. But all is well with me." Then she was lost to him.

## • *48b* • *Living with the* Huldre-Folk *at Aanstad*

*Motif F381.7, "Fairies leave when people do their needs where they live." This legend was collected by J. Hveding in Buksnes, Nordland (western Norway), about 1930 and printed in* Norsk Folkeminnelag, *XXXIII (1935), 52–53.*

• ONE YEAR a man from Holand, in Buksnes, journeyed to Aanstad, in Flakstad, to go fishing. This man was called Hans Jensa. It was autumn, and there were four men in his boat. One of them was from Vaagen, and his name was Peder Björnsa. When they came to Aanstad, they baited their hooks and went out and set their lines the same evening. The next day they hauled them in. In the evening, when they had eaten and were getting ready for bed, Peder Björnsa went out of the house. He was gone for such a long time that they started wondering about it. It grew late, and he had not come back in, so they went out to look for him. At last everyone in the house was out searching, and they kept it up until morning. He had put his wooden shoes out by the doorsill, but he himself was gone and gone he stayed.

Then a long time passed. Peder's mother dreamed about her son several times after this. He wasn't living very far away, she said.

One autumn, just before Christmas, people were out fishing off Balstad. Seven years had passed since this had happened at Aanstad. One morning the fishermen went out and set their lines. The weather was good. As they were busy with the lines, they caught sight of a big, ten-oared boat, which came sailing eastward. The crew sat rowing under the sails. They steered right up to the fishing boat.

"Hallo! Hallo there!" shouted one of the fishermen to the ten-oarer. "Where are you bound?"

"Oh, we're going to Kalle in Vaagen," answered the leader on the ten-oarer. "Do you know Johanna Björnsa in Vaagen?"

Why yes, they knew her, said the men.

"You must give her my regards. I'm her son. I've been living at Aanstad all this time, but now I'm moving to Kalle. The folks at Aanstad grew so thoughtless and careless that they shoveled the dung from the barn right down on my dining table!"

## · 49a ·  *Midwife to the* Huldre-Folk *at Ekeberg*

*Motif F372.1, "Fairies take human widwife to attend fairy woman." R. Th. Christiansen, The Migratory Legends, 5070, "Midwife to the Fairies." This legend was recorded by P. Chr. Asbjörnsen in Christiania in 1838 and printed in Norsk Huldreeventyr og Folkesagn (1870), p. 11; new edition (1949), p. 71.*

· AROUND 1853, Ekeberg was not as cleared and populated as it is now. It was overgrown with trees and shrubs; from the city no other dwellings could be seen except the old Ekeberg farmhouse up on the top of the hill. There was a little red shack farther down the hill. It was on the left side of the road where it turns toward Ekeberg farm. This turn in the road is called "The Swing."

Here in "The Swing," in the little red shack, there lived in the old days a poor old woman who was a basket maker. She was so poor that she barely managed to make both ends meet.

Once, when she went to fetch water, a big fat toad was sitting in the path in front of her. "If you'll get out of my way, I'll be your midwife when you're in confinement," she said as a joke to the toad, which at once started to get out of the way as fast as it could.

Some time after that, when the old woman had come home from the city one evening in autumn and was sitting in front of the hearth spinning, a man came in to her. "Listen," he said, "my wife is soon to be confined. She hasn't much time left. If you'll help her when she's in labor, as you've promised, then you won't regret it."

"So help me God!" said the old woman. "I certainly can't do that. I don't know anything about it!"

"Well, you have to do it as long as you've promised her," said the man.

The woman could not remember having promised to be midwife to anyone, and she told him so.

But the man replied: "Yes, you did promise, for that toad who sat in your way, when you went to fetch water, was my wife. If you will help her," the man went on—and she now realized he was none other than the king of Ekeberg—"then you'll never regret it. I'll pay you what you deserve for it. But you mustn't waste the money I give you, or give it away if anyone asks you for some. And you mustn't talk about it, not even so much as hint about it to anyone."

"Oh Heavens, no!" she said. "I can keep a secret all right, and if you'll just come and tell me when your wife is in labor, I'll try to help as best I can."

Some time passed, and then one night the same man came to the old woman and asked her to come with him. She got up and dressed. He went ahead, and she followed, and before she knew where they were, or how it had happened, she was inside the mountain where the queen lay in labor. And the old woman thought she had never been anywhere so grand before.

But once they were inside, the man sat down in a chair and clasped his hands together around his knees. Now when a man sits like this, a woman in labor cannot be delivered. The basket woman knew this very well, so she and the queen tried to find many errands for him, asking him to fetch first one thing and then the other. But he sat where he sat, and did not budge from the spot. At last the midwife had an idea.

"Now she's delivered!" she said to the husband.

"How did that happen?" he cried, and was so astonished that he let go of his knees. At the same moment the Christian woman placed her hand on the queen, and she was delivered at once.

While the husband was out warming up the water to wash the child, the queen said to the basket woman: "My husband likes you well enough, but when you leave he'll shoot after you all the same, for he must be true to his nature. So you must hurry and pop behind the door the same moment you leave, and then he won't hit you!"

When the child had been washed and tidied up and dressed, the queen sent the basket woman out in the kitchen to get a pot of salve for anointing its eyes. But the like of such a kitchen and such utensils the old woman had never seen before. The most magnificent plates and saucers were lined up in rows, and from the ceiling hung pans and kettles and dishes, all of purest silver and so brightly polished that they shone from all the walls.

But no one can imagine how amazed she was when she saw her own hired girl standing there grinding oats with a hand mill. She took a pair of scissors and clipped a square out of the girl's skirt without her noticing it, and this she hid.

When she had finished and was ready to leave, she remembered what the queen had said, and popped behind the door. At the same moment the king shot glowing phosphorus after her so the fire spluttered from it.

"Did I hit you?" he cried.

"Oh, no," replied the woman.

"That was good!" he shouted.

The sun was high in the sky when the basket woman got

home, but the hired girl, who always complained of feeling poorly and having pains in her back, lay groaning and was still asleep. The old woman woke her up and asked, "Where were you last night?"

"Me, mother?" said the girl. "I haven't been anywhere, as far as I know, except here in bed."

"Well, I know better," said the woman. "I clipped this square out of your skirt inside the mountain last night. See how it fits? But that's the way it is with young people today. In the old days folks said their evening prayers and sang a hymn before they went to bed, so that the trolls wouldn't have any power over them. Now I shall teach you to open your eyes to the Lord. No wonder you're tired and poorly and have a pain in your back. You're no help to me either as long as you work for them during the night and for me during the day!"

From the very day the basket woman played midwife to the queen, she found a pile of silver money outside her door every morning. With this her lot improved so that she was soon a well to do woman. But it so happened that once a very poor woman came and poured out her troubles to her.

"Oh, pooh!" said the basket woman, "Things can't really be as bad as all that; why, if I liked, it would be an easy matter for me to help you, for whatsoever a man soweth he shall reap. I've certainly helped the one who brings me wealth!"

But from that day on, not a shilling did she find outside her door, and it was as if the money she had already received had blown away. And once again she had to take her baskets on her arm and wander to town in sunshine and rain.

## · *49b* · Midwife to the Huldre-Folk at Nore

*This legend is widely known throughout Norway. Some 110 variants have been recorded. This version was collected during the 1870's in Numedal. It is variant F15.2 in the manuscript collection of the* Norsk Folkeminnesamling *and has been printed in* Norske Bygder, VI, *118.*

· THERE WAS a girl from Nore, Gunhild Skjönne, who was at a dance on the Second Day of Christmas. After the dance she set out for home alone. On the way, she disappeared, and for all her parents searched and asked about her, not a trace of her did they find. The father thought she might have fallen in the river and made inquiries all the way down to Kongsberg as to whether they had found a body by the timber boom. But none had been seen.

Then a whole year passed, and on the next Christmas Day, a fine looking young man came in and said he wanted to pay his respects to his in-laws. Their daughter was alive and in the best of health, he said, and if they would come with him they could pay her a visit. At last the mother let herself be persuaded, fixed a gift, and made herself ready. Out in the yard stood a big black horse hitched to a fine sleigh.

After they had driven for an hour, the son-in-law asked if she did not recognize where she was, and she saw that they were not far from her own *seter*. "Well, it's not far now," said the son-in-law, and then they were in the courtyard of a big, fine farm, and he told her to go in while he put up the horse. Inside the parlor sat an old man with a long white beard.

"Welcome, mother," he said. "Now your daughter is going to have a child, but she's not to be reproached for that," he said. In another room she found her daughter in bed, and not long afterward she was delivered.

The mother stayed there for some time, and one evening Gunhild said to her that it was Twelfth Night, and now she had to keep very quiet for the *oskorei* were going to put up at the farm. The mother heard them outside in the yard, saw food and drink being carried out to them, and heard them gambling and dancing until far into the night.

When the young wife was well again, she showed the mother around the farm. Everything was big and well managed, and Gunhild said she would have scarcely been better off if she had married the richest farmer in her own parish. Thus the days passed, and the mother did not keep much track of time. One day the daughter said, "Now papa says that mother is gone too." Then the mother was so uneasy that she wanted to go home. The son-in-law took her back and said that Gunhild was free to come visiting as long as she did not run into the man with the plain white collar around his neck.

## • 50 •   *Married to a* Hulder

*Motif F302.2, "Man marries fairy and takes her to his home"; Motif F377, "Supernatural lapse of time in fairyland"; R. Th. Christiansen, The Migratory Legends, 5090, "Married to a Fairy Woman." Collected by Kjell Flatin in Seljord (Telemark) in 1912 or 1913 and printed in Norsk Folkeminnelag, XXI (1930), 9–13.*

*This legend is widely known in the southern and central districts of Norway; of the 150 variants collected only seven are from the north. Tales about supernatural mistresses are universal; see references under Motif F302. The episode of the woman's fitting on the horseshoe (cf. Motif F862, "Extraordinary horseshoe") seems to be found essentially in Norwegian, Danish, and Swedish versions of this tale; see H. F. Feilberg, Bjaergtagen, p. 87.*

*The reference to the hulder's mother not taking a calf from each pair of twin calves is a remnant of an old folk belief that the second calf belonged to the huldre-folk.*

• ONE SUMMER, Olav Lonar was fishing up in the mountains far to the north. There were plenty of fish in the waters where he had fishing rights, but there was no denying that others fished there after it was dark, and Olav usually remained up there for long periods at a time, to chase away the thieves. He stayed in an old *seter*.

One evening as he was about to go to bed he first had to go outside on an errand. He went out the door, but before he knew where he was, he found himself standing inside a big, richly furnished room. He was bewildered. A fire was burning on the hearth, and around the walls gleamed silver goblets, pewter plates, and copper kettles. Over by the hearth sat an old man and an old woman. A beautiful young maiden went back and forth. She put food and drink of the very best sort on the table and invited Olav to sit down. But he understood that something was wrong here, and he dared not eat or drink.

"You needn't be afraid to eat and drink here," said the old fellow over by the hearth. "We won't do you any harm. You shall leave here as freely as you came."

The maiden was quite sweet tempered; she stole a glance at Olav every now and then, and he thought he had never seen such a beautiful girl before. But he sat there like a block of wood and was not able to utter a word, nor would he eat and drink anything either. All at once, and he did not understand how it had happened, he was standing outside the door of his *seter* again. Everything was dark and cold, and there was barely a faint glow in the coals over in the hearth. For his part, he thought he had only been outside for a little while. But when he went to look, the big birch logs had burned up and only a few coals were left. He had put them on the fire for the night before he went out, and now he understood that it must have been some time ago. He went to bed and had a quiet, restful sleep.

But the maiden he had seen that evening was never out of his thoughts, no matter where he went. He tried to get her out of his mind, but it was no use. All that autumn and winter he went about like a half-wit, and was changed beyond recognition. He did not open his mouth and appeared not to see or hear.

The next summer he was up there again, keeping an eye on the fish. Then one evening he went outside the door. Before he knew it, he found himself in the same room with the old couple and the young maiden he had met the previous summer. Everything happened as before. The maiden went back and forth and was so fine and beautiful that she was a joy to behold. She put the very best food and drink on the table, and now Olav was not careful any longer. He sat down at the table and helped himself. Now the old couple started to speak, and said that they had thought of giving their daughter, the beautiful young maiden, to Olav. And they promised that good fortune and prosperity would follow him and his family all their days. Olav thought he had never heard anything better, and so they were engaged —he and the *tusse* girl. Her name was Torgun.

Olav stayed up in the mountains a long time that summer, and the people back home almost gave up waiting for him. But late in the autumn, when he came down, Torgun was with him. Folks in the parish were not a little surprised that Lonar had found a wife. No one knew where she was from or whether she had any kinfolks. Then the wedding was held, and Olav was married to Torgun in the church. At the wedding people noticed that she had a long tail, and then they understood who she was. But when she went in through the church door, the tail fell off, and Olav never saw anything of it again.

They all thought Torgun was the prettiest and finest looking woman they had ever seen. She was quiet spoken and did not put on airs; she was careful not to do anything wrong and was kind to rich and poor alike. Poor folks who came to the farm begging for food were never turned away; they never left without having something to take with them. She was known for her kindness, and poor folks came from far and wide. Everything prospered after Torgun came there. The cows gave more milk and were so fat and sleek that no one had ever seen anything like it.

The first winter they were at Lonar, she and Olav had a falling-out about what to do with the newborn calves. Olav wanted to follow the old custom of breeding the prettiest calves, but Torgun insisted that they be butchered.

"What are you thinking of, woman? Do you want to take the lives of the ones that'll make the best cows?" said Olav.

"Don't worry about that," said Torgun.

In the spring, when they let out the animals, Olav was not a little surprised, for every one of the cows had a fine calf with her.

"How in all the world can this be," said Olav, "when we've butchered all the calves?"

"Every cow has two calves, but my mother won't take any away from us!" said Torgun. The calves grew and thrived, and became big, splendid looking cows, and no one had ever seen anything like the herd they had at Lonar.

Olav was not nice to his wife. He was quarrelsome and ill-tempered and scolded her from morning till night. She kept quiet and never made a fuss about it. But one Sunday Olav and Torgun were going to church. Olav was out in the yard struggling with the horse. He wanted to put on a horseshoe, but he could not get it to fit the way it should. He cursed and swore and carried on as if he were out of his mind. Torgun could not stand hearing anyone swear, and now she went out to Olav and stood staring at him for a while. Then she took the horseshoe and wadded it up with her bare hands. Then she straightened it out again, fitted it to the hoof, and bent it a little more at the ends.

"This is the way a horseshoe should fit," she said, and looked sharply at Olav.

"You're more than a woman, Torgun," said Olav. "As bad as I've been to you more than once, and you haven't hauled off and given me a thrashing! I think that's strange."

"I've got better sense," said Torgun.

After this, Olav was a different person. He never swore so Torgun could hear it, and was accommodating and kind to her in every way. Torgun and Olav became very rich. They had good luck with everything they did, and there was such prosperity and everything grew so well at the farm that it was downright strange to see. Their descendants were also rich, and have lived in Lonar parish until now, and Torgun's name has remained in the family.

## • 51a • The Interrupted Huldre Wedding at Melbustad

*Motif F303, "Wedding of mortal and fairy"; R. Th. Christiansen, The Migratory Legends, 6005, "The Interrupted Fairy Wedding." Many Norwegian variants of this tale have been*

*collected, in both eastern and western districts. Christiansen cites
similar stories in Swedish and Danish traditions.*

*This legend was collected by A. Faye in Land (eastern Nor-
way) before 1844 and printed in his* Norske Folk-Sagn *(1844),
p. 26. It has been translated in English in F. Metcalfe,* The
Oxonian in Norway, *p. 115. Another variant from Land is to
be found in* Boka om Land, *II, 281.*

• EVERY SUMMER, a long long time ago, they went up to the *seter*
with the cows from Melbustad, in Hadeland. But they had not
been there long before the cows became so restless that it was
downright impossible to control them. Many girls had tried herding them, but it grew no better until a girl who had just plighted
her troth came to work for them. Then the cows were calm
right away, and there was no trouble herding them any longer.
She stayed at the *seter* alone and had no other living soul with
her but the dog.

One afternoon, as she was sitting inside the *seter*, she thought
her sweetheart came in and sat down beside her and started
talking about having the wedding right away. But she sat quite
still and did not answer a word, for she seemed to feel rather
strange. Little by little, people began to come in, and they started
setting the table with silver and food, and bridesmaids carried
in a crown and a beautiful wedding gown which they dressed
her in; and they placed the crown upon her head, as they usually
did in those days, and rings were put on her fingers.

She thought she knew all the people who had come. There
were women from the farms and girls her own age. But the dog
had certainly noticed that something was wrong. It ran away,
straight down to Melbustad, and there it whined and barked
and gave them no peace until they followed it back again.

Then the boy who was her sweetheart took his gun and went
up to the *seter*. When he came to the yard, it was full of saddled
horses standing around. He sneaked over to the cottage and
peeked through a crack in the door at those who were sitting
inside. It was easy to tell that they were trolls and *huldre*-folk,
and so he fired the gun over the roof. At the same moment the
door flew open, and one ball of grey wool after the other, each

one bigger than the last, came rolling out and wound itself around his legs. When he got inside, the girl was sitting there dressed like a bride. He had come in the nick of time. Only the ring for the little finger was lacking, and then she would have been ready.

"For Christ's sake! What's going on here?" he asked, looking about. All the silver was still on the table, but all the good food had turned into moss and toadstools, and cow dung and toads, and other things like that.

"What does all this mean?" he said. "Why are you sitting here dressed as a bride?"

"You should ask!" said the girl. "You've been sitting here talking to me about the wedding all afternoon."

"No, I came just now," he said. "It must have been someone who made himself look like me."

Then she began to come to herself again, but she was not really well for a long time afterward. She told him that she thought both he and the whole party had been there. He took her down to the village right away so that nothing more could happen to her, and they held the wedding at once while she was still wearing the wedding finery of the *huldre*-folk. The crown and all the finery were hung up at Melbustad, and they are supposed to be there to this very day.

## • 51b • The Interrupted Huldre Wedding at Norstuhov

*This story was collected by P. Chr. Asbjörnsen in Romerike (eastern Norway) some time between 1835 and 1837; it was printed in his* Norske Huldreeventyr og Folkesagn (1870), p. 38; *new ed.* (1949), p. 59.

• ELLI BAKKEN was up against the *huldre*-folk one summer before she was married. She was a dairymaid at Norstuhov, and was up at the *seter*. They usually had a loom along with them at the *seter* in those days, for this was over a hundred years ago.

One day, as Elli was sitting by the loom, her sweetheart came in and said that he wanted them to get married right away. She was to come with him now, he said. She stared at him and did not know what to think. Then she saw the dog standing there glaring at him and growling, and she began to have her doubts.

"I'm still my own mistress!" she said. But then there was a rumbling and a humming outside, and in came a whole crowd of people. And among them were two slightly older women, who stood out a little from the others, and it seemed to Elli that they looked at her so mournfully.

"That dog of yours certainly doesn't like people," said one of them, and gave her a queer look. "I think it's best you let it out," she said.

Then Elli understood what the old woman meant. She took the dog out in the woodshed, tied a red ribbon around its neck, and whispered, "Hurry home, Rapp!" And the dog set out.

She would rather have gone with it, but they came out and got her and started dressing her as a bride. One of the old women fastened a big filigree brooch on her breast and whispered, "Just keep calm, help will soon come." Then Elli remembered that two girls had disappeared before at this *seter*, and she understood that they must be the ones who were trying to help her, and so she let them dress her as they liked.

Down at Norstuhov, Anne, the farmer's wife, saw the dog come tearing along with the red ribbon fluttering behind it.

"Oh Lord, Reier!" she said to her husband. "Something's wrong up at the *seter*!" The dog came into the house like the wind, jumped up on the bed, put its paws on the gun which hung on the wall, and barked with all its might. Reier shouted to the boy to saddle the horse as fast as he could so they could ride to the *seter*, for something was wrong up there. He himself took the gun, and the boy took the ax, and they set out as fast as they could go.

Up at Notasen, Lars sat fixing the roof of his *stabbur*, when he saw the two of them come riding by for dear life. "What's up now?" he said.

"Heaven only knows," answered Reier, "but the dog came home and barked for the gun. You'd better come too!"

Well, well, thought Lars, I can't say no; and he took his gun and went with them. A little way up the ridge they tied their horses and went on foot, for it was so steep that they would get there faster without a horse. Soon they were at the *seter*. There stood a long row of saddled horses.

Inside the cottage Elli was already dressed as a bride, and the table was set with all kinds of food, the way it should be for a party. But Elli sat there turning hot and cold, and stared out through the window.

"Aren't we to be married soon?" said the one who was to be the bridegroom.

"No, you'll have to wait a bit," said one of the old women. Then a shot was fired over the roof.

"Cross in Jesus' name!" said Elli, and crossed her hands over her breast. The *huldre*-folk tore off the bridal finery as fast as they could, but they could not take the big silver brooch because her hands were crossed over it. Then they rushed out of the door like balls of grey wool, and Elli was saved.

The brooch is still supposed to exist, for Elli started to work for Madam Schoyen, and she bought it from Elli.

## • 52a • *The Drinking Horn Stolen from the* Huldre *Folk at* Vallerhaug

*Motif F352, "Theft of cup (drinking horn) from fairies"; R. Th. Christiansen,* The Migratory Legends, *6045, "Drinking Cup Stolen from the Fairies." This is one of the commonest Norwegian legends, collected in some 140 variants from all parts of Norway. North and west European traditions about thefts of drinking cups from fairies are treated by E. S. Hartland in* The Science of Fairy Tales, *pp. 148–58. Often a celebrated drinking horn in a village is said to have been stolen from the fairy folk.*

*This story is from Bishop Jens Nielsen's visitation reports from Telemark in the year 1595 while he was traveling in the vicinity of Aase Farm in Hjartdal. He recorded it in his* Visitatsbog, *p. 393.*

• "THERE WE went up to the farm and had a talk with the farmer's wife about a horn which was supposed to have come from a mound just north of the farm called Vallerhaug (Valler Mound). The woman said that after the dividing of the inheritance the same horn was now to be found at a farm called Östenaa in Kvitseid. Here is the story about this horn:

"In days gone by there was a farmer named Gunder Giesemand. On Christmas Eve he set out from Hjartdal on his way home to his farm. When he came to Vallerhaug, he shouted:

" 'Listen, *draug* in Vallerhaug, get up and give Gunder Giesemand a drink!'

"Then, from inside the mound, came the answer: 'Yes!' And to the boy: 'Tap and give him a drink, not of the best and not of the worst!'

"When Gunder heard this, he drove on with the horse. And then someone came out of the mound and threw the horn after him, and it struck the horse on the back between the reins. After that, both hair and hide fell off. The same horn fell on the road, and then Gunder fished it up with a kind of ax, the woman said, and took the horn with him to his farm. And since then, whenever they drank from this horn and struck it on the table, everyone in the room always came to blows.

"Afterwards we journeyed north from the above-mentioned Aase Farm, by way of Vallerhaug, which lies on the right. Big birch trees stand around this mound."

## · 52b · The Drinking Horn Stolen from the Huldre-Folk at Vellerhaug

*This story was collected by Moltke Moe in Böherad (Telemark) in 1878 and printed in* Norsk Folkeminnelag, IX (1925), 63. *Note the persistency of the tradition since 1595 (cf. 52a).*

· BETWEEN Böherad and Nesherad lies a mound which is called Vellerhaug (Veller Mound), and where *draugs* are supposed to live. A man from Gjernes, named Gunnar Gjernes, had heard this, and he wanted to find out if it was true.

So one night, as he rode past this mound, he stopped his horse and said, "Get up, *draug* in Vellerhaug, and give Gunnar Gjernes a drink!"

"Yes, now you'll get it!" came the answer from the mound.

But then Gunnar grew frightened and whipped up the horse with all his might. But the *draug* set out after him, and it was not until they came to Griviveien that the *draug* had to give up. Then he hurled the horn at Gunnar and hit the horse's back, and everything in the horn ran out and singed both hair and hide off the horse.

But at the same moment Gunnar turned and grabbed the horn —or else he picked it up on his way home, I don't remember which—but he got it. And as far as I know, the big golden horn is to be found at Gjernes to this very day.

## · 52c · The Drinking Horn Stolen from the Huldre-Folk at Hifjell

*This variant was collected by Karen Sollie in Rissa (Tröndelag) in 1935. It appeared in R. Th. Christiansen,* Norske Sagn, *p. 92.*

*Christiansen cites a reference to a similar variant of legend type 6045 reported in 1883.*

• THIS IS the legend about the way they got the chalice in Reins church. At the time the church was going to be built, an old troll was living in Hifjell mountain. A hatchet-faced man had promised to get a chalice for the altar. He knew that the troll in Hifjell had a big silver goblet, but the hatchet-faced man needed special skis to get up there, so he had to make some very swift skis. He worked on them for seven Christmas Eves in a row while the trees from which he cut them were standing on their roots. On the seventh Christmas Eve all that was left was to put on the bindings and saw them down.

When the skis were ready, he set out for Hifjell and knocked with his ski pole. The Hifjell troll came out. When he saw who it was, he told him to wait a bit. Then he fetched the big silver goblet, which had been filled to the brim, and offered the hatchet-faced man a drink.

But he was a sly one, this man, and instead of drinking, he emptied the goblet over his shoulder. And it was a good thing too, for the drink in the goblet was so strong that it ate through the skis, and the pieces flew off behind him. Then the hatchet-faced man set out on his skis down the mountain, with the goblet in his hand.

"Hey! Wait a minute until I can get on my rolling breeches!" shouted the Hifjell troll. "Then I'll catch up with you again!"

Now the hatchet-faced man understood that it was a matter of life or death, and he set out as fast as he could. The Hifjell troll did not take long to put on his rolling breeches, and came after him so the sparks flew!

As they went by Aalmo, a cock crowed, and the troll shouted:

> "The white cock doth crow!
> Soon the man I shall throw!"

But down at Modalen, the skis went very fast, and the troll was left far behind. Uphill to Aasen the going was slower, and the troll began to catch up with him again. But on the marshes beyond Aasen, the man was again in the lead.

As they rushed past Solli, a cock crowed again. Then the troll shouted:

> "There crowed the red!
> Soon he'll bleed 'til he's dead!"

On they went, past Berg and Vallin and on to Rissa, and then the troll started catching up with him again.

But then the hatchet-faced man shouted, "Look at that maiden who's coming behind you!"

At the same moment, another cock crowed, and the old troll of Hifjell mountain shouted:

> "There crowed the black!
> Now, my heart must crack!"

At the same moment the sun came up, and the troll burst asunder. The man hurried to Reins and delivered the goblet to the church, where they used it for a chalice.

## • 53a • The Christmas Visitors and The Tabby Cat

*R. Th. Christiansen,* The Migratory Legends, *6015, "The Christmas Visitors." This legend type is extensively known in Norway, with some two hundred variants collected. Only seven have been found in the north.*

*The story given here was collected by P. Chr. Asbjörnsen in Gudbrandsdal (eastern Norway) and printed in P. Chr. Asbjörnsen and Jörgen Moe,* Norske Folkeeventyr *(1852), p. 500. It contains Motif K1728, "The bear trainer and his bear" or Type 1161,* The Bear Trainer and His Bear *which is often, as in this variant, attached to legend type 6015. Christiansen analyzes the relationship between the bear trainer story and the legend about the Christmas visitors in* The Dead and the Living, *pp. 78–87. The theme of the bear trainer and his bear is often found in folk legends about Per Gynt; see* Norsk Folkedikting, III, *"Segner," 122–28, 219–23. Renaissance jestbooks contain the story about*

*the bear trainer whose bear drives the ogre away, and there is a*
*Middle High German poem from the thirteenth century on this*
*subject. Stith Thompson reports that the anecdote is highly*
*popular in northern Europe but nowhere else* (The Folktale,
*p. 205*).

• THERE WAS ONCE a man up in Finnmark who had caught a big
white bear. He set out with this bear to take it to the king of
Denmark. It so happened that he came to Dovre Mountain on
Christmas Eve. There he went into a cottage where a man named
Halvor lived. He asked if they could put him and his white bear
up for the night.

"Oh, Lord bless us!" said the man of the house. "We can't
put anyone up now, for every single Christmas Eve it's so full
of trolls here that we have to move out. We won't even have a
roof over our own heads!"

"Oh, you can put me up regardless of that," said the man.
"My bear can lie under the stove here, and I guess I can lie in
the closet."

Well, he asked so long that at last they let him stay. The people
moved out, and everything was made ready for the trolls. The
table was decked with cream porridge and lutefisk and sausage
and everything else that was good. It was a fine feast.

Soon the trolls came. Some were big and some were small,
some had long tails and some had none, and some had long, long
noses. They ate and drank and took a bite out of everything.

But then one of the troll children caught sight of the white
bear, which lay under the stove. He took a sausage and put it
on a fork and cooked it, and then he went over and thrust the
sizzling sausage on the bear's nose. "Want a sausage, Tabby?"
he shrieked. The white bear flew up with a ferocious growl, and
chased out every single troll, both big and small.

The year after this, Halvor was in the woods at noon on
Christmas Eve to fetch wood for the holidays, for he was expecting the trolls again.

As he was chopping, he heard shouting over in the woods:
"Halvor! Halvor!"

"Yes?" said Halvor.

"Do you still have that big cat of yours?"

"Yes, she's lying under the stove at home," said Halvor. "And now she's had seven kittens, and they're even bigger and meaner than she is herself!"

"Then we'll never come back to your place any more!" shouted the troll. And since then the trolls have never eaten Christmas porridge at Halvor's on Dovre Mountain.

## ·53b· The Christmas Visitors at Kvame

*This legend was collected by T. Mauland in Hjelmeland (western Norway) about 1880 and printed in* Norsk Folkeminnelag, *XVII (1928), 77–79.*

· On Kvame Farm, in Hjelmeland parish, there were *huldre*-folk in the old days. Every Christmas Eve they came in great crowds and put up at the house of a man who lived apart from the others on the farm. Each year, on Christmas Eve, the people at the farm had to move out, and the house had to be put in order and cleaned up by the time the *huldre*-folk came.

But one year they had a farmhand there who was a brave fellow. On Christmas Eve, when all the others were getting ready to move out, he would not go with them. He loaded a musket and stayed in the parlor. When it started growing dark, he climbed up onto the shelf above the oven and lay down. He had not been lying there long when there was such a racket and commotion that he had no doubt that the *huldre*-folk were coming.

First came an old man with a long beard, then came the whole crowd swarming around the old fellow whom they called Old Trond. They started dancing and carousing, and singing and shrieking, as if they were crazy. Old Trond sat down in the high seat, and the others wherever they found a place. It grew late, and they were tired. They sat down around the table. Before they began to eat they wanted a drink, and the horn was handed around. First they put the horn in front of the old fellow.

"Now I'm serving Old Trond," one of them said. The farmhand, who was sitting above them, heard this. So he took the musket and aimed.

"Now *I'm* serving Old Trond!" he cried, and then he fired. Old Trond slumped down in the high seat, and all the *huldre*-folk were so frightened that they started shrieking wildly. Then they jumped up from the table in a flash, and were out of the house like the wind. They were in such a hurry that they did not manage to take the silver goblets which they had put on the table. But they did take along the corpse.

They went up on Valafjell so fast that it took them only a few strides. They wailed and carried on because they had lost their master, and when they were up on the mountain, they shrieked, "A wretched Christmas at Kvame this year!" Then they took three huge boulders and hurled them down at the farm, but they did not come near the houses. The boulders landed on the edge of the fields, and there they lie to this very day. Then they took a golden key and opened a door in the mountain, and went inside.

At the same moment they said, "This door shall be closed and never opened again until Doomsday!" Then they threw the golden key into a rock-fall called *Torurd*. Since then there are many who have searched for the key in the rock-fall, but no one has ever found it.

From that time, the people at Kvame never had any trouble from the *huldre*-folk, and the farmhand got all the silver and gold which they had left behind. No one has ever seen anything of the *huldre*-folk on Valafjell, but the white door through which they went into the mountain can still be seen. It is called Door of the Giants or the *Huldre* Door.

*A Message from the* Huldre-*Folk*
*that Someone Died*

Motif F442.1, *"Mysterious voice announces death of Pan";*
R. Th. Christiansen, The Migratory Legends, 6070A, *"Fairies
send a Message." Collected by P. Chr. Asbjörnsen in Romerike
(eastern Norway) and printed by him in* Norske Huldreeventyr
og Folkesagn *(1870), p. 15; new ed., I (1949), 73.*

    This tale and the two following tales belong to a cycle of
legends about messages from the huldre-*folk. Some of these
stories have a more fully developed epic pattern than others.
Legend type 6070A has been collected in some seventy Norwegian variants and has been found in Finnish-Lappic and
Norwegian-Lappic traditions as well: see J. K. Qvigstad,* Lappische Märchen und Sagenvarianten, Sagen No. 50. *The various
forms of this legend type in Scandinavian, German, Dutch, Belgian, French, and British traditions have been studied by Inger
Boberg in* Sagnet om den Store Pans Død *(København, 1934).*

· A WEDDING WAS ONCE CELEBRATED at Eldstad, in Ullensaker, but
as they had no oven there, they had to send the roasts for the
wedding feast over to the neighboring farm to have them baked.
In the evening the boy from Eldstad was to drive home with
them. As he was driving over one of the moors, he heard someone shout quite clearly:

> "Hey there! If you're driving over to Eldstad,
> Then go tell Feliah
> That Fild fell in the fire!"

The boy laid on the whip and drove so fast that the wind
whistled about his nose. There was a nip in the air, and the
sleighing was fine, and the same message was shouted after him
several times so he remembered it well. He came safely home
with his load, and then he went down to the foot of the table,

where the servants went back and forth whenever they had time, and got something to eat.

"Well, boy, did you get a ride with the Devil himself, or haven't you gone after the roasts yet?" said one of the family.

"Yes, that I've done!" he said. "Here they come in through the door now. But I whipped up the mare and let her run as fast as she could, for when I came up on the moor, someone shouted:

> 'If you're driving over to Eldstad,
> Then go tell Feliah
> That Fild fell in the fire!' "

"Oh, that's my child!" cried one of the wedding guests, and rushed off as if she had lost her mind. She bumped into one guest after the other and shoved them out of the way. At last her hat fell off, and then they could tell that a *hulder* had been there, for she had filched beef and pork and butter and cake and ale and spirits and everything good to eat. But she was so flustered about her child that she forgot a silver ladle in the vat of ale, and she did not notice that her hat had fallen off. They took both the silver ladle and the hat and hid them at Eldstad. And the hat was such that the one who was wearing it could not be seen by any mortal soul—unless maybe he had second sight. But whether it is still there, I cannot say for sure, for I have not seen it, and I have not had it on either.

## ·55·  A Hulder *Calls the Dairymaids*

*R. Th. Christiansen*, The Migratory Legends, *6025, "Calling the Dairy Maid." Collected by S. Solheim from Kari Grimsrud in Valdres (eastern Norway) and printed by him in* Norsk Seter-tradisjon, *p. 450.*

*This tale has been collected in some thirty-five Norwegian variants. Similar stories where the taunt is directed toward a charcoal burner, a miller, a hunter, or a fisherman are common: see* The Migratory Legends, *pp. 163–64.*

• OUT IN BEGNADALEN, there were some girls from Hömern and Strömm who were up at the *seter* in the autumn. One Saturday evening they had visitors, and they had fun and carried on until far into the night. The next morning the dairymaids overslept.

All at once a *hulder* was standing outside on a hill they called Hulder Mound. She looked down at the *seter* and shouted:

> "Lazybones, get up now
> And milk your cows!
> Mine are grazing one and all,
> Yours are standing in the stall!
> The sun his midday watch is keeping,
> And still you lie there soundly sleeping!"

## • 56 • The Huldre-*Folk Tell the Date*

*Motif F346, "Fairy helps mortal with labor"; R. Th. Christiansen, The Migratory Legends, 6030, "Fairies give Information as to the Date." Collected in Valle, Setesdal (southern Norway), and printed in P. Blom, Beskrivelse over Valle Prestegeld i Saetersdalen med Dets Praestehistorie, p. 151; also in A. Faye, Norske Folke-Sagn, pp. 137–38.*

*Some sixty Norwegian variants of this tale have been collected. Texts fairly close to the Norwegian ones have been found in the Faroe Islands; see J. Jakobsen, Faeröske Folkesagn og Aeventyr, pp. 55–56, 556–57.*

• AFTER THE BLACK DEATH, Setesdal lay practically deserted, but gradually people started moving in from the outside and settling up and down the valley. But one old married couple, Tore and Knut, who lived up in Findalen, did not have the heart to leave their homestead. They stayed there quite alone for many years. The only thing they missed was not being able to tell what day of the year it was. Especially in the dark of winter did they grieve over not knowing when it was Christmas, so they could celebrate it at the same time as everyone else.

They had heard that people had started moving back to the
valley, and one year, when the days were at their shortest, they
decided that the wife, Tore, was to go over to Setesdal and find
out when it was Christmas. Tore set out and on the way she sat
down to rest under the wall of a mountain. Then she clearly
heard the sound of singing from inside the mountain:

> "Hurry, hurry Tore,
> Bake your Christmas bread!
> Nights but one, and days but two,
> That's when Christmas Eve is due!"

Tore was overjoyed when she found this out and hurried back
home to bake the bread and make everything ready so they could
celebrate Christmas at the same time as everyone else.

## · 57 ·    Outrunning a Hulder

*Motif F302.3.4, "Fairies entice men and then harm them";
R. Th. Christiansen, The Migratory Legends, 5095, "Fairy
Woman pursues a Man." Collected by schoolteacher Fosse in
Sogn (western Norway) about 1935 and printed in R. Th. Chris-
tiansen, Norske Sagn, p. 217.*

*This and the following legend belong to a group of stories
about the experiences of men with fairy women. Such stories are
usually individualistic, although certain traditional patterns are
discernible (The Migratory Legends, pp. 123–24).*

· A GROWN LAD from Systrand spent a winter snaring grouse up
at a *seter* in the parish. He had a dog with him. One evening, as
he was sitting by the hearth cooking his food, he heard something rattling outside against the wall. It sounded as if someone
were leaning something against the wall. The *seter* was made of
stone and had a turf roof. Shortly after, someone came in the
entryway and knocked at the door. The dog barked and its hair
stood on end, and then in came a beautiful maiden. The boy had
never seen so beautiful a maiden before. She was wearing a red

bodice and a blue skirt, and she had long, fair hair which hung down her back. The boy was quite amazed that a girl would come to the *seter* in the middle of the winter. It was seven miles to the town, and the snow was deep.

She started talking to him and asked if he did not think it was lonely to stay up at the *seter* in the middle of the winter. She laughed and talked, turning and twisting, and showing off to him. He answered back, laughing and joking, and thought this was really fine. At last he asked if she would stay there. Then it would not be so lonely any more. A strange expression came over her face, and she turned away from him, and then the boy saw that she had a long tail which hung below her skirt. Now he understood that she was a *hulder* and that she wanted to marry him. He had heard that *huldre*-folk liked to marry Christians. He became afraid of her and thought he had better watch his step here, for he was halfway engaged to a girl down in the parish. When she turned around, he did not join in the joking any longer. She went on talking and laughing as before and asked if he did not like girls. But he did not say much to that.

After a while, he found some pretext for going outside, and the dog went with him. The moon was full and was shining brightly. Then he caught sight of the *hulder*'s skis, which she had leaned up against the wall of the *seter*. They were made of brass and gleamed and shone in the moonlight. He put them on, took her poles, and set out down the mountain toward the parish. The skis slid over the snow unusually fast, and he went at such a speed that the dog could not keep up with him.

When the boy did not come back in again, the *hulder* grew suspicious and went outside to look. She soon caught sight of him heading down the mountain at a good clip. When she looked for her skis, she found that he had taken them. Then she became furious because he had wanted to run away from her. She put on his skis and took his poles and set out after him. But they were only poor fir skis with willow bindings, so they went much slower than her own. She did not catch up with the boy, but she did catch up with the dog and broke its back with the ski pole. But the boy got home, and the brass skis are still supposed to be at Henja Farm to this very day.

# · 58 · *The Man Who Became* Huldrin

*Motif F362.2, "Fairies cause insanity." Collected by P. Chr. Asbjörnsen in Sörum, Romerike (eastern Norway), in 1836 or 1837 and printed in* Norske Huldreeventyr og Folkesagn *(1870), p. 31; new ed. (1949), p. 57. Asbjörnsen places this story in the mouth of a woman called Berte Tuppenhaug, although she was actually not his informant.*

· MY MOTHER'S BROTHER, Mads, lived at Knae in Hurdalen. He was often up in the mountains chopping wood and felling timber, and whenever he was up there working it was his habit to sleep out in the open too. He would build a shelter of pine branches, make up a fire in front of it, and lie there and sleep during the night.

Once he was out in the forest with two other woodcutters. Just as he finished chopping down a huge tree trunk and sat down to rest, a ball of yarn came rolling down a flat ledge and stopped right at his feet. He thought this was strange. He did not dare pick it up, and it would have been better for him if he had never done so either. But nonetheless he looked up, for he wanted to see where it had come from. Well, up on the hill sat a maiden sewing, and she was so beautiful and fair that she shone.

"Bring that ball of yarn here," she said. Well, this he did, and he remained standing there gazing at her for a long time. She was so lovely that he could not take his eyes off her. At last he had to pick up his ax and start to work again. After he had been chopping for a while, he looked up again, but she was gone. He wondered about this the whole day. It was so strange that he did not know what to make of it. In the evening, when he and his companions were going to turn in, he insisted on sleeping in the middle. But it did not help much, I dare say, for later on in the night she came to fetch him, and he had to go with her whether he wanted to or not. She took him inside the mountain.

Everything there was so fine that he had never seen such riches before, and he was never able to say just how fine it really was.

He stayed in there with her for three days. Later on during the third night he woke up and found himself lying between his companions again. They thought he had gone home after more supplies, but he told them what had happened. After that he was never quite the same. Suddenly, as he was sitting, he would make a couple of hops and rush away. He was *huldrin* (bewitched), I'll have you know!

But a long time after this, he was busy up in the woods splitting logs for a fence. As he stood there, and had driven a wedge into a log so there was a crack all the way down the center, he thought he saw his wife come with his dinner. It was cream porridge, the very rich kind, and the pail she had it in was so bright that it shone like silver. She sat down on the log. He put down the ax and sat down on a stump beside her. At the same moment he saw that she had a cow's tail, and it had slipped down into the crack. Well, he did not touch the food now, you might know, but sat there working the wedge back and forth until he got it out. The log snapped shut on her tail, and he wrote "Jesus" on the pail. But I dare say she had feet now; she jumped up so quickly that the tail snapped off and remained in the log. She was gone so fast that he did not even see what had become of her. The pail and the food were nothing more than a basket of bark with dung in it. After this he hardly dared go out in the forest for fear she would get even with him.

But four or five years after this he lost his horse and had to go out himself to look for it. As he was walking in the forest, he suddenly found himself inside a hut with some people in it, without realizing how he got there. An ugly old hag was busy going about her duties, and over in a corner sat a child who was at least four years old. The hag took the tankard and went over to the child.

"Go over," she said, "and offer your father a drink of beer!"

Mads was so terrified that he took to his heels, and after that he never saw anything of her or the child. But queer and half-witted he was ever after!

## · 59 ·  Outwitting the Huldre Suitor with Magic Herbs

*Motif G303.12.5.6, "Girl wooed by devil is saved by magic herbs she wears"; R. Th. Christiansen, The Migratory Legends, 6000, "Tricking the Fairy Suitor." Collected by P. Chr. Asbjörnsen in 1835 in Christiania and printed in O. A. Överland,* Hvorledes P. Chr. Asbjörnsen begyndte som sagn-fortaeller, *pp. 22–23.*

*More than half of the thirty-five Norwegian variants of this legend come from eastern districts. Stories about women outwitting demon lovers with magical herbs have been known in England from the twelfth century on; see G. L. Kittredge,* Witchcraft in Old and New England, *pp. 119–21.*

• ON A FARM in Asker parish, not far from Christiania, there once worked a girl who was exceptionally beautiful. It was her misfortune that a boy of *huldre* stock fell in love with her and wanted to marry her. He never gave her a moment's peace. If she was alone in the evening or during the night, he always came to her and pestered her with his courting and said that if she would marry him she would be well off and have wealth and luxury all her days. The girl grew so tired of this that she asked everyone if they knew of any way to get rid of her suitor. There was no one who did, but at last she met a wise old woman who knew more than the others. She told the girl to ask the boy if he knew of a cure for a heifer that was always ailing.

When he came the next time, she asked him, and he replied, "You're to put three kinds of plants on her: daphne, honeysuckle, and orchid. Then the heifer will soon be well again."

She got hold of the three kinds of plants, but, as the old woman had advised her, she carried them on herself, and when the *huldre* boy came the next time he noticed it right away. Then he said, "Drat you! If I'd known you were going to use them on yourself like that, I never would have given you such advice!"

After that she was never bothered by this suitor again. She married a cotter. They had lots of children, so it was hard for them to make ends meet.

Late one evening in autumn she was out working in the field. Then the *huldre* boy came over to her and said, "You could have chosen me, you could! Then you wouldn't have had to toil and struggle the way you're doing now!"

## · 60 ·  Outwitting the Huldre Suitor with Gun Fire

*Collected by R. Th. Christiansen in Land (eastern Norway) in 1920 and printed in* Boka om Land, *II, 283.*

*Many stories about ridding oneself of fairy lovers and fairy suitors are told as personal experiences and have no particular epic pattern.*

· OLD NILS had bought Garde farm, at Vest-Torpa, and his sister Marit kept house for him. While she was there, a *huldre* boy started courting her. Only Marit could see him, no one else, and she liked the boy too.

Now one day she was supposed to go home with him to see how he lived. His farm was not far away—right over by the bed —and it had big, red-painted houses, and everything was fine and well cared for, both inside and out.

Nils knew that Marit was up to some kind of *huldre* business, for all at once, as she was going about her duties in the house, she was gone—even if she had been standing right in front of his eyes. He could search for her as much as he liked, but it did not help. She was gone. Then he thought of taking the gun and firing it right up in the air. When he did this, Marit was standing there as she had been before. He knew then that the suitor had been there, but Marit thought it strange that he had not seen either her or the boy.

Nils did not like it one bit, and he kept up with this shooting every time Marit disappeared. At last he sold the farm and bought another one in a neighboring parish and moved there. Marit went with him, but the *huldre* boy did not follow her. Later she married a man from this parish, had lots of children, and all went well with her.

# Part VII
# Legends about
# Household Spirits

## · *61* · Nisse *Fighting*

*Motif F482.7, "House spirits fight each other"; R. Th. Chris-*
*tiansen, The Migratory Legends, 7000, "Fighting Nisse in the*
*Service of a Farmer." Collected by S. Nergaard in Elverom*
*(eastern Norway) between 1910 and 1920 and printed in* Norsk
Folkeminnelag, *XI (1925), 40–42.*

*More than seventy-five Norwegian variants of this legend have*
*been collected, none from the north. This tale is very common in*
*Danish tradition; Laurits Bødker in his* Danske Folkesagn,
*p. 179, cites a variant together with other stories about fights*
*between* nisser.

· THERE WAS A NISSE (household spirit) on every single farm in
the old days. Now an occasional horse can be seen with a *nisse*
plait in his mane, but the *nisse* himself is gone.

On a farm in Elverom there was a black horse that received
extra care from the *nisse*. He was both fatter and sleeker than
the other horses on the farm, and the farmer became angry at
the stable boy because he took better care of this horse than the
others.

"Oh, that's not me at all," said the boy, "it's the *nisse*!"

One evening, after the boy had fed the horses for the night, the
farmer went down in the stall and saw that the black horse had
been given better and more hay than the others. He took some
away and threw it over in a corner, but at the same moment he
received such a blow on the back of his neck that he staggered
across the floor. After that the horse was allowed to have his hay
in peace, for there was no one who dared take it away from him.

Once people heard quite a commotion over in the woods between Öygard and Nerstuhov farms, and when they went over
there they saw two *nisser* fighting. They were the *nisser* from the
two farms. Öygard was a good farm for wheat, while at Nerstuhov the hay was better. So each of the *nisser* had been drawing

from the other farm. The Öygard *nisse* was drawing hay from
Nerstuhov, while the Nerstuhov *nisse* was drawing wheat from
Öygard. Then they had met in the woods, and had come to
blows so hard that hay and wheat flew high in the air. In the
end the Öygard *nisse* lost, and from that time on misfortune
followed the farm.

## • 62 •  *The New Breeches*

*Motif F451.5.10.9, "Ausgelohnt"; R. Th. Christiansen, The
Migratory Legends, 7015, "The New Suit." Collected by Kr.
Bugge in Tjölling (eastern Norway) about 1905. Printed in
Norsk Folkeminnelag, XXXI (1934), 74–75.*

*Twelve Norwegian variants of this legend have been collected,
all from the east. Bolte-Polívka, I, 364–66, in discussing the
Heinzel Männchen in the Grimms' tales give references in north
and east European tradition to stories about the disappearance or
ingratitude of household spirits after they have been given new
clothes.*

• ON A FARM—it was somewhere in Jarlsberg, as far as I know—
they had a *nisse* who was kind and helpful. But he could get
angry too, and then he was not easy to get along with. When
he was angry he would do things like putting new-born calves
down in the bucket and pouring out the milk for the dairymaid
and many other tricks. So both the farmer and the dairymaid
thought it best to satisfy the *nisse* in everything within reason,
and they certainly did not regret it either. The dairymaid took
care to put out really fine cream porridge in the barn every
holiday, and on Christmas Eve she put an extra big lump of
butter in it so the porridge would be rich and good.

It was easy to see that the *nisse* appreciated all the good things
he got, for nowhere did the cows thrive so well as on that farm.
Not to mention the horses! For the *nisse* had bestowed most
of his love on them. When the farmer came home, he did not
even have to put the horses in. He just unharnessed them and

the *nisse* took care of the rest, put them in the stable, rubbed them down with a handful of straw, took down hay to them, and gave them water. The farmer knew this, and so he let the *nisse* take care of the horses the way he liked. And, as he was so well satisfied with the *nisse* in every way, he put a fine pair of white leather breeches out for him one day.

One day the man and the boy were out driving. When they got back it was raining as though the heavens had opened, so they left the horses standing outside and hurried in the house. They thought the *nisse* would put them in the way he usually did. But the one who didn't come, that was the *nisse*. They had gone over to the window to see how the horses were getting along, and there stood the *nisse,* quite content, in the door of the stable, with his hands deep in the pockets of his new leather breeches.

The farmer was annoyed, as you can imagine, and so he went to the door and shouted, "My good *nisse,* what does this mean? Don't you see the horses today?"

The *nisse* slapped his thighs with both hands and laughed so hard he almost fell over. Then he straightened up, stuck out one leg, thrust his hands down in his pockets again, and said, "Well, you certainly don't expect me to go out in this weather with my new white leather breeches on, do you?"

## •63• *The Heavy Load*

*Motif F451.9.1.7, "Dwarfs emigrate because mortals tease them"; R. Th. Christiansen,* The Migratory Legends, *7005, "The Heavy Burden." Collected by Kjell Flatin in Flatdal (Telemark) before 1916 and printed in* Norsk Folkeminnelag, *XXI (1930), 43.*

*Nearly thirty Norwegian variants of this tale have been collected, mostly from eastern Norway and Telemark. Further references concerning the spread of this story in north European tradition are given in H. F. Feilberg,* Nissens Historie, *p. 50.*

• BAD LAVRANS lived in the latter half of the eighteenth century at Meaas in Seljord. One day Lavrans was down in Meaasdalen, when he caught sight of a little *tusse* boy who crawled up toward the barn with a single ear of barley on his shoulder, panting and struggling as if he were carrying an exceedingly big load.

"Why are you puffing and panting like that?" shouted Lavrans. "You haven't got such a heavy load!"

"If I take just as much *from* you as I've given *to* you, you'll find out that the load is heavy enough!" replied the *tusse,* and then he turned with the load and went over to the neighboring farm, Bakken.

Lavrans stood looking after him, and only then could he see that the *tusse* was carrying an unbelievably big load of barley. Up to now, the *tusse* had taken both feed and food from Bakken, so they were poor and needy at that farm. But now he started taking it from Meaas back to Bakken again, so there was great prosperity there. But at Meaas nothing succeeded after that day. Lavrans himself came to an untimely end, and his family suffered great misfortune.

## •64• *The* Nisse's *Revenge*

*Motif F481.1, "Cobold avenges uncivil answer (or treatment)";*
*R. Th. Christiansen, The Migratory Legends, 7010, "Revenge*
*for being teased." Collected by P. Chr. Asbjörnsen in Christiania*
*in 1845 and printed in his Norske Huldreeventyr og Folke-*
*sagn (1870), p. 77; new ed. (1949), I, 15. Asbjörnsen localized*
*the story in Hallingdal in southeastern Norway, although he*
*actually collected it in Christiania.*

*Most of the forty Norwegian variants of this tale are from the*
*southeast. H. F. Feilberg treats the spread of this story in northern*
*Europe in his Nissens Historie, p. 61.*

• AT A FARM in Hallingdal, I think it was, there was a girl who was going to take cream porridge out to the *nisse.* Now whether

it was on a Thursday evening or a Christmas Eve, I can't remember, but I think it was a Christmas Eve. Now she thought
it was a pity to give the *nisse* all that good food, so she ate the
cream porridge herself, drank the drippings into the bargain,
and went out to the barn with oatmeal porridge and sour milk
in a pig trough.

"Here's your trough, you nasty old thing!" she said. But
scarcely had she uttered these words before the *nisse* rushed out
and grabbed her and started to dance with her. He kept it up
until she lay on the ground gasping for breath, and when the
people came out to the barn in the morning, she was more dead
than alive.

All the while he danced, he sang:

> "Oh, the *nisse*'s porridge you did steal!
> So dance with the *nisse* until you reel!"

## · 65 · *The* Tunkall

*Collected by T. Mauland in Hjelmeland (western Norway) about
1880 and printed in* Norsk Folkeminnelag, XVII *(1928), 138–
139.*

*Traditions about and beliefs in the huge and strong* tunkall
*as the guardian spirit of the house belong to the northern and
western parts of Norway, whereas the belief in the* nisse *is confined to the south and east. See Introduction, p. xl.*

· On Steintland farm, in Hjelmeland, there was a *tunkall* in
the old days. Many people lived on the farm, but all the houses
stood close together as was the custom on the big farms at that
time. A little apart from the houses stood a sheepcote, and there
the *tunkall* usually stayed. Whenever people went by this sheepcote in the evening, they could hear him grunting like a pig.
There was an old shack on the farm, and in it was a bed that
always stood ready for the *tunkall*. Otherwise no one else lived
in this shack. There was no bedding in the bed, only some straw

sweepings, and if there was not anything to lie on, they could hear the *tunkall* wailing and carrying on something awful. In the evening at ten o'clock they heard him go in, and they heard him get up and fix the bed in the morning. It always looked as if a dog had been lying there.

Once there were two girls who did not believe what was said about this *tunkall,* and so they were not afraid to go in and lie down in another bed that stood in the same shack. They lay there a long time before they heard anything, but all at once they heard someone come in through the door. It opened and closed the way it does when a human being goes through a door. Then everything was quiet, and they heard no more until the next morning at four A.M. Then they heard the straw rustling, and it sounded as if a dog had sprung out on the floor. The door opened and closed, as it had done the night before, but they saw nothing.

An old woman on the farm said that she could both hear and see the *tunkall.* Yes, she often talked with him, for they were really good friends. When this old woman became sick, they heard the *tunkall* crying and wailing, and when she died, the *tunkall* disappeared, and no one has ever seen him since.

On Tengisdal farm, in Hylsfjord, there was also a *tunkall* who stayed in a shack like that. Whenever strangers came to the farm and were to sleep there, they were usually thrown out onto the floor as soon as they had gone to bed. The farmer was called Njadl. He was an unusually strong fellow, and wanted to be the master of his own house, so once he decided to go to bed in this shack. As soon as he lay down, the *tunkall* took hold of him and wanted to throw him out. But Njadl put up a fight. He took his knife and slashed and carved in the air about him, and he stabbed at the walls with all his might. Then the *tunkall* became frightened and ran out in the pigpen to hide. Njadl went after him. He did not want the *tunkall* there either, and he did not stop until he had chased the *tunkall* away from the farm. When he was some distance away, the *tunkall* looked back and cried. For a while after that they could hear him sobbing and wailing all over the farm.

At another farm they told about a boy who was on his way to a farm after dark when a troll came after him. The boy was brave, he was, and thought he could manage the troll when he went back. On the way back the *gardvord* went with him, and so the troll did not dare come near him. But if he had not done that, it is not so easy to tell how it would have turned out.

## • 66 • *The* Gardvord *Beats Up the* Troll

*Collected by Ivar Aasen in Sogndal, Sogn (western Norway), in 1842 and printed in* Norsk Folkeminnelag, *I (1923), 71.*

*The* gardvord *is another name for the* tunkall *mentioned in tale No. 65 above.*

• A HUNTER—his name, now, was Tore Nabben—was up in the mountains hunting. Night fell, and he went to sleep in a bunk in a *seter*. In the middle of the night he heard shouting from a hill: "Will you lend me that big cauldron? I want to cook ol' Tore Nabben!" Then came the reply: "Yes, if I can taste the broth!" " 'Fore the broth you can try, on the coals he will fry!"

Tore became frightened and hurried off as fast as he could. When he had come a bit on the way he met a *gardvord* with a pole on its back. Tore hurried even faster, and when he had come a bit farther on the way, he heard a terrible shrieking behind him. He dared not look back, but ran and ran until he came home. The next day he took his brother along and went back to the same place where he had been during the night. There they saw blood and all the other grisly things where the *gardvord* had beaten the troll to death.

*Part VIII*
*Fictional Folktales*

# · 67 ·  *The Finn King's Daughter*

*Type 870, The Princess Confined in the Mound; R. Th.*
*Christiansen,* Norske Eventyr, *870, "Kongedatteren i haugen.*
*Finnkongens Datter," No. 13. Collected by Rikard Berge in*
*Kvitseid (Telemark) about 1900 and printed in Sophus Bugge*
*and Rikard Berge,* Norske Eventyr og Sogn, *I, 51.*

*Waldemar Liungman has studied this tale primarily in its*
*Scandinavian versions. He holds that the folktale is based upon*
*a legend and that the oldest form of the narrative in Scandinavia*
*is from Jutland. See Waldemar Liungman,* Prinsessan i Jordkulan. *The wedding party's riding to church, rather than going*
*by carriage, has been a common custom in Scandinavia up until*
*recent times; nineteenth-century folk paintings from Dalecarlia*
*in central Sweden depict such scenes.*

· IN THE OLDEN DAYS there lived a king called the Finn King.
He had a daughter, and he was so fond of her that he always
had to keep her in sight. "Something could so easily happen to
her," he thought. Now it so happened that he had to go to the
wars. To take her along was impossible, but to leave her behind
again was not safe either. Most of all he was afraid of the new
serving boy. It seemed to the king that he had noticed something
going on between those two. He pondered greatly over what
he was going to do with his daughter, and at last it came to
him that he should make a house for her inside a mound over
in the woods. When this house was ready, with food and drink,
clothing and cups and vessels, he accompanied her into the
mound, and nine handmaidens were with her to take care of
her. She cried and wailed and begged to be set free, but it was
like asking a stone. And the boy—poor thing—was no better
off, for the mound was leveled to the ground and sown over,
and it was not long before grass was growing on it. Then the
king set out with all of his men.

"Console and help us, we who must spend all our days here

inside this mound," said the princess, and the handmaidens echoed her words. Soon they made up their minds to dig themselves out, come what may. They had nothing to dig with but their bare hands. After they had been digging for a year, one of the maidens died. But those who were left went on digging and digging, while each year a maiden died. When the ninth year had passed, all the handmaidens were dead. Lonely as she was, the king's daughter did not give up. She dug and cried, and cried and dug, until the blood ran and the nails loosened from each and every finger. Finally at long last she caught sight of a glimmer of daylight. Oh, how happy she was! And she dug and dug, and at last she was standing under open sky. But she did not know where she was. A forest had grown up over the mound, and everything was different from what it had been before. So she wandered off, trying to find some people. She wandered aimlessly, with her little bundle on her back, but she did not know where she was going.

During all these years her father had been away at war. While he was far away, in a foreign land and kingdom, he found out that his serving boy was a king's son, and a really fine one too. The old king longed for home. As soon as the war was over, he would go home and fetch his daughter, and then these two, who really loved each other, would be married. But then he became sick and had to send his men home without him, and scarcely were they well on their way before the king died.

But in the Finn Mound no king's daughter did they find. They searched hill and moor, from mountain to shore, but for all they searched they found no one. Finally one day a woman came to the court. She was actually a troll hag, a slovenly, clumsy creature. But she lied and said she was the king's daughter, and she got everyone to believe her, everyone, that is, but the king's son. He never could accept her, but there was to be a wedding all the same.

The Finn King's daughter came upon some charcoal burners. These were the first people she met. They let her spend the night with them in their shack, and it seemed like Christmas itself to her after what she had been through. The second day she came to a wide river, but she could see no way of getting across.

As she was standing there, a big wolf came up to her and made signs that she was to sit upon its back. This she did, and she shivered and shook where she sat. But the wolf padded on and paid no heed. For ever so long she roamed about the forest, poor thing, and froze and starved so that she was close to dying. At last she came to a king's manor, and then she recognized where she was: house and garden, streams and mountains. She was home again. But no one there recognized her—there were only new people here—but she knew her sweetheart again, of course. She was given a serving job. "We can always use an extra wench here these days," said the one who was to be the bride. But from the servants she found out everything that had happened during these years, both to herself and to her father.

Now one day the king's son was going away. He spoke to the troll hag: "If you're really the Finn King's daughter, you'll finish sewing this seam by the time I come back." "Yes, that I shall," said the troll hag. Scarcely was he gone before she sat down to sew and rip it out again, but to get it finished was quite impossible.

The new serving girl went about there, washing and straightening up, and all at once she stole a glance at the troll hag and her seam. "That pattern there isn't so hard to match," said the girl. "Yes, of course you can do it!" said the troll hag. She was so angry she sputtered. "I've hemmed it before," said the girl. "Well, that would be a sight to see!" The girl sewed, and it became so fine that it was an out-and-out wonder to behold, but she took care not to resew the bit which the troll hag had sewn. Later on in the evening, when the king's son came home, the first thing he wanted to see was the seam. He looked at it with complete astonishment. "How is it that this bit is such a mess?" he said when he saw the part that had been spoiled. "Oh, I didn't get the hang of it right away," she said.

The second day the king's son was going out again. "If you're really the Finn King's daughter, you'll finish weaving this cloth today," he said. Yes indeed, she'd certainly do that, she said, but she could neither thread nor tread, and she broke off the staves, shoved out the thread, and got almost everything on the loom out of order. The serving girl went about there looking on. "Is it so hard to weave on that loom, then?" she said. "Of course you can weave on it!" said the troll hag. "Oh, I've woven on it before. I'll do it for you," said the girl. So she had to let the girl weave it for her. She wove, and the weaving went like greased lightning. And such a cloth had never been seen before. There were roses and lilies, and little birds and four-legged animals, and there were the king's son and she herself as real as life. In the evening, the king's son came, and the troll hag met him with the cloth. Then it was just as before: "I didn't get the hang of it right away," she said, when the king's son wondered why it was so ugly in one place.

"Well, tomorrow we shall be wed, and if you're the Finn King's daughter you'll ride the horse you rode in the old days," he said. The troll hag wanted to try the horse first, but that did not work. The horse became both wild and stubborn and bit and kicked so there was quite a commotion. The serving girl stood watching. "Oh, this horse is easy to bridle," she said. "Yes, you'll bridle it well, I dare say!" said the troll hag. "I've managed Grey Borken before, I have," she said. "Oh, my dear girl, will you dress yourself as a bride and ride the horse in my place?" said the troll hag. "But don't say a word to my lord. Promise me that! One good turn deserves another!" "Well, I suppose I'll have to do it, that," said the girl, and made herself ready. When she was ready to go, the girl took the bridle:

> "Upon your knees, Grey Borken, glide,
>    The Finn King's daughter to church will ride!"

And at once the horse kneeled down so she could mount.

"Take heed and mark ye well!" said the king's son.

When they had ridden a bit, they came to the Finn mound. Then the bride stopped and stared:

> "None knew the tears my cheek had crossed,
>    My maidens in the mound I lost.
> None saw me wipe my tears away,
>    My maidens all behind me lay."

And she was on the verge of tears.

"Take heed and mark ye well!" said the king's son.

After a while the procession was at the charcoal burners' place, and then she said:

"Much have I seen, much have I learned,
There at the kiln the coal I burned."

"Take heed and mark ye well!" said the king's son.

Then they came to the river:

"Much have I suffered, much have I cried,
On the back of a wolf I here did ride."

"Take heed and mark ye well!" said the king's son as before.

In the church the king's son pulled off his gloves and gave them to the bride. "Now you must hide them well, and not give them away until I ask you for them," he said, and this she promised. But the whole time, and most of the way home, the bridegroom was as happy as if he had won a kingdom. As soon as the girl got home, she changed out of the bridal garments and became the serving girl as before. All was now merriment and mirth, but the bridegroom went about downcast and silent, and would not have anything to do with the bride.

As it was getting on toward bedtime, the bridegroom wanted to go to bed. "Come whenever you want to," he said to the bride. When he was well under the covers, the bride came. "Nay, wait a bit!" said the bridegroom. "What did you say when you were going to mount the horse today?" "Did I say anything then?" "Yes, you did, and now you'll say it on the spot! You're not coming in the bed before you do!" he said. "I have to go out again. There was something I forgot to tell my serving girl," she said. "You've made it difficult for me, you've been talking to my lord," said the troll hag to the girl. "What did you say when you climbed up on the horse?"

"I only said:

'Upon your knees, Grey Borken, glide,
The Finn King's daughter to church will ride!'"

The troll hag repeated it just as the girl had said. "Now it came to me!" she said. "Well, what kind of a Finn King's daughter do you think you are?" mumbled the king's son to himself. Now the bride thought she should be welcome in the bed.

"Nay, wait a bit!" said the bridegroom. "What did you say when you came to the Finn mound?" "Did I say anything then too?" "You must say it quickly, as much as you remember!" She went out again as before. "What did you say when you came to the Finn mound? Tell me at once!" said the troll hag, when she came out to the girl.

> "None knew the tears my cheek had crossed,
> My maidens in the mound I lost.
> None saw me wipe the tears away,
> My maidens all behind me lay."

The troll hag repeated it again, just the way the girl had said it. "Well, what kind of maidens have you lost, and what kind of tears did you wipe away?" thought the king's son. Well, now she wanted to go to bed.

"Wait a bit, mother! What did you say when you came to the charcoal burners' place?" "I think you're out of your mind!" she said, and sat down on the bed. But he shoved her away, and she had to go out again. Soon she came back in and repeated:

> "Much have I seen, much have I learned,
> There at the kiln the coal I burned."

"What did you say when you came to the river?" said the bridegroom. He wanted to find that out too. Now she did not even protest. "There's still something I've forgotten to say to my serving girl," she said, and out she went. Then she came in again, safe and sure of herself:

> "Much have I suffered, much have I cried,
> On the back of a wolf I here did ride."

Now, she thought, at any rate she would not have to beg for company for the night, and started taking off her clothes.

"First give back what you got from me today!" he said. She was tired of flying back and forth like this, but out to the serving girl she had to go. "Hand over the gloves you got from my lord today!" And she was so angry and wild with rage that she sputtered. "No, I want to give them to him myself," said the girl. At first it looked as though the troll hag was going to fly at her, but then she made herself sweet again and started begging and pleading. But the girl put her foot down: "Glove and hand belong to me!" Then the troll hag said, "If I can't have the gloves, then you must come in with me and give them to him yourself." She begged prettily, and this the girl did.

"Where are my gloves?" said the bridegroom. He saw them both coming. They went over to his bed. The troll hag tried to squeeze herself in front of the girl, but that trick did not work. When the girl slipped the gloves to him, he was so quick that he took her hands. "I'd rather have the hand than the gloves, I would!" he said, and drew the serving girl onto his lap. Then that troll beast looked ridiculous, I dare say. She had to confess all the wicked things she had done, and was flogged and bound. The next day they put her in a spiked barrel and threw her in the river. But there was soon real rejoicing, for now the Finn King's daughter had been found again.

## • 68 • The Three Princesses in Whittenland

*Type 400, The Man on a Quest for his Lost Wife; R. Th. Christiansen, Norske Eventyr, 400, "De tre prinsesser i Hvidtenland. Östenfor sol og vestenfor maane. Manden some hadde en svart flekk i aakren sin. Jomfru Solea," No. 5. Collected by Jörgen Moe in Ringerike (eastern Norway) in the 1830's and printed in P. Chr. Asbjörnsen and Jörgen Moe, Norske Folkeeventyr, 2nd. ed. (1852), No. 9.*

*This tale is known in most parts of the world. Sixty-five Norwegian versions, some containing the swan maiden motif, have been collected. Lappic variants have their roots in Norwegian oral tradition, according to Christiansen; see his "Noen anmerkninger til samiske Eventyr og Sagn," Svenska Landsmal* och svenskt Folkliv (*1953–54*), *pp. 63–67. Tale No. 23, "The Woman Who Came Down from Heaven," in Keigo Seki's* Folktales of Japan (*a companion volume in this series*), *pp. 63–69, contains the episodes of Type 400 in which the man goes in quest of his wife and performs supernatural tasks.*

• THERE WAS ONCE a fisherman who lived close by a castle and fished for the king's table. One day, while he was out fishing, he did not catch anything; no matter how he went about it, baiting and fishing, fishing and baiting, not a bone hung on the hook. But, as it was getting on in the day, a head popped up out of the water and said, "If I get what your wife is carrying under her belt, you shall get fish enough!" The man agreed at once, for he did not know that she was with child. After that he certainly did get fish during the day, and as much as he wanted too. But when he came home in the evening, and told how he had got all the fish, his wife started to cry and carry on and pray to God to help her out of the promise the man had made, for she was carrying a child under her belt. They soon heard up at the castle that the wife was so sorrowful, and when the king found out about it, he promised to take the child and try to save it. The days went by, and when the time had come, the wife gave birth to a boy. The king took him and reared him as his own son until the boy was grown.

One day the boy asked to be allowed to go out fishing with his father, the king; he would so dearly like to go. The king was not any too willing to permit it, but at last the boy was allowed to go. He set out with his father, and all went well the whole day, until they returned to land in the evening. Then the son forgot his handkerchief. He wanted to run down to the boat to get it, but the very moment he got in it, the boat started moving so that the water foamed, and for all the boy pulled back on the oars, it did not help. It sailed and it sailed the whole night, and at last he came far, far away to a white shore. There he landed, and after he had walked a bit, he met an old man with a long, white beard.

"What's the name of this place?" said the boy.

"Whittenland," answered the man. And then he asked the

boy to tell him where he was from and what he wanted, and this the boy did.

"Well," said the man, "if you go on along the shore here, you'll come to three king's daughters standing in the ground with only their heads sticking out. Then the eldest will shout and beg you so prettily to come and help her, and the second one will do that too; but you're not to go over to either of them. Just hurry on by them as if you had neither seen nor heard them. But the third one you shall go over to, and do whatever she asks you to. That'll be your fortune, it will!"

When the boy came to the first princess, she shouted to him and begged and implored him so prettily to come to her, but he walked on as if he'd never seen her; and he went by the second princess in just the same way; but the third princess he went over to.

"If you will do as I tell you, you shall have which ever of us three you want," said the princess.

Yes, he would do it gladly, and then she told him that three trolls had put them down in the ground there, but before that they had lived in the castle he could see over in the forest. "Now you're to go into that castle and let the trolls beat you, one night for each of us," she said. "If you can stand that, then you'll save us."

Yes, answered the boy, he would try it all right.

"When you go in," said the princess, "two lions will be standing in the gate, but if you just go right between them, they won't do anything to you. Then go straight ahead, into a dark little room. There you're to lie down. Then the troll will come and beat you, but you're to take the bottle which is hanging on the wall and rub yourself where he has beaten you; then you'll be just as good as new again. Then grab the sword hanging beside the bottle and hack the troll to bits."

Well, he did just as the princess said; he went right between the lions as if he did not see them and straight into the little chamber where he lay down.

The first night, a troll with three heads and three birch rods came and beat the boy sinfully, but he held out until the troll had finished. Then he took the bottle and smeared himself.

Then he grabbed the sword and hacked the troll to death. When he came out in the morning, the princesses were standing above the ground to their waists. The second night went just like the first, but the troll that came then had six heads and six birch rods, and it beat him even worse than the first! When he came out in the morning, the princesses were standing above the ground to their calves. The third night a troll with nine heads and nine birch rods came and beat and whipped the boy so long that at last he fainted; then the troll took him and threw him against the wall. When he hit the wall the bottle fell down and sprinkled all over him, and he was just as good as new. Quick as a flash, he grabbed the sword and hacked the troll to death, and when he came out of the castle in the morning the princesses were standing all the way out of the ground. So he took the youngest of them for his queen and lived well and good with her for a long time.

But at last he wanted to go home for a while and see his parents. The queen was not any too happy about that, but, as he was longing so hard, and finally should and would go, she said to him: "One thing you shall promise me: that you do whatever your father says but not what your mother says." And that he promised. Then she gave him a ring, which was such that the one who had it on could make two wishes, whatever he wanted. Then he wished himself home, and the parents could not stop wondering over how splendid and fine he was.

After he had been home a few days, the mother wanted him to go up to the castle so the king could see what a man he had now become. The father said, "No, that he shouldn't do, for then we won't have any joy of him while he's here." But it didn't help; the mother pleaded and begged him so long that at last he went.

When he came up to the castle, he was finer both in clothing and equipment than his foster father. Now the king did not like this at all, and he said, "Well, you can see how beautiful my queen is, but I cannot see yours. I don't think you have so pretty a queen!"

"If only she were standing here, you'd see!" said the young king, and at once she was standing there.

But she was sorrowful and said to him, "Why didn't you do as I asked you to and listen to what your father said? Now I must go home again at once, and you have used up both your wishes!" With that she fastened a ring in which her name was written, in his hair, and then she wished herself home again.

Now the young king was beside himself with grief, and day in and day out he went about thinking of how he was to get back to his queen. I'll have to see if I can't find out where Whittenland is, he thought, and set out in the world. After he had gone a while, he came to a mountain. There he met a man who was lord of all the animals in the forest—for they came when he blew on a horn he had—and so the king asked about Whittenland.

"Well, that I don't know," answered the man, "but I'll ask my animals." So he called them in and asked if any of them knew where Whittenland was; but not one of them knew.

Then the man gave him a pair of skis. "When you stand on these," he said, "you'll come to my brother who lives seven hundred miles away from here. He's the lord of all the birds in the air; ask him! When you get there, just turn the skis so the tips point here, and they'll come home by themselves."

When the king got there, he turned the skis just as the lord of the animals had said, and they went back.

He asked again about Whittenland, and the man called in all the birds and asked if any of them knew where Whittenland lay. No, none of them knew that. A long while after the others, there also came an old eagle; she had been away for ten long years, but she did not know where Whittenland was either.

"Well, well," said the man, "then you can borrow a pair of skis from me. When you stand on them, you'll come to my brother who lives seven hundred miles from here. He's the lord of all the fish in the sea. You'll have to ask him. But don't forget to turn the skis!"

The king thanked him and stepped on the skis, and when he had come to the one who was lord of all the fish in the sea, he turned them and they went back just like the others. Then he asked about Whittenland again.

The man called in the fish, but none of them knew anything. At last there came an old, old pike that he'd had a lot of trouble calling in. When he asked her, she said, "Why yes, I know my way there very well, for I've been cook there for ten years. Tomorrow I'm going there again, for then the queen, who's lost her king, is to wed another."

"Since that is so, I'll give you some advice," said the man. "Over here in a marsh are three brothers who've been standing there for a hundred years, fighting over a hat, a coat, and a pair of boots. Whoever has these three things can make himself invisible and wish himself as far away as he likes. You can say to them that you want to try the things first and then pass judgment among them."

Well, the king thanked him and did as he was told. "What are you standing here fighting about?" he said to the brothers. "Let me try on the things, and then I'll decide for you." This they were only too willing to do, but when he'd put on the hat, the coat, and the boots, he said, "The next time we meet, you shall hear the judgment." And with that he wished himself away.

While he was rushing through the air, he met up with the north wind.

"Where are you going?" asked the north wind.

"To Whittenland," said the king, and then he told him what had happened to him.

"Well," said the north wind, "You can probably go a little faster than I can. I have to go into every nook and cranny and huff and puff, I do. But when you get there, stand out on the steps beside the door, and then I'll come rushing by as though I were going to blow down the whole castle. Then, when the false prince who intends to have your queen comes out to see what's going on, just take him by the neck and throw him out; then I'll try to get rid of him!"

Well, the king did just as the north wind had said. He stood out on the steps, and when the north wind came rushing and blustering and took hold of the castle wall so that it shook, the false prince came out to see what was going on. At the same moment as the prince got to the door, the king took him by the neck and threw him out, and then the north wind took him and flew off with him. When he was rid of him, the king went into the castle. At first the queen did not recognize him, for he had become so pale and thin, because he had been wandering so far and had been so sorrowful. But when he showed her the ring, she was overjoyed. Then the real wedding was held. It was so splendid that it was renowned both far and wide.

## ·69· Svein Unafraid

*Type 810, The Snares of the Evil One; R. Th. Christiansen, Norske Eventyr, 810, "Kontrakt med den onde," No. 7. Collected by Ivar Aasen in Helgeland (northern Norway) in 1846 and printed in Norsk Folkekalender (1859), p. 111. Reprinted in Löland, Norsk Eventurbok, p. 157, and in Norsk Folke-minnelag, I (1923), 7–11.*

*This folktale is found throughout Scandinavia, Great Britain, Ireland, Central Europe, and Russia; it has also entered French-American and West Indian tradition. The promising of a child to the devil through ignorance or desperation is a common introduction to many folktale types, e.g., Type 500, The Name of the Helper (Rumpelstiltskin, Tom-tit-tot). See Bolte-Polívka, II, 329–30.*

· THERE WAS ONCE a man who had fallen into such poverty and distress that he no longer knew how he was going to save himself. Then one day, when things were at their worst, a man came to him and said, "If you will promise to let me have the first gift you receive, then I shall help you."

"Well," said the man, "I can easily promise that." He did not give it much thought, nor did he know of any gift he was to receive. But shortly afterward his wife was brought to bed and gave birth to a son. Then the stranger came back and reminded him of his promise.

"Now you've received a gift," he said, "and this baby boy is what I want to have." Then the man grew both angry and frightened, for he understood whom he had run up against. "Well, there's no way out of it," said the Evil One, "but now I'll arrange it so well for you that you can keep the boy until he's grown."

The man was in a bad way, but he consoled himself with the fact that, when the boy was grown, he might find a way of saving himself.

The boy was christened and was given the name Svein. As he grew he became handsomer and brighter than other youths, so that everyone knew he had a good head on his shoulders. And he was strong and brave too, so that he was never afraid of anything. People usually called him "Svein Unafraid."

Time passed and the boy was full-grown. Then the stranger came again and said that now the time had come for him to have the boy, and he would come back and fetch him on the following night. The father was so upset that he went to the minister, and asked if there was any way out so the boy could go free. The minister said the boy was to come to him on the following evening, and then they would talk it over and try to work out something for the best.

When the boy came to the parsonage, the minister took him into the church, led him before the altar, and gave him a book which he was to hold in his hand. "Now you're to stand here," he said to the boy, "and you mustn't go away from the altar until I, myself, come back. You're not to be afraid if you see anything horrible, and you're not to let yourself be tricked into leaving if anyone comes and asks you to go with him. If you become frightened, just ask him to take that book you have in your hand. If he won't do that, you can just send him away." Then the minister went home again, and everything was quiet.

After a while a man who said he was the minister's hired hand came in and told Svein to return to the parsonage with him right away. There was something the minister had forgotten to tell him, and it would be really too bad if he did not find it out.

Yes, the boy said he would come if the man would take the book he was holding in his hand. He could just lay it on the altar, said the farmhand, but Svein said no. They argued about this for a while, until the stranger said he did not have time to stand there any longer, and then he left.

Shortly after, a maiden came in, and she was so beautiful and friendly that it was downright wonderful. She said she was the minister's daughter, and that it was really too bad that he had not gone with the hired hand, for the minister must talk with him and have his book back again, so he could see what he was to do.

That was clear enough, said Svein, if she would just take the book, he would come with her. It certainly made no difference who carried the book, she said, but it was most fitting that he give it to the minister himself, since he was the one who had been given it. Svein insisted, and they talked about this back and forth until she pretended to be tired of it and left.

Then after a while a man came in. He looked like the minister himself, and he praised Svein for not letting himself be tricked by these messengers. "I scarcely believe," he said, "that anyone else could have managed to come through such a trial. But now the danger is past. You can come with me, and there's nothing more to be afraid of." Then Svein asked if he would take his book. The other one felt there was no hurry about that. He would not be using it, in any case, until the following day. "You can just put it on the altar for the time being." But Svein insisted that he would have to take the book himself, and then they argued for a while until the minister pretended to be angry because Svein was so stubborn, and then he left. But that was not the real minister, you might know.

Now everything was quiet for a while, but then there was a rumbling and a crashing in the church, as if there was life and movement on all sides. First, a flock of black cats came in. Every corner was swarming and teeming with them. Then a great number of terrible animals came creeping up on all sides and crawled around the altar with hideous shrieks and howls. With all this there was such an uproar and such banging in the walls that it sounded as if the whole church was going to collapse.

"This is fun!" said the boy. "I've always liked to see it when things are lively around me and listen to the goings-on, but I never expected to see such dancing and hear such an uproar as there are here tonight!"

Then everything was quiet again, but after a while the wind started blowing, and there was such a storm that the church was swaying like grain in a field. At last there came a gust of wind so hard that it blew the whole church out to sea, where it was battered to pieces by the waves that broke over it. Only the altar remained, and the boy clung fast to it.

"This is fun!" said the boy. "I've always wanted to sail in a howling gale, but I never expected to sail in such a storm as there is tonight!" Then everything was quiet again, and the church was standing in the same place, just as whole as before.

After a while there was a crackling and a flickering up in the ceiling of the church, and when the boy looked up the whole roof was ablaze, and the flames approached the altar from all sides. They came closer and closer, but the boy stood there just as safe as before.

"This is fun!" he said. "I've always liked to have plenty of light and warmth, but I never expected it to be so bright and warm as it is tonight! I had expected to stand here shivering and freezing all night long." Then the fire went out little by little, and the boy could see that the church stood there just as whole and undamaged as before.

Now everything was quiet again. It was already late at night, but there was still a long time until daybreak. Then a man came in. He went right over to the altar, broke up a couple of boards in the floor, and dragged up a coffin with the body of a man in it. He took out the body, flayed off its hide, and put it down in front of the altar while he lowered the coffin down again. When Svein saw that, he leaned over and pulled the hide inside the altar railing.

"Whose skin is this?" he asked.

The man answered, "That was a bailiff who belonged to me and served me long and well. He did many things that people call unjust, but he amassed a lot of money and was a fine fellow. Now let me have the hide back again," he said.

"No," said Svein, "I want to have it to make soles for my shoes."

The other begged and pleaded earnestly to get back the hide. The case was such that this bailiff had done one good deed, when he gave some shillings to a poor wretch, and so the Evil One was not quite sure whether or not the bailiff belonged to him. To make certain, he wanted to have the hide out of the church. He asked to have it, and at last he promised Svein a lot of money if he would give it back again.

"Well," said Svein, "if I can have all the money the bailiff has cheated out of people, then it's the same to me."

Yes, this he would get, said the man. He went out and came back with a huge bag of money on his back. It was so heavy that he was quite worn out.

"I'm sure that's not all the money," said Svein. "He certainly had more than that."

"Only one shilling is missing; it has fallen down through the floor," said the man.

"Well, I want to have it," said Svein. The man went out, and this time he was gone a long while, but at last he came back with the shilling. "That was fine," said Svein, "but all the money still hasn't been found."

"Only one shilling is missing," said the man, "but it's sitting in a crack in the wall."

"Well, I want that one too," said Svein, and the man had to go out again, to look for this shilling. But it lay in the crack in the wall wrapped in a page torn from an old missal, and the man could not take hold of it.

Then Svein understood that he had won, and he would not bargain with him any longer. Now it was broad daylight, and they had to part. The man had been held up so long, searching for this shilling, that the sun was shining and it was another day. Then he could do no more, and the boy was free.

Now the minister came back and took his book, and Svein followed with the bag of money. Then they sent for the poorest people they could find and told them to come to the parsonage to get the money. When they had gathered there, Svein took out the bag of money and divided all the money among them. Not a shilling would he keep himself, and the poor people thanked him and blessed him, and said that no one was as

generous and no one as confident and brave in every way as
Svein Unafraid.

## •70• *Giske*

*Type 1383, The Woman Does not Know Herself. R. Th. Chris-
tiansen, Norske Eventyr, 1383, "Konen kjonder sig ikke selv,"
No. 1. Collected by P. Chr. Asbjörnsen in Röykjen (eastern Norway) in the 1840's and printed in Asbjörnsen and Jörgen Moe,
Norske Folkeeventyr, 2nd ed. (1852), No. 32.*

*Tales in which a man rids himself of a woman by smearing
her with tar and feathers or soot or by cutting off her clothes are
well distributed over Europe; see Bolte-Polivka, I, 341–42, and
also see tale No. 77, "Some Wives are that Way," in this book.*

• THERE WAS ONCE a widower who had a housekeeper called
Giske. She was only too willing to have him, and was after him,
ever and always, to marry her. At last the man grew so tired of
it that he did not know what to do to get rid of her.

So it was, between the haying and the reaping, when the hemp
was ripe, that they were to pull hemp. Giske thought, now as
always, that she was so pretty and so clever and smart, and so
she pulled hemp until her head reeled from the strong odor and
she toppled over and lay there asleep in the hemp field. While
she slept, the man came with a pair of scissors and clipped off her
skirts, and then he smeared her all over—first with tallow and
then with chimney soot—until she looked worse than the Devil.

When Giske woke up and saw how hideous she looked, she
did not know who she was. "Can this be me—this here?" said
Giske. "No, it can't be me, for I've never been so awful. It must
be the Devil himself!"

But now she wanted to find out how this could be, and so
she went over and opened her master's door and asked, "Is your
Giske home today, father?"

"Yes, of course my Giske's home," said the man. He wanted
to be done with her.

"Well, then I can't be his Giske, I can't," she thought, and wandered away, and glad he was to be rid of her.

When she had gone a bit, she came to a great forest; there she met two thieves. "Them I'd better join up with," thought Giske. "As long as I'm the Devil, it's fitting for me to be in a gang of thieves." But the thieves did not think so. When they caught sight of Giske, they took to their heels as fast as they could, for they thought the Evil One himself was after them and wanted to get them. But it was not much help, I dare say, for Giske was long of limb and fleet of foot, and she was after them before they knew it.

"If you're going out to steal, I want to come along and lend a hand," said Giske, "for I know my way well around the parish here."

When the thieves heard that, they thought this was good company and were not afraid any more.

They were on their way to steal a sheep, they said, but they did not know where they should go to get hold of one.

"Oh, that's no problem," said Giske, "for I've been serving a farmer over here by the woods for a long time. I'd be able to find the sheepcote in pitch darkness."

The thieves thought that was fine, and when they got there, Giske was to go into the sheepcote and hand out a sheep; then they were to take it. The sheepcote stood close up to the wall of the room where the man lay sleeping, and so Giske went in quite silently and carefully. But when she was well inside, she shrieked out to the thieves: "DO YOU WANT A RAM OR A EWE? THERE'S ENOUGH TO CHOOSE FROM HERE!"

"Hush! Hush! Just take one that's nice and fat!" said the thieves.

"YES, BUT DO YOU WANT A RAM OR A EWE? DO YOU WANT A RAM OR A EWE? FOR THERE'S ENOUGH TO CHOOSE FROM HERE!" shrieked Giske.

"Hush! Hush, now!" said the thieves. "Just take one that's good and fat! Then it doesn't matter if it's a ram or a ewe!"

"YES, BUT DO YOU WANT A RAM OR A EWE? DO YOU WANT A RAM OR A EWE? THERE'S ENOUGH TO CHOOSE FROM HERE!" shrieked Giske; she did not give up.

"Then shut your mouth and take one that's good and fat, no matter if it's a ram or a ewe!" said the thieves.

In the meantime, the man of the house had been awakened by all the noise and yelling, and came out in just his nightshirt to see what was going on. The thieves took to their heels, with Giske right after them so she knocked the man over.

"WAIT, FELLOWS! WAIT, FELLOWS!" she shrieked.

The man, who had seen nothing but this black animal, became so frightened that he hardly dared get up again, for he thought it was the Devil himself who had been in the sheepcote. He knew of but one remedy, he did. He went in and woke up his family and sat down to read and pray, for he had heard that one could read the Devil away.

Then it was the second evening. The thieves were going out to steal a fat goose, and Giske was to show them the way. Giske was to go in and hand one out, for she knew her way around, and the thieves were to take it.

"Do YOU WANT A GOOSE OR A GANDER? THERE'S ENOUGH TO CHOOSE FROM HERE!" shrieked Giske, when she got in the goose pen.

"Hush! Hush! Just take one that's nice and heavy!" said the thieves.

"YES! BUT DO YOU WANT A GOOSE OR A GANDER? DO YOU WANT A GOOSE OR A GANDER? THERE'S ENOUGH TO CHOOSE FROM HERE!" shouted Giske.

"Hush! Hush! Just take one that's nice and heavy! It doesn't matter if it's a goose or a gander! And shut your mouth!" they said.

While Giske and the thieves were bickering about this, one of the geese started honking, and then another started honking, and all of a sudden they were all honking at the same time. The man came out to see what was going on. The thieves set off as best they could, and Giske after them, so fast that the farmer thought it was the Black Devil, for she was long of limb and she had no skirts to get in her way.

"WAIT A BIT NOW, FELLOWS," shrieked Giske. "WHY, YOU COULD'VE GOTTEN WHATEVER YOU WANTED, NO MATTER IF IT WAS A GOOSE OR A GANDER!"

But they had no time to stop. At the farm where they had been, everyone started reading and praying, both big and small, for they were certain that the Devil had been there.

As it was getting on toward the evening of the third day, they were so hungry—both the thieves and Giske—that they did not know what to do. Then they decided to go to the *stabbur* [storehouse] of a rich farmer, who lived on the edge of the forest, and steal themselves some food. Well, there they went, but the thieves did not dare go in, so Giske was to go into the *stabbur* and hand out some food, and they were to stand on the outside and take it.

Now when Giske got in, the *stabbur* was filled with everything, beef and pork and sausage and bread. The thieves shushed her and bade her just throw out some food, and remember how it had gone the other two nights. But Giske did not give up: "Do you want beef or pork or sausage or bread?" she shrieked until it rang. "You can have whatever you want, for there's enough to choose from here!"

The man at the farm was awakened by this screaming and came out to see what was going on. The thieves were off as fast as they could go. All at once Giske, black and hideous as she was, came running past. "Wait a bit! Wait a bit, fellows!" she shrieked. "You can have whatever you want, for there's enough to choose from here!"

When the man caught sight of that ugly beast, he also thought that the Devil was loose, for by now he had heard what had happened on the other two nights, and he started to read and pray—and this they did on all the farms in the whole parish, for they knew that one could read the Devil away.

On Saturday night the thieves were going out again to steal a fat ram for their Sunday fare, and they certainly could do with one, for they had got hungry for many days; but now they would not take Giske with them. She only made noise and caused trouble with that big mouth of hers, they said.

While Giske was waiting for them on Sunday morning, she became terribly hungry—she had not had much to eat for three whole days either—and so she went in a turnip patch and pulled up some turnips and started eating. When he got out of bed, the farmer who owned the turnip patch felt so uneasy that at last he thought he ought to go down and have a look at his turnip patch even though it was Sunday morning. Well, then, he put on his robe and went down to a marsh at the bottom of the hill where the turnip patch lay. When he got there, he caught sight of something black walking around and pulling up the turnips in his patch. And it did not take him long to believe it was the Devil too. So he saw to it that he got home as fast as he could, and said that the Devil was in the turnip patch. They were scared to death at the farm when they heard that, but then they thought it best to send for the parson and have him bind the Devil.

"No," said the old wife, "it'll never do to go to the parson today. Why, it's Sunday morning. He won't come now, for he's not up so early, and if he is, then he's reading his sermon."

"Oh, I'll promise him a fat loin of veal, I will. Then he'll come all right," thought the man.

He set out for the parsonage, but when he got there the parson was not up yet. The girl bade the man go in the parlor, while she went up to tell the parson that Farmer So-and-So was downstairs and wanted to talk with him. Well, when the parson heard that such a fine man was sitting downstairs he pulled on his pants and came down at once in his slippers and nightcap.

The man told him his errand, that the Devil was loose down in his turnip patch, and if the parson would come with him and bind him, he'd give him a fat loin of veal.

Well, of course the parson had nothing against this and shouted to the boy to saddle the horse while he got dressed.

"Nay, Father, that'll never do at all," said the man, "for the Devil certainly won't stay put long, and you never can tell where he can be taken again, once he's got loose. You'd better come along at once."

The parson went with him just as he was, nightcap and slippers and all, but when they came to the marsh it was so soggy that the parson could not cross it in his slippers. The farmer took him up on his back to carry him over. Now he stepped pretty carefully, on a stump here and a mound there, but when he had come out in the middle, Giske caught sight of them, and thought it was the thieves coming with the ram.

"Is 'e fat? Is 'e fat? Is 'e fat?" she shrieked so the forest rang.

"Damned if I know whether he's fat or lean!" said the man, "but if you want to find out, you'll have to come and feel for yourself." And then he became so frightened that he dumped the parson right in the middle of the soggy marsh and took to his heels. And if the parson has not got up, then he must be lying there still.

## •71• *The Seven Foals*

*Type 471, The Bridge to the Other World; R. Th. Christiansen, Norske Eventyr, 471, "De syv folerne. Gjaete kongens stutar," No. 2. Collected by Jörgen Moe in Aadalen (eastern Norway) in the 1840's and printed in P. Chr. Asbjörnsen and Jörgen Moe, Norske Folkeeventyr (1852), No. 31.*

*This tale has been reported from all continents except Africa. The clever youngest brother called Askelad (Ashboy) is a stock character in Norwegian folktales, comparable to the Spanish Juan, the French Louis, or the English Jack.*

*A largely elaborated Hungarian variant of this tale is given in* Folktales of Hungary, *a companion volume in this series.*

• THERE WAS ONCE a poor couple who lived in a wretched hovel a long way away in the forest. They lived from hand to mouth, and with difficulty at that. But they had three sons, and the youngest of them was Askelad. He was called that because he did nothing but lie by the fire and poke in the ashes.

One day the eldest boy said he wanted to go out and look for work. This he was allowed to do right away, and so he wandered out into the world. He walked and he walked the whole day. Just as it was getting dark he came to a king's manor. The king was standing out on the steps and asked where he was going.

"Oh, I'm just going to look for work, father," said the boy.

"Do you want to work for me and tend my seven foals?"

asked the king. "If you can tend them the whole day, and tell me in the evening what they eat and drink, then you'll get the princess and half the kingdom. But if you can't, then I'll carve three red slices out of your back!"

Well, the boy thought that was an easy job, he would certainly be able to manage it, he thought.

In the morning, as day was breaking, the stablemaster let out the seven foals. They galloped away with the boy after them, and then, if you please, they went over hill and dale, through bushes and shrubs. After the boy had been running like this for quite a while, he started growing tired, and after he had kept it up even longer, he was pretty well fed up with the whole business. But just then he came to a cleft in the mountain. There sat an old hag spinning on a distaff.

When she caught sight of the boy, running after the foals so the sweat was pouring off him, the hag shouted, "Come here! Come here, my dear son, and I'll pick the lice out of your hair!"

The boy was only too willing. He sat down in the cleft with the hag and laid his head in her lap, and she picked the lice out of his hair the whole day, while he took it easy.

As it was getting on toward evening, the boy wanted to go. "I might just as well wander straight home again," he said, "for there's no use my going to the king's manor."

"Wait until nightfall," said the hag, "and the king's foals will come by this way again. Then you can run back with them. There's no one who knows you've been lying here the whole day instead of tending the foals."

When they came, she gave the boy a pitcher of water and a clump of moss. These he was to show to the king and tell him that this was what the seven foals ate and drank.

"Well, have you tended the foals faithfully and well the whole day?" asked the king when the boy came back in the evening.

"Yes, indeed I have," said the boy.

"Then you can certainly tell me what my seven foals eat and drink," said the king.

Well, the boy held out the pitcher of water and the clump of moss he had got from the old hag. "Here's what they eat and here's what they drink!" said the boy.

But now the king could tell how he had tended, and he was so angry that he ordered the boy to be chased home that very moment. But first they were to carve three red slices out of his back and rub in salt.

When the boy came home again, you can certainly imagine what kind of spirits he was in. He had gone out once to look for work, he said, but he would never do that again!

The next day the second son said he wanted to go out into the world and seek his fortune. The parents said no, and told him to look at his brother's back. But the boy did not give up, and at long last he was allowed to go. After he had walked the whole day, he also came to the king's manor. There stood the king out on the steps, and he asked where he was going. And when the boy replied that he was looking for work, the king said he could work for him and tend his seven foals. And then the king set the same punishment and the same reward for him as he had set for his brother. Well, the boy agreed to it at once. He entered the king's service, for he thought he would certainly be able to tend the foals and tell the king what they ate and drank.

In the grey light of dawn, the stablemaster let out the seven foals. Again they galloped away over hill and dale with the boy behind them. But the same thing happened to him as to his brother. After he had been running behind the foals for a long, long while, until he was both sweating and tired, he came to a cleft in the mountain. There sat the old hag spinning on a distaff, and she shouted to the boy,

"Come here! Come here, my dear son, and I'll pick the lice out of your hair!"

The boy thought this was a good idea. He let the foals run their way and sat down in the cleft with the hag. Thus he sat and thus he lay and took it easy the whole day.

When the foals came back in the evening, he also got a clump of moss and a pitcher of water which he was to show to the king. But when the king asked the boy, "Can you tell me what my seven foals eat and drink?" and the boy held out the clump of moss and the pitcher of water and said, "Yes, here's their food and here's their drink!" the king grew angry again and ordered them to carve three slices out of his back and rub in salt and chase him home on the spot. So when the boy came home, he also told how he had fared and said he had gone out once to look for work, but he would never do that again!

On the third day Askelad wanted to set out. He wanted to try to tend the seven foals too, he said.

The others laughed and made fun of him. "As long as it's turned out this way with us, you'll certainly manage it! Yes, that'd be likely. Why, you never do anything but lie and root in the ashes!"

"Well, I still want to do it all the same," said Askelad, "since I've made up my mind." And for all the others laughed, and for all his parents pleaded with him, it helped not one bit. Askelad set out on the way, he did.

Now after he had walked the whole day, he also came to the king's manor at dusk. There stood the king out on the steps and asked where he was going.

"I'm looking for work," said Askelad.

"Well, where are you from?" asked the king, for he wanted to find out a little more about that one before he hired him to work for him.

Askelad told where he was from and said he was the brother of the two who had tended the seven foals for the king. And then he asked if he could not try to tend them on the following day.

"Damn!" said the king. He grew angry just thinking about them. "If you're a brother of those two, you can't do much either. I've had enough of the likes of you!"

"Well, as long as I'm here, I might just as well be allowed to try too," said Askelad.

"All right, if you must have your back flayed, it's all right with me," said the king.

"I'd rather have the king's daughter, I would," said Askelad.

In the grey light of dawn the stablemaster let out the seven foals again, and they set out over hill and dale, through bushes and shrubs, with Askelad behind them.

When he had been running like this for a long time, he also came to the cleft in the mountain. There sat the old hag again, spinning on her distaff, and she shouted to Askelad, "Come here! Come here, my dear son, and I'll pick the lice out of your hair!"

"Kiss my ass! Kiss my ass!" shouted Askelad, hopping and running, and holding onto the tail of one of the foals.

When he was well past the cleft, the youngest foal said, "Sit up on my back, for we've still got a long way to go." And this he did.

Then they traveled a long, long way. "Do you see anything now?" said the foal.

"No," said Askelad.

Then they traveled a long way again. "Do you see anything now?" asked the foal.

"Oh, no," said the boy.

After they had gone a long, long way, the foal asked again, "Do you see anything now?"

"Yes, now I think I see something white," said Askelad. "It looks like a great big birch stump."

"Yes, we're going in there," said the foal.

When they came to the birch stump, the eldest foal took it and broke it aside, and there where the stump had stood was a door. Inside was a tiny room, and in the room there was not much more than a hearth and a couple of stools. But behind the door hung a huge rusty sword and a little jug.

"Can you swing the sword?" asked the foal.

Askelad tried, but he could not do it. Then he had to take a swig from the jug—first once, then again, and still once more. And then he could handle it as if it were nothing.

"Well, now you must take the sword with you," said the foal, "and with it you're to chop off the heads of all seven of us on your wedding day. Then we will turn into princes again as we were before, for we are the brothers of the princess you're to have, when you can tell the king what we eat and drink. But a terrible troll has cast a spell over us, so when you have chopped off our heads you must take good care to put each head by the tail of the body it was sitting on. Then the spell will have no more power over us."

This Askelad promised to do, and they journeyed on.

After they had traveled a long, long way, the foal asked, "Do you see anything?"

"No," said Askelad.

Then they journeyed a good while longer. "Now?" asked the foal. "See anything now?"

"Oh, no," said Askelad.

Then they journeyed many, many miles again over hill and dale. "Now?" said the foal. "Don't you see anything yet?"

"Why, yes," said Askelad. "Now I see a kind of hazy stripe a long way off."

"Well, that's a river, it is," said the foal. "We're going to cross it."

There was a long, magnificent bridge over the river, and when they had come to the other side, they again journeyed a long, long way. Then the foal asked again if Askelad saw anything.

Yes, this time he saw something black in the distance, just like a church tower.

"Well, we're going in there," said the foal.

When the foals came into the churchyard, they turned into people again and looked like king's sons. And their clothes were so fine that they fairly shone. Then they went into the church, and there they received bread and wine from the minister who was standing before the altar. Askelad went in too, and after the minister had placed his hand on their heads and said the benediction, they went out of the church again. Askelad did too, and he took along a bottle of the wine and a loaf of the communion bread. At the very moment the seven princes came out of the churchyard, they turned into foals again. Then Askelad sat up on the back of the youngest foal, and they went back the same way they had come, only much, much faster. First they went across the bridge, and then past the birch stump, and then past the old hag who sat spinning in the cleft in the mountain. They went so fast that Askelad could not hear what the hag shrieked after him, but he heard enough to understand that she was furious.

It was almost dark when they got back to the king's manor, and the king himself was standing out in the yard waiting for them.

"Have you tended faithfully and well the whole day?" said the king to Askelad.

"I've done my best," answered Askelad.

"Then you can certainly tell me what my seven foals eat and drink," said the king.

Askelad took out the communion bread and the bottle of wine and showed them to the king. "This is what they eat and this is what they drink," he said.

"Yes, you have tended faithfully and well," said the king. "And you shall have the princess and half the kingdom!"

Then everything was made ready for the wedding, and this was to be so grand and fine that it would be the talk of seven kingdoms, said the king. But as they were sitting at the wedding table, the bridegroom got up and went down to the stable, for he had forgotten something there and he had to get it, he said. When he came down there, he did as the foals had said and chopped off their heads, all seven of them—the eldest first, and then all the others according to age—and he took care to lay each head by the tail of the foal it had been sitting on. And as he did this, they turned into princes again. When he came back to the wedding table with the seven princes, the king was so happy that he kissed Askelad and pounded him on the back, and his bride was even more in love with him than she had been before.

"You have received half the kingdom now," said the king, "and you shall get the other half after my death, for my sons can get lands and kingdoms for themselves, now that they are princes again." So there can be no doubt that there was rejoicing and merriment at this wedding.

I was there too, but no one had time to think of me. All I got was a slice of cake with butter on it. I put it on the stove,

> And the cake did burn,
> And the butter did run,
> And I got back
> Not a single crumb!

# ·72· All-Black and All-White

Type 303, The Twins or Blood-Brothers; R. Th. Christiansen, Norske Eventyr, 303B, "Aalsvart og Aalkvit," No. 23. Collected *by Moltke Moe in Böherad (Telemark) in 1880. Manuscript by Moltke Moe in Norsk Folkeminnesamling (The Norwegian Folklore Institute), XI, 72. Printed in Löland, Norsk Eventyr-bok, p. 351.*

*Kurt Ranke holds that this widespread folktale originated somewhere in western Europe, probably in France; see his Die Zwei Brüder, p. 348. Often the introduction of this folktale type deals with the magical birth of the brothers in which a man's wife eats from a magical fish and gives birth to twins. The Norwegian variant printed here can be compared to the Icelandic Bjarki-saga.*

*About half of the Norwegian variants of this folktale come from Telemark, where this text was collected. Many story-tellers in Telemark tell their tales in a manner comparable to the Icelandic saga style. See R. Th. Christiansen, "Eventyrvandring i Norge," Arv, II (1946), 75.*

• THERE WAS ONCE a man who lost his horse, and so he went out in the fields to look for it. He walked far and long, but no horse did he find, and then it was nightfall. But all at once he caught sight of a light from a cabin in the forest. He went in and there sat an old hag doing her baking.

"Good evening," the man greeted her.

"Good evening," answered the hag. "Find yourself a seat."

"Thanks," said the man, and sat down on the log chair. "You haven't seen anything of a horse, have you?" he said.

"Why yes, I can tell you where the horse is. It's right over there in the field," answered the hag. "But I've heard you have no wife. I don't suppose you'd have me, would you?"

"No, that would never do at all," said the man. "I have two grown sons by my first wife, and I can't very well give them a stepmother," he said.

"Well, you can do as you like," said the hag, "but you're not getting out of that chair before you say you'll have me." She was a troll hag, you see!

No, he did not dare do that.

But after he'd been sitting there for a while, and could not get free, there was no way out. He had to promise it.

Now after they had celebrated the wedding, she wanted to visit her sisters in the mountain, she did—she had three sisters inside the mountain. She took along All-Black, one of her stepsons, and her own son. He was called Gjermund. But before he left, All-Black made a hole in the doorsill, and then he said to All-White, his brother,

"As long as that hole is full of water, I'm alive. But if it's full of blood, I'm dead."

When they came to the mountain where the first sister lived, All-Black lay down on the bed. "I'm made so strangely," he said. "When I keep my eyes open, I'm asleep. But when I keep them shut, I'm awake." With that, he kept his eyes open. So they thought he was asleep.

"How do you like your marriage?" asked the sister.

"Oh, pretty well," answered the other. "It's just that I don't like those two sons, and especially the one I have with me."

"Oh, I know of a way out," said the sister. "We'll get rid of him. I have a wild pig which I'll ask him to butcher, and then the pig will kill him."

Yes, that was very good indeed.

In the morning the sister said to All-Black, "I'd like to ask if you'd cut the head off my pig. He's quite dangerous, and I can't get anyone else to do it," she said.

"Gjermund can do it," said All-Black.

"Oh, him? That little weakling?" they said.

Well, All-Black took his sword, and the very moment the pig rushed at him, he was ready and cut off its head.

Then they journeyed far and long, through forests and fields, until they came to another mountain. There lived the old hag's second sister.

As soon as All-Black came in, he lay down on the bed. "I'm made so strangely," he said. "I'm accustomed to sleeping with my eyes open. When I shut my eyes, I'm awake." Then he kept them open.

"How do you like your marriage, sister?" she asked.

"Oh, pretty well," she said. "It's just that I don't like those two stepsons of mine, and especially the one I have with me," she said.

"Oh, we can get rid of him. I have a dangerous ox," said the sister. "I'll ask him to cut off its head. Then I think we're rid of him."

In the morning, the troll hag came and asked All-Black if he would butcher an ox for her. "He's quite vicious, and I can't get anyone else to do it," she said.

"Gjermund can do it," said All-Black.

"Gjermund? That's not likely, the idiot! No, he certainly couldn't do it," they said.

Well, All-Black seized his sword and killed the ox too.

Then they set out again and journeyed over hill and dale and high ridges until they came to the third sister.

There, All-Black lay down on the bed again. "I'm made so strangely that I'm almost ashamed of it," he said. "I can't sleep unless I keep my eyes open. But when I wake up, then I keep them shut."

Then he lay there and stared.

"How do you like your marriage?" asked the sister.

"Oh, pretty well. It's just that I don't like the two stepsons, and especially the one I have with me," said the hag.

"Oh, I can do away with him all right. When you go, leave your glove behind and ask All-Black to run back after it. Then I'll be standing behind the door with a bowl of venom, and I'll sprinkle it over him, I will!"

So that was all very well and good.

When she set out in the morning, she left one of her gloves behind. After they had journeyed a while, the hag said, "Oh, now I've forgotten my glove. You'll have to run back and fetch it, All-Black," she said.

"No, Gjermund can run," he said.

"No, he can't run as fast as you can. You'll have to do it, you will," she said.

Well, back he went. When he got there, he shoved the door so hard that the hag who stood behind it fell down, and spilled the venom all over herself. Then he took the glove and ran back.

Then they traveled far, and farther than far, until they came to a king's manor. The king's daughter had been carried off, and there was no end to the wailing and grief. Whoever could save her would have her for a bride, the king promised.

"Now we'll go to the mountain, we will," said the troll hag to All-Black. "Then they'll let you try to find the princess—you and Gjermund."

"I dare not go with you. When my life is at stake, you'll run away from me," said All-Black.

No, not at all. They would not run away, he need not be afraid of that.

Then they came to the mountain, and All-Black knocked. All at once there was such a loud bang that he could hardly hear, and the other two took to their heels so fast that he was showered with moss and pebbles. At the same moment a troll with three heads was standing in front of him!

"My horse and my hound, come to my aid," said All-Black— and suddenly he had his horse and his hound with him.

> And the horse began to kick and bite,
> And the hound began to tear and fight.
> He swung the sword above his head,
> And then he hacked the troll quite dead.

And all the heads rolled away.

Well, now Gjermund and his mother came back.

All at once there was a bang even louder than the first, and at the same moment a troll with four heads was standing in front of him!

"My horse and my hound, come to my aid," said All-Black.

> And the horse began to kick and bite,
> And the hound began to tear and fight.
> He swung the sword above his head,
> And then he hacked the troll quite dead.

Well, then they were back on the spot again, those two. But all at once there was a third bang, so hard that it sounded as if the mountain had cracked. Out came a troll with five heads, and the two of them fled!

"My horse and my hound, come to my aid," said All-Black.

> And the horse began to kick and bite,
> And the hound began to tear and fight.
> He swung his sword above his head,
> And then he hacked the troll quite dead.

When he had put an end to this troll too, he went inside the mountain and fetched the king's daughter. Well, then, there they were again, Gjermund and his mother, and the very moment the princess came out, they grabbed her and rushed off with her.

Well, All-Black did not know what he was going to do. He came to a deep, dense forest, and the troll hag caused him to lose his way. At nightfall he made a big bonfire and sat down in front of it. As he was sitting there, a maiden came up to him, as fair as the sun in the sky, and with hair like pure gold, which shone from afar through the forest.

"Are you sitting here, warming yourself?" she said.

"Yes, that I am," he said.

"May I warm myself here with you?" she said.

"Yes, that you may," he said.

With that she laid her head in his lap. "Will you pick the lice out of my hair?" she asked. Well, this he did.

"Pull a hair out of my head and wind it around your horse. It looks so pretty," she said. So he pulled a hair out of her head and wound it around the horse.

"Pull a hair out of my head and wind it around your hound. It looks so pretty," she told him once again. Well, he pulled out a hair and wound it around the hound.

Then she said a third time, "Pull a hair out of my head and wind it around your sword. It looks so pretty." Yes indeed, he wound it around the sword too.

And now she started to grow until she was as tall as all the tree tops, and so ugly and hideous that it was truly frightening. It was his stepmother!

"My horse and my hound, come to my aid," said All-Black.

"My hair holds well," she said.

"My sword, come to my aid," he said, and tried to draw his sword.

"My hair holds well," she said, and then he was not able to get it out, and she put an end to him—and his horse and his hound too.

Then All-White saw that the doorsill was full of blood. "Now my brother is dead," he said, and taking his horse and his hound, he set out to search for him.

Well, the stepmother caused him to come to the same forest and lose his way. At nightfall, he made a fire and sat down.

Well, the same maiden came back. She was so fair, so fair that she was a joy to behold, and with the golden hair that glittered and shone from afar through the trees.

"Are you sitting here, warming yourself?" she said.

"Yes, I am," he said. His voice was hard and gruff.

"May I sit down beside you and warm myself too?" asked the maiden.

"That you may," said All-White.

"Will you pick the lice out of my hair?" she asked, and lay with her head in his lap.

"That I will," he said.

"Pull a hair out of my head and wind it around your horse. It looks so pretty," she said.

All-White pulled out a hair and threw it in the fire.

"Fie! Fie! What is it that smells so?" she said.

"There are so many things that smell in the forest," he said.

Then she said, "Pull a hair out of my head and wind it around your hound. It looks so pretty."

Well, he pulled out one more hair and burned it up too.

"Fie! Fie! What is it that smells so?" she asked.

"There are so many things that smell in the forest," said All-White.

"Pull a hair out of my head and wind it around your sword," she said. "It looks so pretty."

With that he threw the third hair in the fire.

"Fie! Fie! What is it that smells so?" she said.

"There are so many things that smell in the forest," he said.

Then she started to grow until she was as big and tall as the highest tree.

"My horse and my hound, come to my aid," said All-White.

"My hair holds well," she said.

"Your hair lies burning in the fire," he said.

> Then the horse began to kick and bite,
> And the hound began to tear and fight.
> He swung his sword above his head,
> And then he hacked the troll hag dead.

When he had put an end to her, he started searching about everywhere. Well, he found his brother lying there dead, with the horse and the hound beside him. Over where the stepmother lay stood some crocks. All-White stuck a finger down in one of them to find out what it was, and the finger fell off! It was the troll hag's "sore crock." Then he stuck it down in the other crock, and the finger grew back again. This was the troll hag's healing salve. Then he rubbed the salve on his brother and on the horse and on the hound too, and they awoke and were all as good as new.

Well, then All-Black told what had happened from the very beginning: about the stepmother and the king's daughter and the trolls.

"Now we'll both go to the king's manor," said All-White. This they did, with their horses and their hounds too.

When All-Black came in, the king's daughter knew him right away. "Here's the one who saved me," she said, and told what had happened and showed them where she had marked him— as I remember it, she had probably put a ring in his ear.

With that they took Gjermund and threw him in the snakepit. And then they had the wedding and reveled and drank. They fired salutes as long as they had balls and powder. But when it was all gone, they took me for wadding and stuffed me in the gun barrel and shot me all the way here. That's why I know this story so well!

*Type 870A, The Little Goose-Girl; R. Th. Christiansen, Norske Eventyr, 871, "Vesle Aase Gaasepike," No. 1. Collected by P. Chr. Asbjörnsen in Solör (eastern Norway) in the 1840's and printed in Asbjörnsen and Jörgen Moe, Norske Folkeeventyr (1852), No. 29.*

*This variant form of Type 870 (see also tale No. 67) is found mainly in the eastern mountain areas of Norway. Waldemar Liungman has studied Norwegian, Swedish, and Danish variants of this folktale in the light of Child ballad No. 5, "Gil Brenton," and Scandinavian ballads containing Motif K1843, "Wife deceives husband with substituted bedmate." See Waldemar Liungman, Två Folkminnesundersokningar, pp. 1–40.*

· THERE WAS ONCE a king who had so many geese that he had to have a girl just to tend them; her name was Lucy, and so they called her Little Lucy Goosey Girl.

Now there was a king's son from England who was going out courting. Lucy sat down in the road to wait for him.

"Are you sitting there, Little Lucy?" said the king's son when he came.

"Yes, here I sit, a-patching and a-mending. I'm waiting for the king's son from England today," said Little Lucy.

"You can't expect to get him!" said the king's son.

"Oh yes, if I'm to have him, I'll get him all right!" said Little Lucy.

Now artists were sent to every land and kingdom to make portraits of the most beautiful princesses; the prince wanted them to choose from. He liked one of them so well that he journeyed to see her and wanted to marry her, and he was both delighted and pleased when she became his sweetheart. But the prince had a stone with him, which he put in front of his bed, and this stone knew everything; and when the princess came, Little Lucy Goosey Girl told her that if she had ever had a sweetheart before, or if there was anything she did not want the prince to know, then she must not climb over that stone he had in front of his bed, "for it will tell him everything about you!" she said. When the princess heard that, she was quite upset, you might know, but then she hit upon asking Lucy to take her place and go to bed with the prince in the evening. And when he had fallen asleep, they were to change places again, so he would have the right one with him in the morning when it grew light.

This they did.

When Little Lucy Goosey Girl came and stepped on the stone, the prince asked, "Who's that climbing in my bed?"

"A pure and untainted virgin!" said the stone, and then they lay down to sleep. But later on in the night the princess came and lay down there in Lucy's place.

In the morning, when they were getting up, the prince asked the stone again, "Who's that climbing out of my bed?"

"One who's had three lovers!" said the stone.

When the prince heard this he did not want her, you might know, so he sent her home again and took another sweetheart instead.

When he was going to visit her, Little Lucy Goosey Girl was sitting in the road waiting for him again.

"Are you sitting there, Little Lucy Goosey Girl?" said the prince.

"Yes, I'm sitting here, a-patching and a-mending, for I'm waiting for the king's son from England today," said Lucy.

"Oh, you can't expect to get him!" said the king's son.

"Oh yes, if I'm to have him, I'll get him all right!" said Lucy.

With that princess it went just as with the first, except that when she got up in the morning the stone said that she had had six lovers! So the prince did not want her either and sent her packing. But still he thought he would have to try once more to find a pure and untainted virgin. He searched far and wide, in many a land again, until he found one he liked.

But when he was going to visit her, Little Lucy Goosey Girl was sitting in the road waiting for him again.

"Are you sitting there now, Little Lucy Goosey Girl?" said the prince.

"Yes, I'm sitting here, a-patching and a-mending, for I'm waiting for the king's son from England today!" said Lucy.

"You can't expect to get him," said the prince.

"Oh yes, if I'm to have him, I'll get him all right," said Little Lucy.

When the princess came, Little Lucy told her, like the others, that if she had ever had a sweetheart, or if there was anything else she did not want the prince to know, she must not step on that stone the prince had in front of his bed, "for it'll tell him everything!" she said. The princess was upset when she heard this. But then she was just as sly as the two others and asked Lucy to go in her place and lie down with the prince in the evening, and when he had gone to sleep they were to change places so he would have the right one with him when it grew light in the morning.

This they did.

When Little Lucy Goosey Girl came and stepped on the stone, the prince asked, "Who's that climbing in my bed?"

"A pure and untainted virgin!" said the stone, and then they lay down.

Later on that night the prince put a ring on Lucy's finger, and it was so tight that she could not get it off again, for the prince was certainly able to tell that something was wrong, and he wanted to have a sign so he could recognize the right one again. When the prince had fallen asleep, the princess came and chased Lucy back down to the goose pen and lay down in her place.

In the morning, when they were getting up, the prince asked, "Who's that climbing out of my bed?"

"One who's had nine!" said the stone, and when the prince heard that he became so angry that he sent her packing on the spot. And then he asked the stone how this could be with these princesses who had stepped on the stone, for he was not able to understand it. The stone then told how they had fooled him and sent Little Goosey Girl in their stead. This is what the prince wanted to find out. He went down to where she sat tending her geese, for he also wanted to see if she had the ring. "If she has it, it is best to make her the queen," he thought. When he came down to the goose pen, he saw at once that she had tied a rag around one of her fingers, so he asked why she had done this.

"Oh, I've cut myself so badly," said Little Lucy Goosey Girl.

Then he wanted to see the finger, but Lucy would not take off the rag. So the prince took hold of the finger, but Lucy wanted to draw it back, and with that the rag fell off and he recognized his ring again. Then he took her with him to the king's manor and gave her plenty of beautiful things and fine clothing, and then they held the wedding. And that's the way Little Lucy Goosey Girl got the king's son of England all the same—just because she was to have him.

## •74• *Haaken Grizzlebeard*

*Type 900, King Thrushbeard; R. Th. Christiansen, Norske Eventyr, 900 "Haaken Borkenskjaeg," No. 1. Collected by P. Chr. Asbjörnsen in Sörum, Romerike (Telemark), between 1837 and 1839 and printed in Asbjörnsen and Jörgen Moe, Norske Folkeeventyr (1852), No. 45.*

*This folktale has been reported throughout Europe, from Turkey and India, and from North and Central America. One of the earliest known variants dates from 1260, in a poem supposedly written by the German Konrad von Würzburg. A literary version of "King Thrushbeard" is in Giambattista Basile's* Pentamerone *(1634-36).*

• THERE WAS ONCE a king's daughter who was so proud and haughty that no suitor was good enough for her. She made fun of them all and sent them packing one after the other. But even though she put on such airs, suitors always came to the manor, for she was very pretty—the hateful shrew!

Now one day a king's son came to court her, and he was called Haaken Grizzlebeard. But the first night he was there, she told the court fool to cut the ears off one of his horses and slit the jaws of the other right up to its ears. When the prince came out the next morning to go driving, the king's daughter was standing out on the porch to watch.

"Well, I never saw the like!" she said. "The biting north wind that blows here has taken the ears off one of your horses, and the other has stood here snickering at it so that its jaws have split right up to its ears!" And then she burst out laughing, ran inside, and let him drive on his way.

He went home, but he thought to himself that he would get even with her all right. He put on a big beard of moss, pulled on a wide fur robe, and disguised himself like any other beggar. From a goldsmith he bought a golden spinning wheel and set out with it, and one morning he sat down outside the princess' window and started to file and work on the golden spinning wheel, for it was not quite finished, nor were there any uprights on it either.

When the king's daughter came to the window in the morning, she opened it and called to him and asked if he would sell his golden spinning wheel.

"No, it's not for sale," said Haaken Grizzlebeard. "But it's all the same to me, if I can sleep outside your chamber door tonight, you can have it!"

Well, the king's daughter thought this was a good bargain, and there could not be any harm in that. She got the spinning wheel, and in the evening Haaken Grizzlebeard lay down outside her chamber door. But later on in the night he started to shiver.

"*Huttetuttetuttetu!* It's so cold that . . . Let me in," he said.

"I think you're absolutely out of your mind!" said the king's daughter.

"Oh *huttetuttetuttetu!* It's so cold! Oh, just let me in!" said Haaken Grizzlebeard.

"Shhhh! Shhhh! Keep quiet!" said the princess. "If my father hears there's a man here, I'll be most unhappy!"

"Oh *huttetuttetuttetu!* I'm almost freezing to death! Just let me come in and lie on the floor," said Haaken Grizzlebeard.

Well, there was no other way out. She had to let him in, and once he was inside, he lay down on the floor and slept quite well.

After a while Haaken came again, and this time he had the

uprights to the spinning wheel with him. So he sat down again outside the princess' window and started to file on the uprights, for they were not quite finished either. When she heard him filing, she opened the window and asked what he had there.

"Oh, the uprights to that spinning wheel the princess bought, for I supposed that as long as she wanted the spinning wheel, she just might need the uprights too," said Haaken.

"What'll you have for them then?" asked the king's daughter.

They weren't for sale either, but if he could lie on the floor of the princess' chamber tonight, she could have them.

Well, this he could do, but she asked him to keep quiet and not start shivering in the middle of the night and saying *huttetu.*

Haaken Grizzlebeard promised, all right, but later on in the night he started to shiver and freeze and carry on, and asked if he could not lie in front of the princess' bed. There was no way out, she had to let him do it if the king was not to hear. Then Haaken Grizzlebeard lay down on the floor in front of the princess' bed and slept both good and well.

Now it was a long time before Haaken Grizzlebeard came again, but then he had with him a golden reel. And in the morning he sat down outside the princess' window and started to file on it. When the princess heard that, she came to the window and greeted him and asked what he wanted for the reel.

"It's not for sale for money, but if I can sleep in your chamber with my head on the edge of the bed, you can have it," said Haaken Grizzlebeard.

Well, this he could do all right, if only he would be quiet and not make so much noise, said the princess, and he promised to do his best. But later on in the night he started to shiver and freeze so his teeth chattered.

"*Huttetuttetuttetu!* It's so cold! Oh let me come up in the bed and warm myself a little," said Haaken Grizzlebeard.

"I think you're mad!" said the king's daughter.

"*Huttetuttetu!*" said Haaken Grizzlebeard. "Oh, let me come up in the bed! *Huttetuttetuttetu!*"

"Shhhh! Shhhh! Be quiet, for God's sake!" said the king's daughter. "If my father hears there's a man here, I'll be most unhappy! I do believe he'd put an end to me on the spot!"

"*Huttetuttetuttetu!* Let me up in the bed!" said Haaken Grizzlebeard, and shivered so that the whole room shook.

There was no way out, she had to let him come up in the bed, and then he slept both good and well.

But after a while the princess had a little baby, and the king was so furious that he almost put an end to both her and the child. Some time after this Haaken Grizzlebeard happened to drop by there one day, as if by chance, and sat out in the kitchen just like any other beggar.

Then the king's daughter came out and caught sight of him: "Oh Lord have mercy! What a mess you've got me in!" she said. "My father's bursting with rage. Let me go home with you."

"You're used to too much to come home with me," said Haaken. "All I have is a shelter of pine boughs to stay in. And how I'll be able to get food for you, I don't know, for I struggle hard enough to get food for myself."

"Well, it makes no difference to me how you live," said the king's daughter. "Just let me come with you, for if I stay here any longer I think my father will take my life."

Then she was allowed to go with the tramp, as she called him, and they walked both far and long, and she was not any too well along the way. At last they left her father's kingdom and entered another, and the princess asked whose it was.

"Oh, it's Haaken Grizzlebeard's," he said.

"Oh, indeed?" said the princess. "I could have taken him, then I would not have to be wandering about here like a ragamuffin."

And all the finest castles and forests and farms they came to, she asked who owned them.

"Oh they're his—Haaken Grizzlebeard's," said the tramp. And as she walked, the princess wailed and carried on because she had not taken him, who owned so much.

At long last they came to a king's manor. He said they knew him well there, and he was pretty certain he could get work for her so they would have enough to live on. And then he put up a shelter of pine boughs on the edge of the forest where they were to live. He himself went to the king's manor and chopped

wood and carried in water for the cook, he said, and when he
came home again he had a few crumbs of food, but they did not
stretch far.

Then one day he came home from the castle. "Tomorrow I'll
stay home and mind the child, but you have to go to the castle,"
he said, "for the prince says you must come and help with the
baking in the oven."

"Me, bake?" said the king's daughter. "I can't bake! I've never
done that!"

"Well, you have to go," said Haaken Grizzlebeard, "as long
as he's said so. If you can't bake, you might just as well learn.
You'll have to watch and see how the others go about it, and
when you leave you must steal some bread for me."

"I can't steal!" said the king's daughter.

"You can certainly learn," said Haaken Grizzlebeard. "You
know food is scarce. But look out for the prince, because he keeps
an eye on everything!"

When she had gone, Haaken took a short cut and got to the
castle long before she did. He took off the rags and the beard
of moss and put on his royal finery.

The king's daughter helped with the baking and did as
Haaken had told her and stuffed all her pockets full of bread.
When she was ready to go home in the evening, the prince said:
"We don't know anything about this beggar woman. It's best
to see if she's taken anything with her."

Then he reached down in all her pockets, and dug and searched
about; and when he found the bread, he became angry and
made a terrible row.

She cried and carried on and said, "The tramp asked for it, so
I had to do it!"

"You should be severely punished," said the prince, "but never
mind. For the tramp's sake you shall be forgiven!"

When she was well on her way, he threw off his finery, pulled
on the fur robe, put on the beard of moss, and was back in the
pine shelter ahead of her. When she came, he was busy taking
care of the child.

"Well you've made me do something I regretted!" she said.
"That's the first time I've ever stolen anything, and it'll certainly

be the last time now!" And then she told him how it had gone and what the prince had said.

One evening, a few days later, Haaken came home to the pine shelter. "Tomorrow I'll have to stay home and mind the child," he said, "for you're to help with the butchering and sausage making."

"Me, make sausages?" said the king's daughter. "I can't do that! I've eaten sausages all right, but make them? Never!"

Well, Haaken said she had to go, as long as the prince had said so. She'd have to do what she saw the others doing, and then he said she was to steal some sausages for him.

"No, I can't steal!" she said. "You certainly remember how it went the last time!"

"You can learn how to steal," said Haaken. "It doesn't mean that it'll always go wrong." When she was well on her way, Haaken Grizzlebeard took the short cut and came to the castle long before she did. He threw off the fur robe and the beard and was standing in the kitchen in his fine robes when she came. The king's daughter helped with the butchering and sausage making, and she did as Haaken had said and stuffed her pockets full. But when she was ready to go home in the evening, the prince said, "This beggar woman was light-fingered the last time. It's certainly best to look and see if she hasn't taken anything." And he started searching and rummaging in all her pockets. When he found the sausages, he was angry and made a terrible row again and threatened to hand her over to the bailiff.

"Oh, Lord bless you, let me go! The tramp asked me to do it!" she said, and cried and carried on.

"Well, you should have been punished, but for the tramp's sake you shall be forgiven," said Haaken Grizzlebeard.

When she had gone, he threw off his finery, put on the fur robe and the beard of moss, and took the short cut. When she came home, he was already there ahead of her. She told him how it had gone, and vowed loud and long that it would be the last time he made her do anything like that.

After a while the tramp went to the king's manor again. "Now our prince is going to be married," he said when he came home in the evening, "but the bride is sick, and the tailor can't measure her for the bridal gown. So the prince wants you to come up to the castle and be measured in her place, for he says you resemble her in weight and everything. But after you've been measured, you're not to leave right away. You can just stay there and watch while the tailor cuts it out and then sweep up the biggest scraps and take them along for a cap for me!"

"No, I can't steal!" she said. "You must remember how it went the last time."

"You can certainly learn," said Haaken. "It doesn't mean it'll go wrong this time too!"

She knew it was wrong, but she went and did as he asked. She stood and watched while the tailor cut out the gown, and she swept up the biggest scraps and put them in her pocket. When she was to leave, the prince said, "We'll certainly have to see if the woman hasn't been light-fingered this time too," and started searching in all her pockets. And when he found the scraps, he was furious and started swearing and carrying on beyond words.

She cried and carried on badly, and said, "Oh the tramp asked me to do it, so then I had to!"

"Well, it should have gone badly with you, but for the tramp's sake you'll just have to be forgiven," said Haaken Grizzlebeard.

And then it went just like the other times. When she came home to the pine shelter, Haaken was already there.

"Oh, Lord help me!" she said. "You'll probably be the ruin of me in the end, for you only want me to do what's wrong! The prince was so wild and angry that he threatened me with both bailiff and workhouse!"

Some time later, Haaken came home one evening. "Now the prince wants you to come to the castle and be married," he said, "for his bride is sick and still in bed. But he wants to hold the wedding, and you're so like her that no one can tell you apart. In the morning you must get ready to go to the castle."

"I think you're out of your minds, both you and the prince!" she said. "Do you think I look like a bride? Why, there isn't a beggarwoman who looks worse than I do!"

There was no way out; she had to go. And when she came up to the king's manor, they dressed and fixed her up so that no princess could have been finer. They went to the church, and she was the bride, and when they came back home again there was dancing and revelry at the castle. But as she was dancing with the prince, she caught sight of a glow through the window, and then she saw that the pine shelter was all ablaze.

"Oh no! The poor tramp and the child and the pine shelter!" she cried, and was about to faint.

"Here's the tramp, and there's the child! Now let the shelter burn!" said Haaken Grizzlebeard, and then she recognized him again. Only then was there real merriment and joy; but since then I've neither heard nor asked a word about them!

## •75• *The Blue Band*

*Type 590, The Blue Band; R. Th. Christiansen, Norske Eventyr, 590, "Det blaa band." Collected by Jörgen Moe in Aadalen (eastern Norway) in the 1830's and printed in P. Chr. Asbjörnsen and Jörgen Moe, Norske Folkeeventyr (1852), No. 58.*

*This tale type has spread all over Europe and Asia and has also been carried to North and Central America. Especially interesting is a version collected among the Chipewayan Indians by E. P. Goddard, which closely resembles the present text. Stith Thompson thinks that the Chipewayan tale has been brought to North America by Scandinavians in fairly recent times (European Tales among the North American Indians, Colorado Springs, 1919, pp. 391–95).*

• THERE WAS ONCE a poor woman who went about a certain parish begging. She had a little boy with her. When her bag was full, she headed north up the ridge, and was on her way home to her own parish again.

When they had come a little way up the side of the ridge, they caught sight of a little blue band lying in the pack trail. The boy asked if he could pick it up.

"No," said the mother. "There can be some devilment about it." And then she made the boy come with her.

When they had come a little farther up, the boy said he had to leave the road a bit. In the meantime the woman sat down on a log. But the boy was gone a long time, for when he was off in the wood where the woman could not see him he ran down to where the hoseband lay, picked it up, and tied it round his waist. Then he became so strong that he felt he could lift the whole ridge.

When he came back, the woman was furious and asked what had taken him so long. "You're not worried about the time," she said, "even though it's getting on toward evening. You know we must get over the ridge before it gets dark."

Then they walked for a while, but when they had come half-way or more across the ridge, the woman grew tired and wanted to lie down under a bush.

"My dear mother," said the boy, "may I go up on this high hill here, while you're resting, and see if I can't find some sign of life?"

This he was allowed to do, and when he came up on the top he saw a light shining due north of there. The boy ran back and said to the woman, "We'll have to go on, mother. People aren't far off. I can see a bright light shining just north of here!"

She got up, grabbed the sack, and wanted to go with him to see. But they had not gone far when they came to a spur of the ridge. "I might have known!" said the woman. "Now we can't go any farther. It's probably best to lie here!"

But the boy took the sack under one arm and the woman under the other and headed up the spur of the ridge with them. "Now you can see that people aren't far off. See how bright it's shining," he said.

But the woman said it was not people, it must be a mountain troll. She knew every inch of the bear forest, and there was not a soul to be found anywhere before they came to the bottom of the ridge on the north side.

When they had gone a little way they came to a big red-painted manor.

"We're not going in," said the woman, "a mountain troll lives here!"

"Oh, of course we're going in; we can see a light. No doubt

there are people inside," said the boy. He went in first, and the woman after him, but at the same moment as he opened the door she fainted, for she caught sight of a great big man sitting on a stool.

"Good evening, grandfather," said the boy.

"Now I've been sitting here for three hundred years, but nobody's ever come who called me grandfather," said the man who sat on the stool.

The boy sat down beside the man and started talking with him as if they were old friends.

"But how's your mother getting on?" said the man after they had been talking for a while. "I think she's fainted. You'd better have a look at her."

The boy went over, took hold of the woman, and dragged her in across the floor. Then she came to and crawled over and seated herself well inside the corner where the wood was stacked. But she was so frightened that she hardly dared peek out.

After a bit the boy asked if the man could put them up for the night. Yes he could, said the man. Then they went on talking for a while; soon the boy grew hungry and asked if they could have something to eat too. Yes, the man thought that could certainly be arranged.

When they had been sitting there a bit, he got up and put six loads of dry spruce wood on the fire. The woman grew even more frightened. "Now he wants to burn us up too!" she said over in the corner where she sat.

When the dry spruce had burned down to coals, the man got up and went out. "Lord have mercy on you!" You're so fool-hardy! Don't you see you're with a troll?" said the woman.

"Oh, pooh! That doesn't matter," said the boy.

In a little while the man came in with an ox that was so big and huge that the boy had never seen anything like it. The troll struck the ox with his fist under the ear and it dropped dead to the floor. When this was done, he took it by all fours, put it on the coals, and turned it until it was roasted brown on the outside. Then he went over to a cupboard, took out a silver dish, and put the ox on it, and the dish was so big that the ox did not stick out over the edge on any side. This he put on the table; then he went down in the cellar and brought up a pail of wine, knocked off the lid, and put the pail up on the table, and then he set out two knives that were three *alens* [about 2 ft.] long. When he had done this, he bade them go over to the table and sit down and eat.

The boy went ahead and told the woman to follow him. She started to wail and carry on and wondered how she was going to manage these knives. But the boy grabbed one of them and started carving pieces of meat out of the ox's thigh and handing them over to his mother. After they had eaten for a while, he took the pail of wine between his hands and lifted it down to the floor. Then he told his mother to come and have a drink. It was so high that she could not reach the edge, but the boy lifted her up and held her. And then he climbed up and hung over the edge like a cat while he drank. When he had drunk his fill, he put the pail of wine back on the table, said his thanks for the food, and told his mother that she must come and say her thanks too. And as afraid as she was, she dared not do otherwise than go over and thank the man for the food. The boy sat down beside the man on the stool and started talking with him again.

After they had been sitting there for a little while, the man said, "I'd better get up and have a bit of supper too." Then he went over to the table and ate the whole ox, bones and horns and all. He took the pail of wine and drank from it and then sat down on the stool again.

"I don't know what to do about beds," he said. "I have nothing but a cradle here. It could most likely do for you to lie in that and your mother could lie over there in my bed."

"Yes, thanks, that was good enough," said the boy. He tore off his clothes and lay down in the cradle, which was as big as a huge four-poster bed, and the woman had to follow the man and lie down in the bed, as frightened as she was.

"It's not worth going to sleep here; I'd better stay awake and hear what happens later on tonight," thought the boy.

After a while the man started talking with the woman. "Here we could live quite comfortably and well, if only we were rid of that son of yours," said the man.

"Don't you know of any way to do it?" said the woman.

Oh yes, he would try, he said. He would pretend that he wanted the woman to keep house for him for a few days. Then he would get the boy over in the mountain to dig up cornerstones and turn a mountain over on him.

The boy lay there listening to this.

The next day the troll asked—for it was a troll, that was easy to tell—if the woman could keep house for him for a few days, and later on in the day the troll took a big iron pole and asked the boy if he would go over to the mountain with him to dig up cornerstones.

After they had unearthed some stones, the troll wanted him to go down a little way and look for cracks in the mountain. While the boy did this, the troll turned and twisted with the iron pole until he sent off a whole mountain, which came tumbling down over the boy. But the boy held it off until he got out of the way, and then let the mountain fall.

"Now I see what you want to do with me," said the boy to the troll. "You want to kill me. But now you go down and look for cracks, and I'll stand up above."

The troll dared not do other than the boy had said, and the boy broke down a huge mountain, which tumbled over the troll and broke one of his thighs.

"Oh, what a poor wretch you are!" said the boy. He climbed down and lifted up the mountain and carried the troll out of the way. And then he had to put him on his back and carry him home. He rushed off with him like a horse and shook him so he shrieked as if a knife were sticking in him. When they came home they had to put the troll to bed, and there he lay, and feeble he was.

Later on in the night, the troll started talking with the woman again, wondering how he was going to get rid of the boy.

"Well, if you don't know of a way to get rid of him, then I don't!" said the woman.

Why, yes, he had twelve lions in a garden, said the troll. If they could only get the boy there, the lions would tear him to pieces. The woman thought this wouldn't be so hard. She would pretend to be sick and say that she was so feeble she could not be well again unless she got some lion's milk.

The boy lay there listening to this. When he got up in the morning, the woman said she was feeling feebler than anyone could imagine, and if she did not get some lion's milk she would certainly never be well again.

"Then I dare say you'll be feeling feeble for a long time, Mother, for I don't know where that's to be found."

Well, the troll thought there was no difficulty in getting some lion's milk, if only someone would go after it. His brothers had a garden in which there were twelve lions, and the boy could have the key if he thought he could milk them.

The boy took the key and the milk pail and strode away. When he had unlocked the gate and was inside the garden, all twelve of the lions reared up on their hind legs at him. The boy picked out the biggest one, took it by the forepaws, and dashed it against sticks and stones until nothing was left of it but its paws. When the other lions saw this, they became so frightened that they crawled over and lay down at his feet like cowardly dogs. Afterward they followed him wherever he went, and when he came home they lay down outside with their forepaws on the doorsill.

"Now you'll be well again, for here is lion's milk, Mother," said the boy when he came in, for he had milked a few drops into the pail.

But the troll lying over in the bed swore that it was not true; it took a better man than the boy was to milk a lion.

When the boy heard that, he made the troll get out of bed and then yanked open the door. The lions reared up at the troll and sprang upon him, so that the boy had to go between and loosen their hold.

Later on in the night the troll started talking with the woman again. "I don't know how we're going to take the life of that boy," said the troll. "He's much too strong. Don't you know of a way?" he said to the woman.

"No, if you don't know of a way then I don't," said the woman.

"Well, I have two brothers at a certain castle," said the troll.

"They're twelve times stronger than I am; that's why I was thrown out and got the manor. They use the castle, and there's an orchard there with apples in it that are such that whoever takes a bite out of them will sleep for three days. Now if we could send that boy there after some apples! He would not be able to keep from tasting them, and once he was asleep, my brothers would tear him to bits."

The woman said she would have to pretend she was sick, and say she could not be well until she got some of those apples. Then he would go after them, all right. All the while the boy lay there listening to this.

In the morning the woman was so sick and feeble that she could not be cured unless she got apples from the orchard which lay beside the troll brothers' castle. But she had no one to send there.

Well, the boy was willing to go, and the eleven lions went with him. When he came to the orchard, he climbed up in the apple tree and ate as many apples as he was able, and scarcely had he climbed down again before he went to sleep. But the lions lay down in a ring around him. On the third day the troll's brothers came. But they did not come as trolls; they came bellowing along in the shape of vicious bulls. They had come to find out who this might be who had lain down there. And they said they were going to pluck him to pieces as small as grain, so there would not be a shred of him left. But the lions rushed up and tore the trolls into tiny bits, so it looked as if a scrap heap had been made there. And when they finished, they lay down around the boy again. He did not wake up until late in the afternoon. When he had got to his knees and rubbed the sleep out of his eyes, he wondered what had happened when he saw all the signs of the battle.

But when he came over to the castle, there was a maiden there who had seen what had happened, and she said, "You can thank God that you weren't in that fight, or else you'd have lost your life."

"What? Me lose my life?" said the boy. There was no danger of that, he thought.

Then she asked him to come in so she could talk with him. She had not seen a Christian soul since she came there.

When he opened the gate, the lions wanted to go in too. But she was so frightened that she shrieked and carried on, so the boy made them lie down outside. Then they talked about everything under the sun, and the boy asked how it had come about that such a pretty girl as she was living with those ugly trolls. She had not wanted to live with them, she said; she was not there of her own free will, for they had taken her. She was the King of Arabia's daughter. As they sat there talking, she asked what he would like: either for her to go home, or would he have her? Well, of course he would have her!

Then they wandered about the castle and looked around, and at last they came to a great hall. High up on the wall hung two huge swords which had belonged to the trolls.

"If only you were man enough to use one of those," said the king's daughter.

"Who, me?" said the boy. "Can't I use one of these? That shouldn't be any problem!" He piled two or three chairs on top of one another, hopped up, and took the biggest sword with two fingers. He threw it up in the air, caught it again by the handle, and stood it up in the floor so the whole hall shook. Then when he came down, he put it under his arm and carried it along with him.

After they had been in the castle for a while, the king's daughter felt that she should go home to her parents and tell them what had become of her. They fitted out a ship, and then she set out on her way.

When she had gone, the boy stayed about there for a while, then he remembered that he had come there on an errand; he was to fetch a remedy for his mother. But he thought that perhaps the woman had not been so sick after all and probably was well again. Still, he wanted to go down and see how they were getting along.

The man was well, and the woman had long since got better too.

"What miserable creatures you are to sit down here in this

ramshackle hut," said the boy. "Come with me up to my castle, and you'll see that I'm an important fellow," he said.

Well, both the man and the woman went with him, and on the way she talked sweetly to him and asked how he had become so strong.

Why, yes, it had come from that blue band which had lain on the ridge the time they'd been out begging in the parish, said the boy.

"Do you still have it?" asked the woman.

Yes, he had it, he had it under the waistband of his pants, he said. Then the woman asked if she could see it. Well, the boy pulled up his jacket and his undershirt and was going to show it to her. Then she grabbed at it with both hands, yanked it from him and wound it around her fist.

"What should I do with a wretch like you?" she said. "I ought to beat your brains to a pulp!"

"That's too easy a death for such a scoundrel," said the troll. "We ought to burn out his eyes and put him to sea in a little boat!"

This they did, too, for all he cried and carried on.

But wherever the boat drifted the lions swam after it, and at last they took it and dragged it ashore on an island and propped up the boy under a fir tree. They caught game for him and plucked birds and made a whole bed of down for him. But he had to eat everything raw, and he was blind.

Then one day the biggest lion was chasing a hare. The hare was blind, for it was running into sticks and stones, and at last it ran right into a tree trunk and knocked itself head over heels backward down the hill, right into a little tarn. But when it came up out of the water again, it could see its way quite well, and so it saved its life.

"Well, well!" thought the lion. He dragged the boy to the tarn and pushed him down in it. When the boy recovered his sight, he went down to the sea and made signs to the lions to lie side by side in the water like a raft. Then he stood on their backs while they swam to the mainland with him.

When he was safely ashore, he went up into a grove of birches; there he let the lions lie down again. Then he softly stole over to the castle to see if he could get hold of his band. When he came to the door he peeked in through the keyhole and saw the band hanging over a door in the kitchen. He strode across the floor—for there was no one inside—and got hold of the band. Then he started banging his heels and kicking his legs as if he had lost his wits. At the same moment the woman came rushing out.

"My dear, sweet little boy! Let me have that band!" she said.

"No thanks! Now you shall receive the same sentence you wanted to pass on me," said the boy, and he carried it out at once.

When the troll heard the commotion, he came in and pleaded and begged for his life.

"Yes, you shall live all right, but you shall receive the same punishment you gave to me," said the boy. And then he burnt out the troll's eyes, and put him to sea in a boat—but the troll had no lions to follow him.

Now the boy was alone, and he went about the castle longing for the king's daughter. At last he could hold out no longer. He fitted out four ships and set sail for Arabia after her. For a while they had a good and favourable wind, but then they lay becalmed off a rocky island. Here the sailors went ashore and wandered about to while away the time. After a while they found an enormous egg almost the size of a house. They started hitting and beating on it with large stones but were not able to break it. The boy followed with his sword, to see what all the commotion was about. When he caught sight of the egg he knew it would be an easy matter to break it into pieces. He took a swing with the sword and split the egg wide open, and out came a baby bird as big as an elephant.

"Now we've really got ourselves into trouble," cried the boy. "This may cost us our lives." And then he asked the seamen if they could sail to Arabia in twenty-four hours if they got a good wind.

Yes, they thought they ought to be able to do it.

Then they got a good wind and sailed away and were ashore in Arabia in twenty-three hours. At once the boy ordered the seamen to go up and bury themselves in a mound of sand, so they could just see the ships. The captain and the boy went up onto a high mountain and sat down under a fir tree. An hour later the bird came with the island in its claws, and dropped it over the fleet of ships so they sank. When that was done, it went to the mound of sand and started beating its wings so it almost took off the sailors' heads, and flew up under the tree so fast that the boy was swung around. But the boy was ready with the sword and slashed at the bird until it fell down dead.

Then he went to the city, and here there had been great rejoicing because the king had got back his daughter again. But now he had hidden her away and had proclaimed that the one who could find her could have her, even though she were promised to someone else.

As he was walking along, the boy met a fellow who was selling white bearskins. He bought one of these skins and put it on. He had one of the captains take an iron chain and lead him by it, and so he wandered about the city performing tricks.

At last news of the unusual performance reached the ears of the king. The white bear danced in every possible way just as its master commanded. Then word came that he was to come to the king and perform tricks there, for the king wanted to see him.

When he came in, they all became frightened, for they had never seen such an animal before. But the captain said there was nothing to fear unless they laughed at it. This they must not do or else it would kill them. When the king heard this, he warned the courtiers and told them they must not laugh. But after a while the king's handmaid came in and started showing off and laughing. Then the white bear swung at her so hard that she flew into pieces. The courtiers started crying and carrying on, and the captain most of all.

"Oh, pooh!" said the king. "It's only a matter of a hand-maiden. That's my business, not yours."

When they finished, it was late at night. "There's no point in your taking the bear out now that it's so late," said the king. "It can sleep here tonight."

"Perhaps it can lie behind the stove?" said the captain.

"No, it shall have pillows and quilts to lie upon," said the king, and took out a whole pile of them. The captain was allowed to sleep in a chamber beside it.

In the middle of the night, the king came with a light and a huge bunch of keys and led the white bear with him. He went through porches and covered passageways, one after the other, through doors and rooms, upstairs and down. At last he came out on a pier which headed right out to sea. Here the king started shaking sticks and jolting pegs, dragging first one up and another down, until a little house floated up. Here he had his daughter, for he was so fond of her that he had hidden her so no one could find her. He left the white bear outside the door, while he went in and told her about the bear and the dancing and the tricks. She said she was afraid and dared not look at it. But the king persuaded her to and said there was no danger as long as she did not laugh. Then he let in the bear, and it danced and performed tricks. But all at once the princess' handmaiden started to laugh. With that the boy swung at her so hard that she flew to pieces, and the princess wailed and carried on badly.

"Oh, pooh!" said the king. "It's only a matter of a handmaiden, and I can get you another good handmaiden again. But now it's best that the bear stays here tonight, for I don't feel like running back with it through all the passageways and porches at this time of night."

No, she did not dare stay there then, said the princess.

But the bear curled up in a ball behind the stove, and in the end the princess went to bed and left the lights burning. But when the king was well out of the way, the white bear came and asked her to loosen the collar. The princess was so frightened that she was almost ready to faint, but she fumbled until she found it, and scarcely had she opened it when he threw off the white bear's head. Then she knew him again and was happy beyond words and wanted to tell her father at once that he was the one who had freed her. But he did not want her to do that, he wanted to do her one more favor, he said.

When they heard the king pottering around with the sticks in the morning, the boy pulled on the bearskin and lay down behind the stove.

"Well, has it lain still?" asked the king.

"Heavens, yes!" said the princess. "It hasn't so much as lifted its paw."

Up at the castle the captain took the bear back again. Then the boy went to a master tailor and had himself fitted for a prince's clothing. And when they were ready, he went up to the king and said that he had a mind to seek out the princess.

"There are many who've had a mind to do that," said the king, "but they've lost their lives, every last one of them. For the one who can't find her in twenty-four hours has forfeited his life."

Well, there was no danger in that, said the boy. He wanted to search, and if he did not find her, that would be his business.

But at the castle there were fiddlers to play and maidens to dance with, and the boy danced the time away.

After twelve hours, the king came and said, "I feel sorry for you. You're such a poor searcher that you'll most likely lose your life!"

"Oh, pooh! There's nothing wrong with the corpse as long as it sneezes! We have plenty of time," said the boy, and went on dancing until there was no more than an hour left. Then he said he would start searching.

"Oh, there's no use!" said the king. "Now the time is up."

"Light a lantern and out with your big bunch of keys," said the boy, "and follow me wherever I want to go! There's still a whole hour left."

The boy went the same way the king had gone the night before and ordered him to unlock every door, until he came to the pier which led straight out to sea.

"Now there's no use! The time is up and you're heading right to sea!" said the king.

"There are still five minutes left," said the boy, and yanked and pulled at the logs and sticks so the house floated up.

"Now the time is up!" shrieked the king. "Come now, my fencing master, and take off his head!"

"No, stop a bit!" said the boy. "There are still three minutes left. Out with the key so I can go in."

But the king stood there, fumbling and groping after the key, and, to draw out the time, said he could not find the right one.

"If you haven't got it, then I have one myself," said the boy and kicked the door so that it flew to bits across the floor.

The princess met him in the doorway and said that he was the one who had freed her, and he was the one she would have. So the king agreed, and the boy was wed to the King of Arabia's daughter.

## •76• *Stupid Men and Shrewish Wives*

*Type 1460, The Merry Wives Wager; R. Th. Christiansen, Norske Eventyr, 1460, "Dumme maend og trold til khaer-ringer," No. 4. Collected by P. Chr. Asbjörnsen in Sogn (western Norway) in 1847 and printed in Asbjörnsen and Jörgen Moe, Norske Folkeeventyr (1852), No. 18.*

*This tale has been reported from most parts of Europe, and it is also known in Near Eastern and Anglo-American traditions. A variant from Iraq is No. 69 in* Folktales of Israel, *a companion volume in this series. W. A. Clouston discusses comic stories about foolish people who have been made to believe that they are dead in his* The Book of Noodles, *p. 163.*

• THERE WERE ONCE two wives who were always quarreling, the way some wives do now and then, and, as they had nothing better to quarrel about, they started bickering about their husbands: about which one was the stupidest of the two. The longer they quarreled, the angrier they grew, and at last they were on the verge of coming to blows. For one thing is certain: "A quarrel is more easily stirred than stilled, and it's a bad thing when common sense is lacking."

The first wife said that there was not a thing she could not make her husband believe if she but said it was true, for he was as gullible as the trolls! And the second wife said that no matter how wrong it might be, she could make her husband do any-thing if she said it should be done, for he was the kind who could not see through a ladder.

"Well, let's see which one of us can fool them the best. Then we'll find out which husband is the stupidest," they said, and this they agreed to do.

Now, when her husband came home from the woods, the first wife cried, "Heaven help me! Why, this is awful! You must be sick, if you're not already dying!"

"There's nothing wrong with me that food and drink won't cure!" said the man.

"God save me if it isn't true!" sobbed the wife. "It's getting worse and worse all right; you look as pale as a corpse. You'd better lie down! Oh, you won't last long at all!"

Thus she carried on until she got the man to believe that he was at death's door. She got him to lie down, fold his hands, and close his eyes. Then she stretched him out, put him in a shroud, and laid him in a coffin. But, so he would not suffocate while he was in there, she made some holes in the boards so he could breathe and peek out.

The other wife, she took a pair of carders, sat down, and started carding. But she had no wool on them. Her husband came in and looked at what she was doing.

"It helps little to spin without a wheel, but to card without wool, a wife is a fool," said the man.

"Without wool?" said the wife. "Why, of course I have wool, but you can't see it because it's the finest kind!"

When she had finished carding, she got out the spinning wheel and started to spin.

"Nay! This is going right to the dogs!" said the man. "Why, you're sitting there whirling and spoiling your wheel without anything on it!"

"Without anything on it?" said the wife. "The thread is so fine that it takes better eyes than yours to see it."

When she had finished spinning, she set up the loom and threaded it and wove the cloth. Then she took it off the loom, and cut it out, and sewed clothes out of it for her husband. And when they were finished she hung them up in the *stabbur* loft. The man could see neither cloth nor clothes, but now he had come to believe that they were so fine that he could not see them, and so he said, "Well, well, as long as they're so fine, it's lucky I am to have them."

But one day his wife said to him, "Today you must go to a burial feast. The man at the North farm is getting buried today, so you have to have on your new clothes." Well, well, go to the burial feast he should, and the wife helped him on with the clothes, for they were so fine that he would tear them to pieces if he did it himself.

When he came up to the farm to the burial feast, they had already been drinking hard and fast, and their grief was not any greater when they caught sight of him with his new church-going clothes on, I dare say.

But as they were on the way to the graveyard, and the dead man peeked out through the breathing holes, he almost split his sides laughing. "Well, now I have to laugh!" he said. "If it isn't old Ola South Farm at my burial feast as naked as the day he was born!"

When people in the funeral procession heard that, it did not take them long to get the lid off the coffin. And the one with the new church-going clothes on asked how it could be that he lay in the coffin, talking and laughing, when they were holding a burial feast for him. Why, it would be more fitting if he cried.

"Tears never dug anyone up out of the grave," said the other. But the longer they talked together, the more clear it became that the wives had arranged the whole thing between them. So the husbands went home and did the wisest thing they had ever done. And if anybody wants to know what that was, then he'd better ask the birch rod!

# •77• Some Wives Are That Way

*Type 1384, The Husband Hunts Three Persons as Stupid as His Wife; R. Th. Christiansen, Norske Eventyr, 1384, "Somme kjaerringer er slike," No. 1. Collected by P. Chr. Asbjörnsen in Gjerdrum, Romerike (eastern Norway), in the 1830's and printed in Asbjörnsen and Jörgen Moe, Norske Folkeventyr (1852), No. 10.*

*This tale is known all over Europe and has also been found in the traditions of the New World and in Africa. In the present text the farm woman thinks that the man from Ringerike comes from Himmerike (the heavenly paradise). In a Latin poem of 1509, a monk on his wanderings from Paris to Mecheln asks a farm woman for water; she thinks that he comes from paradise instead of Paris and asks the monk about her deceased husband. See Bolte-Polívka, II, 441–46. A Pennsylvania German variant is in R. M. Dorson,* Buying the Wind *(Chicago, University of Chicago Press, 1964), pp. 132–33.*

• THERE WERE ONCE a man and his wife who wanted to plant corn, but they had no seed corn, nor did they have any money to buy it with. A single cow they had, and this the man was to take to town and sell, to get money for the corn. But, when all was said and done, the wife did not dare let the husband go, for she was afraid he would drink up the money. So she set out with the cow herself, and took along a hen, too. Close to the town she met a butcher.

"Are you going to sell that cow, mother?" he asked.

"Yes, indeed I am," she said.

"What'll you have for it then?"

"I probably ought to have a *mark* for the cow, but you can have the hen for ten *dalers* [ten *dalers* equals one *mark*]," she said.

"Well, I've no use for the hen," he replied, "and you'll probably get rid of it when you get to town. But I'll give you a *mark* for the cow."

She sold her cow and got her *mark,* but there was no one in the town who'd give ten *dalers* for a dry, scrawny hen. So she went back to the butcher again and said, "I can't get rid of the hen, father. You'd just better take it too since you kept the cow."

"We'll work that out all right," said the butcher, and invited her to dine; and he gave her food and poured her so many glasses of wine that she became drunk and lost her wits completely.

While she slept, the butcher dipped her in a barrel of tar and then rolled her in a pile of feathers.

When she awoke, she was feathered all over, and started to wonder, "Is this me, or isn't it me? No, me it could never be!

It must be a big, strange bird. But how am I to find out whether it is me or not? Why yes, now I know; if the calves lick me and the dog doesn't growl at me when I come home, then it's me!"

The dog had never seen such a strange creature before, so it started barking furiously as though both thieves and tramps were at the farm. "No, it certainly can't be me," she said. When she went into the cowshed, the calves would not lick her, for they could smell the tar. "No, this can't be me. It must be a strange bird!" she said. So she crawled up onto the roof of the *stabbur* and started flapping her arms as though they were wings, trying to fly.

When the man saw this, he came out with the gun and started aiming.

"Oh, don't shoot! Don't shoot!" shouted the wife. "It's me!"

"If that's you," said the man, "don't stand up there like a goat! Come down here and give an accounting of yourself!"

Then she climbed down again, but she did not have a single shilling, for in her drunkenness she had thrown away the *mark* she had got from the butcher. When the man heard that, he said, "You're just as crazy as you've always been!" He was so angry that he swore he was leaving her, and he would never come back unless he met three other wives who were just as crazy as she.

He wandered off, and when he had gone a short way he caught sight of a woman who was running in and out of a newly built cottage with a sieve. Each time she ran in, she threw her apron over the sieve, as if she had something in it, and emptied it out on the floor.

"Why are you doing that, mother?" he asked.

"Oh, I only want to carry in a little sunshine," answered the old wife. "But I don't know how it is; when I'm outside, I have the sun in the sieve, but when I come in I've lost it all. When I was in my old cottage, I had sun enough even though I never carried in a drop. If only someone could get sunshine for me, I'd gladly give him three hundred *dalers*!"

"If you've got an ax," said the man, "I'll get you sunshine all right!"

He got an ax and chopped holes for windows, for the carpenters had forgotten them. At once the sunshine poured in, and he got his three hundred *dalers*.

That was the first one, thought the man, and went on his way again.

After a while he came to a house, and there he heard a terrible crying and yelling. He went in and saw an old woman who was beating her husband on the head with a bat. Over his head she had pulled a shirt which had no opening in it for the neck.

"Do you want to beat your husband to death, mother?" he asked.

"No, I just want a hole for the neck in this shirt!"

The man kept shrieking and carrying on. He cried, "Oh, save and preserve the one who has to put on a new shirt! If anyone could teach my wife another way of making a hole for the neck in the shirts she makes, I'd gladly give him three hundred *dalers*!"

"That's soon done, just bring the scissors," said the other. He got the scissors, clipped a hole, and then went on his way with the money.

That was the second one, he said to himself.

At long last he came to a farm. There he thought he would rest for a while, and so he went in.

"Where are you from, father?" asked the old wife.

"I'm from Ringerike," he replied.

"Oh my! Oh my! Are you from Hemmerike [heaven]? Then you certainly must know Per Number Two, my blessed husband?"

The wife had been married three times. The first and last husbands had been bad, and so she thought that only the second one was blessed, for he had been such a kind man.

"Yes, I know *him* well," said the man.

"How's he getting along now?" asked the wife.

"Oh, he's badly off," said the Ringerike man. "He rambles from farm to farm up there, with neither a bite to eat nor a stitch on his body—not to mention money!"

"Oh, mercy upon him!" said the wife. "Why, he needn't go about so wretchedly, as much as he left behind, Why, there's a big attic full of clothes that belonged to him, and there's a big chest of money standing here too. If you'll take it to him, you can have both a horse and buggy to drive it with. And he can keep the horse and sit in the buggy and drive from farm to farm, so he won't have to walk!"

The Ringerike man got a whole buggy load of clothing and a chest full of shiny silver money and as much food and drink as he wanted. He seated himself in the buggy and drove on his way.

That was the third one, he said to himself.

But over in the field, the woman's third husband was ploughing, and when he saw a stranger driving off with the horse and buggy he went home and asked the wife who that was who rushed off with the little bay.

"Oh, him?" she said. "That was a man from Himmerike. He said that Per Number Two, my blessed husband, is so badly off that he goes from farm to farm up there with neither clothes nor money. So I sent with him all those old clothes, which have been hanging here since he died, and that old money chest with the silver *dalers* in it."

The man, who understood at once what was going on, saddled a horse and rushed off at full gallop. It was not long before he was right behind the one who was driving the buggy. When the other noticed that, he drove the horse and buggy off into the woods, yanked a handful of hair from the horse's tail, and ran up to the top of a hill. There he fastened the horse hairs to a birch tree and then lay down under the tree and started staring up into the sky.

"My! My! My!" he said as if to himself, when Per Number Three came riding up. "No, I've never seen anything so strange! No! I've never seen the like!"

Per stood looking at him for a while, wondering if he were crazy or what it was all about. At last he asked him, "Why are you lying there gaping into the sky?"

"No, I've never seen the like of this!" said the other. "There goes a fellow straight up to heaven with a bay horse. Here you can see the horse hair hanging behind in the birch, and up there in the sky you can see that little bay of his."

Per looked at the clouds, and from the clouds to the man, and said, "I don't see anything but the horse hairs in the birch, I swear I don't."

"No, you can't see it there where you're standing," said the other. "But come here and lie down and stare straight up, but you mustn't take your eyes off the clouds."

While Per Number Three was lying there, staring up at the clouds until his eyes ran, the Ringeriker took his horse and mounted it and rode off with both it and the buggy. When Per Number Three heard rumbling of the buggy, up he jumped. But he was so confused, because his horse was gone, that it did not occur to him to set off on foot after the man from Ringerike.

Now he had been left both bare and broke, but when he came home to his wife, and she asked what he'd done with the horse, he said, "I also gave it away to Per Number Two, I did, for I didn't think a buggy was good enough for him to sit on and rattle about from farm to farm in Heaven. Now he can sell the buggy and buy himself a carriage to drive."

"Thanks to you for that!" said the wife. "Never did I think you were so kind!"

Now, when the one who had collected the six hundred *dalers* and the buggy load of clothes and money came home, he saw that all the fields had been ploughed and sown. The first thing he asked the wife about was where she got the seed corn from.

"Oh, I've always heard that whatsoever a man soweth, that shall he also reap. So I sowed the salt which that traveler from the north left here, and if only it rains soon, I think it'll come up fine!"

"Crazy you are, and crazy you'll be as long as you live," said the man, "but it doesn't matter, for the others are no better than you."

## ·78· *Mastermaid*

Type 313, The Girl as Helper in the Hero's Flight; *R. Th. Christiansen, Norske Eventyr, 313,* "Flugten fra trollet. Mestermö. Ranei paa Stinen," *No. 16. Collected by Jörgen Moe in*

*Seljord, Telemark, in the 1840's and printed in P. Chr. Asbjörn-*
*sen and Jörgen Moe,* Norske Folkeeventyr *(1852), No. 46.*

*One of the world's most widespread tale types, this folktale*
*has been extensively collected in Norway. Type 313 is an old*
*folktale well known in ancient Greece, as demonstrated in the*
*Jason and Medea story. R. Th. Christiansen has found two*
*widely distributed Norwegian variants with some apparent*
*Gaelic features, perhaps pointing to old Gaelic-Norse relations.*
*See Christiansen, "A Gaelic Fairytale in Norway,"* Bealoideas,
*I (1927), 107–14.*

*Variants of this tale are given in* Folktales of Japan *and* Folktales of Hungary, *companion volumes in this series. See tale No.*
*23 in the former and No. 3 in the latter.*

• THERE WAS ONCE a king who had several sons. I don't rightly
know how many there were, but there were so many that the
youngest son did not want to settle down at home. He just had
to go out into the world to seek his fortune, and at long last
the king agreed to let him go.

After he had been journeying for several days, he came to a
troll's manor, and there he entered into the troll's service. In
the morning the troll was going out to herd the goats, and as
he was leaving he told the king's son that he was to shovel out
the stable.

"When you've done that, you won't have to do any more
today, for I want you to know you've come to a kind master,"
he said. "But whatever you're set to doing, you're to do both
good and well. And then you're not to go into any of the rooms
beyond the room you were in last night. If you do, I'll take
your life!"

"Indeed he is a kind master too!" said the king's son to
himself. He walked to and fro, and hummed and sang, for
he thought there was plenty of time to shovel out the stable.
"But it would be fun to peek into his other rooms all the same.
There must be something he's afraid of, since I'm not allowed
to go in there," he thought, and then he went into the first
room. A cauldron hung cooking on the wall, but the king's son
could see no fire under it.

"I wonder what's in there?" he thought, and dipped a lock of his hair down in it. When he took it out, his hair looked as if it were made of copper, each and every strand of it. "That is a funny soup. If anyone tasted it, he'd have copper lips!" said the boy, and with that he went into the next room. A cauldron hung bubbling and cooking on the wall, but there was no fire under it either.

"I'll have to try this one too," said the king's son, and stuck the lock of hair down in it. Then his hair looked as if it were made of silver. "They don't have such costly soup at my father's manor!" said the king's son. "But the question is: how does it taste?" And with that he went into the third room. There a cauldron also hung cooking on the wall, and the king's son wanted to try it too. So he dipped the lock down in it, and then it was gilded with gold so brightly that it shone.

"Slays me!" as the old woman said when she meant to say, 'Praise be!' But if he's cooking gold in here, I wonder what he's cooking in the next room." This he wanted to see, and he went through the door into the fourth room. No cauldron was to be seen, but a maiden was in the room, sitting on a bench. She was a king's daughter, that was certain, for she was so beautiful that the king's son had never seen anything like her in all his born days.

"God have mercy!" said the maiden who was sitting on the bench. "What do you want here?"

"I've entered into service here yesterday," said the king's son.

"God help you, for a place you've come to work!" she said.

"Oh, I think I've got a kind master, I have," said the king's son. "He hasn't given me any hard work to do today. After I've shoveled out the stable. I have nothing more to do."

"Well, how do you plan to go about it?" she asked. "If you shovel the way people usually do, ten shovelfuls will come in for every one you throw out! But I'll teach you how to do it. You're to turn the dung fork upside down and shovel with the handle. Then it'll all fly out by itself."

Well, he'd be sure to do that, thought the king's son, and then he remained sitting in there all day, for the two of them soon discovered that they loved one another—and so the first day he served the troll certainly did not seem long to him, I dare say.

But as it was getting on toward evening, she said that now he had better shovel the stable clean before the troll came home. When he got out in the stable, he wanted to see if what she had said was true. First he started shoveling the way he had seen the stableboys doing at his father's manor. But I do believe he had to stop that, for after he had been shoveling a little while there was scarcely any room left to stand in. Then he did as the king's daughter had said; he turned the dungfork upside down and shoveled with the handle. And then it did not take a moment before the stable was as clean as if it had been scrubbed. When this was done, he went back into the room where the troll had said he could stay, and there he paced back and forth and started to hum and sing.

Then the troll came home with the goats. "Have you shoveled out the stable?" asked the troll.

"Yes, now it's clean and tidy, master!" said the king's son.

"This I have to see!" said the troll, and went out to the stable. He saw that it was just as the king's son had said. "You must have been talking to my mastermaid, for you could never have sucked this out of your own breast!" said the troll.

"Mastermaid? What sort of thing might that be, master?" said the king's son, pretending to be as stupid as a fool. "That would be fun to see."

"Oh, you'll get to see her soon enough!" said the troll.

On the second morning, the troll was going out again with his goats. Then he told the king's son that today he was to bring home his horse, which was grazing up on the mountain. And when he had done this, he could take it easy the rest of the day, "for I want you to know you've come to a kind master," the troll said again. "But if you go into any of those rooms I told you about yesterday, I'll wring off your head!" he said, and then he left with his herd of goats.

"Indeed he is a kind master too," said the king's son, "but I dare say I'd like to go in and talk with Mastermaid all the same. Maybe she'd just as soon be mine as thine!" and then he went in to her.

Then she asked him what he was to do today.

"Oh, it's not such a hard job, I dare say," said the king's son. "I just have to go up on the mountain and fetch his horse."

"Well, how do you plan to go about that?" asked Mastermaid.

"Oh, it's certainly easy enough to ride home a horse," said the king's son. "I dare say I've ridden horses as spirited as this one before."

"Well it's not such an easy matter to ride that horse home," said Mastermaid, "but I'll teach you how to do it. When you catch sight of it, it'll come rushing toward you with fire and flames pouring from its nostrils, as if you were looking at a pine torch. See to it that you take along the bridle hanging over there by the door and throw it right in its mouth. Then it'll be so tame that you could easily lead it with a piece of thread!"

Yes, he would certainly remember that, and then he sat in there with Mastermaid all that day too. They talked and chatted about one thing and another, but first and last they talked about how fine and wonderful it would be, if only they could have each other and get safely away from the troll. And the king's son would certainly have forgotten both the mountain and the horse, if Mastermaid had not reminded him of it when it was getting on toward evening. She said that now it was best he set out after the horse before the giant came home.

This he did. He took the bridle that was hanging in the corner and strode up on the mountain. And it was not long before the horse came rushing at him, with fire and flames pouring from its nostrils. But the boy bided his time, and at the same moment as the horse rushed at him with gaping jaws, he threw the bit right in its mouth. Then the horse stood there as patiently as a lamb, and it was not much of a job to get it home in the stall, I dare say. Then he went in the house again and started to hum and sing.

The troll came home with his goats in the evening. "Have you fetched home my horse from the mountain?" he asked.

"Yes, that I have, master. It was a nice horse to ride on, but I rode straight home and put it in the stall all the same, I did," said the king's son.

"This I have to see!" said the troll. He went out in the stall, but the horse was standing there as the king's son had said.

"You must have been talking to my Mastermaid, for you never sucked this out of your own breast!" the troll said again.

"Yesterday master talked about this Mastermaid, and today it's the same talk. Oh, God bless you, master, won't you show me this thing? I know I'd really enjoy seeing it," said the king's son, and pretended to be just as stupid and half-witted again.

"Oh, you'll get to see her soon enough!" said the troll.

On the morning of the third day, the troll was again going out in the forest with his goats. "Today you're to go to hell and fetch the fire tax," he said to the king's son. "When you've done this, you can take it easy the rest of the day, for I want you to know you've come to a kind master." And then he left.

"Yes, you're such a kind master that you still give me all the dirty work to do," said the king's son. "But I'd better try to find your Mastermaid. You may say she's yours, but she just might even tell me how to go about it." And then he went in to her.

Now when Mastermaid asked what the troll had given him to do today, he told her he was to go to hell and fetch the fire tax.

"How do you think you'll go about this?" said Mastermaid.

"Well, that's for you to tell me!" said the king's son. "I've never been to hell before, and even if I knew the way, I wouldn't know how much to ask for!"

"Oh, yes, I shall tell you all right. You're to take that club lying there, go over to the mountain, and knock on the wall," said Mastermaid. "Then someone will come out with sparks flying off him. Tell him your errand, and when he asks how much you're to have, just say, 'As much as I can carry!'"

Well, he would certainly remember that, he said, and then he sat in there with Mastermaid the whole day, until it was getting on toward evening. And he'd be sitting there yet if Mastermaid had not reminded him that he had better go to hell after the fire tax before the troll came home.

Then he had to go, and he did exactly as Mastermaid had said. He went over to the mountain wall and knocked with the club.

Then someone came out with sparks flying out of both eyes and nose. "What do you want?" he cried.

"I've come here from the troll to fetch the fire tax," said the king's son.

"How much are you to have?" said the other one.

"I never ask for more than I can carry with me, I don't!" said the king's son.

"It was good you weren't to have a cartload!" said the one who came out of the mountain wall. "Come with me now!"

The king's son did so, and in there he saw gold and silver, I'll have you know. It was piled up inside the mountain like stones in a rock-fall. And when he had been given as big a load as he could carry, he went on his way.

Now when the troll came home with the goats in the evening, the king's son was in the room, singing and humming, just as on the other two nights.

"Well, have you been to hell and brought back the fire tax?" asked the troll.

"Yes, indeed I have, master," said the king's son.

"Where is it, then?" said the troll.

"The sack of gold is standing over by the bench," said the king's son.

"This I have to see!" said the troll, and went over to the bench. But the sack was standing there, and it was so full that gold and silver poured out of it when the troll but loosened the string. "You've certainly been talking to my Mastermaid," said the troll. "If you have, I'll wring off your head!"

"Mastermaid?" said the king's son. "Yesterday master talked about this Mastermaid, and today he's talking about her again. And the day before yesterday it was the same kind of talk. I wish I could see this thing, I do," he said.

"Well, well, wait until tomorrow, and I'll take you to her myself!" said the troll.

"Oh, thanks shall master have! But I wouldn't want to put him to any trouble," said the king's son.

The next day the troll took him in to Mastermaid. "Now you're to butcher him and cook him in that big cauldron you know well. And when the broth is ready, you can let me know," said the troll. He lay down on the bench and went to sleep, and all at once he was snoring so hard that the mountain rumbled.

Then Mastermaid took a knife, cut the boy in his little finger, and let three drops of blood fall onto the stool. Then she took all the old rags and shoe soles, and all the vermin she could lay her hands on, and put it in the cauldron. Then she filled a whole chest with powdered gold, and she took a salt stone and a bottle of water which was hanging by the door and a golden apple and two golden hens with her too, and she and the king's son set out from the troll's manor with it as fast as they could go. When they had come a bit on the way, they came to a sea; then they set sail—but where they got the ship from, I've never been able to find out.

Now after the troll had been sleeping for some time, he started to stretch on the bench where he was lying. "Is it soon ready now?" he said.

"Just started to boil," said the first drop of blood on the stool.

Well, then the troll went back to sleep again and slept for a long, long while. Then he turned over again. "Is it soon ready now?" he said. He did not look up—he did not do this the first time either—for he was still half asleep.

"Half-cooked!" said the second drop of blood, and the troll thought it was Mastermaid again, so he turned over on the bench and went back to sleep.

Now after he had been sleeping for many hours, he started to move and stretch. "Hasn't it cooked yet?" he said.

"All ready!" said the third drop of blood.

Then the troll got up and started rubbing his eyes, but he could not see who had been talking, and then he called for Mastermaid. But no one answered. "Oh well, she's probably popped out for a moment," thought the troll. He took a ladle and was going over to the cauldron to have a taste, but there was nothing but shoe soles and rags and other foolishness in it, and it had all cooked together so he could not tell whether it was porridge or gruel. When he saw this, he could figure out what had happened, and he was so angry that he did not know which leg to stand on, and he set out after the king's son and

Mastermaid as fast as he could go. And it was not long before he was standing by the water, but he could not get across.

"Well, well, I know a way out of this! I'll just call my River-sucker," said the troll, and this he did. Then his River-sucker came and lay down and drank one-two-three gulps, and the water went down so much that the troll could see Mastermaid and the king's son out on the ship.

"Now you must throw out the salt stone," said Mastermaid, and this the king's son did. Then it turned into a mountain so big and high, all the way across the sea, that the troll could not come over it, and the River-sucker could not suck any more either.

"Well, well, I know a way out of this!" said the troll. He sent for his Mountain-borer, and it bored a hole through the mountain so the River-sucker could start sucking again. But at the same moment as there was a hole, and the River-sucker lay down to drink, Mastermaid told the king's son to pour out a drop or two from the bottle, and then the sea was just as full again. And before the River-sucker could take another gulp, they were on the shore, and then they were saved.

Now they were going home to the prince's father, but the prince in no way wanted Mastermaid to walk, for he thought it was not fitting either for her or for himself.

"Just wait here for a little while, and I'll go home after the seven horses standing in my father's stall," he said. "It's not far, and it won't take me long either. But I don't want my sweetheart coming home on foot!"

"Oh no, don't do that! If you come home to the king's manor, you'll only forget me. I know that you will," said Mastermaid.

"How could I forget you after all we've suffered together and as much as we love one another?" said the king's son. He insisted on going home after the carriage with the seven horses in front, and she was to wait there by the shore in the meantime.

Well, at last Mastermaid had to give in to him, as long as he really had to go. "But when you get there, don't even take time to greet anyone. Just go right in the stall and hitch up the horses and drive as fast as you can. For they'll all gather around you now. But you must pretend not to see them, and you mustn't

taste a thing. If you do, you'll bring misfortune upon us both,"
she said, and this he promised.

But when he came home to the king's manor, one of his
brothers was just celebrating his wedding, and the bride and all
her kinsfolks had already come to the manor. They all crowded
around him and asked first one thing and then the other, and
wanted him to come in. But he pretended not to see them and
went straight to the stall and got out the horses and started
hitching them up to the carriage. Now when they in no way
could make him come inside with them, they came out to him
with both food and drink and all the good things they had prepared for the wedding. But the king's son would not taste a
thing. He just hitched up the horses as fast as he could. But at
last the bride's sister rolled an apple across the yard to him.

"As long as you won't taste anything else, you can just take
a bite of that, for you must be both thirsty and hungry after
your long journey," she said. And this he did. He picked up the
apple and took a bite out of it. But scarcely was the taste of it
in his mouth before he had forgotten Mastermaid and the fact
that he was going to drive down to get her.

"I do believe I'm mad! What do I need the horses and carriage
for?" he said, and then he put the horses back in the stall and
went into the manor with them. And in the end it turned out
that he was to have the bride's sister, the one who had rolled the
apple to him.

Mastermaid sat down by the shore and waited and waited for
ever so long, but no king's son came. Then she left, and after
walking for a while she came to a tiny cottage lying off to itself
in a pasture close to the king's manor. She went in and asked if
she could be allowed to stay there. An old hag owned the cottage,
and she was an angry and a wicked old shrew too. At first she
would not let Mastermaid stay with her at all, but after fair
words and good payment, she allowed her to stay all the same.
But it was as dirty and as ugly as a pigsty inside. Then Mastermaid said she was going to fix it up a bit, so it would look like
other houses. The old hag did not like this one bit; she fretted
and was angry. But Mastermaid paid no attention to that. She
took out the chest of gold and threw half a firkin or so over in

the fire, so the gold sputtered out over the whole cottage, and it was gilded both inside and out. But at the same moment as the gold began to sputter, the old hag became so frightened that she set out as if the Evil One himself were after her. But she forgot to bend down in the doorway, and broke off her head against the lintel.

The next morning the sheriff came riding by. He was downright amazed at the golden cottage, that sparkled and glittered there in the pasture, as you can imagine. And he was even more surprised when he went in and laid eyes on the lovely maiden sitting there. He was so smitten by her that he proposed on the spot and asked both prettily and well if she would be his wife.

"Well, if you have plenty of money," said Mastermaid.

Oh, he did not have so little after all, said the sheriff. He would just go home after the money; and in the evening he brought half a barrelful with him in a sack, which he put over in the corner.

Well, as long as he had so much money Mastermaid would have him. But scarcely had they gone to bed before Mastermaid had to get up again. "I've forgotten to stoke the fire," she said.

"Lord! Must you get up for that?" said the sheriff. "I'll do it." And then he was out of the bed and over by the hearth in one jump.

"Tell me when you're holding onto the poker," said Mastermaid.

"I'm holding onto the poker now," said the sheriff.

"Then hold onto the poker and the poker onto you, and shower yourself with fire and embers until daybreak!" said Mastermaid.

And then the sheriff had to stand there the whole night, and shower himself with fire and embers. And for all his crying and begging and pleading, the embers grew no colder for that. But when day was breaking, and he was able to let go the poker, he did not stay there any longer, you might know. He set out as if the bailiff or the Devil was at his heels. And everyone who met him gaped and stared at the sheriff, for he ran as if he had lost his wits, and he could not have looked worse if he had been tanned and flayed. And then they all wondered where he had been. But do not say anything about that, for goodness sake!

The next day the scrivener came riding past the cottage where the Mastermaid lived. He saw it glittering and shining over in the pasture, so he too had to go in to see who lived there. And when he caught sight of the lovely maiden, he was smitten even more than the sheriff and started proposing on the spot. Well, Mastermaid answered him just the way she had answered the sheriff: if he had plenty of money, then perhaps . . .

Money, said the scrivener, was what he had not little of, and he would go right home and fetch it. In the evening he came back with a great big sack of money—I think it weighed four firkins, I do—and put it on Mastermaid's bench. Then he was to have her, and so they went to bed. But now Mastermaid had forgotten to shut the door to the porch. She must get up and shut it, she said.

"Lord! Are you going to do that?" said the scrivener. "No, lie down. I'll do it." And he was out of the bed as lightly as a pea on a piece of bark, and out on the porch.

"Tell me when you're holding onto the door handle," said Mastermaid.

"I'm holding onto the door handle now," shouted the scrivener out on the porch.

"Then hold onto the door handle, and the door handle onto you, and rush back and forth from wall to wall until daybreak!" said Mastermaid.

Then, if you please, the scrivener had to dance that night. Such stepping and hopping he had never done before, nor was he tempted to do it afterward, either. First he was ahead, and then the door, and it went from one corner of the porch to the other, so the scrivener was almost battered to death. First he started to swear, and then to cry and pray. But the door paid no attention to anything. It kept on with what it was doing until the grey light of dawn. When the door let go its hold, the scrivener took to his heels as if he were going to be paid for it. He forgot both the sack of money and the courting, and was glad that the door did not come dancing after him. Everyone he met gaped and stared at the scrivener, for he ran as if he were mad, and what is more he looked worse than if he had been butting with rams all night.

On the third day the bailiff came riding by. Then he also caught sight of the golden cottage over in the pasture. Well, he had to go over and see who lived there too, and when he caught sight of Mastermaid he was so taken with her that he proposed as soon as he had paid his respects. Mastermaid told him, as she had told the two others, that if he had plenty of money she would have him all right. And he did not have so little of that, the bailiff said. He would go home and fetch it right away, and this he did. When he came back in the evening, he had an even bigger sack of money than the scrivener—it held six firkins, to be sure —and he put it on the bench. Well, then he was to have Mastermaid.

But scarcely had they gone to bed before Mastermaid said she had forgotten to let in the calf. She would have to get up and put it in the bin.

No, of course she was not to do that, the bailiff would, he said. And as big and fat as he was, he was out of the bed as nimbly as a young boy.

"Well, tell me when you're holding onto the calf's tail," said Mastermaid, and this he did.

"I'm holding onto the calf's tail now!" shouted the bailiff.

"Then hold onto the calf's tail and the calf's tail onto you, and run all over the world until daybreak!" said Mastermaid.

And then I dare say the bailiff managed to make use of his legs. They went up and down, over mountains and deep valleys; and the more the bailiff swore and shrieked, the faster the calf ran. When it started growing light, he was on the point of collapsing, and he was so glad to let go of the calf's tail that he forgot both the sack of money and everything else. Now he went ever so much slower than the sheriff and the scrivener, but the slower he went, the better time people had to stare and gape at him. And this they did too, you might know, as worn out and tattered as he was after dancing with the calf.

On the following day the wedding was to be held at the king's manor, and then all the brothers were going to the church, the eldest with his bride, and the youngest, who had served the troll, with the bride's sister. But when they had seated themselves up in the carriage and were going to drive away, one of the harness

pins broke; they put two and three in its place, but they all broke.
It did not help, no matter what kind of pin they used. Time
dragged on and on, but they were not able to leave, and at last
they were all beside themselves. But then the sheriff said—for
he had been invited to the wedding too, you might know—that
over in the pasture lived a maiden, "and if you can borrow the
poker she rakes the coals with, I guarantee it will hold," he said.

Well, they sent a messenger to the cottage and asked so prettily
if they could not borrow the poker the sheriff had spoken of.
She did not say no to this, and now they had a harness pin that
did not break. But at the same moment as they were going to
drive, the bottom of the carriage fell out. They started making
a new carriage bottom both quickly and well, but no matter how
they hammered it together or what kind of wood they used, it
did not help. Scarcely had they put a bottom in the carriage and
were going to start, before it broke again, and now they were in
an even worse fix than with the harness pin. But then the
scrivener said—for if the sheriff had been invited, then you can
be certain the scrivener was at the wedding in the king's manor—
"Over in the pasture lives a maiden. If you could only borrow
one of the doors to her porch, then I know it will hold."

Well, they sent a messenger to the cottage again and asked so
prettily if they could not borrow one of the gilded doors the
scrivener had spoken of, and they got it right away. Then they
were to set out again, but now the horses would not pull the carriage. They had already hitched six horses to it. Now they hitched
up eight, and then ten and twelve; but no matter how many they
hitched up, and for all the coachmen laid on the whips, it did
not help. The carriage would not budge off the spot. Now it was
already late in the day, and to the church they would and should
go, so everyone at the king's manor was out-and-out disheartened.
But then the bailiff said that over in the gilded cottage in the
pasture lived a maiden. If they could only borrow her calf, "for
I know that it could pull the carriage, even if it were as heavy as
a mountain!"

They certainly did not think it was proper to drive to church
behind a calf, but there was no other way out. They had to send
a messenger again, and ask so prettily from the king's daughter

if she could borrow that calf the bailiff had spoken of. And Mastermaid let them have it. She did not say no this time either. When it was hitched up, I dare say that carriage started to move! It went over hill and dale, over stock and stone, so fast that they could hardly catch their breaths. And sometimes they were on the ground and sometimes they were up in the air. And when they got to the church, the calf started running around and around it—just like a yarn-winder—and it was only by the skin of their teeth that they managed to get out of the carriage and into the church. And on the way back, they went even faster than they had come, for they were at the king's manor before they knew it.

Now when they were seated at the table, the king's son—the one who had served the troll—said he thought they ought to invite the maiden in the pasture up to the king's manor. She had loaned them the harness pin, the porch door, and the calf, "for if we hadn't gotten those three things, we wouldn't have been on our way yet," he said.

Well, the king thought this was only fair, and he sent five of his best men down to the gilded cottage. They were to give her the king's best regards and ask if she would be so kind as to come up to the manor and eat dinner.

"Give my regards to the king and say that if I'm not good enough for him to come to me, then he's not good enough for me to come to him," answered Mastermaid.

Then the king himself had to go down, and now Mastermaid went back at once. The king certainly thought there was more to her than met the eye, and he seated her in the high seat, next to the youngest bridegroom.

After they had been sitting at the table for a little while, Mastermaid took out the two hens and the golden apple which she had taken from the troll's manor and put them on the table in front of her. And scarcely had she done this before the hens started fighting over the golden apple.

"My, look at the way those two are struggling over that apple!" said the king's son.

"Yes, that's the way the two of us also struggled to come out, that time we were in the troll's manor," said Mastermaid.

Then the king's son recognized her again, and he was happy, you might know. The troll hag, the one who had rolled the apple over to him, he had torn to pieces by twenty-four horses so there was not a shred of her left. And now they really celebrated the wedding; and as sore-winged as they were, the sheriff and the scrivener and the bailiff attended this time too!

## •79• *The Hen Is Tripping in the Mountain*

*Type 311,* Rescue by the Sister; *R. Th. Christiansen, Norske Eventyr 311,* "De tre sostre som blev indtat i berget. Gull-skjaeren. Risen og de tre sostre," *No. 2. Collected by Jörgen Moe in Ringerike (eastern Norway) in the 1840's and printed in P. Chr. Asbjörnsen and Jörgen Moe,* Norske Folkeeventyr *(1852), No. 35.*

*This tale, which is widespread in Europe and also known in North American and Central American traditions, has been collected in fifty-four Norwegian variants. R. Th. Christiansen in his paper "The Sisters and the Troll: Notes to a Folktale," has written "The distribution of the variants within the Scandinavian countries ... points to the conclusion that this folktale belongs to a Western-Nordic traditional group which was never to any great extent accepted by Swedish storytellers" (p. 33).*

• THERE WAS ONCE an old widow who lived with her three daughters in a corner of the parish, way up under a mountain ridge. She was so poor that she owned nothing but a hen, and this was the apple of her eye. She cackled to it and took care of it from morning to night.

But one day, all of a sudden, the hen disappeared. The old woman went all around the cabin, searching and calling, but the hen was gone, and gone it stayed.

"You'll have to go out and look for our hen," said the old

woman to the eldest daughter. "We've got to get it back, even if we have to dig it out of the mountain."

Well, then the eldest daughter went out to look for it. She went both here and there, searching and calling, but no hen did she find. But all at once, over in a wall of the mountain, she heard a voice saying:

> "The hen is tripping in the mountain!
> The hen is tripping in the mountain!"

She was going over to see what it was, but by the mountain wall she fell through a trap door, deep, deep down into a vault under the ground. Down there she made her way through many rooms, each one finer than the last, but in the innermost room a big, ugly mountain troll came up to her.

"Will you be my sweetheart?" he asked.

No, she said, not at all. She wanted to go back up and look for her hen which had disappeared.

Then the mountain troll became so angry that he took her and wrung off her head and threw body and head down in the cellar.

The mother sat at home, waiting and waiting, but no daughter came back. She waited a good while longer, but when she neither heard nor saw anything of her, she told the middle daughter that she would have to go out and look for her sister, "and you can call the hen at the same time," she said.

Then the second sister went out, and the same thing happened to her as to the first: she walked and searched and called, and all at once she also heard a voice over in the wall of the mountain saying,

> "The hen is tripping in the mountain!
> The hen is tripping in the mountain!"

She thought this was strange, and was going over to see what it was when she also fell through the trap door, deep, deep down into the vault. There she went through all the rooms, but in the innermost room the mountain troll came up to her and asked if she would be his sweetheart. No, she would not at all. She wanted to go back up at once and look for the hen that had disappeared, she did. But then the mountain troll became angry. He took her and wrung off her head and threw head and body down in the cellar.

Now after the old woman had been sitting and waiting a long, long time for the second daughter, and no daughter was to be heard or seen, she said to the youngest, "Now you'll really have to go out and look for your sisters. It was bad enough that the hen disappeared, but it would be even worse if we never found your sisters again. But you can always call the hen at the same time!"

Well, then the youngest daughter went out. She went hither and thither, and searched and called, but she did not see the hen, nor did she see her sisters either. At long last, she also came over toward the mountain wall, and then she heard a voice saying:

"The hen is tripping in the mountain!
The hen is tripping in the mountain!"

She thought this was strange, and was going over to have a look, and then she also fell through the trap door, deep, deep down into the vault. Down there she went through one room finer than the other. But she was not so frightened. She took her time and looked at both one thing and the other, and then she caught sight of the cellar door. She looked down in there, and at once she recognized her sisters who were lying there.

At the same moment that she closed the cellar door, the mountain troll came over to her.

"Will you be my sweetheart?" he asked.

"Yes, gladly!" said the girl, for she was able to figure out what had happened to her sisters.

When the troll heard this, she was given fine, fine clothing—the finest she could desire—and everything else she wanted to have, so happy was he that someone would be his sweetheart.

But after she had been there for a while, there was a day when she was very downcast and silent. Then the mountain troll asked what she was moping about.

"Oh," said the girl, "it's because I can't go home to mother. She's probably both hungry and thirsty, and she has no one to stay with her, either."

"Well, you can't go to her," replied the troll, "but put some food in a sack and I'll carry it to her."

Well, she thanked him for this, and said she would do it. But at the bottom of the sack she put lots of gold and silver, then she put a little food on top. Then she told the troll that the sack was ready, but he must not look in it at all, and this he promised not to do.

When the mountain troll left, she peeked out at him through a tiny hole in the trap door. When he had gone a bit of the way, he said, "This sack is so heavy, I'll just see what's in it!" and was going to untie the string.

But then the girl shouted, "I can see you all right! I can see you all right!"

"Those are damned sharp eyes you've got in your head!" said the troll, and then he did not dare try that any more.

When he came to where the widow lived, he threw the sack in through the door. "There's some food from your daughter! She has everything she could wish for!" he said.

Now one day, after the girl had been in the mountain a good while longer, a billy goat fell down through the trap door.

"Who sent for you, you shaggy beast?" said the troll. He was wild with rage, and he took the goat, wrung off its head, and threw it down in the cellar.

"Oh, no! Why did you do that?" said the girl. "I could have had it to amuse myself with down here."

"You needn't sulk about that," said the troll. "I can soon bring the goat back to life, I can." With that he took a crock which hung on the wall, put the head on the goat, and rubbed salve on it from the crock. Then the goat was just as good as new.

"Aha," thought the girl, "that crock is certainly worth something!"

After she had been with the troll a good while longer, she waited one day until the troll was away, then she took her eldest sister and put her head back on. She rubbed her with salve from the crock, the way she had seen the troll do with the billy goat, and at once the sister came back to life. Then the girl put her in a sack with a little food over her, and as soon as the troll came home she said to him, "My dear friend, now you must take some food home to mother again. She's probably both thirsty and hungry, poor thing, and quite alone she is too. But don't look in the sack!"

Yes, he would take the sack all right, he said, and he would not look in it either. But when he had come a bit on the way, he thought the sack had grown so heavy, and when he had gone a bit farther, he thought he would see what was in the sack. "No matter what kind of eyes she's got in her head, she can't see me now!" he said to himself.

But at the same moment as he was going to open the sack, the girl who was sitting inside it said, "I can see you all right! I can see you all right!"

"Those are damned sharp eyes you've got in your head this time too!" said the troll, for he thought the girl in the mountain was talking. Then he dared not try to look in it any more, but carried the sack to the mother as fast as he could. When he came to the cabin, he threw it in through the door. "There's some food from your daughter! She has everything she could wish for!" he said.

Now when the girl had been in the mountain a good while longer, she did the same with the second sister. She put her head on her body, rubbed on salve from the crock, and put her in the sack. But this time she filled the sack with as much silver and gold as there was room for, and on the top she placed a little food.

"My dear friend," she said to the troll, "now you must take some food home to mother again, but don't look in the sack!"

Well, the troll was only too willing to let her have her way about this, and he also promised that he would not look in the sack. But when he had come a bit on the way, he thought the sack had become terribly heavy. And when he had gone a bit farther, he was downright worn out. He had to put the sack down and catch his breath, and then he thought he would untie the fastenings and look in the sack.

But the girl who was in the sack shouted, "I can see you all right! I can see you all right!"

"Those are damned sharp eyes you've got in your head this time too," said the troll, and then he dared not look in the sack any more, but hurried as fast as he could and carried the sack straight to the mother. When he was outside the cabin, he threw the sack in through the door. "There's some food from your daughter! She has everything she could wish for!" he said.

Now when the girl had been there even longer, the troll was going out one day. Then the girl pretended to be poorly and sick, and she whimpered and carried on. "There's no use your coming home before twelve o'clock," she said, "for I won't be able to have the food ready before then. I'm feeling so miserable and feeble," she said.

Now when the troll was out of sight, she stuffed her clothes with straw and stood this straw girl over in a corner by the hearth with a stirrer in its hand, so it looked as if she herself were standing there. Then she hurried home and took along a hunter to stay with them in her mother's cabin.

When it was twelve o'clock or more, the troll came home. "Bring the food!" he said to the straw maiden. But there was no answer. "Bring the food I say!" said the troll again. "I'm hungry!" Again, she didn't answer.

"Bring the food!" shrieked the troll a third time. "Listen to what I say, or else I'll wake you up!" No, the maiden just stood still.

Then he became so angry that he gave her a kick so the straw flew about the walls and ceiling. But when he saw that, he suspected some mischief and started searching both high and low, and at last he went down into the cellar. There, both sisters were gone, and now he understood at once what had happened. Well, she would soon pay for that! he said, and set out for the mother's cabin. But when he got there, the hunter fired a shot. Then the troll dared not go in. He thought it was the thunder. He set out for home again as fast as he could, but just as he came to the trap door the sun rose, and then he burst asunder.

There is plenty of gold and silver left there, if only there were someone who knows where the trap door is!

The One Who Is Loved by
Womankind Will Never
Find Himself in Need

*Type 580, Beloved of Women; R. Th. Christiansen, Norske
Eventyr, 580, "Det har ingen nod med den som alle kvindfolk
er glad i," No. 2. Collected by Jörgen Moe in Seljord (Telemark)
in the 1840's and printed in P. Chr. Asbjörnsen and Jörgen Moe,
Norske Folkeeventyr (1852), No. 38.*

*This tale is known throughout Scandinavia, and scattered
variants have been reported in other parts of Europe. Some versions have a definitely obscene character (Norske Eventyr, p. 88).*

· ONCE THERE WERE three brothers: I do not rightly know how
it had come about, but they had each been given a wish so that
they could have one thing, whatever they liked. The two eldest
did not take long to think it over: they wished that every time
they stuck their hands in their pockets they would always take
hold of money, "For whenever you have as much money as you
like, you'll always get on in the world!" they said.

But the youngest, who was called Askelad [Ash Boy], knew
how to wish for something better: he wished for all womankind
to fall in love with him if they but saw him. And this, as you
shall hear, was better than both goods and money.

Now when they had made their wishes, the two eldest brothers
wanted to set out in the world. Then Askelad asked if he could
go with them, but this they did not want at all. "No matter
where we go, we'll be welcomed as counts and princes," they
said. "But you, you miserable hungry wretch, nothing do you
have and nothing will you get. Do you think anyone will trouble
about you?"

"But I certainly ought to be allowed to go with you all the
same," said Askelad. "I dare say a bite of meat just might fall

off to me too, as long as I was in the company of such high and mighty gentlemen."

At long last he was allowed to go with them, if he would be their servant; otherwise they would have nothing to do with him.

Now when they had journeyed a day or so, they came to an inn. They put up there, the two who had money, and ordered both a roast and fish, both spirits and mead, and all that was good. But Askelad was to keep an eye on everything that belonged to the two bigwigs.

As Askelad sauntered back and forth out there in the yard, the innkeeper's wife happened to look out through the pane, and she caught sight of him. She thought she had never laid eyes on such a handsome fellow before; she stared and stared at him, and the longer she stared at the boy, the handsomer she thought he was.

"What in the Devil's skin and bones are you standing over there by the window staring and gaping at?" said her husband. "It'd be better if you saw about roasting the pig instead of hanging about here! You see the kind of folks we have with us today, I dare say!"

"Oh, I don't care about that pack of trash, I don't!" said the wife. "If they don't want to stay, they can just go back where they came from! But come here and you'll see someone walking out in the yard! Such a handsome fellow I've never seen before in my life. If it's the same to you, we'll ask him in and treat him to a little something to eat, for he certainly hasn't got much to pay with, poor thing!"

"Have you lost what few grains of sense you had, wife?" said the man—he was so angry he fumed. "Quick, out in the kitchen with you and fire up the hearth! And don't stand here gaping at strange men!"

There was nothing else for the wife to do but go out in the kitchen and start fixing the food. She was not allowed to look at the boy, and she dared even less to give him something to eat. But just as she had put the roasting pig on the spit in the kitchen, she pretended to have an errand out in the yard. And then she gave Askelad a pair of scissors which were such that if he but clipped in the air with them, they clipped out the fanciest clothing anyone could wish to behold, of both silk and velvet and everything fine.

"You're to have these because you're so handsome!" said the wife.

Now when the two brothers had put an end to all the good things to eat, both baked and fried, they wanted to be on their way again, and Askelad stood on behind the carriage and was their servant. Then they journeyed a long way again until they came to another inn. Here the brothers wanted to go in, but they did not want Askelad, who had no money, inside with them. He was to stay outside again and keep an eye on all their belongings.

"And if anyone asks whose servant you are, just say we're two foreign princes!" they said.

But then it happened just like the first time. While Askelad was lounging about in the yard, the innkeeper's wife came over to the window and caught sight of him, and then she was just as smitten by him as was the first innkeeper's wife. She stood and gazed at him and could not get her fill of looking at him. Then her husband came rushing through the room with something the two princes had demanded.

"Don't stand there gaping like a cow on a barn door! Go out in the kitchen to your fish kettle, woman," said the man. "You see the kind of folks we have with us today!"

"Oh, I don't care about that pack of trash, I don't!" said the wife. "If they don't want what they get, they can just take what they had with them. But come here too, and you'll see. Such a handsome soul as the one out there in the yard, I've never seen on earth before. If it's the same to you, we'll ask him in and treat him to a little something to eat; he looks like he needs it, poor thing. Oh, how truly handsome he is!" said the woman.

"You never did have much sense, but what little you had has now flown away, I can tell!" said the man. He was even angrier than the first innkeeper, and drove the wife out to the kitchen. "Quick, out in the kitchen with you, and don't stand here gaping at boys!"

Then she had to go out to the kettle of fish, and she dared not give Askelad anything to eat for she was afraid of her husband.

But all at once, as she stood fixing the fire, she pretended to have an errand out in the yard. And then she gave Askelad a cloth which was such that it served up the best things imaginable, if he but spread it out.

"You're to have it because you're so handsome!" she said to Askelad.

Now when the two brothers had tasted everything there was to eat and drink, and paid for it through the nose, they set out on their way again and Askelad stood on behind. When they had traveled so long that they were hungry again, they put up at an inn and demanded the costliest and best things they could name: "For we are two journeying kings, and we've got money to spend like grass," they said.

Well, when the innkeeper heard this, there was a frying and a roasting, so they could smell it all the way to the neighboring farm, and the innkeeper could not do enough for the two kings. But Askelad had to stay outside here too and keep an eye on what was in the carriage.

Then the same thing happened as the other two times: the innkeeper's wife happened to look out the window. Then she caught sight of the servant who stood out there by the carriage, and such a handsome fellow she'd never seen before. She stared and she stared, and the more she stared at him, the handsomer she thought he was.

The innkeeper came running through the room with the food the two journeying kings had demanded, and it did not make him any happier when he saw the woman standing by the window, gazing outside.

"Don't you know better than to stand there gaping when we have such folks in the house?" he said. "Out in the kitchen to your cream porridge this very minute!"

"Oh, those guests don't matter at all. If they don't want to wait until the cream porridge is done, then they can just leave!" answered the wife. "Now, come here and you'll see. Such a handsome fellow as the one standing out there in the yard, I've never laid eyes on before. If it's the same to you, we'll ask him in and treat him to a little something to eat. He certainly looks like he needs it! Oh, how truly handsome he is!"

"You've been a man-chaser all your days, and you are one still!" said the man. He was so angry that he did not know which foot to stand on. "But if you don't see about getting out to your porridge pot, I'll try to put feet under you, I will!"

Then the wife had to hurry out to the kitchen as fast as she could, for she knew her husband was not to be fooled with. But all at once she popped out in the yard, and then she gave Askelad a barrel tap.

"If you just give the tap a twist," she said, "you'll get the finest there is to drink, both mead and wine, and spirits. You're to have it because you're so handsome!" she said.

Now when the two brothers had eaten and drunk their fill, they left the inn, and Askelad stood on behind their carriage and was to be their servant. Then they drove far and long until they came to a king's court, and here the two brothers passed themselves off as emperor's sons. They were received both good and well, for they had plenty of money, and they were so fine that they shone from afar. They were to stay at the castle, and the king could not do enough for them.

But Askelad, who went in the same rags as he had had on from home, and who did not have a shilling in his pocket, was taken by the king's guards and rowed out to a little island. Here they took all the beggars and tramps who come to the king's court. The king had ordered this to be done because they went about so tattered and ugly and might disturb the merrymaking at the castle. The brothers saw the guards row Askelad out to the island all right, but they were glad to be rid of him, and did not pay the least bit of attention to it.

But when Askelad came out to the island, he took out his scissors and clipped in the air with them. And then the scissors cut out the finest clothing anyone could wish for, of both velvet and silk, so the tramps out on the island were much more finely dressed than the king and everyone at the castle. Then Askelad took his cloth and spread it out, and now I dare say the tramps got something to eat too. There had never been a feast at the king's court like the one they had on the island that day.

"You must be thirsty too," said Askelad. He took out the barrel tap and gave it a little twist, and then the tramps got something to drink as well; and the king himself had never tasted anything like that ale and mead in all his life.

Now when the guards, who were to bring the food to the ragged tramps on the island, came rowing out with their scrapings of cold porridge and whey—this was the food they were to have—the tramps would not so much as taste it. The guards thought this was strange, but they were even more astonished when they took a good look at the tramps, for they were so dressed up that the guards thought they were emperors and popes, every single one, and they had rowed out to the wrong island. But when they took a better look, they knew where they were. Then they understood that the fellow they had rowed out on the day before must have got all this finery for the tramps on the island. When they came back to the court, it did not take them long to tell how the fellow they had rowed out with on the day before had dressed up all the tramps. They were so elegant and fine that the finery fairly dripped off them.

"And they've become so high and mighty that they wouldn't so much as taste the porridge and whey we brought!" they said. One of the guards had also managed to find out that the boy had a pair of scissors with which he had clipped out the clothing.

"When he sticks the scissors up in the air and clips with them, he cuts out silk and velvet!" he said.

When the princess heard this, she did not have a moment's rest until she had seen the boy and the scissors that clipped both silk and velvet out of the air. Those scissors were certainly worth having, she thought. With them she could get all the finery she wanted. So she pestered the king for such a long time until he had to send for the boy who owned the scissors. When he came to the king's court, the princess asked if it were true that he had a pair of scissors that were thus-and-so, and if he would sell them.

Well, he certainly did have a pair of scissors like that, said Askelad, but he did not want to sell them. And then he took the scissors out of his pocket and clipped in the air with them so the pieces of silk and bits of velvet flew about her ears.

"Well, you just have to sell them to me!" said the king's

daughter. "You can ask whatever you like for them, but I must have them!"

No, he would not sell them at any price, for he could never get a pair of scissors like those again, he said. But as they stood there bargaining for the scissors, the king's daughter took a better look at Askelad, and, like the innkeepers' wives, she thought she had never seen a handsomer man before.

Then she started bargaining for the scissors again and begged and pleaded with Askelad to sell them. He could ask for as many hundreds of *dalers* as he liked. It did not matter as long as she got the scissors.

"No, I'm not going to sell them," said Askelad. "But it's the same to me; if I can lie on the floor of the princess' bedchamber tonight, right by the door, she can have the scissors. I won't do her any harm, but if she's afraid, she can have two men stand guard inside the chamber."

Yes, that could certainly be arranged, thought the king's daughter. As long as she got the scissors, she was satisfied. Then Askelad lay on the floor of the princess' bedchamber during the night, and two men stood guard. But the princess did not sleep very much, for every so often she thought she had to open her eyes and peek at Askelad again. And this kept up all night; scarcely had she closed her eyes before she had to peek over at him again, so handsome she thought he was.

In the morning Askelad was rowed out to the tramps' island again. But when the guards came with the porridge scrapings and the bottles of whey, no one would so much as taste it on that day either. The guards were even more surprised at this, but one of them managed to find out that the boy who had the scissors also owned a cloth. And he only had to spread it out and it served up the best things to eat one could wish for. When the guard came back to the king's court, it was not long before he told about this too:

"At the king's court there's never been anything like the roast meat and cream porridge that the cloth serves up!"

When the princess heard this, she went to the king again and told him and begged and pleaded for such a long time that at last he had to send out to the island for the owner of the cloth.

And then Askelad came up to the castle again. The king's daughter just had to get the cloth from him and promised him anything under the sun. But Askelad would not sell it at any price.

"But if I can sit on the stool beside the bed in the princess' chamber tonight, she shall have my cloth," said the boy. "I certainly won't do her any harm. But if she's afraid, she can have four men stand guard there."

Well, the princess agreed to this, and four men stood guard. But if she had not slept very much the night before, she slept even less that night. She could hardly shut her eyes; she had to lie and gaze at the handsome boy the whole night through, and even then she did not think the night was long enough.

In the morning Askelad was again rowed out to the tramps' island. It was certainly against the princess' will, for she was so fond of the boy already. But there was no use asking, he had to go out there again.

Now when the guards came with the porridge scrapings and the whey which the tramps were to have for food, not one of them would have what the king had sent; nor were the guards any too surprised about that either. But they did think it strange that none of the tramps was thirsty. Then one of the king's men managed to find out that the fellow who owned the scissors and the cloth had a barrel tap too. And it was such that if he but gave the tap a twist, he had the finest things to drink imaginable, both ale and mead, and wine. When the guard came back to the castle, he could not keep his mouth shut any better than the time before. He told everyone he met about the barrel tap and how easy it was to get all manner of things to drink from it.

"Nothing like that ale and mead has ever been tasted at the king's court!" he said. "It's sweeter than both honey and syrup!"

When the king's daughter heard that, she wanted to get hold of the barrel tap at once, and she certainly had nothing against bargaining with the one who owned it either. So she went to the king again and asked him to send out to the tramps' island for the fellow who owned the scissors and the cloth, for he still had something even better, she said. And when the king heard it was a barrel tap that poured out the best ale and wine that anyone

could wish to drink, just by giving the tap a twist, it certainly
did not take him long to send for him, I dare say.

When Askelad came up to the castle, the princess asked if it
were true that he had a barrel tap that was thus-and-so?

Yes, he had it in his vest pocket, said Askelad. But when the
king's daughter wanted to buy it at any price, Askelad said, just
as on the other two times, that he would not sell it at all—even if
the princess offered him half the kingdom for it.

"But it's the same to me," said Askelad. "If I can lie on the
edge of the princess' bed, on top of the bedclothes, she shall have
my tap. I won't do her any harm, but if she's afraid, she can just
have eight men stand guard in the bedchamber."

Oh no, that was not needed, thought the princess, as well as
she knew him. And so Askelad lay on top of the bedclothes,
beside the princess, during the night. But if she had not done
much sleeping on the other two nights, there was even less that
night. She could not shut an eye. The whole time she had to lie
and gaze at Askelad, who lay beside her on the edge of the bed.

When she got up in the morning, and they were going to row
Askelad out to the tramps' island again, she told them to wait
a bit. Then she ran in to the king and asked him so very sweetly
if she could not have Askelad, for she loved him so much that
if she did not get him she did not want to live, she said.

"Why, of course you can have him, if you really must," said
the king. "Anyone who has such things is just as rich as you
are."

Then Askelad got the princess and half the kingdom—he
would get the other half when the king died—and so everything
turned out all right. But his two brothers, who had always
treated him badly, he put out on the tramps' island.

"There they can stay until they find out who is better off, the
one whose pockets are full of money or the one who's loved by
womankind!" said Askelad. And then I dare say it did not help
much to reach down in their pockets and jingle their money out
there on the island. And if Askelad has not taken them off the
island, they are still there eating cold porridge scrapings and
whey to this very day.

## · 81 ·  Bird Dam

*Type 310A, Quest for a Vanished Princess; R. Th. Christiansen, Norske Eventyr, 301, "De tre rövede prinsesser. De tre prinsesser i berget det blaa. Klöverhans," No. 7. Collected by P. Chr. Asbjörnsen in Röyken (eastern Norway) in the 1840's and printed in Asbjörnsen and Jörgen Moe, Norske Folkeeventyr (1852), No. 3.*

*This variant from Röyken of one of the world's most widespread tale types is, according to Asbjörnsen, very unusual (Norske Eventyr, p. 29). R. Th. Christiansen has pointed out that tale types connected with a quest for stolen princesses have a tendency to take on complicated patterns. In Norway this popular story is often told in broad saga or chronicle style or is embroidered in other ways by individual tellers. In Ireland Type 301 is commonly told by Gaelic storytellers in a stylized literary manner. See R. Th. Christiansen, "Eventyrvandring i Norge," p. 75.*

· THERE WAS ONCE a king who had twelve daughters. He was so fond of them that he wanted them always to be around him. But every day at noon, when the king slept, the princesses went out and took a walk. One day, while the king was taking his nap and the princesses were outside, they suddenly disappeared and did not come back again. Then there was great mourning throughout the land, and the king was the most sorrowful of all. He sent out heralds both in his own kingdom and in foreign lands; proclamations were read at all the churches, and church bells were rung. But the king's daughters were gone, and gone they stayed, and no one knew what had become of them. Since they never returned, everyone supposed that they had been taken into a mountain.

It was not long before this was known far and wide, both in town and parish, yes in many parishes and foreign lands, and at last word of it also reached a king in a far off land. This king had twelve sons. When they heard about the twelve princesses, they asked their father for permission to journey out and search for them. He was not very willing to let them go, for he was afraid he would never seen them again. But they fell down on their knees before him, and begged so long that at last he had to let them go. He fitted out a ship, and put the Red Knight at the helm, for he was familiar with the sea.

They sailed for a long time. They went ashore in every land they came to and searched and asked for the princesses, but they neither heard nor saw anything of them. Now, in a few days, they would have been sailing for seven years. Then one day there was a great storm, and the weather was so bad that they thought they would never come to land again. They all had so much to keep them busy that they were not able to close their eyes as long as the storm lasted. The storm lasted for three days, then suddenly the wind died and there was a dead calm. Everyone was now so tired after the toil and the storm that he fell asleep on the spot. But the youngest prince was restless and could not sleep at all.

As he was pacing the deck, the ship came to a little island. A little dog ran back and forth on the island, barking and whining as if it wanted to come out to it. On the deck, the king's son called and whistled to the dog, but it only barked and whined all the more. He knew it would be a shame for it to stay there and perish. He thought it probably came from a ship that had been wrecked in the storm, but he did not see how he could rescue it. He did not think he could lower a boat alone, and the others were sleeping so soundly that he did not want to wake them just for the sake of a dog. But the weather was calm and still, and he decided, "I'd better go ashore and save the dog all the same." So he tried to lower a boat, and it went easier than he had imagined. He rowed ashore and went over to the dog, but each time he grabbed at it, it ran away, and it kept this up until, before he knew it, the boy found himself inside a castle. Here the dog turned into a beautiful princess. Inside the castle there was a man sitting on a bench. He was so big and ugly that the king's son was downright afraid.

"You've no reason to be afraid," said the man—and the boy

was even more frightened when he heard his voice—"for I know very well what you're after. There are twelve princes of you, and you're searching for the twelve princesses who have disappeared. I know where they are; they're at my master's place. Each one is sitting on a golden chair picking lice out of his hair, for he has twelve heads. Now you've been sailing for seven years, but you'll have to sail for seven more before you find them. You could just as well stay here instead," said the troll, "and have my daughter. But if you go to seek the princesses, first you must slay the master with twelve heads for he's a hard master to us. Now try to swing that sword."

The king's son took hold of an old rusty sword which was hanging on the wall, but he could hardly budge it.

"Then you'll have to take a swig from this bottle," said the troll.

When he had done this he was able to move it, and when he had taken another he could lift it, and when he had taken still another swig, he could swing the sword as lightly as a rolling pin.

"Now when you go on board," said the troll prince, "you must hide the sword carefully in your bunk so the Red Knight doesn't catch sight of it. He certainly wouldn't be able to swing it, but still he would be jealous of you and would put you to death. Now, three days before the seven years are up," he went on, "the same thing will happen again: a great storm will blow up, and when it's all over you'll all be sleepy. Then you must take the sword and row ashore, and you'll come to a castle. Outside, all kinds of animals are standing on guard, wolves and bears and lions. But you're not to be afraid of them, for they'll fall down at your feet, every single one. When you come into the castle, you'll see the troll sitting in a richly furnished chamber. He has twelve heads, and each princess is sitting on a golden chair, with one of the heads in her lap, picking the lice out of his hair. And you can just imagine what they think of that job! You must hurry and chop off one head after the other. If he wakes up and catches sight of you, he'll swallow you alive!"

The king's son went on board with the sword, taking good care to remember what he had been told. The others still lay sleeping, and he hid the sword carefully in his bunk so that neither the Red Knight nor any of his brothers would catch sight of it. Now the wind started to blow again, and he woke them up and said that they were fine ones to lie there idling now that there was such a good breeze. No one had noticed that he had been away.

Now, three days before the seven years were up, it happened as the troll had said. A bad storm blew up that lasted for three days, and when it was over they were so worn out after the hard struggle that they lay down to sleep, every single one. But the youngest prince rowed ashore, and the animals on guard fell down at his feet as soon as he came to the castle. When he came into the chamber the twelve-headed troll sat sleeping, as the troll prince had said, with each of the princesses sitting on a golden chair and picking the lice out of his hair. The king's son motioned to the princesses to move out of the way, but they pointed at the troll and signaled to the king's son to go away and stay away. But he kept making signs to them to move out of the way. Finally they understood that he wanted to free them, and moved away as silently as they could, one after the other. And just as quickly, the king's son chopped off the troll's heads until at last the blood was flowing like a brook.

When the troll had been killed, the king's son rowed back to the ship and hid the sword. Now he thought he had done enough, and as he was not able to get the body out of the way alone, he did not think it was expecting too much for the others to help him a little too. So he woke them up and said it was a shame for them to lie there taking it easy, now that he had found the king's daughters and freed them from the troll. The others only laughed at him, and said he had probably slept just as soundly as the rest and dreamt he was such a hero. If anyone was going to save the princesses, it would more likely be one of them. But the youngest prince told them how everything had happened, and then they followed him ashore. But not until they had seen the rivulet of blood, the castle, the twelve heads, and the princesses did they realize that he had spoken the truth. After this they helped throw the heads and the body into the sea.

They were all happy now, but no one was as happy as the

king's daughters who no longer had to sit the whole day picking lice out of the troll's hair. Of all the gold and precious things that were there, they took along as much as the ship would carry, and then they went on board, each and every one. But when they had come a bit out on the sea, the princesses said that, in their joy, they had forgotten their golden crowns. They had left them lying in a cupboard, and now they wanted so much to have them.

As no one else would fetch them, the youngest prince said, "Oh well, as long as I've already taken such risks, I can just as well go back after the crowns. Please take down the sails and wait until I come back again."

Yes, this they would do. But when the youngest prince was out of sight, the Red Knight, who wanted to rank first and have the youngest princess himself, said that there was no use lying still and waiting for him. They certainly ought to know that he would never come back again. They knew, he said, that the king had given him, the Red Knight, power and authority to sail whenever he wanted to. Moreover, they were to say that the Red Knight had saved the princesses. And if there was anyone who said anything to the contrary, he would lose his life. The princes dared not go against the Red Knight's wishes and so they sailed off.

In the meantime, the youngest prince rowed ashore and went up to the castle. He found the cupboard with the golden crowns in it and dragged it along until he got it down to the boat. But when he had rowed out to where he could see the ship, it was gone. Now when he could not see it anywhere, he knew what had happened. There was no use rowing after it, and so he turned around and rowed back to shore again. He was afraid to stay in the castle alone during the night, but there was nowhere else to go. He locked all the doors and gates, and, with his heart in his mouth, he lay down in a room where there was a turned-down bed. He was thoroughly frightened, and he became even more afraid after he'd been lying there for a while. There was a creaking and a crashing in all the walls and ceilings, as if the whole castle would fall apart. Suddenly something plumped down beside the bed like a load of hay. Then every-

thing was quiet again, but he heard a voice which told him not
to be afraid, and it said:

> "Bird Dam is my name,
> And I'll help you back from whence you came!

But as soon as you wake up in the morning, you must go out
to the *stabbur* and get me four barrels of rye for my breakfast,
or else I won't be able to do anything!"

When he awoke, the prince laid eyes on an enormously large
bird, which had a feather on its neck as big as a half-grown
spruce log. The king's son went down to the *stabbur* after four
barrels of rye for Bird Dam. When it had eaten it all, the bird
told the king's son to hang the cupboard with the golden crowns
in it on one side of its neck and hang as much silver and gold
as would balance it on the other, and he himself would have to
sit up on its back and hold on tight to the feather in its neck.

Then they set out through the air so the wind whistled, and
it was not long before they flew past the ship. The king's son
wanted to go on board to get the sword, for he was afraid someone would find it, and the troll had said that no one must see
it. But Bird Dam said that would have to wait.

"The Red Knight certainly won't see it," said the bird, "but
if you go on board, he'll kill you, for he wants the youngest
princess for himself. But you needn't worry about her. She lays
a drawn sword in front of the bed every night!"

At long last they came to the troll prince, and hére the king's
son was given a welcome beyond description. There was no end
to the things the troll wanted to do for him, because he had
killed the master and now the troll was king. He would gladly
have given him his daughter and half the kingdom, but the
prince was now so in love with the youngest of the twelve princesses that he could think of no one else; he wanted to set out
after her immediately. The troll told him to take it easy for a
while. He said that those on board the ship had almost seven years
to sail before they reached home. He reassured the king's son
about the princess in the same way as Bird Dam had done. "You
needn't worry about her. She places a drawn sword in front of
her bed. If you don't believe me," said the troll, "you can go

on board when they sail past here, and see for yourself. At the same time please fetch the sword I gave you, for I must have it back."

When the ship sailed past, there was again a terrible storm. After it was over, the king's son went on board and found them all asleep. Each of the princesses was sleeping with her prince, but the youngest princess slept alone with a drawn sword in front of her bed, and on the floor at the foot of the bed lay the Red Knight. The king's son took the sword the troll had given him and rowed ashore again without anyone noticing that he had been on board.

But still the king's son was restless. He wanted to set out immediately. At last, when the seven years were almost up and there were only about three weeks left, the troll king said, "Now you can get ready to leave, since you want so badly to go. You shall borrow my iron boat, which goes by itself if you but say 'Boat go forth!' In the boat is an iron club. You're to lift this club when you sight the ship just ahead of you, and they'll have such a wind that they'll forget to keep an eye on you. When you come alongside the ship, lift the iron club again, and there'll be such a storm that they'll certainly have more to do than think about you. And when you're past them, you're to lift the club a third time. But you must always put it down carefully, or else there'll be such a storm that both you and they will be lost. Now when you've come to land, you needn't worry about the boat. Just shove it out and turn it around, and say: 'Boat go back home the way you came!'"

When the prince left, he was given a great lot of gold and silver, and many other precious things and clothing, and all the linen which the troll princess had sewn for him during all this time, so that he was much richer than any of his brothers. Scarcely had he seated himself in the boat and said, "Boat go forth!" before the boat went skimming over the water. When he caught sight of the ship straight ahead of him, he lifted the club. Then there was such a wind that they forgot all about him. When he was alongside the ship, he lifted the club again, and then there was such a storm and such a tempest that the water frothed around the ship. The waves beat over the deck, so they had more than enough to do than look about for him. When he had sailed past them, he lifted the club a third time, and then they were kept so busy that they did not have any time to see who might have passed them. He came to land long, long before the ship arrived. He took all his things out of the boat, then he shoved it out again, turned it around, and said, "Boat, go back home the way you came!" And the boat sailed off.

He disguised himself as a sailor and went up to a wretched hut belonging to an old woman. He let her believe that he was a poor sailor, telling her that he had been on a great ship which had gone down and he was the only survivor. Then he asked if she would let him stay there with the things he had saved from the ship.

"Heaven help me!" said the old woman. "I can't put put anyone up here. You can see how it is. I have nothing to sleep on myself, much less anything for anyone else."

"Well, it makes no difference," said the sailor. As long as he had a roof over his head, it did not matter what he slept on. Then she could not refuse to put him up, as long as he would be content with what she had.

In the evening he moved in his things, and scarcely were they inside before the old woman, who was only too willing to have something new to gossip about, started asking who he was, where he was from, where he had been, where he was going, what he had with him, what errand he was on, and whether he had heard anything about the twelve princesses who had disappeared many a long year ago—and more, which would take plenty of time to talk about and figure out. But he said he was so weak and had such a pain in his head after the terrible storm that he did not remember a thing. She would have to leave him alone for a few days until he got over all he had been through. Then he would tell her everything she wanted to know, and more.

The next day the old woman started prying and questioning again, but the sailor still had such a pain in his head that he did not know a thing. But he did drop a hint that he knew a little about the king's daughters. Right away the old woman rushed out to all the gossips in the parish with what she had found out. And one after the other they came running and asked for news of the king's daughters: had he seen them? were they coming soon? were they on their way? and more like it. He pretended that he still had a pain in his head after the storm, so he could not answer everything. But he did say that if they had not been wrecked in the terrible storm, they would be arriving in fourteen days, if not sooner. But he could not say if they were still alive, for he had not seen them afterward. They might have gone to the bottom.

One of the gossips rushed to the king's manor with this news and said that in so-and-so's house lived a sailor who had seen the princesses, and they'd be coming in fourteen days, or maybe eight! When the king heard this, he sent word to the sailor to come and tell him himself.

"I look a sight," said the sailor. "I haven't the clothes to appear before the king." But the king's messenger said he really had to come. The king would and must talk to him no matter how he looked, for no one had yet been able to bring him news of the princesses.

Well, then he had to go to the king's manor. He was brought before the king who asked if it were true that he'd seen something of the princesses.

"Yes, that I have," said the sailor. "But I don't know if they're still alive, for when I saw them there was such a storm that our ship went down. But if they are alive, they'll be coming in fourteen days, if not sooner."

When the king heard this, he was almost beside himself with joy. And when it was close to the time the sailor said they were coming, the king went down to the shore to meet them. There was great rejoicing over the whole kingdom when the ship arrived with the princesses, the princes, and the Red Knight. But no one was happier than the old king who had got back his daughters again.

The eleven eldest princesses were happy and merry, but the youngest, who was to have the Red Knight, cried and was always sad. The king did not like this and asked why she was not happy like the other princesses. She had nothing to mope about now that she had got away from the troll and was getting a man like the Red Knight. But she dared not say anything, for the Red Knight had threatened to take the life of the one who told what had happened.

But one day, as they were busy sewing on the bridal finery, a man wearing a huge sailor's suit came in. He had a pedlar's chest on his back and asked if the princesses would buy finery for the wedding from him. He had so many rare and costly things, of both gold and silver. Why, yes, they might buy something from him. They looked at the finery and they looked at him, for it seemed to them that they recognized both him and many of the things he had.

"Anyone who has so many fine things," said the youngest princess, "must have something finer, and which suits us better."

"That could be," said the pedlar. But the others made her be quiet, telling her to remember what the Red Knight had threatened.

Some time later, the princesses were sitting by the window one day when the king's son came again, wearing the big sailor's suit and with the cupboard with the golden crowns in it on his back. When he came into the big parlor of the king's manor, he opened the cupboard for the princesses. And then each one recognized her golden crown.

Then the youngest princess said, "I think it's fitting that the one who saved us receives the reward he deserves. The one who saved us was not the Red Knight but the one who has brought our golden crowns!"

Then the king's son threw off the sailor's suit and stood there much more richly dressed than anyone else. Immediately the old king had the Red Knight put to death.

Only then was there real rejoicing at the king's manor. Each prince took his princess, and then there was a wedding that was the talk of twelve kingdoms.

## ·82· *Mop Head*

Type *711*, The Beautiful and the Ugly Twin; *R. Th. Christiansen, Norske Eventyr, 711, "Lurvehaette," No. 4. Collected by*

*Jörgen Moe and printed in P. Chr. Asbjörnsen and Jörgen Moe,*
Norske Folkeeventyr (*1852*), No. 54.

*This is not one of the common Norwegian folktales. Christian-*
*sen reports six variants in his* Norske Eventyr, *p. 99. The story*
*is known in Sweden, Iceland, and Ireland; some variants are*
*reported from southeast European and Anglo-American tradi-*
*tions.*

• ONCE THERE WERE a king and queen who had no children. The
queen was so unhappy about this that she hardly ever laughed
or smiled. Ever and always she complained about how dreary
and quiet it was at the court. "If only we had children, things
would be lively here," she said.

No matter where she journeyed throughout her kingdom, no
end of children was to be found, even in the poorest cottage.
And everywhere she went, she heard the mother of the house
scolding the children and saying that now they had done such-
and-such a thing wrong again. The queen thought this was fun,
and she wanted to do the same thing too.

At long last the king and queen took a little girl into their
palace. They wanted to rear her at the court and scold her as
if she were their very own.

One day the little maiden was down in the yard in front of
the castle, playing with a golden apple. Then a beggar woman
came wandering by. She also had a little girl with her, and it
was not long before the little beggar girl and the little maiden
were good friends and started playing together and rolling the
golden apple back and forth between them. The queen, who
was sitting by a window up in the castle, saw this and tapped
on the pane for the foster daughter to come up. This she did,
but the beggar girl came with her. When they came in the hall
to the queen, they were holding each other by the hand.

The queen scolded the little maiden. "It's not for you to run
and play with a ragged beggar child," she said, and wanted to
chase the little beggar girl out.

"If the queen knew what my mother can do, she wouldn't
chase me away," said the little girl, and when the queen questioned her more closely, she said that her mother could fix it so

the queen could have children. The queen would not believe it, but the little girl insisted and said that every word was true, and that the queen should just try to get her mother to do it.

Finally the queen sent the little girl down to fetch her.

"Do you know what your daughter says?" she asked the woman when she came in the door.

No, the beggar woman did not know.

"She says you can fix it so I can have children, if you like," said the queen.

"It's not for the queen to listen to what a beggar child makes up," said the woman and strode out.

The queen became angry and was going to chase the little girl out again, but she insisted that every word she said was true.

"If the queen just gives my mother something to drink, she'll be in good spirits, and then she'll certainly know of a way."

The queen wanted to try. The beggar woman was brought back up again and served both wine and mead, as much as she could drink, and it was not long before her tongue was loosened.

"I certainly ought to know of a remedy," said the beggar woman. "The queen is to have two vats of water brought in during the evening when she's going to bed. She's to wash herself in them, and afterward she's to empty them out under the bed. When she looks under the bed in the morning, two flowers will have grown up, a pretty one and an ugly one. She's to eat the pretty one, but she's to leave the ugly one standing. But don't forget the last!" said the beggar woman.

Well, the queen did as the beggar woman had advised: she had the water brought up in two vats, washed herself in it, and emptied it out under the bed. And when she looked in the morning, two flowers were standing there. One was disgusting and ugly and had black petals, while the other was so pretty and fair that she had never seen anything like it, and she ate it at once. But the pretty flower tasted so good that she could not help herself, she ate the other one too.

"It certainly can't make any difference one way or the other," she thought.

After a while the queen was brought to confinement. First she gave birth to a girl child who had a ladle in her hand and was riding on a billy goat. She was ugly and hideous, and as soon as she came into the world, she shouted, "Mother!"

"If I'm your mother, Lord have mercy upon my soul!" said the queen.

"Don't grieve about that. There's another one coming right behind me who's prettier," said the one who rode on the billy goat.

In a little while the queen gave birth to another girl, and she was so pretty and fair that no one had ever seen such a lovely child, and you may be sure the queen was fond of her.

They called the eldest girl Mop Head, because she was hideous and tattered and had a mop of hair that stood out in tufts all around her head. The queen did not like to look at her, and the serving girls tried to shut her into another room. But it was no use. Wherever the pretty child was, she also wanted to be, and they were never able to keep them apart.

When they were both half-grown, it happened one Christmas Eve that there was a terrible commotion and hubbub on the porch outside the queen's room. Mop Head asked what was the pounding and rumbling out on the porch.

"Oh, there's no use asking about that," answered the queen. But Mop Head did not give up. She would find out what it was, and at last the queen told her that the troll hags were playing their Christmas games out there. Mop Head said she was going out and chase them away, and for all they begged her not to, it did not help. She would go out and chase the troll hags away. But she asked the queen to keep all the doors closed, so that no one could even so much as peek out once. Then she went out with her ladle and started driving and sweeping the troll hags away. And there was such a rattling out on the porch that you never heard anything like it. There was a creaking and a crashing as if the whole palace were going to fall apart. Somehow, one of the doors came open a crack. The sister wanted to see how Mop Head was getting along, so she stuck her head through the crack in the door. Swish! Along came a troll hag and took off her head and put a calf's head in its place, and at once the princess went in and started mooing. When Mop Head came in again and caught sight of her sister, she was furious and scolded them for not taking better care of her, and asked if they thought it was better now that her sister had turned into a calf. "Well, I'd just better restore her," she said.

She asked the king for a ship that was fully equipped and ready to sail, but mate and crew she would not have. She wanted to sail with her sister alone, and in the end they had to let her do it.

Mop Head sailed away and steered the ship right to the land where the troll hags lived. And when she had come to the pier, she told her sister to stay on the ship and keep very quiet. But Mop Head herself rode up to the troll hags' castle on her billy goat. When she got there, one of the windows to the great hall was open, and there stood her sister's head on the windowsill. Then she rode up on the porch at full speed, grabbed the head, and set out with it. The troll hags rushed after her and tried to take back the head. They swarmed and teemed around her, but the billy goat pushed and butted with its horns, and Mop Head herself beat and struck them with the ladle, and at last the flock of troll hags had to give up. Mop Head came down to the ship again, took the calf's head off her sister, put the real head back in its place, and the sister became a mortal maiden again. Then Mop Head sailed far, far away to a foreign kingdom.

The ruler of this kingdom was a widower and had an only son. When he saw the foreign ship, he sent messengers down to the shore to find out where it was from and who owned it. When the king's men got down there they did not see a living soul except Mop Head. She was riding around the deck on the billy goat, with the tufts of hair standing up all around her head. The messengers were amazed at the sight and asked if there was anyone else on board. Oh yes, she had a sister with her, said Mop Head. They wanted to see her, but Mop Head refused to allow it.

"No one will see her before the king himself comes," she said, and rode around on the billy goat so the deck thundered.

Now when the messengers came back to the king's manor and told what they had seen and heard down on the ship, the king wanted to set out at once to look at the one who was riding on the billy goat. When he got there, Mop Head led out her sister. She was so beautiful and fair that the king was taken with her on the spot. He took them both with him up to the castle, for he wanted to make the sister his queen. But Mop Head said no, the king could not have the sister, unless the king's son would have Mop Head. Well, you might know the king's son was not any too willing, as ugly and nasty a troll as Mop Head was. But the king and everyone else at the castle talked to him for such a long time that at last he gave in and promised to take her for his princess. But he did not want to at all, and he was downcast and sad.

Then they baked and brewed and fixed everything for the wedding, and when it was all ready they were to go to the church. But the prince thought this was the dreariest church-going he'd ever been to in his whole life. First the king drove off with the beautiful sister. She was so lovely and so fine that everyone stopped and stood staring down the road after her as long as she was in sight. Behind them rode the prince with Mop Head by his side. She trotted along on the billy goat with the ladle in her hand, and he looked more as if he were on his way to a funeral than to his own wedding. He looked so mournful and did not utter a word.

"Why don't you say something?" asked Mop Head, after they had ridden for a while.

"What should I talk about?" asked the prince.

"Well, you could ask why I'm riding on this ugly billy goat," said Mop Head.

"Why are you riding on that ugly billy goat?" asked the king's son.

"Is this an ugly billy goat? Why, it's the finest horse any bride could wish to ride upon," answered Mop Head, and at the same moment the billy goat turned into the finest horse the king's son had seen in all his days.

Then they rode a bit farther, but the prince was just as down-cast and could not utter a word. Then Mop Head asked again why he did not say anything, but the prince answered that he did not know what to talk about.

"Well, you could ask why I'm riding with this ugly ladle in my hand!" said Mop Head.

"Why are you riding with that ugly ladle?" asked the king's son.

"Is this an ugly ladle? Why, it's the finest silver fan any bride could wish to carry!" said Mop Head, and at the same moment the ladle turned into a silver fan that was so bright that it shone.

Then they rode even farther, but the king's son was just as gloomy and did not say a word. After a little while, Mop Head again asked why he did not say anything, and this time he was to ask why she had that ugly grey mop of hair on her head.

"Why do you have that ugly grey mop of hair on your head?" asked the king's son.

"Is this an ugly mop? Why, it's the shiniest golden crown that any bride could wear," answered Mop Head, and at the same moment it turned into a crown.

Now they rode for a long time, and the prince was mournful and sat there without saying a word, just as before. Then his bride asked again why he did not say anything and bade him ask why her face was so grey and ugly.

"Well, why is your face so grey and ugly?" asked the king's son.

"Am I ugly? You think my sister is pretty, but I am ten times prettier," said the bride, and when the king's son looked at her she was so beautiful, that he did not think there could be such a beautiful maiden in the whole world. Now, I dare say, the prince got back his voice and no longer rode with his head hanging down.

Then they celebrated the wedding both long and well, and afterward the king and the prince journeyed with their brides to visit the sisters' father, and here they celebrated the wedding again without end. If you hurry to the king's manor, there still might be a drop of the wedding ale left!

# Glossary

*Aesir*  Plural of *as*, the generic name for the ancient Nordic gods.

*Alen*  A unit of measurement originally calculated as the distance between elbow and finger-tips; now fixed at 2·058 feet.

*Askelad*  "Ash Boy." The clever youngest brother who appears as the hero in many Norwegian folktales.

*Bergfolk*  "People of the hills." The term is common in eastern Norway. See *huldre*-folk, *underjordiske, hauge*-folk.

*Daler*  Old Scandinavian coin.

*Dovre Mountain*  Known in Norwegian folklore as the home of different kinds of supernatural beings, such as *trolls* and *jotuns*. Thus *Dovregubben* (The old man from Dovre) in Ibsen's play, *Peer Gynt*.

*Draug*  Malevolent beings which exist on land or in the sea. Their appearance is an omen of impending disaster. In old Norse the word *draugr* meant "a living dead person"; in some dialects *draug* is still used in this sense.

*Finns*  The Finns, that is, the Laplanders, are famous in Norwegian folklore for their abilities in witchcraft. Especially are they able to let the soul travel to foreign places while the body is in a trance.

*Fossegrim*  Supernatural being inhabiting waterfalls and rivers. See *nökk*.

*Gangferd*  A term in northern Norway for "the wild hunt." It refers to restless, unhappy ghosts who sometimes compel living persons to follow them about. See *oskoreien*; *jolereien*. They are similar to the Gaelic *"sluagh."*

*Gardvord*  A guardian spirit of the house. The term is used in the western and northern parts of Norway. Also called *godbonde*.

*Godbonde*  See *gardvord*.

*Gudrun Gjukesdatter*   A heroine of the Volsunga cycle. Folk tradition has associated her with the *gangferd* or the *oskorei* and given her the name of Guro.

*Guro* (Rysserova)   Leader or member of *gangferd* or *oskorei*.

*Gyger, Gjöger*   Female troll, giantess.

*Haug(e)-folk*   "The hidden folk," "the unseen beings," "people of the mounds." They are comparable to elves and fairies. See *huldre*-folk, *berg*-folk, *underjordiske*.

*Haugetusser*   See *haug*-folk.

*Hellig Olav*   King Olav ruled Norway 995–1030. He is the national saint of Norway and is exceedingly popular in Norwegian oral tradition, being especially well known as an adversary of trolls and giants. This trait he seems to have inherited from the pagan Norse god Thor, who was at one time more celebrated in Norway than in any other area of Scandinavia.

*Himmerike*   The heavenly paradise.

*Huldre-folk*   "The hidden people," "the invisibles." A group of supernatural beings, similar to elves or fairies. It is hard to distinguish this group from other beings such as *haug*-folk, *vetter*, or trolls. Sometimes they are believed to be similar to human beings in appearance. They generally live at the fringe of an area inhabited by human beings. This is perhaps the most common Norwegian term for all kinds of supernatural beings. See *hauge*-folk, *berg*-folk, *underjordiske*.

*Hulder* (*huldre* maiden, *huldre* woman)   A supernatural maiden belonging to the *huldre*-folk, a fairy or wood nymph. Traditions about her marital and other relations to human males are common. She is beautiful but her cow's tail reveals her true nature. The term derives from *hylja*, "to cover" or "conceal." The participle *huldrin* means "bewitched by the *huldre*-folk."

*Huldrin*   To be bewitched by the *huldre*-folk. From *hylja*, "to conceal."

*Ildjern*   The steel used with flint in striking fire.

*Imber Evening*   One of the last three days before Christmas Eve.

*Jagt*  A kind of fishing boat.

*Jolerei*  A form of *"oskorei"* (the terrible host). The word especially stresses the connection of the terrible host with *"jol"* or *"jul"* (Christmas).

*Jotun*  According to old Norse mythology the *jotuns* are the traditional enemies of the *aesir* (the gods; cf. Indian mythology *almras*, the adversaries of the *vedas*, the gods). The *jotuns* are giants closely related to the *trolls*.

*Jutul*  Another term for *jotun*.

*Kjellerman*  "The cellar man." This term is sometimes used for a man belonging to the *underjordiske*, "those under the ground."

*Landsmaal*  New national Norwegian language based on valid dialects. The current term is *nynorsk*.

*Linnormen, Lindormen*  A form of dragon well known in north European folklore (folk etymology: *"Der Wurm unter einer Linde"*; see *Handwörterbuch des deutschen Aberglaubens*, II, 387).

*Lure* (Norwegian *lur*)  A wind instrument used especially by girls at the *seter* in order to call cattle.

*Lut(e)fisk*  Fish steeped in lye. Traditional Christmas dish in Norway and Sweden.

*Mark*  A coin of high value. The word also signifies a measure of weight equal to eight ounces.

*Mjölnir*  The hammer belonging to the old Norse god, Thor.

*Mönsås*  The crossbeam of a house.

*Nisse*  A household guardian of diminutive size. He is well known in Norway, Denmark, and western Sweden. See *gardvord*, *tunkall*, and *godbonde*.

*Nökk*  Spirit of waterfall and rivers. See *fossegrim*.

*Odin*  An old Norse pagan god. According to the Eddas he is the foremost god in the pantheon of *aesir*.

*Old Erik*  A common west Scandinavian euphemism for the Devil. "Old Jerker" is another common name etymologically related to "Old Erik."

*Oskorei*  "The terrible host," "the wild hunt," a group of evil spirits, often spirits of dead people which sweep through the valleys of Norway at Christmas time. See *jolerei*, *gangferd*.

*Osku* An old Norse word meaning "terror." See *oskerei*.

*Rawga* Lappish counterpart of *draug*.

*Seter* An outfarm in the mountains inhabited only in summer. Unmarried women generally take care of the cattle and do churning and cheesemaking there.

*Shilling* A coin equal in value to a half-penny.

*Stabbur* A storehouse raised above the earth; it usually stands on wooden pillars.

*Stallo* A hero in Lappish folktales who takes on many forms. He often appears as the clever youngest brother.

*Thor* Old Norse god. The main adversary of giants and trolls; the owner of the hammer of *Mjölnir*. According to folk belief he is a rather stupid character.

*Troll* Malevolent ogre of superhuman size and strength. Sometimes, however, the term denotes any kind of demon. This is particularly true in international usage where the word *troll* has come to stand for all types of Norwegian supernatural beings.

*Trollebotn* The ice-covered bay which was assumed to connect Greenland to the north of Scandinavia.

*Tunkall* A household guardian. The term is especially common in the western and northern parts of Norway. Cf. *gardvord*, *nisse*, *godbonde*.

*Tufte-folk* A vaguely defined group of supernatural creatures. Related to or the same as the *huldre*-folk or the *hauge*-folk.

*Tusse-folk* A term sometimes used to denote *huldre*-folk.

*Tusse* A term for a supernatural being, a gnome or a goblin.

*Underjordiske* "Those under the ground." The term is used for *tusse*-folk, *hauge*-folk, *huldre*-folk, and is probably a euphemism.

*Utröst* "The blessed lands," "the land beyond Röst." Visits to this place, and to other dwellings of supernatural beings, are often described as actual experiences.

*Vardögr* The soul that appears before a person's death. It is similar to the Scottish *fetch*.

*Vetter* Supernatural beings living at the fringe of an area inhabited by human beings. The term is often synonymous with *huldre*-folk. See also *tusse*-folk, *tufte*-folk, *hauge*-folk.

# Bibliography

AARNE, ANTTI. *Estnische Märchen und Sagen Varianten*. Helsinki, 1918.

———. *Finnische Märchen Varianten*. Helsinki, 1920.

———, and THOMPSON, STITH. *The Types of the Folktale*. Helsinki, 1961.

ASBJÖRNSEN, P. CHR. *Norske Huldreeventyr og Folkesagn*. 3rd ed., Christiania, 1870. (Ed. Knut Liestöl.) Oslo, 1949.

———, and JÖRGEN MOE. *Norske Folke Eventyr*. 1st ed., Christiania, 1842. 2nd ed., Christiania, 1852.

BERGE, RIKARD. *Norsk Sogukunst*. Kristiania, 1924.

BLOM, P. *Beskrivelse over Valle Prestegield i Setersdalen med dets Prestehistorie og Sagn*. Gjövik, 1896.

BOBERG, INGER. *Sagnet om den store Pans Død*. København, 1934.

BØ, OLAV. *Heilag-Olav i Norsk Folketradisjon*. Oslo, 1955.

BØDKER, LAURITS. *Danske Folkesagn*. København, 1958.

BOGGS, RALPH STEELE. *Index of Spanish Folktales*. Helsinki, 1930.

BOLTE, JOHANNES, and POLÍVKA, GEORG. *Anmerkungen zu den Kinder- und Hausmärchen der Brüder Grimm*. 5 vols. Leipsig, 1913–32.

BRASET, KARL. *Hollra-Öventyra*. Sparbu, 1910.

BRINCH, D. *Prodromus Norvegiae Sive Descriptio Loufoudiae*. Amsterdam, 1676.

BUGGE, SOPHUS, and BERGE, RIKARD. *Norske Eventyr og Sogn*. 2 vols. Christiania, 1909–13.

CHRISTIANSEN, REIDAR TH., and KOLSRUD, OLUF. *Boka om Land*. 2 vols. Oslo, 1948–52.

———. "The Dead and the Living," *Studia Norvegica*, II (1946), 1–96.

CHRISTIANSEN, REIDAR TH. "Eventyrvandring i Norge," *Arv*, II (1946), 71–96.

———. "Gaelic and Norse Folklore," *Folk-Liv*, II (1938), 321–335.

———. "A Gaelic Fairytale in Norway," *Béaloideas*, I (1927), 107–114.

———. *The Migratory Legends*. Helsinki, 1958.

———. *Norske Eventyr*. Kristiania, 1921.

———. *Norske Sagn*. Oslo, 1938.

———. "The Sisters and the Troll: Notes to a Folktale," *Studies in Folklore in Honor of Distinguished Service Professor Stith Thompson* (ed. W. Edson Richmond), pp. 24–39. Bloomington, Ind., 1957.

———. "Noen anmerkninger til Samiske Eventyr og Sagn," *Svenska Landsmål och Svenskt Folkliv* (1953–54), 61–74.

CLOUSTON, WILLIAM A. *The Book of Noodles*. London, 1888.

DÉGH, LINDA (ed.). *Folktales of Hungary*. Chicago and London, 1964.

DORSON, RICHARD M. *Buying the Wind*. Chicago, 1964.

———. *Negro Folktales in Michigan*. Cambridge, 1956.

ERBE, A. *Skipperlögne og andre historier fra Skjärgaarden*. Christiania, 1892.

FAYE, ANDREAS. *Norske Folke-Sagn*. Christiania, 1844. Repr. *Norsk Folke-Minnelag*, LXIII (1948).

FEILBERG, H. F. *Bjaergtagen*. København, 1910.

———. *Nissens Historie*. København, 1920.

GRIMM, JACOB. *Deutsche Mythologie*. 3 vols. Graz, 1953.

HARTLAND, EDWIN SIDNEY. *The Science of Fairy Tales*. London, New York, 1914.

*Hedmarks Historie*, I. Hamar, 1957.

HOFFMAN-KRAYER, E., and BÄCHTOLD-STÄUBLI, H. (eds.). *Handwörterbuch des deutschen Aberglaubens*. 10 vols.

JAKOBSEN, JAKOB. *Faeröske Folkesagn og Aeventyr*. København, 1898–1901.

KRAFT, J. E. *Historisk topografisk thaandbog over Norge*. 6 vols. Christiania, 1845.

KRISTENSEN, EVALD TANG. *Danske Sagn*, Vol. VI. København, 1936.

LABERG, I. *Balestrand en Bygdebok*, I. Bergen, 1934.

LIUNGMAN, WALDEMAR. *En Traditionsstudie över Sagan om Prinsessan i Jordkulan*. Göteborg, 1925.

——. *Två Folkminnesundersökningar*. Göteborg, 1925.

METCALFE, F. *The Oxonian in Norway*. London, 1865.

MICHAELSEN, E. *Historisk Beskrivelse af Telemarken*. Kjöbenhavn, 1777.

NIELSSEN, JENS. *Visitatsbog*. (Ed. Yngvar Nielsen.) Kristiania, 1893.

*Norske Bygder*, I, *Setesdal*. *Norsk Folkemuseum*. Bygdöy, 1921.

*Norsk Folkediktning*, Fol. III, *Segner*. (Introduction by KNUT LIESTÖL.) Oslo, 1939.

*Norsk Folkekalender*. Christiania, 1847, 1851.

*Norsk Folkeminnelag*, Vols. I–LXXXVII. Oslo, 1921–63.

ÖDEGAARD, O. K. *Gamal Tru og Gamal Skjik ifraa Valdres*. Christiania, 1911.

OLSEN, OLE TOBIAS. *Norske Folkeeventyr og Sagn samlede i Nordland*. Kristiania, 1912.

ÖVERLAND, O. A. *Hvorledes P. Chr. Asbjörnsen Begyndte som Sagn-Fortaeller*. Kristiania, 1902.

QVIGSTAD, J. K. *Lappiske Eventyr og Sagn*, 4 vols. Oslo, 1927–29.

——. *Lappische Märchen und Sagen-varianten*. Helsinki, 1925.

RAMUS, J. *Norriges Beskrivelse*. København, 1735.

RANKE, KURT. *Die Zwei Brüder*. Helsinki, 1934.

SANDE, OLAV. *Segner fraa Sogn*, 2 vols. Bergen, 1887–90.

SEKI, KEIGO (ed.). *Folktales of Japan*. Chicago, 1963.

SKAR, JOB. *Gamalt fra Setesdal*, 8 vols. Oslo, 1903–16.

SOLHEIM, SVALE. *Norsk Setertradjsion*. Oslo, 1952.

THOMPSON, STITH. *The Folktale*. New York, 1946.

TVEDTEN, H. *Sagn Fra Telemarken*. Kristiania, 1891.

# Index of Motifs*

## A. MYTHOLOGICAL MOTIFS

## B. ANIMALS

## D. MAGIC

## E. THE DEAD

## F. MARVELS

\* From Stith Thompson, *Motif-Index of Folk Literature* (6 vols.; Bloomington, Ind., 1955–58).

## G. OGRES

# Index of Tale Types*

* From Antti Aarne and Stith Thompson, *The Types of the Folktale* (Helsinki, 1961).

# Index of Migratory Legends*

* According to Reidar Th. Christiansen, *The Migratory Legends: A Proposed List of Types with a Systematic Catalogue of the Norwegian Variants* (Helsinki, 1958).

# Index of Places

# General Index

Aarne, Antti (Finnish folklorist), xvii, 27, 30, 33, 41

Aasen, Ivar (Norwegian author, philologist, folklore collector), 16, 93, 97, 102, 143, 159

Adam, xxxviii, 90, 91

Africa, 169, 209

Altars, 12, 18–19, 160, 162

Andersen, Hans Christian (Danish author), xvi

Animals, magic, supernatural, or unusual. *See* individual species

Anglo-American tradition, 206, 253

Arabia, 200, 202, 206

Archives. *See* Norwegian Folklore Institute

Asbjörnsen, Peter Christen (Norwegian folklorist), v–xi, xv–xviii, xl–xli, 18, 28, 30, 35, 37, 38, 45, 55, 61, 84, 105, 115, 121, 125, 130, 132, 140, 153, 164, 169, 183, 186, 193, 206, 208, 214, 228, 234, 243, 253

Asia, 47, 193

Askeladden, x, 169, 172–75, 234–42

Bätzman, F. (collector), 67

Bailiffs, 33, 38, 162–63, 192, 223, 225–28

Ballads, xv, xvi, xx, xxxiv, 13, 183

Barbeau, Marius (French Canadian folklorist), 48

Basile, Giovanni Battista, 186

Bear, 12, 48–49, 96, 121–23, 245

Beggars, 78, 187, 189, 193, 238, 253–54

Belgian tradition, 125

*berg*-folk, xxxiii

Berge Rikard (Norwegian folk-

lorist), 9, 40, 147

Bishops, 71

*Bjarki-Saga,* 176

Björnson, Björnstjerne (Norwegian author), as informant, 67

Black Book, xxv, xxvi, 19, 28, 32

Black Death; xxii–xxiii, 8–12, 127

Black School, xxv, 27

Blacksmiths, 23

Blom, P. (collector), 127

Bö, Olav (Norwegian folklorist), 3

Boberg, Inger (Danish folklorist), 125

Bødker, Laurits (Danish folklorist), 137

Böyum, S. (collector), 48

Boggs, Ralph Steele (American folklorist), 27, 35

Bolte, Johannes (German folklorist), 91, 92, 138, 159, 164, 209

Braset, K. (collector), 41

British tradition, 125

Bugge, Kristoffer (collector), 17, 138

Bugge, Sophus (Norwegian philologist), 147

Bull, Ole (Norwegian composer), 4

Bulls, xxxi, 199

Burial feast, 208

Burial mounds. *See* Grave mounds

Butchers, 209–10

Calves, 110, 112

Captives, of fairies, xxxiii, xxxvii–xxxviii, xxxix, 65, 102–105, 107, 109–10, 116; of robbers, 15–16; of "the terrible host," xxxiii, 78; of trolls, 179–80, 200, 215–20, 230–33, 243–46

Dogs, xiii, 114, 116–17, 128–29, 179–82, 210, 244

Dohn, Peder (minister), 27

Dorph, Niels (minister), 32

Dorson, Richard M. (American folklorist), 82, 209

Dragons, 42. *See also* Trolls

*draug,* xxx–xxi, 53–54, 56–57, 66, 118–19

Dreams, 47–48

Dublin, xviii

Dutch tradition, 125

Easter, 38

Edinburgh, xi

*egentlige sagn,* xi

Emperors, 39

Enchantment, by fairies, 130–31

England, xi, 18, 132, 183–86

English tradition, 30, 38, 169

Escapes: from "Black School", xxv–xxvi, 27; from fairies, 64–65, 102–103, 129; from robbers, 16; from trolls, 180, 200, 220–21, 231–33, 246

Estonian tradition, 33, 41

Etiologicial legends, 118–21; endings, 3, 6, 9, 11, 14, 17, 36, 42, 87, 92, 98, 115, 117, 124, 129

Europe, v, x, xii, xiii, xvii, 91, 164, 186, 193, 206, 208, 228, 234; central, 159; northern, 42, 67, 117, 122, 139, 140; north-central, 45; northwest, xxxii; southeast, 253; west, 47, 176

Eve, xxxviii, 91

*eventyr,* viii, ix, x, xi, xv, xvi, xvii

Evil Eye, 38

Exorcism, of the devil by various means, xxxvi, 28–31, 166–68; of "evil powers" by cross, 117; of fairies or trolls by gunfire, 64, 103, 114, 116–17, 124, 133–34, 233; of snakes by fire, xxvii, 41–42

*fabulat,* xvii, xxiv

Fairy tale, fallacy of the term, xx

Farmers, xxxi, xxxv, 3, 20–22, 23, 56, 61–62, 67–68, 100–101, 118, 137, 138–39, 165–69

Farmhands, 53–54, 123–24

Faroe Islands, 127

Faye, Andreas (Norwegian folktale collector), vi, xxii, 4, 7, 11, 14–15, 86, 114, 127

Feilberg, H. F. (Danish folklorist), 110, 139, 140

Ferrymen, 8

*fetch,* xxviii

Fictional folktales. *See* Folktales

Fiddlers, 4, 205

Fieldwork. *See* Collecting

Fights, between animals, 227; between mortals, 158; between mortals and supernatural beings, 137, 142; between supernatural beings, 53–54, 69, 137–38, 143

Finnish tradition, 5, 27, 30, 33, 41

Finns, as magicians, xii, xxvii, 13–14, 39–42

Fishermen, 55–56, 61–62, 104–105, 126, 154

Flatin, Kjell (collector), 110, 139

Folk beliefs, xx–xxii, xxiv–xl

Folklore, discussed as a cultural complex, xix; genres of, xix–xxi; status of subject in Norway, xliii; relation to Norwegian national romanticism, v–vi

Folktales, discussed, v–xlv; artistic value of, ix; as a genre of folklore, xix–xx; characteristics of Norwegian folktales, xiii–xiv, xl–xlv; collecting of, in Norway, vii–viii, xv–xvi, xl–xlii; comparative studies of, xviii; cultural traits in, xiv; diffusion of, xii–xiii; distinction between legends and fictional folktales, ix, xi, xvii, xx, xl; distribution of Norwegian

Swedish tradition, 28, 30, 48, 54, 84, 110, 114, 183, 228

Sydow, Carl von (Swedish folklorist), xvii

Tabu: against working, 76; against working on Fridays or Sundays, 75–76; not to eat, xxxviii, 131, 222, 254; not to eat ugly flower, 254; not to listen to mother, 156; not to look back, 83, 85; not to look out, 255; not to speak, 12, 20, 221; not to waste money, 106

Tabu, breaking of, 85, 108, 156, 222, 254, 255

Tailors, 192, 205

Tasks, difficult or unusual, xxvi, xxvii, 149–50, 169–75, 177, 198–200, 214–19; assigned to the Devil, 29, 32

Tasks, failure to perform, 149–53, 170–72

Tell, Wilhelm (Swiss folk hero), xiii

Tests; guessing name, 5–7

Thieves, 15, 30, 163–69, 210

Thompson, Stith (American folklorist, xvii, 122, 193

Thor, 86

*Thrymskvida,* 86

Tramps, 189–93, 210, 238

Transformations, of the human soul, discussed, xxvii, xxviii–xxix; billy goat into horse, 257; dog into princess, 244; foals into princes, 174–75; food into dung, 131; human soul, into a mouse, 47; into a fly, 48; ladle into fan, 258; man into bear, xxviii, 48–49; mop hair into crown, 258; princes into foals, 174; salt stone into mountain, 221; toad into fairy, 106–107; trolls into bulls, 199; troll girl into maiden, 258

Travelers, 61, 62

Treasures, 20–24, 247, 249

Trolls, xxxiii–xxxiv, xliii, 4–7, 81–87, 114, 119–21, 122–24, 143, 155–56, 173, 179–80, 182, 194, 204, 206, 213–21, 225, 227, 229–233, 244–49, 251, 257

Troll hags, 8, 148–53, 131, 170–72, 174, 176–82, 222–23, 228, 255–56

*tufte*-folk, 63–66

*tusse,* 6, 89–90, 140

*tusse*-folk, 18, 90, 102

*tusse*-girl, 112

*tunkall,* xl, 141–42

Turkey, 186

Tvedten, H. (collector), 87, 92

*underjordiske,* xxxiii, xxxv

United States, xviii

University of Christiania. *See* University of Oslo

University of Oslo, xv, xlii, xliii

Urashima Taro (Japanese folktale character), 56

*Vatnsdöla saga,* xxvii

Vetter. *See huldre*-folk

Voices, of invisible beings, 6, 67, 100, 103, 104, 122–23, 125, 128, 248

Wagers, 4, 206–208

Warnings, 54

Wars, 13–14, 19, 23

Weddings, 13–14, 86–87, 115, 125–126, 175, 177, 182, 186, 192–93, 222, 226, 228, 252, 257–58; of mortal to fairy, 112–17

Werenskiold, Erik (Norwegian artist), xlii

Werewolves, 48–49

West Indian tradition, 159

Wildhaber, Robert (Swiss folklorist), 67